Sign up for our newsletter to hear
about new and upcoming releases.

www.ylva-publishing.com

DEFENSIVE MINDSET

WENDY TEMPLE

ACKNOWLEDGEMENT

Firstly, I want to thank Astrid Ohletz, without her patience, encouragement and guidance, this novel would never have been published. I'd also like to thank my editors, Andrea Bramhall and Lee Winter, and all the people who work behind the scenes at Ylva Publishing.

I want to say a special thank you to Trish Whelan, who, for the past thirteen years, has offered encouragement in my writing. It's been a long journey to get to this stage and she has taken every step with me.

To Mum, Annie, Tricia, Michael, my nieces and nephews—Jodi, Robyn, Connie, Jed, Evan, Olivia and Charlie—and also, Pete, Mike, and Bev, thanks for making the last seventeen years of my life a lot more joyful than I could have imagined. Your support has been incredible.

DEDICATION

This book is dedicated to my dad, Pat. We miss you everyday.

CHAPTER 1

"OOF!" JESSIE GRAINGER'S LUNGS SCREAMED for air as she landed face down in the lush vegetation. Loose blades of grass invaded her mouth, making her cough and splutter. She got to her hands and knees, caught her breath, and turned her head as an extended hand came into her line of vision.

The curse she was about to emit died on her lips as she glanced up into a face devoid of expression. But the hand offered was a gesture in itself. She accepted the assistance and was swiftly pulled to her feet. Play continued with no foul awarded—the referee deemed it a fair, full-blooded challenge.

Usually a meaningless, end-of-season encounter was played out with a little less fervour. Obviously, this opponent had other ideas if that last tackle was anything to go by. A knee in the back, a stray elbow to the jaw—this was getting ridiculous. Jessie had never come across this player; she would have remembered. She'd be hard to forget given the way she was stamping her authority all over this match and quite literally leaving her mark. Jessie's irritation began to simmer just below the surface. The best way to get back at an opponent, she reminded herself, was to win.

She received the ball on the halfway line in the middle of the first half and ran straight at the two central defenders, hoping to confuse them and leave them uncertain as to who should challenge her. It was on. A quick one-two with the right winger, and she'd be in on goal. She knocked the ball out wide but never collected the return pass. Instead, she ran into the human equivalent of a brick wall as her match-day nemesis stepped right into her path. The impact dumped her onto her backside. This defender was deceptively strong for someone so tall and slim.

Once again, Jessie found herself staring at the outstretched hand. Shaking her head, she accepted the offer and was pulled to her feet.

"No hard feelings?" The voice was surprisingly quiet.

"Sure," Jessie said to the defender, then whispered "not" under her breath. The slight stiffening in her opponent's shoulders told Jessie she'd heard her. *Oops.*

The referee took appropriate action to the deliberate obstruction—a yellow card to the opposition number four and a free kick in the centre of the park, twenty yards from the goal. Jessie grinned. Perfect.

The wall lined up ten yards away, but Jessie could go either side with this. She took a short run up and struck the ball. She curled it around the wall and into the top left-hand corner of the net. Pinpoint accurate and with pace. The keeper had no chance.

"Yes!" Jessie leapt into the air, pumped her fist, and accepted the congratulations of her teammates.

Lothian Thistle, Jessie's team, won a corner with only three minutes left of the first half. Everyone bunched together in the box, jostling for position. The number four had her hands firmly on Jessie's waist. She struggled, feinted movement one way, then the other, but the woman's hands were firmly fixed. She couldn't get away from her, and the ball sailed harmlessly over their heads and out for a goal kick. All Jessie could do was glare fruitlessly at the back of the woman's head while she refused to make eye contact. She was the most infuriating player Jessie had ever come up against. The whistle blew for half-time, and both teams made their way to their respective dressing rooms.

"Nice goal, Jessie," Tom Matthews—the manager of Lothian Thistle—said. "We're doing well out there, ladies. Keep passing the ball, and try to avoid injuries or bookings. Nothing reckless or rash."

"Tell that to the opposition," Jessie griped.

"I noticed you're having a tough time with their number four."

"Yeah." Jessie waved her hand in frustration. "Who the hell is she anyway?"

"Fran Docherty, according to the team sheet. I've never heard of her before." He looked around. "Anyone?" A few shrugs and shakes of the head along with a couple of "nos" was the collective response. "Maybe come up from down south," Tom suggested as he scanned the dressing room, more laid-back than usual and a little subdued.

It had been a long, hard season for Thistle, and once again they'd come up agonisingly short of the league title. It was difficult to maintain any intensity with nothing left to play for. Jessie couldn't blame her teammates. Most of them wanted to get this game over with and enjoy the off season. Personally, she wanted to increase her individual goal tally and finish the season as the league's top goal scorer.

Tom's team talk continued with less fire than usual. Clearly, he needed the break as much as the rest of them. Jessie knew he'd put his heart and soul into managing them this season. He'd taken Thistle from mid-table last season to league runners-up. But nine points between them and the league champions was a big gap. They still had plenty of room for improvement.

Jessie stretched her legs out in front of her, sipped from a water bottle, and mentally prepared for the final forty-five minutes of the season.

"Okay, go out there and enjoy the rest of the game, ladies," Tom said. "Pass the ball around and keep possession. Don't lose concentration and another goal or two would be great. All right, let's go. One last effort!"

The second half began as the first had ended, until the Ayr Hawks team was awarded a corner. Fran Docherty came up from the back to add her considerable height to the penalty box. As the ball swung in from the left, Jessie knew they were in trouble. In the ensuing melee, Jessie was blocked, allowing Docherty to rise unchallenged and head the ball past the stranded keeper. The distinctive swish of the ball hitting the net was both familiar and unwelcome in its finality.

Docherty's celebration was low key; her teammates patted her on the back as she jogged back into her defensive position with a nod. Jessie watched her adjust her socks, apparently more interested in her attire than the adulation of the small home crowd, enthusiastically clapping and chanting her name. She was tall, maybe six foot three, and skinny, with long black hair scraped back into a ponytail. Jessie thought she'd do better with a bit more muscle on her, but Docherty could play.

The game continued at half pace, both sides content to play the ball around without being overly zealous in challenges. Tackles were at a minimum, removing any real competitive edge from the encounter.

With twenty minutes left on the clock, the atmosphere of the game changed in a flash. A shot from Lothian's captain, Andrea Miller, was deflected for a corner. Jessie again found herself being marked by the number four. Arms around her body kept her from breaking free and running into space. She attempted to shake off her marker, but those hands moulded to her breasts. Frustrated and embarrassed, Jessie swung around, and her palm connected with her opponents face in a flash.

The slap was so hard it echoed in the late spring air. Jessie's palm stung, and a shrill blast on the whistle brought everyone to a standstill. There was none of the usual pushing or shoving that accompanied violent conduct. Fran Docherty stood rubbing her rapidly reddening cheek, while Jessie stared wide-eyed, shocked by the incident.

"Damn, you pack a wallop," Docherty muttered. The handprint now showing on her face.

"Right, number nine, that's enough from you." The referee produced a red card and pointed to the changing rooms.

Jessie blinked once, staring at the red card, not quite believing it. She'd never been sent off before.

"Go on, you're off."

The referee's words rang in her ears as Jessie made her way to the sideline and the home crowd erupted into a chant of "Cheerio, cheerio, cheerio." Tom stared straight ahead, not returning her glance. Jessie dropped her gaze and walked to the changing room to wallow in her shame, self-pity, and anger.

She sat down on the wooden bench and removed her sweaty shirt, then pulled at the orange lace of her Nike boot. She held the boot in her hand for a moment before she launched it across the empty changing room. It smacked the wall with a satisfying thunk, spun across the tiled floor, and settled a few feet away from her.

Why had she let this opponent get the better of her? She'd been accidentally groped many times before in the heat of a match. It had been different this time. It had been overt and deliberate. The anger bubbled up within Jessie again. That woman had violated her on purpose and she'd instinctively lashed out.

Docherty had been trying to get under her skin throughout the game. To throw her off balance. To get her out of the game one way or another.

She doubted that Docherty had expected to get her off the pitch, but she had certainly done everything in her power to nullify the threat that Jessie had posed to their team. And she'd managed it more successfully than any other defender Jessie had ever come up against. Jessie shook her head. She never lost her temper like that. Never.

Jessie was dressed and waiting when her teammates trudged into the dressing room. She plucked up the courage to ask. "What was the final score, guys?"

"We lost, 2-1," Andrea Miller informed her, the tone of her voice carrying a hint of chastisement.

Jessie groaned. "I'm sorry I lost it out there."

There were a few replies of "don't worry about it" and "these things happen", but not from the manager.

"I'm sorry, Tom. I let everyone down."

"We'll talk about it later," he said, turning to address the room. "Good effort, girls. Third in the league isn't too bad, we'll do better next season. Now, get showered and dressed, and I'll see you all in the clubhouse before we head back home."

Today's result had cost them second place as the team behind them had won their match and leapfrogged Thistle to the runner-up spot.

Jessie didn't think she could possibly feel any worse as she sat among her teammates. Her melancholy stopped her enjoying the end-of-season high jinks, so she wandered outside to get some of the late spring air.

She made her way along the corridor to the entrance, where she saw a lone figure dressed in faded black jeans with a worn black leather jacket. Everything was black actually, including the scuffed boots and the wet hair.

Fran Docherty. Leaning casually on the side of the building, smoking.

The player who had groped, mauled, elbowed, pushed, and pulled her all over the football park. Jessie wanted to confront her, but she knew it was a bad idea. Having been sent off, she hadn't had the chance to go through the custom of thanking and congratulating the opposition at the end of the game. She pushed her anger aside and went up to the tall woman. "I'm sorry I slapped you."

Docherty stared at her as she took a long draw from her cigarette. Inhaling deeply, her gaze never left Jessie as she exhaled. "Don't worry about it." With those words she turned from Jessie and continued to stare out over the park, casually flicking ash from her cigarette tip.

Clearly, the conversation was over. While her apology had been acknowledged, Jessie wished she had never bothered. The woman infuriated her, on and off the pitch, and the sooner she got home and ended this day, the better.

CHAPTER 2

PARKING IN AN EMPTY SPOT, Jessie removed the keys from the ignition of her Volvo and gazed out over the open playing fields bathed in sunshine. Hope rose within her. A new season, a new start and, right now, anything was possible. A shiver of anticipation ran down her spine.

She loved pre-season training, especially the first day. Seeing her teammates again, meeting new ones, catching up on the off-season news, and falling back into the familiar camaraderie. But also, the hard work started today. The team would begin laying the foundation for the season ahead, the season in which Thistle would win the league—she could feel it. She knew Tom had it in him to push this team all the way to the top. It was one of the reasons she'd had no problems turning down offers from other clubs. Arsenal and Liverpool, the top two clubs in English women's football, and Lyon, champions of Europe and probably the best football club in the world right now, had all asked to speak to her in regards to a move. But her life was here. Her business, her family, and her team. This was where she felt most at home. This was where she belonged.

She slid off her sunglasses and stowed them in the glove compartment before climbing out of the car and walking towards the clubhouse. A casual ease descended upon her as she entered the building to greet the many familiar faces she had missed over the past eight weeks.

"Hello, Mrs Jackson." Jessie's smile was wide. Ruth Jackson had that effect on everyone around her.

"Jessie!" The diminutive woman wiped her hands on a dishtowel and made her way around the counter to greet her visitor. Grabbing Jessie around the waist, she delivered a swift kiss to her cheek and squeezed tightly. "Stand back; let me get a good look at you."

Jessie laughed. "It's only been eight weeks, Ruth."

"I know, but I need to be sure you've been taking care of yourself. Eating properly, not working too hard, and all that malarkey." Ruth cast a judicious eye over Jessie, nodding her approval as she let go of her hands. "Not as tanned as I would've expected, but you'll do."

"Busy with the new office we opened, so no summer holiday for me this year." Jessie picked an apple from the large bowl of fruit on the counter.

"How's work? The newspapers keep saying that house sales are down. Are you and your dad doing all right? Do you want breakfast?" Ruth asked as she made her way back behind the serving counter. "I have scrambled eggs, wholemeal toast, some of those vegetarian sausages."

"Thanks, Ruth, but I had a good breakfast before leaving." Jessie bit into the juicy red apple. "And business is good. House sales are down, but the rental market is booming. People always need somewhere to live."

"Truer words, Jessie. I'm glad it's going well for you." Ruth leant forward. "And I'm so glad you're back. I thought we might be losing you to bigger and better things this time." Ruth busied herself in the kitchen. She was like a mother to all the players, making sure there was always plenty of food to eat, and washing and ironing all the kit they used.

"I'm not going anywhere, Ruth. I've got all I need right here." She took another bite of her apple. "Did you and George get away?"

"Lanzarote." Ruth removed a tray from the oven, bringing it over to the hot plates. "It's lovely. We have found a new favourite destination. The Spanish mainland was becoming too busy and noisy for us. We needed a change of pace. Now that the kids are grown up, we can relax and not worry about keeping anyone else entertained. We met some lovely couples too, more our age you know, early thirties." She winked.

Jessie laughed. "You don't look a day over twenty-five, Ruth." Ruth was in her early fifties, but had a lovely complexion. That soft, almost wrinkle-free skin some women were lucky to have would always make her look younger than her years.

Exuberant voices from the hallway alerted them to new arrivals. "Here we go, Ruth, the new season is about to kick off."

"Looking forward to it."

"Jessie! Ruthie!" A dark-skinned woman came running towards them.

"Hey, Soph, how you doing?"

Sophie Laing was a muscular, fit, central midfielder, with a broad Scottish accent honed on a Lanarkshire council estate. The engine room of the team, dependable and measured in her approach, she rarely made mistakes on the ball. She was a gym junkie, with a love for fast food and cakes.

"I'm good. Full English please, Ruthie."

"Are you growing your hair?" Jessie rubbed the tight black curls in question.

"Kind of. I thought I might go for a bit of a 'fro."

"I like it." Jessie eyes moved to the counter as a large plate of food was deposited there. Sausage, beans, egg, bacon, tomatoes, and mushrooms.

"Any toast with that, Sophie?" Ruth asked.

"Just the two slices of white, with a large glass of fresh orange, please."

Ruth beamed her endorsement "Coming right up."

"Cheers, Ruth, I've really missed your cooking." Sophie winked and grabbed her plate from the counter.

Jessie followed, glancing around the room as they went. It appeared that most, if not all, of her teammates were now in attendance, scattered around various tables chatting and finishing breakfast. One table in particular was extremely boisterous. "What's going on over there?"

Sophie grinned. "Morven asked her girlfriend to marry her while they were in Barbados."

Jessie's eyes widened. The policewoman was forever stating she would never get hitched, that she was not the settling-down type. "How romantic."

Sophie laughed. "She's being teased rotten about it."

"No wonder, given the bravado that comes out of her mouth." Jessie looked over at the woman in question, trying to smother a smirk, but failing as she witnessed the ribbing going on. Morven deserved everything she was getting today, but it wouldn't last for long. She had broad shoulders.

Tom had yet to make an appearance to get the season under way. He'd popped his head in a couple of times and left, Jessie assumed back to his office.

"Who are the new signings?" Sophie asked as she loaded food onto her fork.

"Honestly, I have no idea."

"Seriously? Tom hasn't said a word to you?"

"Truly, not a thing. I'm as anxious as you are to see who walks through the door today."

"I thought you two were close?"

Jessie nodded. "We are, but he doesn't share everything with me."

Sophie grinned. "Some of the players are convinced you two are more than close."

Jessie was fed up with the familiar gossip. "How many times do I have to say they're wrong?"

She played with the salt shaker, twirling it round on the table top. It didn't help that she had gone on a few dates with Tom as his plus-one. "He's a lovely guy; he'll make someone very happy."

"Not you, though."

"We really are just friends."

The double wooden doors opened and Tom once again popped his head into the room, his eyes scanning the tables. Jessie caught his gaze and raised an eyebrow. Tom offered a weak smile in return before walking back out.

"What's up with him?"

Jessie shrugged. "No idea." She pinched a mushroom from Sophie's plate. "How was Corfu?"

"Hot."

Jessie laughed. "I bet you spent most of your time in the hotel gym."

"You know me, if a hotel doesn't have a good gym, I don't book it." Sophie placed her knife and fork together on the plate. It was almost empty, apart from a handful of sliced mushrooms. She drained what remained of her orange juice before sitting back in her chair and patting her stomach. "God, I needed that."

Shaking her head, Jessie smiled. "We have a tough day's training ahead. I don't know how you can eat all that before we start."

"Fuel, Jessie, that's what will get me through the day." Sophie grinned as she stretched her arms above her head.

There was no doubting Sophie's fitness, despite her diet. Jessie was sure she would pile on the pounds if she attempted to eat the way her friend did. She was certain Sophie would be having a hearty lunch followed by a large piece of cake, whereas Jessie would opt for a healthy option every time with yoghurt and fruit.

"Heads up, Tom's back." Jessie nodded to where Tom stood at the top of the hall glancing at his watch, then back at the doors. The girls were getting restless, and Jessie knew he couldn't stall any longer.

"If I can have everyone's attention, please." Some continued to chat. "Ladies!" That shut them up. "Good. Now I'm sure you're all desperate to meet the new signings, so let's give it up for a new talent—England under-twenty-one international, Abby Jones!"

In walked a young girl, no more that eighteen, brown hair, medium height. She gave a small wave as generous applause rang out around the hall. She was understandably nervous as she stood next to Tom, her cheeks flushed as a she bit her bottom lip.

"Abby's signed for us for three years. A left-sided midfielder, with a sweet left foot. She's moved to Edinburgh to study, and we're delighted to have her."

Jessie thought Abby Jones could prove to be a good signing, the team needed to strengthen their left side, especially with players leaving. Time would tell.

"Next we have Danika Kaminski!" Where Abby was youthful and shy, Danika oozed confidence. She was very self-assured, tall, with dark hair and tanned skin. "Danika is a utility player who has spent eight years playing in Poland's top league, and has signed for the next two years."

Tom introduced three more players, not stand-out signings, but they would add depth to the squad. As the girls applauded and welcomed the new players, Tom again darted to the double doors. Jessie picked up on his agitation, assuming there must be another player, for which she was grateful, as none of the newcomers were outstanding defenders and they desperately needed one.

The door opened a few inches and Tom smiled. At first no one else seemed to notice the woman who walked over to stand beside him, then slowly, the room became quieter. Taller than Tom, she stood there with a motorcycle helmet clasped under her left arm. Faded black jeans tucked into black motorcycle boots, a leather jacket open revealing an aged grey T-shirt.

Jessie stared in disbelief. Why did it have to be her? As some of the players recognised the new arrival, lots of eyes shifted gradually towards Jessie.

"Oh, Jessie, it's your pal," Sophie said, laughing.

"It's a walking cliché," Jessie muttered under her breath. The statement made Sophie laugh all the harder.

"Glad you could make it, Fran." Tom's joke evoked no response from the new arrival. He turned to face the room. "Ladies, I would like to introduce Fran Docherty. A central defender. Some of you may remember her from last season's final game against Ayr Hawks. Fran joins us on a two-year deal." Tom allowed a few moments for friendly greetings and the applause to recede. "Everyone, go get changed, you have two tough days in front of you. See you on the playing fields in fifteen minutes."

Jessie hung back as everyone filtered out of the hall. "You've got to be kidding me!" She stood before Tom, arms folded. "She got me a three-match ban!"

"I don't want to hear it, Jessie. You got yourself a three-match ban because you let her get to you."

"She was groping me. That's sexual assault or something!"

"She's not the first defender to get a bit friendly with you. Nor is she likely to be the last, now that you've shown it works. You reacted. You got yourself red-carded. End of story."

"But…"

"No, Jessie. Think about it, she is a good signing."

"I am thinking about it, and," she said, pointing to the dressing room, "*it* has disaster written all over it."

"I'm working with a limited budget here. Laidlaw agreed to put in £50,000 for the next three years. With limited TV revenue, I have to be creative. There wasn't enough to sign a big name. I couldn't go with three unknowns. Docherty is a good defender. We know what we'll get from her."

"I'll tell you exactly what you'll get from her." Jessie's voice increased in volume. "You know what she did to me on the pitch."

"I do and that's why I signed her," Tom continued before Jessie could say any more. "Jessie, she handled you better than any other defender in the league. Yes, some of her methods are questionable. She treads a fine line, but…" he held up his hand to prevent another objection, "she's clever, Jessie. I believe with the two of you in the team, and Sophie and Andrea controlling the middle of the pitch, we can win the league. That would mean European football and more money from TV rights. Which means better players for next season. This is the start of something big."

Her earlier anticipation and good mood had evaporated. She shook her head. "I don't know, Tom."

"Believe me, there is a lot more to come from her. Her best will be better than anything else out there." Tom held eye contact. "Trust me on this."

She couldn't doubt the sincerity and confidence in his voice. His eyes practically danced with excitement at the thought of the capture of this player's signature. Some of Jessie's anger deflated and she followed him out. "You'd better be right."

Three hours later, Jessie was bent over, hands on hips, getting air back into her lungs after the strenuous workout. "Well, that was a waste of lunch," she said to Sophie who'd stopped beside her, hands on knees, pulling in lungfuls of fresh air.

"Huh?"

Jessie pointed to where Docherty was clinging to the perimeter fence, retching, as more of her lunch was deposited onto the pale green grass. "Look at her puking over there, and we haven't even finished yet." Jessie continued to breathe rapidly as she monitored her heart rate on her sports watch.

Sophie chuckled as she caught her breath. "I think she's hung over. I heard her say something about a late night."

"Christ. That's all we need, someone who likes to party."

"Ah, cut her some slack, Jessie. It's the start of the season. Most of us need the fitness training, and it's not like it's the day before a big game or anything."

"Not yet," she grouched. It was fine coming into pre-season training lacking fitness, but that meant you had a tough month in front of you before the start of the season. They were all part-time footballers; the onus was on each individual to find time in their schedule to work on their own fitness. Jessie wasn't convinced Docherty possessed the necessary discipline or commitment required.

"Not everyone is as fit as you."

"You are," Jessie said pointedly. She shook her head as the dark-haired woman finally managed to stand up and let go of the fence as she wiped her mouth with the back of her hand. "Our rivals will have a field day if they get wind of this."

Sophie gave her a playful shove. "Come on, I'll race you to the water bottles." She took off, with Jessie close on her heels.

Fran winced as a muscle in her buttock went into spasm. God help her, the weekend training had been hard and she hurt like a bastard. She sat in the empty changing room, resting her weary body for a few minutes before she could contemplate making the journey home.

She stretched her long legs out along the wooden bench, crossed her booted feet, and rested her back against the wall. Next, she fished around in the pocket of her leather jacket and found her cigarettes. She ignored the tremor in her fingers as she removed one from the packet and flicked the cheap plastic lighter until the flame sparked to life. Fran lit the cigarette, drew smoke deeply into her lungs, closed her eyes, and let her body relax. As she exhaled slowly, the door opened. She squinted through her right eye and observed Jessie Grainger walk into the changing room.

The other woman's nose wrinkled in displeasure before her eyes focused on Fran.

Aw, for fuck's sake, it had to be her.

"Smoking is banned in this building."

Fran waved ineffectually at the smoke. "Sorry, I thought everyone had gone." In truth, she wanted to enjoy a quick puff away from any prying eyes. The new players were expected to do a short interview for a local radio station and Fran was desperate not to give one. Despite what her contract said, she wasn't into that stuff.

Jessie walked over to the shelves where the clean towels were stacked, forcefully removing one before turning back to Fran. "It doesn't matter if the building is empty, it's no smoking at any time."

Fran stared at her. Everything about her screamed conformity. She wore the right clothes, had the right haircut, the latest iPhone, and everyone liked her. Why wouldn't they? She was polite, warm, and friendly. Well, to everyone except Fran, and Fran knew why.

The corner of her mouth crept up as she recalled the last match of the previous season. She had honestly had no intention of playing football this season, and had thrown caution to the wind when it had come to marking the serious striker. It had been a meaningless match, and Fran hadn't expected to come up against an opponent who played as though her life depended on the result. So she'd fucked with her. Driven the polite and serious woman to the point where she had slapped her. That she hadn't anticipated. Just as Fran hadn't expected to ever meet the woman again. Now here she was, standing in front of Fran. Glaring. Again.

"Could you please finish your cigarette outside?"

Fran shrugged. It wasn't really a request, but Jessie had good manners. Fran had to give her that. She had even apologised to Fran for slapping her, when, truth be told, Fran knew she deserved that slap—and probably more.

She rose carefully from the bench. Despite the fact that her thigh muscles screamed their objection and she was seizing up by the minute, she was determined not to show the uber-fit Jessie her plight. It was bad enough she had caught Fran throwing up after one lap of the grounds while Jessie was finishing her second. Without another word, Fran grabbed her helmet and left the building, but the pain was considerable. Sweat broke out on the back of her neck with the effort it took for her to walk to her motorbike. She'd give almost anything for a beer right now to take the edge off.

Fran flicked the cigarette butt to the tarmac, crushed it under the heel of her boot, and put her helmet on. Only then did she allow the pain to show on her face. With gritted teeth, she threw a leg over the bike and started the engine.

Chapter 3

"Shit," Fran hissed as the light turned green and her bike stalled. A car horn blared behind her. She had no choice but to ignore it as she put the bike into neutral, opened the choke, and attempted to kick-start it.

On the third kick the engine briefly spluttered to life, then died. She sighed and got off the bike, waited for the lights to turn green, and then attempted a running start. Her legs ate up the tarmac. She jumped on the bike, pulled in the clutch, and put it into first gear. The back wheel locked, but the bike refused to spurt into life.

"Fuck!" She took a deep breath and tried once again, but there wasn't a flicker of life coming from the old machine. She walked with the bike to the side of the road.

Fran removed her helmet and gloves and unzipped her jacket. Her hair stuck to her head as sweat coated her back. She searched her pockets to locate her phone.

"Oh, for fuck's sake!" She'd only pocketed her cigarettes before running out of her room. No phone. No cash. And the team bus due to leave for their away match any minute. "I'm screwed."

Fran shook her head. The first competitive game of the season, and this had to happen. She didn't want to let Tom down. He'd made her a generous offer to play for Lothian Thistle. And she needed every penny. And more.

She ran a hand through her damp hair. They'd all be bad-mouthing her. Jessie Grainger no doubt giving it a big "I told you so". It's what they were all expecting, and the combination of her bike breaking down, and her forgetting cash and a phone would be all the ammunition the doubters needed.

The thought of Jessie giving her that holier-than-thou look made her want to knock the beautiful blonde down a peg or two. She smirked to herself. Again. She pushed her broken motorbike onto the pavement and leaned it against a fence. She was going to do everything she could to get to the match. She didn't care how long it took, she wasn't giving up. She couldn't give up.

Fran walked quickly, fighting her own thoughts with every step. Each yard away from her bike seemed to be a yard closer to the dark recesses of her soul. Her mind wandered into dangerous territory.

You always fuck it up. You never get anything right. You haven't even played a single match for them and you're already letting everyone down. Just like always. Why bother? You know how it will end up. Useless, stupid arsehole.

Fran gritted her teeth, and tried to ignore the thoughts swirling around her head. She reached for her safety net. Her cigarettes. She lit one and inhaled deeply. *Stay calm and breathe.* The nicotine hit her bloodstream and took the edge off. She focused all her efforts into getting to the clubhouse, and held on to the faint hope someone would be waiting for her.

Over the hill, a black cab idled toward her. Fran shielded her eyes from the sun, but she couldn't tell if it was for hire. The orange light didn't show against the bright sunlight. She put out her hand, praying it would stop.

"Where the hell is she?"

The first competitive game of the new season and Docherty was late. Andrea Miller, the captain of Lothian Thistle and their best midfielder, was becoming increasingly impatient. "We need to get going, we can't wait any longer."

She was right. Andrea led by example both on and off the pitch. She expected players to turn up on time, and put their all into both training and games.

At twenty-nine, she was one of the more experienced players in the squad. Jessie had looked up to her ever since Andrea had arrived almost five years ago and was immediately handed the captaincy by the previous manager. She blew the dark fringe on her forehead, her hands stuffed in the pockets of her tracksuit bottoms, foot tapping; her frustration clear.

Two buses were waiting for them. One full of supporters and the other filled with the team and staff, many of the occupants staring out the windows at the three of them.

Tom shook his head. "Ten more minutes."

"For God's sake, Tom, we need to get going," Andrea protested.

"Wait." Jessie hated what she was about to do, but it made the most sense. "I'm not playing. I'll stay here and if she turns up, I'll drive her to the game."

Andrea beamed at her. "Sounds like a plan, right, Tom?" She had a distinct edge to her voice as she addressed Tom, indicating she had reached the end of her patience.

Tom looked at his watch, pursed his lips, and nodded. "Thanks, Jessie." He turned to Andrea. "Right, let's go."

Jessie stood in the car park as the buses left, a sense of loneliness draping over her. She'd serve the first of her three-match ban today, and her flat mood was now plunging to new depths. The last thing she wanted was to drive for two hours sitting next to the woman who had caused her predicament. If she even bothered to turn up. Jessie shook her head. No, she'd do this for Tom. He'd put his faith in this Fran Docherty, and she was letting him down at the first hurdle. They'd tried calling her mobile. No answer. As she leaned against her car, a taxi pulled into the car park with Docherty in the back. A balding, heavyset taxi driver was gesticulating to her, as she spoke back to him. He powered down his side window.

"Excuse me? She says you'll pay." The irate driver threw his thumb back towards Fran.

Jessie blinked, then slowly nodded as she walked towards the cab. "How much?"

"Twelve pounds seventy."

Jessie pulled her purse from her bag and handed him a twenty-pound note, doubting she'd see the money again as the driver handed her change and released the locks so Docherty could exit the vehicle.

"My bike broke down," Docherty muttered by way of apology accompanied by a lift of her left shoulder as the helmet dangled from her right hand.

"We tried calling you."

"Lost my phone."

Jessie shook her head. What was the point? She doubted Docherty even cared that she'd caused the entire team and a bus full of supporters to set off late for the game.

"I'm driving you," Jessie said curtly as she walked towards the car and unlocked it. "You can put your helmet in the boot. All your kit is on the bus."

Docherty followed her instructions and got into the passenger seat, removing her cigarettes from her leather jacket before she pulled on her seatbelt. She held the pack of cigarettes in her hand, making eye contact with Jessie.

Jessie stared at the woman, not quite believing the audacity of her. She shook her head. "No. No smoking in my car."

Docherty tossed the pack of fags onto the dash and pulled peppermint gum from the pocket of her jeans. She popped two white tabs into her mouth before offering the packet to Jessie.

"No, thanks."

Docherty raised an eyebrow and put the gum back in her front pocket.

Jessie drove out of the car park and headed towards the motorway. She slipped her sunglasses over her eyes as the early morning sun shone brightly. Docherty reached for the sun visor.

"There are sunglasses in the glove compartment," Jessie told her.

Opening the compartment, Fran removed a pair of Aviators. She offered Jessie a nod before she eased back in her seat and slid them on, then yawned and closed her eyes.

As they sat in a queue at traffic lights, Jessie had no idea if she was awake. She stared over at her, noting the relaxed position and entwined fingers resting on a flat, T-shirt-clad stomach that rose and fell in a soft rhythm. Her head was turned away from Jessie, affording her the opportunity to study her further.

Docherty was skinny, too skinny, Jessie thought. Her arms were littered with scars. Nothing deep, but lots of marks of varying shapes and sizes covered her arms and hands. She was pale and there seemed something unhealthy about her. It went beyond the piercings and tattoos, though Jessie found her stretched ears particularly revolting. *Who does that to themselves?*

Jessie knew there was a pierced navel under those entwined fingers and as her eyes drifted up, the outline of two nipple rings were visible under the T-shirt stretched across her modest chest. Jessie knew she wore a bra to train and play in, but the rest of the time she didn't bother.

Jessie didn't get it. All that ink and metal…what was the attraction? Why would someone want to abuse their body like that? To deface it? To take something as truly wonderful and beautiful as a woman's body and make it something grotesque?

She flicked her gaze away from the road and over her dozing passenger again, and was surprised to find Docherty's head turning towards her. Jessie's image was reflected in the Aviators she wore. Damn, she suited those sunglasses better than Jessie ever had.

"Oh, you're awake."

Her lip curled ever so slightly in reply.

Jessie looked back at the road. "So where are you from?" Her Scottish accent had Jessie puzzled as it seemed to have no distinctive regional twang.

"Edinburgh, I suppose." Docherty stretched her arms out in front of her.

"You suppose?"

"Long story."

"Where did you go to school?"

Docherty sighed. "Heriots."

"George Heriots?"

"That's the one."

Jessie didn't know what to make of her travelling companion. Everything was so vague. She was surprised Docherty had been privately educated. *Maybe the old saying's right after all. You shouldn't judge a book by its cover.*

"What did you do when you left school?" Jessie waited a few moments but no reply was forthcoming. "I'm sorry, I don't mean to pry. I went to Knox Academy, in Haddington, that's where I grew up. Then I did a business and finance degree at Heriot-Watt University. I knew I would be working for my dad when I finished. He runs an estate agent's in Haddington and we've just opened new premises in Edinburgh."

Jessie felt like she had to fill the silence. She was used to people chatting with her, making an effort, doing their share of the small talk. Docherty seemed to have zero interest in the social niceties. She was so closed off, it made Jessie uncomfortable. And that made her ramble until she ran out of words.

After a lengthy pause, she sighed and answered, "I went to London."

"Did you play football there?" Jessie latched on to the common thread, hoping the other woman would open up.

"A bit."

"What team did—"

"Enough questions, okay."

It wasn't a sharp reply, but there was finality to the request. Docherty either wasn't in the mood to chat or she didn't like talking about herself. Either way, Jessie knew she had to shut up.

"Sorry."

Docherty folded her arms and turned away. They spent rest of the journey in silence. When Jessie pulled into the football ground, there was still an hour to go before kick-off. Jessie climbed out of the car, glad to be away from the increasingly claustrophobic atmosphere that had descended around them. Docherty followed her to the away changing room, head down, hands stuffed in her pockets. There was something in the set of her shoulders that made Jessie look again, look closer.

She looks like a teenager expecting to be bawled out in front of everyone. She looks...vulnerable. Jessie wasn't sure where the impression had come from, but instead of the difficult woman she was used to seeing, she saw one who had difficulty dealing with things. Sullen transformed in Jessie's mind to shy, moody became scared, and distant became a shield that protected the world from Fran as much as Fran from the world.

When did she become Fran? Jessie shook her head, decided not to think about it, and plastered on her smile.

"Room for two more?" Jessie asked cheerily as she popped her head around the door.

"Jessie! Fantastic!" Tom declared.

"Fran's motorbike broke down and she didn't have her phone with her." Jessie had no idea why she was explaining on the other woman's behalf. *Probably because Fran won't bother.*

"Right, well, Fran, get yourself changed then join us for the warm-up," Tom instructed as he led the team out of the changing room.

Jessie went outside, where her teammates were warming up. She hated missing a game, and missing one through suspension smarted like hell. It was bad enough when it was injury related, but this was an injustice. She shook her head. *No, that's not fair, Jessie. Tom's right. She was doing her job for the team and I let her get to me. It's my own fault. Blaming someone else for my mistake won't make this any better.*

Fran chose that moment to join the rest of the team. Jessie watched every player on the pitch avidly. Fran didn't exactly put much effort into warming up, and Jessie doubted she could appear any less enthusiastic as the players went through their drills with the fitness coach.

Tom joined her on the touchline. "Thanks again, Jessie."

"Don't mention it. We want to win and getting her here will help make that happen."

Tom nodded. "All the same, I appreciate it."

"I hope she works out."

Jessie had her doubts. Nothing about Fran's behaviour over the past month had convinced her she could make a difference for them in the league. Lazy and uninterested sprang to mind, but Tom was convinced otherwise. Fran continued to put in minimum effort during the warm-up, and Jessie wondered what it would take to get her to try. *What makes you tick, Fran Docherty?*

"So do I. I know her signing is tough on you." Tom clapped her on the shoulder. "Two more games after today, Jessie, and you are back where you belong."

"I can't wait!" Jessie answered with as much enthusiasm as she could muster. All morning she'd moped around, trying to be part of the game, but it was difficult. She'd missed games before, but never when she was fit to play.

As the game unfolded, Jessie mentally kicked every ball from the sidelines. Lothian Thistle were proving to have too much in their armoury for the newly promoted opposition. At half-time Thistle were leading 2-0, with Elaine Travers, Jessie's replacement for the day, finishing off a slick passing move for the second. Before the final whistle, the team added three more goals without conceding. A comprehensive victory. Thistle had been solid in defence and potent in attack.

Jessie lamented the loss of goals, knowing she could have easily scored a hat-trick, and watching Fran receive the congratulations of her teammates left a bitter aftertaste. She was pleased with the outcome, and she had to admit, reluctantly, that Fran had been impressive. Her no-nonsense approach to the game was so unlike her off-field appearance. She was efficient with the ball and tidy when it came to clearing up at the back. Even her kit reflected her approach, nothing flashy, hair tied back, and plain black boots. She was fast winning friends and support from her teammates and the sidelines.

The buses were full of her team and supporters. The trip back to Edinburgh would be fun, with everyone in a buoyant mood after the win. She walked back to her car, a feeling of melancholy settling over her as she stepped away from her friends, only to look up in surprise at the black-clad figure standing beside the Volvo. "You could have gone back with the team."

Fran shrugged as she took a final drag from her cigarette, before dropping it to the tarmac and stamping it out with a booted foot. Jessie's nose twitched, picking up the smoke clinging to her passenger's clothing once she'd unlocked the doors and they were both in the car. Fran rifled through her pockets and found the pack of peppermint gum. She offered one to Jessie, who declined, before popping one into her mouth.

The car was quiet as she drove along the motorway, and Fran was twitchy, restless. Her hands in constant motion, stretching her fingers, as her right thigh bounced rapidly as though the nerve was constantly being tapped.

"You got a hot date tonight?"

"No, I'm working."

"Oh, whereabouts?"

"A bar."

Jessie briefly closed her eyes wondering why Fran continually rubbed her the wrong way. "You had a good game today."

Fran rolled her head to look at Jessie. "Thanks," she said before staring out of the window again.

Jessie took a slow, cleansing breath and tried to concentrate on driving. Fran obviously didn't want to pass the time with small talk, and that was fine. She pressed a button on the console to play a radio station, selecting an easy listening preset and settled in to enjoy the relaxing tunes. She was sure it wouldn't suit her rock-chick teammate, but right now she didn't care. Movement caught Jessie's eye as long, slim fingers tapped a denim clad thigh in time to the beat. Well, at least they could enjoy the music together. But the idea of the surly Fran enjoying an old eighties power ballad was as perplexing to Jessie as the woman herself.

On the outskirts of Edinburgh, Jessie finally broke the silence.

"Where's the pub?"

Fran frowned. "Why?"

"How else are you going to get there?" Jessie asked sharply as they were running out of motorway. She already knew Fran had no money.

"Portobello."

Jessie took the inside lane and slipped onto the city bypass, the quickest route to the other side of town. Thirty minutes later, she entered Portobello. It was a place she knew well. Her new office was there and her house was in Joppa, right at the end of the seaside town. The very last stop in Edinburgh before you entered the harbour town of Musselburgh.

"Just say where."

Jessie thought Fran must have been daydreaming, as they got closer to Joppa and had passed all the bars on the high street without Fran asking her to stop.

"Here's good."

She pulled in at the top of a residential street lined with large Victorian houses that led down to the seafront. "Remember your helmet's in the boot."

"Thanks," Fran said.

The boot slammed shut and Jessie watched Fran walk down the street towards the promenade, a plume of smoke billowing behind her as she lit a cigarette.

Jessie shook her head and turned the car around. She knew everyone would be arriving back at the clubhouse any time now. Her day had been strange enough, and now she wanted to hang out with her friends and teammates. She wanted it to feel like a normal match day.

The clubhouse was boisterous, with lots of people in high spirits. They'd won after all. Jessie spotted her teammates in the corner they usually sat in after a game. Sophie waved when she saw her.

"Hey, Jessie. Where's Fran?" Sophie asked, nodding towards the door in expectation of the other woman's arrival.

"She's working tonight."

"Aw, shame she isn't here to celebrate. We voted her best player today."

"I'm sure she'll be ecstatic to hear that." Jessie struggled to keep the sarcasm from her response. She doubted Fran would give two figs about the accolade. "You all did well today. Congratulations, girls."

"You too, Jessie. If you hadn't stayed behind, Fran would have missed the game. You get an assist." Andrea Miller raised her glass of juice in salute, as other team members echoed her sentiment. This cheered Jessie a little. She'd felt so detached and completely out of sorts. A small smile crept on to her face as she took a seat next to Sophie.

"How was your trip?" Sophie asked.

"That woman drives me mad."

Sophie chuckled. "What did she do?"

"We spent over four hours alone today and I doubt she said more than a dozen words to me."

"Mm, she is the strong silent type."

Something in Sophie's tone caught Jessie's attention. "Please tell me you aren't interested in her?"

"She's all dark and mysterious." Sophie shrugged. "Makes you want to get to know her better."

"Yeah, good luck with that," Jessie said. She knew conversation was going to be a barrier for anyone wanting to get to know Fran Docherty.

"So what did you do, dump her in the car park?"

"No, I gave her a lift to work."

"Really?" Surprise laced Sophie's question.

Jessie shrugged. "She arrived here today in a taxi that I had to pay for. How else was she going to get there?"

"That was very sweet of you, Jessie."

She shook her head. "I had no option. I either took her there or gave her bus fare."

"Still…"

"Anyway, I'm starving. I hope Ruthie has some nice soup and sandwiches ready." That effectively put an end to the conversation about Docherty. Jessie had had more than enough of the woman for one day.

Chapter 4

The following Tuesday evening, Jessie pulled into an almost empty car park. Training didn't start for another forty-five minutes, but it was such a lovely night. She had left work a little early after spending most of her day envying everyone who had a reason to be outdoors. Jessie exited her car and stretched to remove some of the kinks from her back. Sitting in front of a computer screen all day had left her with a mild tension headache lurking. Nothing a good workout wouldn't take care of. She lingered a moment in the fresh air and let the gentle evening breeze filter around her body and cool the back of her neck. She closed her eyes and enjoyed the simple pleasure.

"Jessie."

Peace and quiet never lasted long. Smiling, she turned to greet Tom. "Lovely evening."

Tom was one of the people she envied. He had most likely sunbathed between working out at the gym and having an alfresco lunch at a designer restaurant. The owner would probably have fawned over his arrival. Although he was polite, she knew Tom didn't care much for the attention he received almost everywhere he went. He stood in front of Jessie like a catwalk model, in his pastel shorts and brilliant white T-shirt, complete with Wayfarer sunglasses and flip-flops. Not many men in Scotland could pull off that look, but a tanned and toned Tom achieved it effortlessly. Modelling would have been an easy choice for him after the car accident that shattered his right leg had ended his football career at the age of twenty-eight. But he'd already made enough money to last him a lifetime, and the superficiality of the catwalk didn't appeal. He was too driven and needed a goal, a focus. So instead of drowning his sorrows, he took his coaching badges and the rest, as they say, was history. Now Jessie considered herself lucky to count herself among his friends.

"It sure is. Listen, I wanted to thank you again. You bailed me out big time."

"Apparently, it'll be listed officially as an assist," Jessie joked.

Tom laughed. "I don't know about that, but you certainly played your part."

Jessie rolled her eyes. "Yeah, at least I contributed something."

"Hey," Tom put an arm around Jessie and guided her towards the club house. "Two more, then you're back in the team."

"Aye, can't come quickly enough," she grumbled, pushing open the changing room door. She pulled up short at the sight of Fran Docherty already in her training gear. Fran stood, gathering her hair into a ponytail, her initials emblazoned on the top she had selected. A pair of grey shorts also with F.D. on them and white ankle socks completed her outfit. Someone had been artistic with a black marker and written the letters 'UCKE' between Fran's initials on her training gear.

She nodded to Fran as she walked to her own part of the dressing room where her clean training kit was laid out. A crisp ten pound note and three pound coins sat on top. Jessie swallowed the shock she felt, turned to Fran, and gestured to the money. "Thank you."

"No worries," Fran answered as she removed a steel earlet from her lobe.

Why did she feel like Fran was doing her a favour instead of simply returning what she'd borrowed?

Jessie slipped on her kit and trainers, then grabbed her boot bag, before making her way back outside to practice taking free kicks before training started. Anything rather than spend time alone in the changing room with Fran.

Training went well. A two-hour session working on cohesiveness, lots of passing drills, and movement off the ball after a solid hour of fitness. The onus was on each player to work on her conditioning outside of the three training sessions a week. Jessie knew some worked harder than others, and Fran still lacked fitness.

She grabbed her towel from the peg outside the showers. The changing room was empty but that wasn't unusual. She'd stayed out on the pitch after training to put in some extra cardio work. Not playing at the weekend meant she was missing out on match fitness.

Jessie slipped on some loose sweats, towel dried her hair, and then dropped her kit in the laundry basket. She briefly debated going into the clubhouse for a chat, but it held no appeal.

Match fitness wasn't the only thing she was missing after not playing in the weekend's game. She felt distanced and apart from the rest of the squad. Usually she enjoyed chatting tactics with her teammates or Tom. Coming up with strategies for their upcoming opposition, their strengths and weaknesses, visualising how she might play against a certain opponent she knew. But right now Jessie's heart wasn't in it. She was simply passing time until her ban was served.

Jessie drove out of the car park, indicated to turn left, and waited for a gap in the traffic. Fran was standing leaning against the bus stop. Jessie sighed, pulled out of the junction and stopped next to Fran. She dropped the passenger window and leaned across the car so she could see Fran's face. "You heading to work?"

Fran nodded, exhaling smoke from her lungs.

"Hop in."

Fran stubbed out her cigarette and pulled open the door. "Cheers."

Jessie waited until Fran had her seat belt on before pulling away from the kerb. "Is your bike being fixed?"

"Naw, had to scrap it." Fran slouched and crossed one ankle over the opposite knee. The motorbike boots had been replaced by well-worn, black suede ankle boots. The rest of her outfit consisted of various dark garments and the usual leather jacket.

"You're bussing it to training?"

"Yup."

There were dark circles under her eyes. Working in the bar probably entailed a lot of late nights, but surely she could sleep longer in the morning? "Where do you live? If one of the team lives nearby then we'll definitely be able to organise you a lift with them. That'll make life easier."

"Portobello."

Christ. "Oh, I'm only in Joppa." *Bloody hell. Why couldn't she live on the other side of town? Why my side?* Jessie knew that she was by far the closest member of the team to where Fran lived and worked. After offering her fellow teammates up for lift duties, she could hardly shirk the responsibility now. She swallowed, then pasted on her smile. "I can give you a lift to training and drop you back. Be at the Town Hall at 5 p.m. for training, and on match days we can arrange something depending on the time of the game."

Fran's eyes were closed, her head back against the seat. She looked like she was dozing again. One eye popped open. "Nice one."

Jessie expected to drive the rest of the way in silence. She wasn't disappointed, but found the silence less oppressive than before. She didn't feel anger or frustration welling as the miles ticked by. Instead, she felt a little of the peace and quiet she'd enjoyed at the empty football ground return. Something she'd never experienced in the presence of one of her teammates before. Where did you come from Fran Docherty? Where were you before? Jessie's curiosity was piqued. Perhaps Sophie was on to something. The less Fran gave, the more you wanted to know.

A few minutes later she pulled up on the corner where she'd dropped Fran on Saturday evening. "Here we are."

Fran rubbed her eyes, trying to wake herself up.

"Remember, 5 p.m. at the Town Hall."

"Sure, cheers."

"See you tomorrow," Jessie said as the door slammed shut and Fran headed towards the promenade with long strides, quickly disappearing out of sight.

Jessie sighed, put the car into gear, and pulled away from the kerb. At least now she was picking her up for games, the team wouldn't suffer a repeat of last week's palaver. Still, why did she have to live and work on her doorstep? Sophie would've been delighted to drive Fran around all the time. Or Tom. Then he'd have the opportunity to keep a closer eye on his new signing.

Jessie parked in her driveway as dusk began to settle over the seaside town. She loved the view down over the salty waters of the River Forth. The nights were drawing in and the temperature had dropped. The season was changing, but Jessie welcomed it. Summer, though pleasant, meant no football. This time of year was always the most thrilling for her. A new season, full of promise and expectation, and everything to play for. Right now, anything was possible. They could win the league. The cup. Both. Nothing was beyond their reach, and Jessie couldn't wait to be a part of it all again.

Chapter 5

Jessie walked up the path of the large Victorian house that was the Beachcomber bar and hotel. The front door was open. *At least someone's awake.* Walking into the vestibule, she tried the handle of the glass-panelled door just inside. It opened. There were quiet voices coming from the room on the left.

Entering, Jessie stood in the main room not quite believing her eyes. There was a portly man in his late forties standing behind the bar, pouring a pint, while another man sat chatting to him, sipping from a pint of beer. At a quick glance, there were at least four other men in the bar asleep on various chairs. They had obviously been there all night. The smell of stale beer hung in the air, mingling with the distinct whiff of body odour.

"Excuse me?"

"Aye, hen," the man pouring a pint said.

"I'm looking for Fran."

The man indicated with his head as he replied, "Upstairs." His companion joked about something, causing him to laugh. Another man lying in a chair stirred and rubbed his face, opened one eye, and then staggered from his seat towards the toilet.

They paid her no more attention as she walked, frowning, to the bottom of the wide staircase, taking the steps two at a time. On the first-floor landing she called Fran's name, but received no reply. There were at least six doors visible to her. She started with the one straight ahead as it sat slightly ajar.

She stepped into the room. The stale odour of cigarette smoke mixed with the unmistakable smell of sex assaulted her. It took a moment for Jessie to process what she was seeing. Fran was naked on top of the sheets, a small blonde woman partially draped over her.

The unexpectedly explicit scene flustered Jessie, her cheeks warming with embarrassment. *Nothing you can do about it now.* She screwed her awkwardness into a ball and rapped her knuckles firmly on the door. "You're late!" she called out to Fran. "I'm at the bottom of the street waiting. You've got five minutes, then I'm leaving without you."

"What the fuck!" the blonde woman exclaimed, lifting her head to stare at Jessie, who turned around and started to walk away.

"Who the fuck is she?" she growled.

"Five minutes!" Jessie called back, then jogged down the stairs and out of the front door.

Jessie waited impatiently in her car for Fran to arrive. She was angry with her on so many levels. For being late, for making her have to enter the bar, for planting the picture of the two of them into her brain. But mostly she was mad because she was mortified. She had not expected to be greeted by the sight of Fran and another woman. Naked. In bed together. And it troubled her. Everything about Fran troubled her. And now she couldn't get the image of Fran's naked body out of her mind.

The passenger door opened and Fran got in. "Sorry," she mumbled.

Jessie didn't reply. Instead, she started the engine and drove in silence. Fran as usual, closed her eyes and rested, seemingly content not to talk. When they got to the ground, Jessie didn't pay any attention to Fran. She locked the car and joined her teammates inside, hoping to relax with the girls and enjoy a late breakfast before they set off for their away game. As she stood at the counter, Ruth fussed over Fran, making sure she had a heaped plate of bacon, sausage, and eggs. Fran smiled her thanks.

"Morning, Jessie." Ruth smiled brightly, her voice cheerful.

"Hi, Ruth." Jessie tried to appear upbeat, but the narrowing of Ruth's eyes told her she had failed.

"Everything okay?"

The older woman's concern was touching. "I'll be fine. Just had a bad start to my morning."

Ruth nodded. "I heard Fran was late." The statement held no question or censure—that wasn't Ruth's way. "It's good of you to be giving her a lift. She needs a wee bit of help."

"I'd do it for any member of the team, Ruth." She didn't want Ruth to assume she was going out of her way to accommodate Fran.

Ruth nodded. "I know you would, Jessie." Her reply was sincere. "Now what can I get you?"

The warm smile that accompanied the soft words caused Jessie to melt a little. "Fruit salad, please, Ruth, and plain yogurt." That would be enough to keep her going. The bus trip would only take an hour to Glasgow.

"Your first game back today. I bet you're excited?" Ruth asked as she put Jessie's food on a tray.

"You have no idea."

Laughing, Ruth placed the tray in front of Jessie. "Here you go. Are you sure that's filling enough?"

"I've already had muesli." Jessie patted her stomach.

"That's my girl. You have a good one, Jessie."

Taking her food over to the table where Sophie sat with a couple of the other girls, Jessie joined them. She wanted to avoid Fran at all costs today unless it was completely necessary.

"Hey, Jessie, glad you could make it," Sophie joked.

"Don't start," Jessie warned her friend.

"Come on, it was only twenty minutes."

Fran was tucking into the hearty breakfast Ruth had cooked. Why did everyone make excuses for her? It was Jessie who was constantly being put out by her, not them.

"Don't want to talk about it." Jessie speared a strawberry aggressively, warning Sophie that she really wasn't in the mood to be teased.

"Looking forward to the game?"

"Oh yeah." The spark of anticipation rekindled in the pit of her stomach. Jessie couldn't wait to get back into the action.

"Nice one," Sophie replied with a grin.

✦

Fran entered the tunnel. The tension was palpable. Both teams lined up in the small space, like amazons waiting to enter the arena. Each player focused, bursting with anticipation. The air crackled with energy as nerves jangled. Andrea stood at the front of her troops, her yellow armband indicating she was the leader. Staring straight ahead, she refused to make eye contact with the opposition. She was still, focused, while others around her bounced and shouted.

Jessie resembled a tightly coiled spring waiting to be unleashed. It seemed her time on the sidelines had wound her up more than usual. All the pent-up anger and frustration was probably about to explode. It needed an outlet, and the cauldron of the football pitch would provide it.

Fran, slouched at the back, casually leaning against the concrete wall, arms folded. She and Jessie couldn't have been more different.

Jessie was pissed at her. Again. She hadn't meant to sleep in, but last night had been tough, and the warm body had kept her out of trouble. Then Jessie had rapped on her bedroom door. She sighed. Once again she'd given Jessie the wrong impression. Shit always seemed to happen when Jessie was around. Nothing she could do about it now, there was a game to play.

Fran closed her eyes and cleared her mind. She stood up straight, squared her shoulders, and walked out of the tunnel. Football was a welcome distraction, ninety minutes that effortlessly occupied her mind, giving her a purpose and focus. Enjoyment was irrelevant to her. Winning would be nice, but a loss wouldn't put a damper on her day the way it would the rest of the team. She would give it her all, football was a team sport, after all, but she was waging a one-woman war. With herself.

Christ! Fran hissed. The opposition striker left her mark as they both went to ground in a challenge for the ball. She'd won it, but the stud marks from the striker showed clearly on her thigh. Fran stood and hobbled back to her defensive position, trying valiantly to run the injury off, but to no avail. A few short minutes later, she saw Danika getting ready on the sideline, probably to replace her. She was a liability, the injury hampering her movement. Not to mention that it bloody hurt. Her number flashed up on the electronic board and she limped off the pitch.

Tom briefly patted her on the shoulder as she passed him. Maggie Kennedy was waiting to assess the injury, quickly strapping an ice pack to her thigh. Mo Cunningham passed Fran a jacket as she took a seat in the dugout, elevating her injured leg on a cool box. Folding her arms, Fran leaned back against the fibreglass and watched the final ten minutes play out.

Tom Matthews spun on his leather-soled shoe, turning away from the action. Like Jessie, he knew how to dress for each occasion.

"What part of 'keep the ball' don't they get!" he complained in the general direction of the Lothian Thistle bench, gesturing wildly. Fran had to agree the team had been poor on the ball all game, turning possession over cheaply on several occasions. It had been tough against last season's champions, but they were making life more difficult for themselves.

"Jessie! Jessie!" Tom bellowed as he cupped his hands around his mouth projecting his voice loudly to get her attention. "Stay at the halfway line!" He gestured with his right hand, urging her back up the field. "We've no chance of scoring with her all the way back there!" Another pass went astray, once again handing possession to their opponents.

"Dammit!" Tom's skinny charcoal tie whipped over the shoulder of his expensive fitted dark suit as he once again spun inside the designated technical area. "We went over the tactics all week!"

Jessie had drifted deep again in an attempt to get on the ball. Fran knew it was instinctual. Jessie wanted to affect the game, and being isolated and receiving little of the ball meant she came searching for it.

"Jessie! Stay up!" Tom turned to the substitutes bench. "Elaine."

Elaine Travers stood up, surprise written on her face. "You'll be going on for Jessie. Stay the hell up the park. Play on the shoulder of the defence, keep the ball, and wait for support. Draw a foul if you have to, but don't you dare come back over the halfway line."

Elaine nodded. "Sure boss."

Tom rubbed his forehead. "Get yourself ready."

"Ah, Christ!" Tom cursed as Sophie, normally so dependable, played a rushed pass to Jessie, which was easily cut out, and now Glenleven players were again on the attack. Fran watched the drama unfold. While Sophie was working hard to get back, Danika was rooted to the spot, stuck out on the right touchline. Sophie extended a muscled leg and passed the ball back towards Louise Fisher, Danika's central defensive partner. The opposition player tumbled to the ground as Sophie made contact with her, and Fran expected the whistle to blast awarding a free kick to Glenleven. Much to her surprise, the challenge went unpunished and the hesitation in Glenleven allowed Louise to play an accurate pass out to Danika who had remained on the touchline.

Danika cut inside and passed to Jessie, who had only the goalie to beat with the choice of shooting or dribbling around her.

With Tom in Fran's line of vision, she didn't quite see what happened next.

"Penalty!" he screamed, his arms wide in appeal, awaiting the referee's decision. He pumped his fist when she pointed to the penalty spot and stepped back inside the technical area.

The back-pedalling defender had brought Jessie down. She picked herself up from the grass while the referee produced a straight red card for the challenge, the player having clearly prevented a goal-scoring opportunity.

Jessie placed the ball on the penalty spot as the opposition players did their best to interrupt her preparation. Two deep breaths, no eye contact with the goalkeeper, she took four strides, and calmly stroked the ball into the bottom left corner of the goal. With only seven minutes of the game remaining and the opposition a player down, Fran was confident they would now win this game.

Tom waited four more minutes before making his substitution, bringing Jessie off to help run down the clock. At the final whistle, the bench breathed a collective sigh of relief. It was a victory. They didn't all come the way you expected, but any win was welcome.

———— ⊷⊶ ————

The changing room was full of excited chatter. They were buoyant. Then Tom entered. Closing the door behind him, he took up a prominent position in the middle of the room. The frivolity continued among the smell of fresh sweat, VapoRub, and massage cream.

Sucking in his top lip, Tom slowly turned around the room making eye contact with the players who had become aware of his presence, instinctively knowing to pay attention. As the room quietened, a yelp and giggle in the corner stood out in stark relief to the descending silence, the two players immediately sitting as they became aware something was going on.

"What. The hell. Happened out there?" With a pinched thumb and first finger punctuating each word, Tom looked around the room. The euphoria of beating the current champions was evaporating faster than a summer rain.

"We had a game plan," he continued, hands on hips, visibly struggling to contain his anger. "I worked hard on that game plan. I studied the opposition." Again he paused. "Drove all over Scotland taking in games, watched countless videos on YouTube. For what?" Tom yelled. "For you to go out on the pitch and ignore it?"

Fran hid her smile as two players jumped at Tom's raised voice.

"Don't stare at the floor, keep your eyes on me." Tom pointed towards himself. "We got lucky today. We should've lost, instead we stole three points." Some players were nodding, beginning to take on board the reality of the situation. "How many times did we give the ball away? Sophie? Morven?" Sophie shook her head, while Morven stared at him, nostrils flaring. Fran was certain she wanted to jump up and punch him.

"Jessie," he said and waited a beat. "When I tell you not to come deeper than the halfway line for the ball, I bloody well mean it!" Jessie's cheeks flushed pink, but Tom's eyes remained hard. "You got lucky. One good pass from Danika, a rarity today, and it's just as well the defender brought you down, because you were never going to make up your mind whether to shoot or dribble around her."

Tom turned. "Fran, Pauline, well played. Without your performances we would definitely have lost today."

Pauline Elliot nodded briefly, the only sign of acknowledgement as Fran sat with her legs stretched out in front of her, her sock-clad feet crossed, arms folded, staring at the opposite wall. She hated to be singled out for praise. She would far rather be scolded along with the rest of the team. Uncomfortable with the attention, she refused to look at anyone, especially Jessie. She was clearly pissed off today for all kinds of reasons. Fran being praised was only going to make that worse.

"As for the rest of you," Tom said, "you need to get your act together. I want you all to take time over the next forty-eight hours to think about what went wrong, because come Tuesday, we are going to work on making sure next time we get it right." A finger punctuated the air to emphasise his point. "Learn the sheets. I mean it. If anyone went on that pitch today unsure as to what her role was, that must never happen again. Every one of you assured me you knew what you were doing."

Tom appeared to be building up a head of steam again. "Was it too complicated?" Frustration was building in his speech. A few murmurs of "no" greeted the question. "All you had to do was keep possession, keep it simple. Work for each other to make sure the player on the ball had options, frustrate the opposition. I told you the mistakes would come from them."

He shook his head. "There was no patience. You forced the game from the first whistle and made mistake after mistake. We lacked belief in our ability out there, collectively." Tom stopped for a moment. "You need to trust me. I know what you're all capable of and how to achieve it."

He turned to face the opposite direction. "You went out there today believing you weren't good enough. On paper, they have the stronger team. They do. But the game isn't played on paper, ladies. It's played on grass, and I put together a game plan that would beat them. You need to believe in yourselves, and you need to trust me, otherwise what's the point of me being here?" Tom opened his arms. "You're good enough, as a team, to win this league. To play European football next season. If you don't want that, then I'm wasting my time here."

Tom put a hand on his chest. "I'm ambitious. I'm competitive. I want more than to be an also-ran. I can and I will make you winners." He met the gaze of every woman in the room. "If you let me." Tom walked from the dressing, the subdued silence hanging in the air. His words had clearly hit the mark.

Fran stood and stripped off the remainder of her kit. She didn't want to hang around in the flat atmosphere.

❖

Jessie stared out the window as the coach sped along the motorway, taking the team back to Edinburgh. She sat alone, preferring the solitude of the moment. Normally, the team would be boisterous after a good away win, but the dressing-down Tom had delivered had left all of them in a sombre mood. The open fields dotted with trees passed by in a blur as Jessie stared out without focusing on the beauty outside. She turned her head when someone sat in the seat beside her.

"Oh, hi, Soph."

Sophie inclined her head towards the back of the bus where Fran was asleep. "You'd think after a long lie-in this morning she wouldn't need any more."

"Trust me, I don't imagine she got much sleep last night," Jessie muttered.

Sophie's dark brown eyes sparked with interest. "How would you know?"

She shook her head, then focused fully on Sophie. "Listen, have you been in the place where she works?"

"No, what's it like?"

"It's a hotel, with a bar. Well, was a hotel, it's only a bar now. Anyway, this morning when I arrived, the front door was open, and there were folk asleep and a guy was pulling a pint."

Sophie shrugged. "Was Fran asleep in the bar?"

"No, she was upstairs, naked, with a blonde plastered to her."

"A woman?" Sophie asked, grinning.

"Yeah, with a potty mouth on her. She was not pleased to be woken up."

Sophie laughed. "What did you do?"

"Got out of there! I was mortified."

"You are such a prude."

"It was just…" Jessie gestured helplessly, throwing her hand in the air. "Unexpected."

Sophie grinned. "I'm sure it was."

"Cup draw's being made!" Zoe Wood declared as she skipped past them towards the back of the bus.

Jessie and Sophie made their way towards the rest of the team, who were gathered around Tom's seat. The Scottish cup was a welcome distraction from the weekly pressures of the league, especially in the early rounds, where they were likely to draw a lower ranked team.

"Who've we got, Tom?" Zoe asked excitedly, her short red hair perfectly styled with gel.

"Hang on, the draw is happening. My mate's there, he's going to text the name of our opponents."

Everyone waited. Anticipation hung in the air, a couple of her teammates literally bouncing in their seats.

"So long as we avoid a big name first round, I'll be happy." There were a few nods of agreement with Andrea's statement.

"Come on, come on," Zoe added as she grasped the back of the seat tightly.

"Patience, ladies," Tom joked. When his phone beeped, everyone stopped chatting, all eyes on him as he read the text. The energy around the manager was palpable, a mixture of excitement and trepidation. Tom's face held no expression as he scanned the expectant faces gathered around him. "Orkney Ladies."

"Please, no," Morven said, the hint of dread in her voice mirrored by most of the players.

"Get on with it, Tom." Andrea was clearly losing patience. "Put us out of our misery."

"Away." With that simple word chaos ensued around him. There were groans and curses, and someone punched a seat.

"What does this mean?" Danika asked, confusion written all over her face.

"It means a thirty-six-hour trip, Danika," Andrea replied.

"For a football game?" The normally cool woman's voice went up a notch.

"We have to travel to the Orkney Isles."

Jessie stared at Tom. "I hope your friend has a warped sense of humour, or our sponsor stumps up for plane tickets." She knew there was no way David Laidlaw would pay for them to fly. "Two bloody days away to play a football match that we'll win at a canter." She sat down heavily on her seat, arms folded.

"I'm not even sure our team could all fit on one flight. It's those little propeller things."

"That's not helpful, Sophie," Jessie chastised.

"Look, regardless, there's no way he'll pay for flights. You know this from previous experience. So it's going to be bus, boat, and a cheap hotel. It'll be half the price." Tom tried to diffuse the situation, now standing to restore order and focus among his players.

"I'm flying. Then I can be in and out of there in the one day," Morven declared, the policewoman's time was more precious than most, especially with shift work.

"I'd prefer the team stay together," Tom countered. The assistant manager, Mo, was already making plans for the trip ahead, her wavy brown hair, covering her face as she used her phone to surf the net.

Jessie closed her eyes and leaned her head back against the seat. A trip to Orkney, probably one of the easiest teams, but the worst possible draw. The only good thing about today had been the win.

Chapter 6

The howling wind caused the rain to sting like pinpricks as it hit Fran's face. She stood in a recess next to the Town Hall, sheltering from the foul weather. She zipped her leather jacket to her chin and upturned the collar, trying to protect herself against the elements as best she could. She cupped her hand around a cigarette and attempted unsuccessfully to light it as the wind whipped viciously into the recess. Eventually, she gave up and returned the cigarette to the packet.

The estate agent's office was only twenty metres from where she was standing and it would be ten more minutes until Jessie would leave work. *Ah, fuck it.* Fran ran to the door, the warmth blanketing her as she entered the premises. Silence and relief greeted her, along with a young woman who lifted her head from the computer screen, the heavy-rimmed black glasses adding an air of studiousness to an otherwise pretty blonde.

"Hello, may I help you?" A warm smile accompanied the polite enquiry.

"Jessie's giving me a lift to training," Fran replied as she wiped away damp, long black strands of hair that stuck to her face.

"Oh, hiya, I'm Meadow." Politeness was instantly replaced by excited exuberance.

Fran smiled at the friendly girl. "Fran. Nice to meet you, Meadow," she replied, offering her hand in greeting.

"That weather's horrible. You were right to come in and wait. Have a seat and I'll let Jessie know you're here."

"Thanks."

Fran took in the modern office. There was a desk that Meadow was using and two others that were currently unoccupied. Obviously, there was a back office for Jessie, offering more privacy. The front window and the main wall were lined neatly with A4 panels advertising property for sale. Two large canvas landscapes hung on the wall on either side of the recess leading to the back office. One depicted the seafront and the other a vast open green space. Fran found both images relaxing, no doubt what they were designed for.

"Five more minutes, Fran, and Jessie will be ready to leave. Would you like a tea or coffee while you wait?"

Fran offered Meadow a lopsided grin. "I'm good, thanks."

Meadow's smile in return was a little bashful. Fran tried to relax on the comfortable sofa, but her damp jeans clung uncomfortably to her thighs, so she stretched her long legs out in front of her to ease the stiff denim. She closed her eyes, took a deep breath, and the gentle clacking of a keyboard hypnotically lulled her towards slumber.

Fran peeked from under half-closed lids as the muted thud of heels on carpet reached her ears, and Jessie entered the outer office. She wore a dark grey trouser suit over a crisp white blouse, finished off with black heeled ankle boots. Jessie always dressed smartly. Neat and pristine, with each occasion in mind, whether it was work or football. Fran thought it must take a hell of an effort to be that co-ordinated at all times. A light dusting of make-up with a hint of floral scent that barely tickled Fran's nostrils finished the ensemble. Despite her aversion to Jessie's orderly life, mirrored by the attire, Fran couldn't help but admire her. Something kept pulling her in, much to her annoyance.

"Let's close up. Meadow, you get yourself off home. Rod won't be returning today, and I doubt anyone else is going to drop in. The weather will put them off."

"Thanks, Jessie."

Meadow removed her glasses and popped them into her desk drawer before grabbing her coat and bag from the back office. She was out of the door in under a minute with a wave and a smile. Jessie picked a large black umbrella from a bucket near the door and handed it to Fran.

"We're going to need this."

Outside, Fran valiantly held on to the umbrella as the wind caught it, holding it over Jessie while she locked up and then as they walked to the car. She was tired and cold, the dampness seeping deep into her bones. Since leaving the Beachcomber, a weariness had descended upon her. She could blame the weather, but Fran knew she was suffering a dip in mood. She sensed the darkness creeping in, bringing with it agitation, unsettling her. She had to keep moving forward. Focus on each day and not let her mind wander to dark places. She needed to put one foot in front of the other and not look back. That's where the danger lurked, in the past, waiting to enter the present.

As they travelled towards the training ground, she was grateful Jessie had taken the hint and now remained fairly quiet for the duration of their car journeys. When she did speak, it was with purpose, not the incessant, space-filling, idle chit-chat that caused Fran to grind her teeth. Or the probing questions about her life, which were nobody's business but her own. Fran closed her eyes as the car wound its way through the miserable, drenched Edinburgh streets, grateful for the heater blasting warm air onto her damp legs.

Jessie hung her trouser suit on a hanger and placed it inside a suit cover. Fran was in her usual spot in the corner of the changing room, removing her piercings. The club physio, Maggie Kennedy, inserted silicone discs into Fran's stretched ears, swabbing the area with alcohol wipes. Jessie shook her head. The preparation that physios had to do that fell outside their usual remit was on the increase. After a brief discussion between the two of them, Maggie nodded and left. Jessie dressed appropriately for the wet, muddy weather. Training wasn't going to be that enjoyable, but she didn't mind the rain.

Maggie returned a few moments later with a pair of compression shorts, which Fran put on, indicating she had some kind of problem. Most players were carrying a niggle of some sort, but usually you could play through the smaller injuries. Maggie would work her magic to restrict training and offer treatment that would aid recovery. Sometimes, very rarely, a player made the most of an injury. Jessie hoped Fran wasn't that type.

As the players funnelled out of the changing room, Tom was waiting.

"No chance of using the indoor plastic pitch, Tom?" Zoe asked.

"You know the rules, Zoe. A match would go ahead in this weather, so we train in it."

"We could catch pneumonia," she complained.

"Wrap up warm then," was Tom's retort.

Grinning at the verbal exchange, Jessie opened the door. Despite being wrapped up against the elements, she shivered as the wind and rain hit her full force. She broke out into a slow jog to ward off the chill. Nothing would keep her from the training pitch unless it would do her harm, and even then she would train in a reduced capacity.

Training was brisk and busy. Tom had obviously decided that it was best not to let the players cool down between drills, deliberately keeping them warm to avoid injury. Fran trained lightly, but after a brief discussion with the physio, the two of them left the outside pitch. Jessie pursed her lips, as they returned to the clubhouse.

"Lucky bitch! We are all out here freezing our arses off and she's getting to go back into the warmth," Zoe declared, her normally coiffed hair plastered to her head. She attempted to intercept a ball as it was passed from Jessie to Morven, then on to two other players as the one-touch drill increased in pace.

"Concentrate on winning the ball, Zoe. You are staying in there until you do," Tom called out.

Without discussion, the six players in the training drill increased the pace of their passing until Zoe fell over from exhaustion.

"Get up, Zoe! Go again!" Tom bellowed.

As Zoe got to her feet, Jessie hit her on the backside with a stinging pass, causing the group to laugh at their teammate's predicament, as she yelped and cursed.

"You're all sadists!" Zoe screamed as she rubbed her backside.

Taking pity on her, Jessie, took her spot in the centre, relishing the challenge of the intense workout.

"Come on then, let's see what you all have?" Taunting her teammates produced the expected response. They were going to try and keep her in the middle, chasing the ball as long as possible.

As the players made their way back inside after training, it was a welcome relief to get out of the rain. Jessie stopped in the doorway of the treatment room, hesitating. Fran was lying mostly naked on the treatment table. Jessie took in her body, the long, lean legs, the tattoos on her back, head tilted to one side, eyes staring at Jessie as Maggie worked on her right buttock. The image sparked an unwelcome twinge in the pit of Jessie's stomach, a visceral reaction beyond her control.

She pushed the sensation back, determined to bury it. To cage it like a dangerous beast. Arousal and yearning had no place in her life, especially not where Fran was concerned. It was unexpected, but Jessie knew it wasn't real. It couldn't be. Fran did not interest her in that way. *It must just be some residual feeling to seeing her with that blonde,* Jessie reasoned with herself.

It was a joy to peel off her wet training clothes, and the hot shower was heavenly, melting away the cold as the water sluiced over her body, carrying with it the intermingled sweat, dirt, and unwelcome arousal. It swirled and disappeared down the drain, leaving Jessie cleansed and clean. As she dressed, Fran walked into the changing room wearing only a sports bra and briefs. The back of her right thigh glistened with massage oil in the light, indicating that Maggie had worked on her hamstring.

Jessie wondered absently if Fran might not be fit for the weekend game, and despite her early season misgivings, she knew that Fran would be missed if that was the case. She was getting fitter, and despite her laid-back attitude, she brought a solidness to the defence that hadn't been there last season.

CHapteR 7

THE TRIUMPHAL MARCH FROM *AIDA* roared upliftingly from the speakers as Jessie sat parked next to the promenade waiting for Fran. She was early and it was a beautiful autumn afternoon. A light breeze carried a nip in the air. She hoped the weather in Orkney would be similar—it was perfect for football.

Jessie relaxed as she hummed along with the music. She loved opera. She closed her eyes and let herself forget where she was for a moment. When she opened her eyes, Fran walked past, pushing an elderly man in a wheelchair. The pair made their way up the pavement before they disappeared into one of the large Victorian houses.

Jessie checked her watch, but Fran still had ten minutes before they were due to meet. She closed her eyes again and relaxed back into the music.

The passenger door opened, causing Jessie jump and reach for the button to shut off the music. A hand covered hers, stopping her. Jessie turned, confused, eyes on her companion.

"Please leave it on."

The quiet request surprised Jessie. She simply nodded once and started the car. The familiar scent of mint and smoke filled the interior as Fran settled back in the passenger seat, eyes closed and hands clasped loosely over her stomach.

As Jessie drove, she remained silent, sensing that it would ruin what was a connection of sorts for them. She didn't know who the man in the wheelchair was, but she knew Fran cared for him and she liked classical music. For now, that was enough.

The drive to the club was pleasant. The solitude they shared while they were both lost in their own thoughts was one of the most peaceful moments

Jessie could remember in a long time. So much so that she wished she had more time to just drive around. Instead, she pulled into the parking lot and the music died as she shut off the engine.

Fran turned to her. "Thank you," she said quietly before undoing her seatbelt and reaching for the passenger door.

"Do you have a favourite?" Jessie asked softly.

Fran stopped. Her back to Jessie, she answered, "Stravinsky." Then she was gone. The moment over and the spell broken.

Travelling the evening before a game on the team bus was a rowdy affair. Players were bored and full of energy. It was still too early to focus on playing the next day, and they were all in a relaxed, playful mood. Some were hanging over the back of their seats, chatting with each other. Some had headphones on to drown out their rowdier teammates. Fran was stretched out on the back seat, probably asleep. Everyone left the seat empty for her, knowing she liked to rest.

"Listen up, ladies!" Morven shouted as she walked up the bus, pulling headphones off the players who were enjoying music and giving Fran a playful push with her foot. She was rewarded with an eye popping open and a shoe being thrown her way. "Although I'm sure most of you already know," she went on, glancing up and down the bus as she stood in the middle, making sure she had everyone's attention, "Jessie is still in the lead on Twitter with over 12,000 followers."

"That's because she's an Olympian!"

Jessie couldn't be sure who the dissenting voice belonged to, but there was truth in the reason for her accumulating more followers than most of the team combined. Being in the 2012 Olympic squad had contributed to a huge surge in her Twitter followers.

Morven paused to allow the usual congratulations and abuse to be hurled. Jessie nodded her thanks and ignored the more ribald comments.

"Fran's gained the most followers this season with almost 3,000."

"Fran has a Twitter account?" Jessie blurted, shocked at this news.

"And a Facebook page," Morven replied.

Jessie frowned. "She doesn't even own a smartphone."

"She doesn't have a computer, either," Morven added, which caused laughter among the players. "Me and Zoe run the accounts." Fran sat up, though not quite fully, on the back seat. "Fran, your Twitter followers love that you interact with them so freely."

A raised eyebrow was the slouching woman's reply.

"I'm joking. We're keeping it very professional, as per Mo's instructions."

"And I'm keeping a close eye on it, Morven," Mo Cunningham, the assistant manager warned.

Jessie was surprised that Mo allowed Morven any part in running the accounts. Morven had a streak of devilment in her that couldn't be tamed. The only time she was serious was when she was on duty as a police officer and on the pitch. Jessie suspected that social media accounts in Fran's name were a disaster waiting to happen.

Why did everyone assist Fran? Everyone. All doing their part and enabling her to simply turn up and train or play. She refused to do media. Just refused. Jessie thought it unlikely she would say much beyond a few grunts anyway, but that wasn't the point. Everyone else had to do media along with promotion and skills coaching for kids to get them into the game. Fran strolled around avoiding all extra responsibilities, and everyone accepted that. She suspected Fran had stipulated what she would and wouldn't do in her contract, and Tom had agreed in order to secure her signature.

Jessie only half listened as Morven continued to update the team on the various activities that were coming up. Apparently, she was taking her job heading up the social committee very seriously. Jessie leaned her head against the bus window, staring out into the darkening sky as they hurtled towards the northerly tip of Scotland, and tried to forget how much Fran and the whole situation bothered her.

———— ◦━◦◦━◦ ————

Fran lay in her hotel bed wide awake as a foghorn blared in the distance. They'd arrived in Scrabster around two hours ago and Fran guessed it was a little before midnight. The team would be catching the first ferry in the morning over to Orkney for a 1 p.m. kick-off. Then all they had to do was win the game and get back on the evening ferry, before they got to enjoy the bus journey all the way home to Edinburgh. What the fuck was she doing here? She'd signed on for two seasons of this, and then she was done with it.

The revelry coming from the wedding reception in the hotel bar below her room wasn't to blame for her insomnia. Jessie snored lightly in the twin bed adjacent to hers. The faint, sweet scent of Jessie's perfume tickled her nose causing an unwanted jolt of arousal, and she cursed her own libido.

It was unwelcome, this attraction to Jessie. It had been there since she had first laid eyes on her in the final game of last season. The confident woman with the cute curls had grabbed her attention.

Fran sighed. Jessie was off limits for so many reasons. She was a teammate and it would complicate life. Assuming Jessie would even agree to share her bed, which, she had to admit, seemed unlikely, she didn't seem like the one-night-stand type. And Fran didn't do anything else. She briefly entertained the notion of pleasuring herself, but Jessie was sleeping less than three feet away, and while the idea of Jessie catching her or hearing her was damn exciting, it brought her straight back to complicating her life. Jessie had only just got over seeing her in bed with...what was her name again?

Fran turned away from Jessie and tried to force sleep to come for her. It was no good. She craved sex.

The bed sheets irritated her skin. She was uncomfortably hot. Sitting up, she searched in the dark for her discarded clothing. She knew she should stay in bed, but she couldn't— her body was wired. She needed space, but she also knew danger lurked outside the door. She located her jeans with trembling hands, and pulled them on slowly so as not to alert her roommate. Jessie would be so unimpressed with her slipping out at this hour.

Her dark T-shirt was impossible to find without light, but she spotted a white shirt hanging over the back of a chair. Fran grabbed the shirt and slipped it about her shoulders, picked up her leather jacket and ankle boots, and eased the door open just enough to slip out.

Fran stood outside the main bar full of revellers. She took a deep breath. She wanted to step inside, to join them. To join the fun. But that would be a mistake. Her mouth was dry. Her tongue ached for the first taste, for the burn that would follow. She was so close to caving. She wanted to. She wanted to walk up to the bar and order a drink. Instead, she clenched her fists and forced herself towards the main entrance on stiff legs.

Outside the front entrance to the hotel, Fran tucked into the corner and allowed the cold air to cool her heated skin. Less than fifty yards away was the well-lit harbour, quiet at this hour. She lit a cigarette and tried to relax as the smoke filled her lungs and the nicotine entered her bloodstream. She had avoided the danger. For now.

A woman stumbled out of the hotel, her gait unsteady, and her lopsided grin infectious. She stood apparently oblivious to Fran's presence, staring up into the starlit night.

"Oh, could I bum one of your ciggies?" The smiling woman teetering towards her wore only a thin, sleeveless, ivory dress. She rubbed her bare arms in an attempt to protect herself from the chilly October night air. Her dark hair was in a bun, but several strands had come loose throughout the evening. *Cute, in a wholesome kind of way.*

Fran offered a cigarette from her packet, then lit it for the clearly inebriated stranger, who swayed as she tried to stand still.

The woman took a deep draw from the cigarette, exhaling the long stream of smoke up into the air. "Thanks. I've not seen you around here before, I'm Jenny." She thrust an uncoordinated hand towards Fran.

"Fran, going to Orkney." She shook hands then flicked ash from the tip of her smoke.

"Family?"

Fran shook her head. "Football."

Scrutinising Fran, the woman appeared doubtful. "You don't look like a footballer. I love your ears by the way." Jenny leaned in and pointed at Fran's ear, her eyes unfocused.

"Cheers."

The woman shivered. "Jesus, it's freezing."

Fran stubbed out her cigarette and removed her jacket, then draped the leather over her shoulders causing Jenny to moan in pleasure. "Mm, that's hot."

Jenny stumbled backwards into Fran, who caught her around the waist. Her backside nestled into Fran's pelvis. They stood so close that the woman's hair tickled Fran's lips. Placing her mouth next to the brunette's ear, she spoke softly. "So are you."

The words caused a shiver to run through the stranger, and she leaned back into Fran's body. Fran's left arm snaked around the woman's waist, pulling her in close. "Do you want to get a room?" she whispered in her new friend's ear.

The woman stiffened in her arms and Fran was aware of someone standing next to them. As she raised her head she saw a smartly dressed man staring at them, his hand holding an unlit cigarette, frozen in mid-air. A myriad of emotions passed over his face, confusion, suspicion, until he settled on one. "What the fuck!"

At those words, the woman in Fran's arms also reacted, pushing her away. "I'm the bride!" she shrieked.

"Did she try and pick you up?"

Before either woman could answer, the man lunged at Fran and they both ended up hurtling into the bushes next to the front door. Jenny, the bride, was screaming at the man to stop.

"Leave her alone, Drew!"

Fran managed to free herself from the bushes before he did and rolled to her feet. Guests from the wedding had gathered around the front entrance to find out what the shouting was about. Fran stood, not sure which direction to move in as her attacker remained entangled in the shrubbery.

"What's going on, Jen?" asked a man who resembled the one in the bushes. With his thick wheat-coloured hair and generous lips, they were both built like farmers. Fran swallowed hard.

Drew answered as he tried to untangle himself from the bushes. "Magnus, she tried to pick up your wife!" He pointed at Fran.

Jenny put a comforting hand on Magnus' chest, rubbing affectionately. "She didn't know it's was my wedding. Did you?" She frowned at Fran.

Fran held up her hands in a gesture of surrender. "No, not a clue. Sorry."

"See? She didn't know." Jenny swayed in Magnus' arms and accidentally headbutted his chest. "So let's all calm down."

Magnus gazed at Jenny, his eyes softening. "Jesus, these city folk." He stood in front of Fran. "I'll say this for you, you have good taste, but your timing could do with a little work."

Fran grinned. "Sorry about that and congratulations." She knew not to add anything to that comment.

Jenny took her new husband's hand. "Well, this'll be some story for the grandkids. A woman tried to pick me up on my wedding night." Her

50

comment caused laughter among the guests, though Magnus didn't seem to find it quite so funny.

Fran wiped the dirt from her hands on her jeans and offered her hand to Magnus. "I'm sorry for any offence caused."

Magnus shook her hand. "No harm done, hen."

Fran said goodnight and went back inside, only to find herself confronted by some of her teammates. Jessie among them, arms folded, glaring at her.

"Is that my blouse?"

Fran had forgotten she was wearing Jessie's shirt. It was now ripped, covered in dirt and spots of blood. She was about to speak when a hand rested on her shoulder.

"Here's your jacket, Fran. I hope you don't hurt too much in the morning."

"Thanks, Jenny." Fran took the jacket, holding it in one hand. What could she say to Jessie? She hadn't envisioned ending up in a fight when she slipped out for a cigarette. "I'm sorry."

Jessie shook her head before turning on her heel and presumably heading back to the room.

"Come on everyone, let's get back to bed," Mo suggested. "We have a busy day tomorrow."

"Fran, come with me. I'll clean up those cuts and scratches," Maggie offered.

Fran followed Maggie, refusing to make eye contact with anyone else as she made her way to the stairs.

--- ✧ ---

Weary, tired, and a little sore, Fran inserted her key card into the room door. After a quiet beep, she pulled the handle. Jessie was sitting up in bed using her iPad. Fran had hoped she'd be asleep. She quietly started to undress.

"What kind of person tries to pick up the bride at her wedding reception?"

She sat on the edge of her bed. "I didn't know she was the bride."

"Thank God for that." Jessie closed the cover on her iPad and put it on the side table.

Fran pulled off her boots and jeans, then finally removed the white shirt. Holding it up she gestured helplessly at the damaged garment. "Sorry."

Jessie waved off the apology, staring intently at Fran's semi naked body. She appeared to be scrutinising the various scratches marking her skin. "Do you enjoy playing football?"

Fran lay back on the bed, propping her head and shoulders up on the pillows. "It's all right."

"Why do you bother?"

Fran covered her face with both hands, she attempted to rub away the tension gathering at her temples. "I need the money."

"Are you in debt?"

"Something like that." She was too tired to keep her guard up.

"You owe someone money?" Jessie continued probing.

"I owe a lot more than that," she answered cryptically.

"Do you own the Beachcomber?" Jessie's voice held more than a hint of frustration.

Fran shook her head. "No."

"If you do…"

"It's a long story and I'm tired." Her reply was terse. She'd had enough of Jessie's questions. Talking to her was dangerous. It made Fran want to tell her everything. Made her want to open up and bare her soul. Something else she would never—could never—do. She turned her back and waited for Jessie to turn off the lamp and plunge the room into the darkness to match what she felt inside.

⁕

"Quick, lock up your wives!"

Jessie raised her head as an eruption of laughter followed the comment from Zoe. Fran had arrived in the breakfast room where most of her teammates were already gathered.

"Hey, Fran, it's the bridesmaids you're supposed to try and shag, not the bride," Sophie said to more chuckles. "Come on over and join us."

Fran did as requested, making her way to the table where some of the more exuberant characters in the team sat.

Morven slapped Fran's back as she took a seat. "You've got some pair on you, missus."

"I only went out for a cigarette." Fran's simple explanation caused more laughter.

"You have scratches all down the side of your neck." Zoe helpfully pointed out. "Where did you get them?"

Jessie knew there were many more scratches over Fran's torso. The other woman must be in some discomfort.

"I fell into a bush."

"Oh my God, I'm going to pee myself. I'm actually going to pee!" Zoe crossed her legs and bit her lip, indicating she was serious.

As the hilarity unfolded a couple of tables away, Jessie thought the saddest part was the only person at the other table not laughing was Fran herself. She turned to Tom. "What are you going to do?"

"What do you mean?" He frowned as he buttered his toast.

"She broke curfew."

"Jessie, she couldn't sleep and went out for a smoke." Tom shrugged then put a forkful of scrambled eggs into his mouth.

"Did you miss the part where she tried to pick up the bride?" Jessie glared, waiting for him to finish his mouthful of food, disbelieving his lack of concern.

He shrugged. "What can I do?"

"She is a walking disaster. You're making allowances for her that you wouldn't for any other player."

"I would make the same allowances for you because you're valuable to the team. So is she." Tom's answer, though delivered in a quiet voice, held a hint of warning.

"So that's it? She gets away with her behaviour because of the talent?"

"That's always the way, Jessie. We want to win; she's a key part of that. She always turns up for training, and she always puts in a solid performance on match day. That's what she's paid to do."

Fran was eating breakfast while the players at her table spoke of the previous night. "She doesn't love the game." She turned back to Tom, wishing he could comprehend what she did.

"There are lots of people who love the game but don't have an ounce of her talent. Life's not always fair, Jessie. Your career could be over by the final whistle today. The wrong impact or angle in a tackle, a bad bit of the pitch when you plant your foot. An accident." Tom shrugged. "Then what?"

Jessie knew the point he was making, Tom loved the game, but he could no longer play. Now he was sharing his knowledge and passion while satiating his competitive spirit in a whole new way.

"Not everyone has the dedication and passion that you do, Jessie. You need to find a way of accepting that and move on."

"I know." She was angry at herself for allowing Fran Docherty to constantly get under her skin. "But it's unfair."

"My job is to get the best out of each player. If I punish her financially, she is likely to tell me to stuff it. If I bench her, she will sit there and watch us lose. It won't bother her in the slightest, but it will hurt the team. There is no punishment that will motivate Fran. I have to manage each player in a way that will get them to produce their best on the pitch. Once Fran has done something wrong, it's too late to do anything about it. She knows if she misses training or a game and it's not down to injury or illness, she won't get paid, and so far she has not missed one session or match."

"So she gets to do what she wants?"

"Come on, Jessie, it's not that bad."

Jessie pushed her empty plate away. "I give up."

Chapter 8

"Get out of my car." Jessie stood outside with the driver's door open. When she'd pressed the key fob to open the doors, some of her teammates had jumped in. Now she stood in the cold, on a dark frosty night, sober, with a car full of drunk women.

"We need a lift," Zoe stated from a busy backseat.

"There are too many of you." Jessie counted five of her teammates crammed into the car. "I'll get stopped by the police."

"I am the bloody police!"

"Morven?" Jessie couldn't see the policewoman, "Where are you?"

"I'm on the floor. Now I'm ordering you to get in your car and drive."

"You're all drunk."

"For God's sake, Jessie, just drive the car!" Morven shouted.

It was the Christmas night-out for the team, and all Jessie wanted to do now was go home. However, some of her teammates obviously had other ideas. Jessie sighed, climbed into the car, and started the engine. "Where are you going?"

"The Beachcomber. Since Fran couldn't make our night-out, we're going to her." Sophie was sitting in the passenger seat.

"I'm sure she'll be thrilled."

"Shut up and drive," Morven called. "Zoe, get your foot off my face!"

The smell of alcohol was overpowering, and Jessie decided it was best to get rid of them as quickly as possible. She pulled out of the car park and tried to ignore the hilarity that was going on in the confined space. "Morven, if I'm stopped by the police, you get to explain what's happening here." She couldn't drive the three miles quickly enough, inwardly cursing every red light that halted her progress.

"Bit heavy on the brakes there, Jessie!" Morven complained from somewhere in the back.

"Sorry, my foot slipped."

"My arse!"

Jessie was angry at being hijacked, and the anger was transferring to her driving. Just a few more minutes, and she'd be rid of them. But something wasn't right. The atmosphere in the car had changed.

"What are you lot whispering about?" Jessie glanced in the rear view mirror.

"Nothing," Zoe answered sharply.

"Sophie?"

"I have no idea," Sophie said.

Jessie pulled onto Brunstane Road and parked at the bottom next to the prom where she usually dropped Fran off.

"Everyone out."

Jessie waited as her car emptied and Morven finally sat up from the floor behind her. Sophie opened the driver door and leaned in to give Jessie a hug.

"Thanks, for the lift, Jessie."

"You're welcome, now let me go home."

As Jessie reached for her door, her seatbelt slackened and Morven pushed her towards Zoe.

"What the hell!"

"Quick grab her!" Morven shouted.

Quick as a flash, Jessie was pulled from the car by her teammates as Morven crawled out behind her, car keys in hand. "You're boring, so we're taking you for a drink."

Jessie struggled, but she was no match for the six of them.

"Grab her legs," Morven instructed as she locked the car.

"Put me down! I'm not being carried into a bar!"

"Don't, she'll run." Morven was clearly in charge of this stunt and calling the shots.

"I promise. I won't run."

"Sorry, Jessie, I don't believe you."

"Give me my car keys!"

Morven held them in front of her, but not close enough for Jessie to grab them. "Don't worry, the Volvo is all locked up safe. By the way, that car is as boring as you. This is an intervention."

"*This* is ridiculous!"

"Have a drink with us," Sophie pleaded. "Go on, you never let your hair down."

"That's because she has a stick up her arse."

Jessie glared at Morven. They were almost at the bar and Jessie was still being carried. A handful of patrons standing outside smoking, appeared bewildered by the scuffle.

"This is embarrassing," Jessie hissed.

"If you promise to have a drink, we'll let you walk in," Morven stated.

"I promise, one drink."

"Alcohol!"

"Good thinking, Alex," Morven replied, clearly impressed.

Alex McMann, normally quiet and introverted, had leapt out of her shell with alcohol-infused confidence.

Jessie huffed. "Fine. I promise, one alcoholic drink." Jessie's legs were lowered to the ground, but the players kept a tight hold on her upper body and she was literally frogmarched into a busy pub on a Friday night.

Fran was behind the bar, pouring a pint, but her eyes were firmly on Jessie, a small smirk playing on her lips as she dipped her eyes just as the pint glass was almost full. Placing it on the counter, she turned to give her full attention to the new party of revellers.

"Hey, Fran. Since you couldn't make the night-out, we've come to you," Morven said by way of an explanation. Behind her, Jessie mumbled something about a "Fran club", but the policewoman ignored her.

Fran studied Jessie with mirth in her eyes. "Okay."

"Six tequilas and whatever Jessie wants?" Morven threw a thumb back towards her.

Jessie shrugged of the last grip from her teammates and straightened her clothing. "I'll have a…" She didn't know what to order, but something about the way Fran's right eyebrow raised up really irked her. "A port."

"Do you want a cigar with that?" Morven joked, causing the rest of the team to laugh.

"A port?" Fran was clearly sceptical as she stood with her arms wide, palms flat on the mahogany counter.

"Yes. Port. Don't you have it?"

Fran shrugged and nodded, then turned to get the drinks order.

They found an empty table at the back of the bar, and the seven players crammed around it. Jessie stared at her teammates, all of whom rarely drank much alcohol, but tonight they had really let their hair down. They were entitled to let off steam every once in a while. They all worked or studied full-time on top of training hard and playing each weekend.

Morven leaned back in her chair, eyes glassy, as she appeared to be having trouble focusing. "Look at you, with your safe car and your practical clothes. Someone is going to get your number Jessie Grainger and your head's going to spin." Morven made a spinning motion with her index finger to emphasise her point. The rest of her teammates laughed.

Jessie sipped the port in front of her, not questioning the arrival of yet another glass of the claret liquid. It was smooth, easy to drink, but coated her tongue in a pasty substance. "I'm happy the way I am, Morven."

"Seriously, that white shirt of yours saw more action in the thirty minutes Fran wore it than in a lifetime with you." That comment caused outright laughter around the table, and Zoe snorted drink all over herself.

Jessie slumped back in her chair. She wasn't used to being taken apart so thoroughly without reply. She usually gave as good as she got, but tonight she didn't have any fight in her.

"Aw, Jessie, I'm only joking. I know I sometimes take it way too far, but listen, seriously." Morven moved to within an inch of Jessie, putting an arm around her shoulder. "All I'm saying is, you need to live a little. I think the world of you, Jessie. You're a top woman, but you need some romance in your life. I mean, you're gorgeous, plenty are interested. Men and woman, you can take your pick." Jessie remained silent. "Okay, okay. I'll shut up now." Morven hugged Jessie to her and ruffled her hair. "At least now we know what shuts you up, Jessie. Alcohol. You are never this quiet."

Jessie groaned. Her head was fuzzy and the room tilted at an odd angle. She was drunk. "I need the loo."

"Where's Jessie?" Sophie asked her very drunk friends, loud enough for everyone, including Fran, to hear her. "It's time to go, the bar's closing."

Morven waved a hand limply. "She'll have snuck out ages ago."

"Fran, have you seen Jessie?"

Fran, who'd agreed to sit with them for a few minutes since the bar closed, frowned. She hadn't seen Jessie for at least a half hour. "Have you checked the toilets?"

"No, I'll go do that," Sophie said, with a definite slur to her words.

"Nice one. Fran, could you call us a cab? Wait, how many are there. Who is still here?" Morven attempted to count.

"I'll get you two cabs," Fran said, knowing they wouldn't all fit in the one vehicle.

Morven saluted her teammate. "Thanks, chief."

"I can't find Jessie. She's not in the toilet," Sophie said. "Anybody know where Jessie is? Has anyone seen Jessie?"

Morven pursed her lips and raised her hands as if in defeat. "Jessie's gone home, Sophie. We brought her here against her will. Oh shit." Morven laughed, placing her hands on her head. "Wait until training, she is going to go nuts." She wobbled in her seat laughing at the prospect of Jessie's ire. "I can't believe we kidnapped her."

"And made her drink," Alex added remorsefully.

"That was your fault, Alex. You pointed out it had to be alcohol."

"It was your idea to kidnap her, Morven!"

Morven waved a hand randomly. "Ah, she'll come round." She sat back in her seat. "Those taxis here yet, Fran?"

"Few more minutes." Fran licked her lips, the urge to cut loose for a few hours and join in the festivities had been strong. To release all the pent-up emotion in an alcohol-induced buzz...bliss.

Now she was desperate for the taxis to arrive and take her teammates home while she cleaned up. Sitting idle surrounded by drunk people was too tempting. Her right leg bounced, the only outward sign of her inner turmoil. She envied her teammates their ability to do this for a night. To be able to let their guard down, drink, be merry, be stupid, and be able to pick up their lives the next day. She couldn't, she didn't trust herself. She was too terrified to try. But the craving for one night of alcohol-induced frivolity was strong. That trouble-free buzz. But she daren't. It had never been just one night with her. It was never enough…

The policewoman pointed a finger at her. "By the way. You are one sexy woman. And," she whispered, drawing the word out as a precursor to a huge declaration, "Sophie fancies you."

"Morven!" Sophie protested.

Morven put a finger to her lips. "Shh, I wasn't supposed to tell you that." She attempted a wink. "What can I say, I'm a drunk pain in the arse. You're safe with me, Frannie, I have a girlfriend. She's a firewoman and she's hot." Morven started laughing again. "Did I tell you I proposed to her? I'm getting married in June." Morven placed an uncoordinated hand on Fran's upper chest. "You better be coming to my wedding."

"Please tell me the taxi is here," Sophie groaned.

Fran dipped her head. She knew Sophie was interested, but she had no plans to spend a night with the woman. She was a teammate. That was too close to home for a one-night stand.

"Morven, isn't Jessie dating Tom?" Alex asked.

Morven exploded into laughter. "Tom? Let me tell you about Tom. That man is further in the closet than our Jessie."

"What!" Alex appeared shocked.

"Oops, did I say that out loud?" Morven put a hand over her mouth.

"Morven!" Sophie chastised.

Fran had had her suspicions about Tom, but his sexuality was none of her business.

"Maybe we should all keep that information to ourselves. It's not easy for an ex-professional footballer to be gay," Sophie suggested, and everyone around the table nodded.

"Fuck, I'm in so much trouble. My mouth runs off when I'm drunk." Morven leaned her elbows on the table, closing her eyes. "I need to get to my bed." She put a hand in the pocket of her jacket. "Fran, you better take these. I'll text Jessie to let her know you have them." Morven placed Jessie's car keys on the table. "Shit, she's going to kick my arse at training for this."

Ten minutes later, they were gone, leaving Fran alone to close up. She was tired and desperate for a good night's rest. Wearily, she made her way around the bar, collecting glasses, and briefly debated leaving the rest until morning. Knowing it would only be worse if she did, she shook her head and started washing up. With the last glass clean and on the drainer, she stretched her tired muscles and yawned. It had been a busy evening, with seven drunken teammates adding to her workload.

Fran switched the lights off and made her way upstairs, pausing on the landing when she saw legs protruding from the top of the stairs, across the carpeted floor. Black satin straight-legged trousers with a pair of patent leather heels were sticking out beyond the staircase. Fran frowned and took the last few steps two at a time to find Jessie sitting with her back against the wall...asleep.

She took a moment to observe Jessie. Her face was peaceful, relaxed, her mouth slightly open. It made a welcome change from the way her jaw was usually set and accompanied by frown lines in the centre of her forehead whenever Fran was around her. Fran was tempted to leave her there, but she might fall down the stairs. Gently shaking her shoulder, she was rewarded with one eye opening and incoherent mumbling.

"Hey, wake up." Fran shook her harder this time.

Jessie's eyes opened wide. She appeared dazed and a little confused. As her gaze settled on Fran, her eyes cleared, a hand going to her forehead.

"Are they still downstairs?" Jessie's voice was hoarse.

"No, I've closed up for the night."

Jessie stood up so quickly, she swayed precariously at the top of the stairs. Fran reached out to place a steadying hand on her upper arm.

"Sorry, I'll get out of your way." Jessie rubbed her forehead, grimacing. "How much did I drink?"

"Four glasses of port."

Shaking her head produced a groan. "I don't normally drink, usually only a glass of wine or two, and I've never even tasted port before." Closing her eyes Jessie held her stomach. "I don't feel too good."

Fran still with a hold on her arm encouraged Jessie to follow her. "Come on." She was clearly in no condition to travel home.

Fran led a stumbling Jessie to her bedroom, sitting her on the edge of the bed, she assisted her with the removal of the heels, black dress jacket and monochrome silk top, then handed Jessie a T-shirt.

"Why can't we be friends?"

"Put that on, I'll be back in a minute," Fran said, ignoring the question.

Fran returned to the room to find Jessie lying spread eagled on the bed asleep. Her trousers open, but still on. She put the glass of water on the bedside table and encouraged Jessie to lift up her hips while she completed the abandoned task. Fran pulled the duvet over her teammate, who snuggled into the comfort it provided. With a sigh, she turned and walked over to the large glass doors that led out to the balcony. She grabbed a dark grey hoodie and slipped it on before opening one of the doors and closing it quickly behind her.

Fran smoked her last cigarette of the day with one foot firmly on the balcony and a long leg stretched along the top of the stone rail. It was a ritual she enjoyed. It helped her to unwind after yet another busy day. The blustery December wind blew her long hair across her face. She didn't mind the cold. She glanced back into the bedroom as she flicked ash from the tip of the cigarette, and lamented the loss of her comfortable bed. With a shake of the head, she exhaled the last of the smoke via the side of her mouth, and crushed the cigarette stub under her booted foot.

Once inside, she removed her boots and jeans, and then lay down on the large chaise longue that dominated the top of the expansive room. She pulled a blanket over herself and attempted to get some well-needed rest.

Chapter 9

She hadn't even opened her eyes and Jessie knew she was in a strange place. A vacuum cleaner being used somewhere and the smell of coffee were the first clues. She usually woke to silence. Snippets from the evening before started to come back to her. She prised her tongue from the roof of her mouth. The Christmas dinner, her teammates bundling into her car demanding a lift. Being kidnapped. That's when the clarity of her memory reduced greatly.

She opened her left eye and waited for her surroundings to come into focus. She knew the room and who it belonged too. The knowledge and realisation hit her like a sledgehammer. Jessie sat bolt upright, grabbing at her upper body. Relief flooded her when she found herself clothed and alone. Releasing a breath, she slumped back on the pillow, her head throbbing.

There was a glass of water on the bedside table along with a packet of paracetamol. Grateful for both, she drank the much-needed water and fumbled with the painkillers.

Searching for clues as to what had happened, she glanced around the room. Her jacket was hanging on a high-backed antique chair, her trousers and top folded neatly on the cushioned seat, shoes tucked below. Jessie doubted she'd managed to do that judging by the hangover she was sporting.

The room was neat, unlike the last time she'd seen it, when Fran was naked with a blonde, empty bottles of alcohol around, and clothing strewn all over the floor. The furniture was aged and well used—it was probably over fifty years old, but sturdy, and could last at least that long again.

A large chaise longue dominated the top of the room. Solid oak carved beautifully with a padded, faded green covering, it needed some repairs, part of the base thatching hanging down. A beige blanket was draped over the side. Jessie imagined stretching out on the piece of furniture, a good book in hand, while intermittently looking out across the sea. Its placement was no accident. In the summer, with the balcony doors wide open late into the evening, watching the sunset would be glorious.

Swinging her legs over the side of the bed, she rubbed her eyes. The dark grey T-shirt she was wearing caught her eye and she pulled at it to study the faded, sinister graphics. A skull with roses in the eyes covered most of the front. Jessie grimaced at the image as she stood up and padded over to a set of oak drawers, and rummaged for a pair of jogging bottoms or shorts. Despite the dishevelled appearance of the owner, the clothing in the drawers was folded neatly and orderly. She found a pair of grey cotton shorts and pulled them on before she walked barefoot to the bathroom.

Once finished, the kitchen was easy to find. A pot of coffee sat warming on the machine. She ignored the brew, looking around for teabags instead. She guessed it was Fran vacuuming, so with tea in one hand and a coffee in the other, Jessie headed downstairs.

Inside the main bar, she sat at a table while Fran moved chairs as she cleaned. Her hair was in a loose ponytail and she was dressed in tracksuit bottoms and a black T-shirt. A fine sheen of sweat coated her face as she worked quickly. Jessie checked the clock behind the bar. Half past eight.

A worn, navy converse trainer hit the base of the vacuum cleaner and it shut off. Fran stood tall and stretched. Jessie cleared her throat, hoping not to startle the other woman. Arms stilled above her head, then slowly released back down to her sides as she turned towards Jessie.

"Morning. I, ah, brought you a cup of coffee." Jessie gestured to the cup on the table.

"Thanks." Fran took a seat at the table Jessie occupied and reached for the warm brew.

"I'm sorry for last night. I never get drunk."

Fran made no acknowledgment of the apology. "How are you feeling?"

"I've been better." Jessie sipped her tea. "How much did I drink?"

Fran shrugged. "About four glasses of port."

Jessie's face contorted with disgust. "I've never drunk port before and I doubt I will again."

Fran stared at Jessie as she drank her coffee. Jessie found the scrutiny and silence unnerving. "Is it the cleaner's morning off?"

"No."

Jessie was confused. "How many people work here?"

Fran shrugged. "Mostly me."

Jessie was surprised by this answer. It appeared that Fran was almost running the place solo and not doing the best job of it. Why the owner would allow such a thing? Unless.... "Do you own this place?" She had asked before, but nothing else made sense.

"Nope."

"Then w…"

Fran held up a hand, forestalling the questions. "I need to finish cleaning. I've still got a lot to do. Hang around as long as you like. There's food in the kitchen." With those words effectively cutting off all conversation, she rose from the chair and unplugged the hoover. Jessie sat there stunned and a little angry. An emotion that was prevalent whenever she was around the moody woman for more than a few minutes. Any time she tried to speak to Fran, she found a way to shut down the conversation. Over the past few months of giving her lifts and being on the same team with her, Jessie had learned not to bother. But since Fran had been kind enough to allow her to spend the night here, she'd broken her own rule.

Gathering the cups she headed back upstairs, still fuming as she washed up. When she returned to the bedroom, she stood in the middle of the floor and counted to ten. Her headache, which had been starting to recede, had returned, and she felt queasy. She picked up her bag from the chair and searched for her car keys. She slammed the bag back down on the chair. "Bloody Morven." Jessie lay down on the battered chaise longue and stared out at the sea. The water was a greyish blue as it swirled and undulated, reflecting her mood. She pulled the blanket over her bare legs and drifted off to sleep.

———————◆✄◆———————

Fran shut off the vacuum cleaner and gathered the cord, wrapping it around her arm before packing it neatly onto the back of the machine. It was silent again. She half expected Jessie to be lurking somewhere. She'd disappeared back upstairs and Fran was grateful. She was still trying to purge Jessie's confused "why can't we be friends?" question from her ears.

Jessie had no idea how dangerous her request was. She shook her head. She couldn't be a friend to Jessie. Friendship would never be enough, and she couldn't afford to pursue anything else. She was inexplicably drawn to her, no longer able to deny or pass it off as a fleeting attraction that would wane with time. The more time she spent around Jessie, alone with her, the more the attraction was growing, until the only option Fran had left was to push her away. But the pushing was becoming more and more difficult.

Jessie was attractive, amiable, and genuinely nice, but above all that, she was damn well persistent. Fran could destroy all that was good about Jessie and drag her into the gutter, a place Fran had only recently managed to crawl out of and had fought hard every hour of every day not to return to. There had been too many relapses, too many mistakes, countless people hurt. How many times could a person forgive?

She'd lost more friends than she could count. Some she was better off without, but she had hurt and let down many good people. People like Jessie. She didn't want that anymore. She couldn't handle the guilt or the shame any longer. And she certainly couldn't risk it with Jessie. Better that Jessie hate her for being a dick than hate her for being a junkie. But Jessie kept chipping away at Fran's defences, and keeping her at arm's length was difficult. Fran knew she couldn't let Jessie in. For both of their sakes. For her own sanity.

She was suddenly drained and it had little to do with her morning chores. She put the vacuum cleaner into a large cupboard, then headed upstairs to get ready for opening up in a couple of hours.

She walked into her bedroom and found Jessie asleep on the chaise longue, the blanket Fran had used the night before draped over her. She was beautiful. So beautiful. Fran had to resist the urge to reach out and move a strand of blonde hair from Jessie's face. Too much temptation.

Fran moved quietly so as not to disturb her guest. She took clean clothes from the chest of drawers and headed to the bathroom for a quick shower.

Knowing Jessie was asleep on the other side of the door as she removed her clothing caused an unwelcome twinge between her legs. Angrily she stepped into the shower and welcomed the hot water hitting her skin. She closed her eyes and put her face under the spray as she tried to clear the image of a naked Jessie in the shower with her.

Fran vigorously rubbed shampoo into her hair, attempting to wash the images down the drain with the soap suds.

After towelling dry, she threw on her jeans and T-shirt, leaving her hair wet. She went to the kitchen and couldn't stop herself from preparing breakfast for Jessie.

The banging of crockery brought Jessie out of her slumber. Blinking awake, she stared at the tray on a side table next to her. A tall glass of fresh orange juice sat alongside several slices of wholemeal toast covered in banana. Jessie looked up from the tray into the face of Fran Docherty.

"It'll help with the hangover."

Jessie sat up and took a drink of the juice before biting into a slice of toast and banana. She chewed slowly and hoped her stomach wouldn't rebel. Fran had showered and changed into her usual dark ensemble of jeans and a T-shirt with a faded Celtic design emblazoned on the front. She went out to the balcony and lit a cigarette, her wet hair whipping in the wind. The cold didn't appear to bother her as she stood with her back to Jessie, staring out over the Firth of Forth.

When she eventually came back inside, Jessie had to admit that the food was making a difference.

"Thank you."

"No bother."

"May I ask you a question?"

Fran froze, her back to Jessie, shoulders slumped. Not receiving a reply, but with Fran standing waiting, Jessie forged ahead.

"Why can't we get along?"

Fran turned her head to the side. Jessie knew she was being studied. The moment stretched out between them and Jessie waited patiently. Fran stood with her hands in her pockets, before taking a seat on the edge of the bed. She rubbed the side of her face. "As you might have noticed I'm not much of a talker."

Jessie almost laughed at the understatement, but knew it would not go down well. "I know that, but you go out of your way not to have a conversation with me."

"I'm not the kind of person you want to get to know." Fran was rubbing her left bicep with her right hand, leaving a mark on the skin. The silence between them stretched out. Jessie knew instinctively not to push for more. She changed the topic.

"Let's talk about the bar then."

Fran leaned her elbows on her knees. Jessie sensed she had an opening and seized upon it.

"Who owns this place? They aren't too fussed about making money. You're not letting rooms. You're doing all the jobs yourself, so they must be paying you a fortune."

"I can't run a hotel. I'm barely running the bar." Fran's voice was deceptively quiet.

"I've noticed…" Jessie held up a hand in apology. "Sorry, but I've seen people sleeping in the bar and helping themselves to alcohol."

"Sometimes, I'm too tired at the end of the night." She sounded weary.

Jessie couldn't disagree. There were times at training when Fran appeared ready to drop. Now she understood a bit more about the woman and why she was constantly napping as the team travelled.

"You told me a few weeks ago that you were in debt to someone. Is that why you won't hire any staff?" Jessie knew she was being pushy, but she needed to gain some sense of understanding.

Fran rubbed her face. "That's part of the reason."

Jessie was becoming increasingly frustrated with the lack of clarity. She gestured forcefully with her hands as she spoke. "I'm trying to help you here."

Frown lines appeared on Fran's forehead as her eyes narrowed. She seemed to be weighing Jessie up. Jessie had a hard time reading Fran. She gave so little away. It was frustrating. Annoying. Disconcerting.

"My grandfather owns this place."

"So you're running it for him? Where is he?"

"He's in a nursing home." Fran's voice was quiet.

Jessie thought back to the day she saw Fran walk past her with an older man in a wheelchair. Things were beginning to make a little more sense. "The gentleman in the wheelchair?"

Fran nodded. "I had no idea he was so ill. He had a stroke in the summer. The first I knew about it was when I got a call from one of his friends to say he had been admitted to hospital. I was his next of kin, that's why I was contacted. They weren't sure he was going to make it."

Fran rubbed her chest as she spoke those words. Jessie guessed this was difficult for her to talk about. She stayed quiet, hoping Fran would continue.

"The hospital said he wasn't well enough to come home, he needed too much care. But he was determined to get back here. He begged me not to let this place close." She turned her eyes fully on Jessie. "I owe him so much, I couldn't refuse."

Still puzzled Jessie enquired further. "So your grandfather is in a nursing home and you're keeping this place open. Why don't you hire more help?"

"He's getting all the care he needs in the nursing home. I bring him here every afternoon and take him back every evening for his dinner. That's why he agreed to the nursing home. I can't run the place and take care of him. I can't afford to pay anyone wages."

Now Jessie understood some of Fran's cryptic answers. "So the debt you owe is to your grandfather?"

Fran nodded.

"But you're not making enough money here. Are you going to be closed down?"

Fran sighed. "It's the nursing home fees. I'm struggling to clear the £600 pounds a week I need."

"And you won't sell the place because you promised him you wouldn't?"

"It would destroy him to see this place sold." Fran put her head in her hands, appearing defeated.

"You need to let the rooms."

Fran shook her head. "I don't have any experience running a hotel. We're talking breakfasts, clean bedding, it's too much." Fran stared at the ceiling as if searching for answers there.

Jessie licked her lips. Where Fran saw defeat, Jessie saw opportunity. "I mean, rent the rooms out on a more permanent basis."

"I've thought about it. It would be a shambles. Me as a landlady. I can't have kids running about the place, it's a pub."

"Let them out to students." Jessie sat up, leaning forward, sensing an opening.

"I wouldn't even know how to go about it. It's part way through the academic year. I'd have to wait until September."

Jessie smiled. "You may not know how to go about it, but I do. Students are always looking for accommodation. There are queues outside every student let that becomes available. They're desperate for decent digs. There's a college and a university, both less than two miles away from here."

Fran stared at her, and Jessie sensed she was being pulled in by the idea. She knew she had the gift of the gab and was relentless.

"You can make this happen?" Fran asked, scratching her cheek.

Jessie nodded. "I'm an estate agent, this is part of what I do. You won't have to do a thing, and you'll get a nice lump sum of cash every month, upfront."

Fran's eyes narrowed, her suspicion returning. "What's in it for you?"

"I'm the letting agent, I get a percentage. We both win." Jessie studied Fran intently. Emotions ran rampant across her face. Fear, doubt, and hope. "I could come by sometime and assess the rooms you have for rent, then I'll give you some actual figures to look at. If you're happy, I'll go ahead and organise everything."

Fran rubbed the back of her neck. "I don't have time to prepare rooms, I'm too busy here."

"You won't have to. I'll organise what needs to be done in order to have the rooms ready for letting. If you agree, I can also arrange the work. Let me draw up the plans. It won't cost you anything and you won't be committing to anything either."

Fran nodded slowly, a little dazed by the turn of events. "Okay."

"Great!" Jessie said, and then she frowned. "You don't happen to have my car keys do you?"

Chapter 10

WHY WAS SHE NERVOUS? JESSIE took a deep breath and rubbed her stomach in a feeble attempt to quell the unsettling pangs contracting within. So what if it was Christmas Eve? It wasn't like she had anything else to do. Now was as good a time as any, this was business.

Jessie raised the camera to her face and started to take pictures of the exterior of the Beachcomber, hoping the activity would set aside her unease. It was a magnificent building, bathed in the early-morning winter sun. Jessie stood on the short concrete wall that ran the length of the prom, separating it from the sandy beach. She snapped a handful of pictures before putting the camera into her pocket and jumping down from the wall.

The bar wouldn't open for another couple of hours, but she knew Fran was inside cleaning the place, readying for the new day. The heavy red wooden door was open as she approached.

She knocked and called "Fran?" as she pushed the door open wider. She waited a beat, but there was no answer. She poked her head around the massive frame. The bar was empty, the floor immaculate, and the tables clean. New beermats were neatly laid on the wooden surfaces, and the scent of polish hung in the air with the dust motes she could see dancing in the shafts of sunlight. Fran had already been down to get the bar ready. Jessie passed the large Christmas tree with its lights off, giving the place a cold, empty sensation on her way to the bottom of the stairs.

"Fran?"

The dark-haired woman appeared at the top of the staircase. A frown on her face, her hair still damp from the shower, and already dressed in her usual attire.

"I thought I would take a look at the rooms available for rent. You know, evaluate their condition, check what work may be required to get each of them ready for renting." The butterflies had returned. Fran had a knack of triggering Jessie's anxiety.

Fran paused, rubbing her damp hair. "I'll get the keys."

Jessie wasn't sure why she'd expected a warmer reception. Just because they'd spent some time together the day before and Fran had opened up a little didn't mean the barriers were going to stay down this morning.

With a little less enthusiasm and her nervous anticipation disappearing fast, Jessie climbed the stairs to the first floor, where she met Fran holding a large bunch of keys.

"The rooms are numbered, as are the keys."

Jessie hesitated, but Fran remained silent while maintaining eye contact. It was as unsettling as it was irritating. She took the keys, her fingers momentarily touching Fran's. "Okay then, I'll come and find you when I'm finished."

"Right."

Jessie stared at the bunch of keys in her hand as Fran disappeared back into her bedroom. She closed her eyes and drew in a calming breath. She had wrongly assumed they had made progress after the night she spent in Fran's room. She was here for work, nothing else. Fran was a client and a teammate, not a friend. It appeared that nothing was going to change that fact.

Sorting through the keys, she located the number that corresponded with the room in front of her, number six. She unlocked the door and entered, not knowing quite what to expect. The double bed, fitted wardrobes, en-suite bathroom, and wall-mounted flat-screen television was a pleasant surprise. She hadn't expected modern. The room was in good decorative order, and finished off with a dressing table and chair, which could double as a desk. It was perfect for renting.

She went through each room thoroughly, one by one. All of them were in good order, with only minor work required to get them ready for renting, a faulty smoke detector in one, a leaking shower cubicle in another. Some of the rooms had twin beds, while others had doubles. It left the possibility of students sharing the twin rooms, meaning more revenue for Fran but a cheaper rent for the students choosing to share.

Jessie deliberately left the turreted room for last. Every room had been different and unique due to the architecture, but this one promised to be special. She inserted the key and opened the door. As expected, her attention was immediately grabbed, but not in the way she had anticipated. While the layout was special, what left her open-mouthed were the contents of the room. She felt like she'd gone back in time.

She knew she should turn around, close the door, and lock it. As though her intrusion into this inner sanctum was not wanted. Despite the goosebumps erupting on her arms, Jessie couldn't stop herself from stepping inside.

It was a snapshot of the past. One she could walk around and explore. Though the room mirrored Fran's style, she knew it didn't belong to her. This was an Aladdin's cave full of memories and memorabilia from a bygone era. An era full of rich fashion and music that left its footprint on history with the solid stamp of a Doc Marten boot, safety pins, and spiked, dyed hair.

The walls were adorned with posters, some faded from years of catching the sunlight. Many were female icons, strong, fierce, independent, and intimidating. Jessie could only put names to a couple. Among the many posters were prints that Jessie recognised, but had no idea who the artists were.

One in particular caught her eye. A naked woman in a foetal position with long red hair. A dark patterned silk scarf surrounded her and a river of gold cascaded down between her legs. This was familiar because Fran had a tattoo of this woman on her upper arm. The significance struck Jessie immediately. This place was important to Fran. The bedroom of a teenage punk rocker, remaining untouched for all these years, was not lost on her. Everything had been left waiting for the return of a daughter. Now it was her shrine.

Carefully, Jessie stepped further inside, intruding respectfully, if such a thing were possible. There was a desk with a row of books on it—school novels, no doubt. *To Kill A Mockingbird, Brave New World, Animal Farm,* mixed with more obscure titles, *On The Road, Junkie, A Clockwork Orange, The Green Brain.* Some Jessie had never heard of, but a few of the authors' names were familiar.

The books were well thumbed, particularly *Animal Farm* and *A Clockwork Orange*. Jessie reached for the copy of *Animal Farm*. A quick flick through the pages revealed pencilled marks in the margins—study notes.

She eased the book back into place and studied the wall above the desk. Concert ticket stubs were pinned to every available space around a cork noticeboard full of badges. An anarchy symbol, a peace symbol interspersed among the many band names. On the floor was a long row of albums. One sleeve lay next to an old record player, the black vinyl on the turntable. The lack of dust indicated this had been in action recently, and closer inspection revealed not a punk band as Jessie had expected, but Stravinsky, *The Rite of Spring*.

Oh, Fran. Something in Jessie's heart melted at the thought of a sullen Fran sitting in this room all alone listening to the music.

Jessie knew she shouldn't, but couldn't resist opening the wardrobe. A few empty wire hangers hung limply on one side of a rail. The other side held a navy school blazer, adorned with the George Heriot's crest on the left breast pocket, a green tartan kilt hung beside it.

Jessie wasn't sure what she had expected to find in there, but an old school uniform had been disconcerting. It indicated a more innocent time; most of the room's contents did. A glimpse offered into a point in someone's life when young dreams and ideologies came thick and fast. Possibilities were endless, and anticipation burned bright in the soul. This room pointed to a teenage girl on the precipice of life and all it had to offer.

Jessie made her way to the room's main feature, which was prominent from the outside of the building—the round turret. There was wooden seating built in a semicircle. She imagined the girl sitting here with her friends, chatting as they listened to music. The wood was worn, scraped in places, marked with cigarette burns and some names carved into it— "DeeDee + Ross" inside a heart, with an arrow shot through it.

She imagined Fran sitting on the bench, Stravinsky playing on the record player, and she ached for the loneliness she sensed in her. The fear that kept her locked away in a tower. Jessie wiped a tear away from her cheek and stared out of the window towards the shore, where white frothy waves danced in the water. The sea was choppy and sand churned in the waves, making the water appear dirty as it spilled its contents on to the beach. A sadness washed over her with every caress of water on the shore, and Jessie knew without doubt that this room wasn't for renting.

She made her way slowly to the door, stopping in front of a dressing table devoid of any personal belongings but a photograph tucked into the join at the top of the mirror.

Two boys, probably in their late teens, stared at the camera, attitude pouring from them and matching the clothes they wore. Leather and denim jackets embellished with badges and writing, jeans and boots; one had tartan trousers on, both had spiked hair. In the middle were two girls. One with long black hair and dark make-up, wearing a black dress with zips covering it. The other had dyed blonde hair, dark eye make-up, a black T-shirt with the sleeves ripped off, and a leather jacket draped over her arm. She wore a dog collar around her neck, and a leather bracelet with spikes coming out of it. She was the only one not staring into the camera. Almost like she was bored of having her picture taken. Or maybe she was bored with life? Was this girl Fran's mum? Could this be DeeDee? On closer inspection, the guy next to her had his arm around her waist. Was she leaning away from him? Was he Ross? Something stood out about him, maybe his eyes.

A prickling sensation at the back of her neck caused her to turn her head toward the door. Fran stood with her arms folded, leaning in the open doorway.

"Not this one," Fran said quietly.

"Of course." She had snooped around wanting to know more about the enigma that was Fran. Now she had more questions. And knew not to ask. "I'm sorry," she whispered as she handed the keys back.

Jessie walked down the stairs with Fran following behind her.

She cleared her throat. "The rooms are in great condition. There isn't too much work required, but I'll give you a detailed account in the next few days of the costs, and a time scale of how long the repairs will take. We can let out eight rooms by the end of January. I don't know what you plan to do for the summer. Some students may want to let the rooms straight through until the next academic year, but for any that will be empty, you have the option of short-term summer lets. You could make a killing during the Edinburgh festival. People will pay crazy prices for rooms in August."

Jessie was running off at the mouth more than usual. She knew it was because she had been caught snooping. Chatting animatedly was preferable to the strained silence that had developed between them from the moment Fran had found her in the turreted room. Fran didn't answer, but Jessie wasn't expecting her to. "I'm going to my parents' for Christmas. Do you have any plans? Will you be keeping the bar open over Christmas? I don't suppose you will get much custom on Christmas day?"

"The bar will be open."

"Oh, well…" Jessie was flustered, she wanted to get out of the Beachcomber and as far away from Fran as possible. "Anyway, enjoy your Christmas, and I'll see you at training next week." She wanted to bolt right out the front door, but good manners stopped her from doing so. Instead, she stood awkwardly at the door, waiting for Fran to do or say something.

"Thanks for doing this."

"Oh, you're welcome. It's a great opportunity, for both of us." Jessie was surprised to be thanked—she had anticipated silence—but this was a pleasant change from the usual one-word answers.

Fran nodded, but her face remained neutral.

"Well, I'll see you next week."

Jessie left, no longer wanting to run. Instead, a kind of calm settled over her. Fran hadn't exactly engaged in sparkling conversation, but there had been progress. Of sorts. A tiny chink of light shining through the dull clouds that constantly hovered.

CHapteR 11

JESSIE SAT ALONE IN THE sitting room of her parents' house. Normally, she loved the thirty-minute drive along the east coast to her parents', but today her mind had been preoccupied with Fran.

Flicking through the TV channels, she couldn't settle on a programme. Christmas-day television couldn't hold her attention, and where the hell were her parents? They'd been acting strange all afternoon. Tiptoeing around her, sneaking off to the kitchen, talking in hushed tones. Something was up, and she was determined to find out what.

Jessie tossed the TV remote onto the sofa and headed for the kitchen. Both her parents stopped talking, and greeted her with what she perceived to be forced cheeriness.

"What's going on?" She glanced from her mum to her dad, who automatically deferred to his wife by manoeuvring her in front of him with a hand on her back.

Her mother reluctantly stepped forward, throwing a withering look back at her husband, before plastering a smile onto her face. "It's nothing, darling."

Jessie wouldn't continue the charade any longer. She shook her head, exasperated, and replied, "Something's wrong. You're both acting weird, and I need to know why. I'm sorry, but whatever it is you believe I don't need to know now, I do, so please tell me. Is someone ill? Is the business failing? I thought I was doing a good job with the new office in Edinburgh. The figures are decent, and I'm working hard to bring in more business."

"No, Jessie, please, it's nothing like that," her dad interrupted her rant. "You're doing a great job with the expansion, especially considering the current downturn we're in."

"And your dad and I are in good health," her mother added.

"Gran?" she asked, her only living grandparent.

"Oh, she's fine, I promise you," her mum replied, with mock exasperation. Her maternal grandmother was a feisty individual and certainly wasn't slow to let her opinion be known.

"Then what's going on? If you don't tell me, I'm only going to fret and worry until you do."

Her parents stared at each other and appeared to come to a wordless decision. It was a knack they had perfected over the years, one she'd often found herself on the receiving end of when they'd presented a united front, catching her off guard as she'd made a request they hadn't agreed with.

"We've come to a decision, me and your dad…" Her mum started, then made eye contact with her dad, who nodded his agreement, a tenderness in her eyes.

"Let's sit down at the table," her mum suggested. When everyone was comfortable, she continued. "Your dad and I have reached a point in our lives where we want different things."

A buzzing began in Jessie's ears. Fundamentally, she already knew where this conversation was leading, but the child in her refused to acknowledge it.

Her father continued, "It's not anyone's fault, Jessie, there's no blame here. We've simply grown apart. Neither of us really noticed it was happening. Certainly I didn't, until your mum sat me down one day and we talked." Her dad stopped, swallowing hard, pain etched on his face. He was one of those rare men who, the older they got, the better looking they became. Like George Clooney. Many of her friends had remarked that her dad was a silver fox. He suited his greying hair, but she knew they weren't alluding to his hair. He was handsome, with his full lips and straight nose, set off by his deep brown eyes. They carried a warmth and vulnerability, and women appeared to fall into the deep pools swirling there. Like herself, her dad was always well turned out. Whereas Jessie resembled her mother physically, she definitely had her father's dress sense. Her mum was more at home in frilly, flowery patterns that spoke of peace and being at one with Mother Nature.

"Jessie, it's never easy to end a marriage, even…"

She interrupted her mum, shock and disbelief flooding her senses. "You're getting divorced?"

"Darling, please don't be upset. We still love each other, we're just not 'in love' anymore."

The way her mum had emphasised the not "in love" part unsettled her further. "What happened?" Jessie asked, bewildered and shocked.

Her father shrugged his large shoulders. "We grew apart."

"You mean, you did?" Jessie accused.

"Jessie, your dad isn't to blame. Yes, he has someone new in his life, but it's with my blessing."

Her father turned sharply to stare at his wife, clearly unhappy with her revealing that information.

Who were these people sitting across the table from her? They looked like her parents, but her parents loved each other, always had. She'd barely ever witnessed them having a cross word. They'd always got along so well.

They were Mark and Suzanne, the nice couple that had the lovely home and the great summer barbecues. Mark owned the estate agent's and Suzanne's watercolours were hanging in the little gallery on the village high street. People like that didn't get divorced after almost thirty years together.

Jessie's ears were ringing. This was like a bad dream, but she knew she wasn't going to wake up from this. They were serious, but why was her mother happy that her dad was with someone else? She was thoroughly confused.

"You approve?" she asked, needing to understand more. Her mother bit her bottom lip, something Jessie couldn't recall her ever doing before.

"Yes, I approve. I encouraged your dad to move on."

Jessie was horrified. "Why?"

"Because I want to move on," she replied.

Jessie covered her face with her hands, unable to accept the calmness with which they were talking. She addressed her mum in an attempt to clear up the confusion. "Do you have someone else?"

Her mum shook her head. "No, but I want to be free to pursue other things in my life."

"Like what?" There was edge of panic in her voice now.

"I'm not exactly sure yet." Her mum's eyes, gentle and kind, held her in their gaze.

"Dad?" Jessie was practically pleading with her father to shed some further light on this.

"I'm sorry, Jessie, I know it's difficult to understand, and we don't want to hurt you. That's why we haven't told you until now." He took his wife's hand in a show of solidarity.

"Why now?" Jessie was trying not to fall apart in front of them. She swallowed, blinking back the tears that threatened to come. Her breathing increased as her bottom lip quivered, her throat tight, anger and pain flooding her.

She knew that this news, in real terms, wouldn't affect her life. It's not like she still lived at home and depended on her parents for anything. She had her own life. Her own dreams. What was wrong with them pursuing theirs? Nothing. Her mind could grasp the concept, but her heart ached, questioning all the memories of her happy childhood. Had that all been make-believe? A show her parents had put on for her benefit? Had they ever loved each other the way she thought they had?

Her parents' relationship, their love, had always been something she had looked up to. It was a bond she'd aspired to. And it had been a sham. A façade. They'd always seemed so happy with each other, so right together. If they couldn't make a relationship work when they had everything going for them, what hope was there for everyone else? What chance did Jessie have of finding someone to love?

"Your dad is moving out of the house in the new year. That's why we're telling you now. We don't want you learning this from anyone else. Although we had planned to wait until tomorrow."

Jessie slumped back in the wooden chair and stared wide-eyed at her parents as she attempted to somehow absorb this information.

"I'll make some coffee," her mum suggested as she stood, leaving Jessie alone with her dad.

Jessie stared across at her father, as if seeing him for the first time. She looked at him as a man, not just as her dad. His strong shoulders seemed slumped, the lines on his face a little deeper, the hair at his temples a little greyer than she remembered.

He reached across the table and took her hand in his larger one. "We're still your parents. That will never change."

"But it won't be the same," she whispered.

He squeezed her hand tighter and smiled. The lines around his mouth were tight and the smile didn't reach his eyes "No, it won't be, but our love for you will always remain the same. I still love your mum, Jessie. We'll always be great friends." His smile was sad, there was pain etched around his eyes. "And we'll always have you." She watched as he blinked back tears, a genuine smile of pride across his face. "Our greatest achievement."

A sob broke free, and Jessie put a hand to her mouth in an attempt to stall it. But it was to no avail as fat, salty tears rolled down her cheeks. A second, then a third sob broke free.

Her dad stood up to get some tissues and asked his wife to hurry up with the coffee. Jessie thought he always was a wimp whenever it came to her tears. He'd always told her he couldn't bear to see his little girl cry, and that made her cry harder.

"Come on, Jessie, it'll be alright." He handed her a tissue and sat down next to her, rubbing her back. And in her head, she knew he was right. There were worse things in the scheme of it, but something in her felt shattered, disillusioned. Where was the happily ever after?

Jessie reached for fresh tissues and blew her nose noisily. Her dad put his arm around her shoulder as she brought her emotions back under control. Her mum returned to the table with three cups of coffee. She placed one in front of Jessie cautiously, casting a sidelong glance at her husband, before taking a seat opposite the pair.

As Jessie stared into the dark brown liquid, she came to a decision. She cleared her throat to gain the attention of both her parents. "Since this is a day for confessions, I have one of my own." She sniffed noisily, dabbing at her eyes with a soggy tissue. She took a deep breath and sat straighter in her chair, determined to speak clearly and confidently. "I like women." Jessie stared directly at her mother, then her father, awaiting their response.

"Well, that makes three of us," her dad declared, before raising the cup to his lips.

Her mother pinned him with a withering look, to which he raised his eyebrows.

"What?" he said with mock innocence.

"Mum?" Jessie wasn't exactly sure what was going on, but her ears were buzzing again.

"Your dad's just being facetious. I may have, in the heat of the moment..." She shook her head, her colour high. "For God's sake, Mark, that was a flippant, throwaway comment, I wasn't serious!" Taking a deep breath she continued, "Jessie, we've both long suspected that your romantic interests lay with women, and we agreed some time ago that we'd wait until you were comfortable enough to tell us."

"Jesus!" Jessie had worried about coming out to her parents, not because she'd feared a backlash or that they were homophobic, but because she hadn't wanted to disappoint them in any way. She'd lost count of the amount of times she'd wanted to blurt it out over Sunday dinner. But she'd never envisioned her coming out being the least shocking news that day. It was a total anti-climax.

"Maybe you two can exchange dating tips," her dad helpfully added.

"Not funny, Mark."

He started shaking his head and laughing. "Alison had a pregnancy scare, but it was a false alarm."

"What?" her mum asked.

"Who's Alison?" Jessie asked.

"Alison Byers, that's who I'm dating."

"Oh my God!" Jessie knew Alison. She worked in the main office for her father. She'd worked alongside Jessie before she'd opened the new office. "Is she even older than me? Are you planning to start a family?"

"About four years older, and I don't know. But Alison is only twenty-nine. If we stick together, she may want children in the future." Her father blushed, which was completely out of character.

Jessie slumped back in her chair, a hand going to her forehead, completely stunned. Her mum looked thoughtful, but if she was shocked, she was hiding it well.

"Does anyone have anything else to add?" her mum asked. "Might as well get it out now."

Jessie prayed nothing more would come out of their mouths, but she did have a question. "Who's going to tell Gran?"

⊷ ⬦ ⊶

Jessie sat staring at the flames licking the logs, the fire crackling as it roared in the hearth. The earlier revelations had thrown her. Today could be the last Christmas they would spend as a family. What would the next year be like? She couldn't imagine they would all be here, in her parent's house, with her dad's girlfriend. Would her mum be alone? It was inconceivable,

82

unimaginable, that her parents would be with different people. Would she be alone? Or maybe she'd have a girlfriend of her own? Her head was spinning

"Jessie?"

Her dad stood in the open doorway of the sitting room, two mugs in his hand. "Hey, Dad." She struggled to muster up any enthusiasm, her smile weak.

"Thought you might like a cuppa." He held the cups up a little higher, his eyebrows raised in question.

"Come and join me." She nodded to the armchair opposite her own.

He handed Jessie the mug of hot chocolate, then took the fireside chair opposite.

"Thanks, Dad." Jessie blew on the hot drink out of habit, before turning back to the flames.

"We still going to the New Year derby?" her dad asked, trying to inject some hope into the conversation. Going to the Hearts versus Hibs game at New Year had been a father–daughter tradition since Jessie had been eight years old. They'd never missed a derby yet.

"Of course." Jessie stared into her hot chocolate. She didn't want to think about how that might change in the future. Would her dad have another daughter, or a son even, to take to matches? Would he still want to go with her? To spend time with her? "As long as you want to go with me."

Her father shook his head. "Jessie, that will never change. I wouldn't miss it for the world." He stood and knelt beside her, taking her free hand in both of his. She never could seem to hide what she was feeling from him. "I remember when I bought you your first Hibs strip, for your seventh birthday." He smiled and squeezed her hand tighter. "Every time we passed the sports shop, you would spend ages staring at the football strip in the window. I wasn't sure back then how long your love of football would last." He shook his head. "I never imagined you'd become one of the best players in the country." Jessie detected a tremor in his voice as he sniffed back tears. "You're so talented and you make me so very proud." The emotion in his voice was raw, leaving Jessie in no doubt of his sincerity.

"Me too." Her mum's voice was soft, like she didn't want to disturb the air around them.

Jessie turned her head towards the door and smiled as her mum joined them.

"We'll both still come and watch you play for Scotland. We'll be there together as a family, your family. When you line up in the dark blue, and 'Flower of Scotland' plays, I get a lump in my throat." Her mum's eyes filled with unshed tears. She sat on the arm of the chair and rubbed Jessie's back. "My little girl standing there so strong and beautiful, so talented." She shook her head. "I don't know where the sporting prowess comes from, certainly not me, and your dad never showed any talent for it. He's got two left feet." They all laughed at the truth of that statement, despite the emotion in the air. Her dad always danced to his own beat as he could never keep time with the music.

"You make us both so proud, you show such dedication in everything that you do. Your work and football. Your dad and I may be getting a divorce, but you are the success from our marriage. We had almost thirty happy years of marriage." Her mum's lip trembled. Clearing her throat, she continued. "We gradually fell out of love, but the love we have for you will always bind us together."

Jessie hugged both of her parents close. How could they just stop loving each other? The foundation her world, her confidence, had been built on, crumbled and washed away like a sandcastle before the tide. She'd dreamed of finding a love like theirs. One that had stood the test of time, and was still going strong. One that was built on loyalty, honesty, and trust. She sighed as some of that dream ebbed away.

Chapter 12

Jessie sat in the maroon plastic seat next to her dad, behind the goal. There were still twenty minutes until kick-off, and the stadium was starting to fill up. It was icy cold despite the sun shining brightly.

"I prefer the home games," she remarked to her dad, as he perused the match programme. Although less than four miles separated the grounds of Heart of Midlothian and Hibernian, being at Tynecastle Stadium meant the Hibs fans would be outnumbered three to one.

"The pitch looks like it might cut up a bit," he remarked.

Jessie nodded her agreement. There had been a lot of rain in the last few days, and parts of the pitch were heavy. Tucking her chin further into her green-and-white Hibs scarf, she sniffed back a runny nose. The away end was situated behind one of the goals. Jessie spotted some of her teammates a good few rows in front of her. She sent a quick text to Morven.

I'm looking at the back of your head.

Morven turned around and waved. A few seconds later Jessie's iPhone signalled an incoming text.

"Morven says hello."

Her dad looked to where Jessie motioned with her head and waved back to the familiar faces as another text came in.

Are you and Mr G. Coming to The BC?

Jessie glared at Morven, the impudent grin unmistakable, knowing she was taunting Jessie over the last time they had been in the Beachcomber. Morven had been very apologetic the day after the kidnapping incident, but that hadn't lasted long. Her irrepressible personality was back at full throttle. Morven nodded towards her dad, raising her eyebrows. Jessie sighed. "Morven would like to know if we are going to meet them in the Beachcomber after the game?"

Mark Grainger smiled at Morven as he nodded in the affirmative. "The place you're setting up as student accommodation?"

"Yes." She had run her plan by him and he had heartily approved.

"I'd love to see it and have a catch up with your friends."

Jessie texted the reply even though Morven had already given her a thumbs up. She and her dad usually met up with the girls after the New Year derby. She knew he wouldn't refuse the rare opportunity to spend some time with her friends and teammates.

With kick-off imminent, the Tynecastle Stadium was full, the ground tightly packed with fans, the atmosphere electric. It was a compact stadium, with little space between the sidelines and the front row. Maroon versus green, in a city divided by its football affiliation. It was a sell-out. Jessie smiled at her dad as they both soaked up the atmosphere. She loved the surge of anticipation as kick-off loomed ever closer.

Her dad always looked dapper and today was no different. A dark grey wool overcoat worn over straight blue jeans and dark brown brogue boots. With neatly cut greying brown hair and a clean shave, Jessie knew women found him attractive, and idly considered if that was why he and her mum were getting a divorce. Her attention was drawn back to the pitch. A crescendo of noise erupted around the ground as the two teams ran out of the tunnel. The Hearts anthem blared out from the Tannoy speaker, and the fans twirled maroon-and-white scarves above their heads.

This was what she loved about football. The atmosphere that started with the fans and carried you along on the pitch. The camaraderie, not just with the players, but the hundreds or thousands of people watching, cheering you on when you thought you couldn't do any more. Where one person was a cog in a wheel that made each one better than any single individual could hope to be alone.

The first half passed quickly as Hibs took an early lead and held on by dominating the midfield and taking the game to the higher-placed Hearts. When you played with passion and belief, a higher place in the league meant nothing. What happened on the pitch was what counted.

The whistle for half-time blew. Rubbing her hands together in an attempt to warm them, Jessie stood next to her dad as fans all around them headed for hot food and drinks.

"Excuse me?"

Jessie turned to where a young girl of around ten years stood clutching a match programme in a gloved hand. She smiled at the youngster. "Hello."

"My dad says you're Jessie Grainger and you are really good at football." The girl was bundled up against the cold with a pink scarf with the Hibs colours woven through it and a matching hat, with blonde locks peeking out.

"Yes, I'm Jessie Grainger and I play football." Jessie sat down in her seat so she was closer in height to the youngster. "Do you play?"

The little blonde nodded enthusiastically. "For my school."

"That's great. What position do you play?"

"I score goals."

Jessie smiled. "That's what I do too."

"Have you been on telly?"

Laughing, Jessie nodded. "I'm on sometimes, usually when I play for Scotland." The little girl's eyes went round. She pressed the programme closer to Jessie.

"Would you sign this?"

"I'd love to. What's your name?"

"Shannon."

Jessie signed the programme with a special message for Shannon. "There you go, Shannon. We run football camps during the summer holidays. You should come along."

Shannon turned to her father, an eager expression on her rosy-cheeked face. "Could I go, Dad?"

Shannon's dad, a fair-haired guy in his early thirties, nodded. "You want to be a footballer like Jessie?"

"Yes!"

"Okay then." He smiled at his daughter, as he rubbed her head.

"Thanks, Dad!" Shannon said as she tilted her head backwards to smile up at him.

"Thanks, Jessie. She loves football. Who knows if she will still be playing it when she leaves primary school, but right now she's out in all weathers kicking a ball." He put a hand on his daughter's shoulder. "You want to get a burger now?" Shannon nodded enthusiastically and her dad laughed. "She loves hamburgers as well."

"See you in the summer, Shannon, and I'll ask you how many goals you've scored for your school."

Shannon waved as she and her dad went up the steps towards the food kiosks at the back of the stand.

"I remember when that was you," her dad said, his eyes twinkling.

Jessie smiled fondly at the memory. "Yeah, I was thinking the same."

"Was really nice that she met you and got your autograph. I'd never have known any of the female footballers when I was taking you to games all those years ago."

"True, but the women's game has made a lot of inroads, especially in the past five years."

Her dad nodded. "It certainly has."

Jessie recognised his smile—indulgent. He was proud of her and had enjoyed the meeting with little Shannon as much as she had.

"Did you see that goal scored by Stephanie Roche?" he asked.

Did she? It was the type of goal all strikers dreamed of scoring. A three-touch, no bouncer, volley into the top corner of the net, the keeper helpless to do anything about it. You then turn to accept the congratulations of your teammates as the crowd chants your name. A moment when everything comes together—time, place, and technique. The truth was, Roche's goal was scored in the Irish women's league on a cold, blustery day in front of about eighty people, the moment captured on a shaky camera. There was no crowd chanting her name, no replays of the goal showing it from various angles, no close-up of Stephanie Roche's face as she celebrated.

Jessie took heart from the fact that despite the lack of fans and big-game atmosphere, the quality of the strike had been recognised and shortlisted by FIFA for the Goal of the Year award. Right alongside two men whose goals had been seen live on television by millions worldwide at the prestigious World Cup. Many of the male professionals in the game and those who had now retired from football believed Roche's goal should be the winner. Jessie thought so too. A woman winning the best goal would be amazing, and it would be, without doubt, deserved. The goal was an absolute screamer.

"You could do that," her father stated with confidence.

Turning to face her dad, smiling, she hoped that if she ever produced a finish like that in a game, the moment would be captured on film. "Thanks, Dad."

———◆◇◆———

"A draw wasn't a bad result I suppose, but we did have the better of the game." Jessie kept her eye on the road as she idly chatted with her dad. He'd been quiet since they left the stadium. It wasn't like him. She took after her dad in that respect—they both liked to talk. "The Beachcomber's in Portobello, right on the promenade. We should be there in about twenty minutes." Jessie glanced at her dad as she stopped at a set of traffic lights. He was staring out of the passenger-side window, his head turned away from her. "Dad?"

"What? Sorry, Jessie, did you say something?" His voice was flat.

He was sad, and that was an emotion Jessie had rarely seen in her dad. A beep from the car behind alerted Jessie to the fact the lights had turned green. She held a hand up to apologise as she pulled away. "Is everything okay, Dad?" Her eyes flicked briefly to him as he let out a long sigh.

"Ah, Jessie." He paused, "I don't even know where to start."

Concerned, Jessie frowned. "Just tell me, whatever it is."

"I never wanted the marriage to end." There was a note of resignation in his voice.

"You didn't?" Jessie was shocked. "But you're with Alison now."

"I know, I know, but I loved your mum, still love her. She changed."

"What do you mean, 'changed'?"

"Over time she just became distant. I felt like she didn't really need me anymore, didn't want me anymore." He shook his head. "I fully intended to spend the rest of my life with her."

"I'm confused. Why did you start an affair with Alison?"

"Because your mum didn't want me any more." The words were laced with pain.

"Aw, Dad," Jessie whispered. She saw it now. The truth, the hurt, written on his face, a face etched in pain. She pulled over to the kerb and stopped the car.

She turned in her seat to face him. "Do you want to be with Alison?"

"We've been in a relationship for almost a year now."

That information surprised Jessie. How could she have missed all this going on with her parents, not even suspecting anything was wrong. "A year?" Her voice went up a notch.

He nodded. "I confessed to your mum back in the summer that I was seeing someone else. She told me she was glad."

She stared at her dad, searching his face, waiting for him to continue.

"She was relieved. She'd never have ended the marriage, but me having an affair with Alison allowed her to say what she wanted to." He tilted his head back. "She admitted what she hadn't been able to say with words, but had carried through in her actions. When I confessed to the affair, she spoke openly about her feelings for the first time."

"And she wanted a divorce?" Jessie clarified.

He nodded. "She was suffocating and couldn't stand the monotony of her life. She felt like she was dying inside." The tremor in his voice was unmistakable.

Jessie's bottom lip trembled. She had genuinely thought that her dad's affair had led to the divorce. Now she wasn't so sure of that at all.

"I would rather we parted than have her feel like that." His voice cracked.

"I'm so sorry, Dad." She sniffed back her own tears, wanting to stay strong for him, but it was heartbreaking.

"I've known for over a year that the marriage was in trouble. You're the one finding all this out for the first time, but I want you to know there is no blame, Jessie. Really, your mum fell out of love with me, and I don't want to spend the rest of my life alone."

"Will you stay with Alison?"

He nodded. "I could, if she'll have me."

"She'd be mad not to, Dad. I really hope it goes well for you."

He took a deep breath. "Thanks, Jessie. I know it's a lot for you to take in, especially with Alison being a part of my life, now that everything is out in the open."

"Will you be moving in with her?"

"I've already got a place for us. It's in Longniddry. Your mum is going to keep the family home."

Jessie squeezed the steering wheel tightly in her hands. This was all still so surreal. She had never imagined her parents would divorce. It had never occurred to her that they would. "Dad, are you sure you want to go to the pub?"

He nodded. "I want to keep everything as normal as possible. Besides, I like meeting your friends. They'll cheer me up." He injected a note of positivity in his voice.

Jessie had to agree. There was rarely a dull moment around that bunch, and with tomorrow being a public holiday, they were sure to enjoy themselves this evening. She started the car. "So long as you're sure. We can leave any time. All you have to do is say, and I'll drive you home."

Why was everything at the Beachcomber these days? It was fast becoming the new place for the players to hang out, especially when Morven was around. Jessie knew she shouldn't be so petty. The players were including Fran and sending business her way, both of which were positive, but Fran had an effortless habit of upsetting Jessie's day. She mentally steeled herself for another meeting with her as her dad held the bar door open for her. She saw Fran's eyes flicker towards her as they approached the bar. She finished serving one of the regular customers Jessie recognised and turned her full attention on the new arrivals.

Jessie smiled out of politeness. "Hi, Fran." She gestured towards her dad, believing the formalities would be wasted on Fran, but, nonetheless, she had been brought up with good manners. "This is my dad, Mark Grainger." She addressed her father. "Dad, this is Fran Docherty. She plays for Thistle and runs the Beachcomber."

Fran offered her hand to Jessie's dad. "Hi, pleasure to meet you, Mr Grainger." Jessie was stunned. She was sure Fran was being overly friendly— no, simply friendly—just to piss her off.

"Oh, please, call me Mark. Lovely to meet you too, Fran."

Fran smiled at Jessie's dad. "What would you like to drink, Mark?"

"Oh, you have real ale." He paused, apparently unsure which ale to choose. "Which one would you recommend, Fran?"

Fran took a tall pint glass from below the bar placing it under the nozzle of the tap and began to pull the lever slowly then placed the full glass in front of him. "Give that a try. I'm sure you'll like it."

Jessie wanted to say something like "you have to be kidding me!", or roll her eyes, but it occurred to her that this could be Fran's usual way with customers. It was a business after all. Fran was now staring at her expectantly. Jessie could swear there was a hint of challenge in that gaze.

Jessie cleared her throat. "A coffee please, Fran."

"What a lovely young woman." Her dad remarked as they made their way from the main bar to the lounge where the rest of her teammates were gathered.

Jessie plastered a smile on her face, the one she usually reserved for difficult clients, to stop her from saying something she would regret. Her dad didn't appear to notice as he sipped his drink.

"This ale is really good. We'll need to come back sometime."

Jessie continued to smile, as she nodded. "Mm," was all she could manage before they were greeted by a handful of Thistle players already seated in the lounge.

Jessie drove towards home. Well, what had been the family home. It would never be the family home again, regardless of her mum remaining there. Normally, they would be looking forward to a bowl of homemade soup dished up as they walked in the door. Her mum asking how the game went, and listening to them complain about decisions that didn't go their way, or the jubilation at a victory over Hearts.

Today, it felt hollow. She and her dad had enjoyed a couple of hours at the Beachcomber. He was pleasantly drunk after three pints of ale, but he was quiet as they drove back to Haddington. Jessie left him to his thoughts as she followed the coastal road, preferring its winding route over the more direct A1.

She pulled into the paved driveway of her parents' home. It didn't have a number, it had a name. But for Jessie it no longer mattered what the house was called. She'd moved out two years ago, but this had still been home. Until now. Now it was a broken home, situated on this peaceful leafy street, where everyone's lawn was immaculate. Not even a chewing-gum wrapper to upset the pristine facade of this affluent suburban road. No one really knew what lay behind each genteel family home. The veneer of respectability was difficult to crack. Unfortunately for Meadowfield, there was now a chasm running the length of the single-storey well-proportioned family property.

How on earth was her mum going to live there alone? If it was only to allow Jessie to hang on to the last vestiges of her upbringing, what was the point? It was a house, no longer a home. She wouldn't be popping out to the converted garage to play pool with her dad. He would be somewhere else.

"Are you coming in?"

"Hmm?" Jessie had been lost in thought. She shook her head. "I'm tired. Tell Mum I said hello." He was about to protest, but Jessie stilled him. "I'll call her."

"Okay, Jessie," he sighed, his eyes troubled.

"I'll call her, I promise." After today's revelations, she wasn't ready to visit her mum. Her heart wasn't in it. Jessie hugged her dad, and they said their goodbyes before she made the thirty-minute journey back to Joppa.

Chapter 13

Fran stretched her cramped body as Jessie shut off the car engine. She had slept most of the journey back to Portobello. She was groggy, and it took a moment to orientate herself. She shook her head and rubbed her hands together. She turned to Jessie, who had been unusually quiet all day. She was staring out into the darkness with a white-knuckled grip on the steering wheel. Fran reached for the door handle, not interested in prying. Then she stopped and frowned at the unfamiliar surroundings. She turned back to Jessie for an answer, but she looked as confused as Fran felt. The tightness around her eyes conveyed tension and pain.

"I'm sorry, I've driven straight home." Jessie raised her hands from the wheel, and stared at them.

Fran shrugged. "No bother. I'll walk." She got out of the car.

The driver door opened and Jessie climbed out of the car. "You don't even know where you are."

Fran zipped up her leather jacket. They were on the crest of a hill overlooking the sea. The view was inky black, with a sprinkling of lights peppering the opposite shore. Fran knew where she was, she had always possessed a good sense of direction. A frost glittered the pavement as the temperature continued to drop under the cloudless night sky. Fran shivered in her jacket—she wore only a threadbare T-shirt underneath.

"For God's sake, get back in the car. I'll drive you, it's freezing." Jessie folded her arms across her chest, her shoulders hunched.

"I'm not in any hurry." Fran's breath billowed in front of her, crystallising in the cold air. She was desperate to leave Jessie to whatever problems she was experiencing. Fran had enough of her own troubles to deal with. She didn't have room for more.

Jessie slammed the car door shut, pressed the fob to lock the doors, and stormed past Fran towards her single-storey Georgian property. She thrust her key into the front-door lock, opened the door, and slammed it behind her. Fran stood awkwardly, hands in the pockets of her jacket, staring at the front door. She hesitated a moment, confused as to what had just transpired. She considered knocking on the door, before shaking her head and walking along the empty street.

Fran fumbled in the pocket of her leather jacket, found the pack of cigarettes, and removed one of the three that were left. She placed the tip between her lips as she searched for her lighter. She stopped what she was doing and pulled the unlit cigarette from her mouth. Fran stood at the end of the street. All she had to do was turn right and she would be home in a few minutes. She closed her eyes and let out a long frustrated breath. "Dammit!"

Fran turned and retraced her steps. She didn't know why, but she just couldn't walk away. She knew going back wasn't a good idea, but slowly, and against her better judgement, she found herself standing in front of Jessie's door. Why was she here? What the fuck was she doing? She should have kept walking.

Fran hesitated, hand poised, and knocked on the door. It opened and Jessie stood before her, confusion on her face. Fran could tell she had been crying. The puffiness around her red-rimmed eyes, swollen and watery, gave her away.

"Did you forget something?" The question was short and impatient. And not at all like the Jessie she'd come to know.

Fran stood with her hands in her pockets, trying to hide the awkwardness she felt. "I thought you might like some company." Fran sniffed and swallowed, continuously moving her feet in the freezing temperature. She was reaching out. Normally, she barely spoke beyond the minimum words required to convey an answer. Her heart thumped in her chest and a cold sweat dampened the back of her neck. She trembled, awaiting a reply, until Jessie stepped aside and offered entry to her home.

Fran stood in the hallway. What the hell was she doing there? Yes, it was cold outside, bloody freezing in fact, and the warmth of Jessie's home was inviting. But Fran was not a social animal. This was completely alien to her. It was one thing for her to be invited in, but quite another for her to initiate a social situation. But she sensed…she knew…that Jessie needed someone. That Jessie was hurting and she was the only person there. She had no idea if she could be what Jessie needed, but figured she was better than nothing. It didn't stop her wanting to bolt right back out and get down to the Beachcomber as fast as her legs would take her. She hovered awkwardly and waited for instructions from Jessie.

"Eh, well then." Jessie rubbed her forehead. "I'm hungry. Would you like something to eat?"

"Sure." It had been a while since either of them had eaten anything, both having skipped the clubhouse when the team bus returned, instead opting to get home early. Concentrating on food was a whole lot better than focusing on each other.

Jessie nodded. "Great, that's great. Let's go to the kitchen."

Fran followed her, taking in the interior as her gaze wandered skittishly around the house. Modern furniture lined walls painted in light shades, allowing the building's intricate cornice and ceiling rose to push through. Everything was neat and tidy, from the coat rack to the gloss paint on the skirting boards. Much like the woman herself, fashionable with a practical twist. Fran sat at the kitchen table and hung her jacket on the back of a wooden chair as Jessie removed items from the fridge.

"I made mushroom risotto yesterday. It won't take long to heat in the microwave." Jessie glanced over her shoulder at Fran.

"Sounds good."

Jessie busied herself with the food, while Fran attempted to make herself comfortable. She wanted a cigarette, but knew it would be rude to step outside just after she had arrived. Fran drummed her fingers on the table as Jessie made a side salad while the risotto rotated in the microwave. She debated offering to help, but Jessie appeared to have everything under control as she efficiently chopped tomatoes and added them to the salad bowl. The microwave pinged and the kitchen went silent, making Fran more uncomfortable. Having put herself in this situation, she had no real idea what to do next.

"Parmesan?"

"Huh?"

Jessie stared at Fran, a lump of hard cheese in one hand and a small grater in the other. "Parmesan cheese, on your risotto?"

"Oh, yeah, sure." Fran watched Jessie efficiently grate the cheese onto the hot risotto. The noise of the hard cheese being shredded in the silent kitchen almost caused her to wince.

"Would you like some wine?"

"Ah, no thanks, just water."

Jessie stared at her before nodding and turning to the fridge to remove a large bottle of mineral water. Fran would have been happy with tap, but said nothing. She wished she could be of some use, but not knowing this kitchen, she couldn't even set out cutlery and glasses. She sat in silence as Jessie placed the bowl of salad in the middle of the table before returning with two plates of risotto. She placed one in front of Fran.

"Thank you."

Jessie smiled as she placed cutlery on the table, then poured the water into two wine glasses, and placed the bottle in the middle of the table, before she sat down opposite Fran.

"Please, help yourself to salad."

Fran nodded, forgoing the vegetables for a mouthful of risotto. She ate in silence, while Jessie focused intently on her plate, only lifting her head to sip water. Fran knew there was something on her mind, something outside of football, but she was no good at this sort of thing. She wasn't sure she wanted to know her teammate's business. But if Jessie needed to talk, she would listen.

The food was good, really good. She rarely ate a proper sit-down meal. It was usually takeaway food and sandwiches, or even a packet of crisps, when she was working. Fran enjoyed silence, but witnessing Jessie, head down, staring at her food, was unnerving. She was usually so together and organised, casually chatting to pass the time, even when she knew Fran wouldn't reply. To see her preoccupied and hurting...yes, that's what Fran saw, pain, not physical, but the kind that ate you up inside. The kind that occupied your thoughts and caused sleepless nights. Well, seeing that on Jessie made her stomach clench into knots.

Fran finished her food and sipped her water as Jessie continued to stare at the plate in front of her. Finally, she lifted her head, her expression solemn.

"Do you get along with your parents?"

Fran blinked in surprise. The question was so unexpected. Jessie waited for an answer. Fran had no idea where the question had come from or why it was being asked, but she sensed it was leading somewhere. Usually, she was reluctant to discuss her life, but something in Jessie's eyes made her answer truthfully. "I was brought up by my grandparents."

Jessie's eyes narrowed. "You grew up in the Beachcomber?"

"Mostly, yeah."

"Was that strange, being brought up by your grandparents?"

Fran shook her head. "Not really. I didn't know any different."

"Why?"

"Sorry?" The way Jessie was asking the questions, so directly, would normally have Fran closing up, but the tone of the questions was so different. A flat, no-nonsense delivery compared to Jessie's usual friendly conversational style.

"Why were you brought up by them?"

Fran closed her eyes and stretched the back of her neck, trying to alleviate some of the tension building there. When she opened her eyes, Jessie was still staring right at her, her face unreadable. Fran sighed. "I don't have any parents."

"Are they dead?"

She shrugged. "I don't know about my father."

Jessie frowned but pressed on. "You don't?"

Fran could understand why her teammate was confused, but she hadn't come here to be scrutinised. She'd made a rash decision, and now she wished she had gone straight home. "I'm not really comfortable talking about this stuff."

"I'm sorry, I shouldn't pry." Jessie slumped back in her chair and rubbed her temples. "My parents are getting a divorce."

"Oh." Fran understood now where all the questions had come from, but had no idea how to address the problem.

"Thirty years of marriage and now it's coming to an end. My dad's dating a younger woman." Jessie laughed, but it was brittle. "I used to work with her before I moved to the office in Portobello. She's not much older than I am." She shook her head. "I'm still trying to take it in. I thought my mum would be devastated, but she isn't." There was a puzzled expression on her face. "She told me she feels lighter. Free to do what she wants, when she wants. Apparently, they've been living separate lives for over a year, but sharing the same house. They were more concerned about breaking the news to me than the actual divorce. It's amicable." Jessie paused. "It's like my childhood was a lie. Does that make sense?"

Fran had no complaints about her childhood. Her grandparents had done their best, provided well for her and loved her. "I don't know. I mean, it's not like they were planning a divorce while you were growing up, were they?"

"No, God, no." Jessie shook her head. "I'm sorry for being so melodramatic. I'm trying to make sense of it. I never imagined they would separate."

As Jessie stared at the ceiling, Fran tried to consider what it must be like to have the rug pulled out from under what she suspected was a perfect life. But she had no frame of reference. Her grandparents had provided her with a stable, loving environment, as had Jessie's parents. The difference between them was Fran knew from as far back as she could remember what her situation was. She had never been under any illusion that life was perfect. As a young child, her life had been touched by the pain and darkness that in some way came to everyone eventually.

"I don't know who my father is. He could be dead, or he could be happily married with a family. I have no idea, no one does." Fran wasn't sure who was more surprised by her statement. It had slipped out before she could stop it, and Jessie was now completely focused on her, no longer staring off into space.

"And your mum?"

"Dead."

"God, I'm sorry." Jessie's voice was a whisper. "Do you have any memories of her?"

"Some." Fran smiled involuntarily as she thought about them. Most of her memories were fragmented, but there were a precious handful that she clung to like gold dust. "I was four the last time I saw her." A shiver rippled through her at that memory.

"It must have been hard. Growing up without her."

Fran rubbed the back of her neck. She was in uncomfortable waters, having shared more than she ever intended, and in such a short space of time. She glanced at the patio doors. "Can I pop outside for a cigarette?" It was a distraction, but she desperately needed to divert the conversation away from herself.

"Oh, of course." Jessie stood and opened the sliding door. "It's freezing out there." She remarked, rubbing her bare arms.

Fran shrugged as she grabbed her jacket. She zipped it up and walked out onto the decking. Jessie closed the glass door behind her and Fran welcomed the solitude.

Jessie stood at the sink washing the dishes and watching the recalcitrant Fran outside. The smoke billowed from her mouth, mixed with her breath in the cold night air. The light shining from the patio doors highlighted Fran, otherwise she'd morph into the darkness around her. Jessie submerged her hands in the hot soapy suds, the action strangely comforting. Outside, she could see Fran's legs twitching against the cold, one hand in the pocket of her leather jacket as the other held her cigarette. Jessie would've loved to know what was going through her head. Knowing Fran had used the excuse of needing a cigarette to prevent Jessie from asking more about her life brought the comment preceding her escape into focus.

The turreted room back at the Beachcomber and the shrine-like quality of it fell into place. The room must have once belonged to Fran's mother. Her death could explain the reason for the room remaining untouched, a place where a family member, maybe a mother, maybe a child, could go and mourn a lost loved one.

She left the clean dishes on the rack, filled the kettle with water, and set it to boil. The patio door slid open and Fran stepped back inside, the cold clinging to her like a damp cloak as she stood awkwardly in the kitchen.

"I was about to make some coffee." She gestured towards the kettle.

Fran rocked on her heels, hands in the front pockets of her jeans. "I better get going. I'm doing the late shift."

Jessie was disappointed but not surprised. It had astonished her that Fran had come into her home in the first place. It was out of character. "Of course, sorry. Let me get my jacket and I'll give you a lift." Jessie walked into the hall, with Fran following her. As she reached for a jacket hanging on a peg inside the front door, Fran stopped her, placing her hand on top of Jessie's as it stilled on the hanging jacket.

"I'd rather walk."

Jessie frowned. "It's freezing outside."

Fran shrugged and offered a crooked grin. "I don't mind the cold, and it's only a short walk from here."

Jessie realised she didn't want her to go. She had enjoyed Fran's company; it didn't matter that she wasn't exactly great when it came to small talk. Fran had offered an ear and Jessie appreciated the overture. As the seconds ticked by in the hall, the moment became awkward. Jessie sensed that Fran was desperate for her to open the door so she could flee into the safety of the night. Jessie reached for the door to allow her to leave, but turned impulsively at the last moment. They would have collided had Jessie not pulled Fran close and buried her face into the now warm leather covering Fran's shoulder. She inhaled the faint scent of the ageing material as Fran stiffened in her arms, before returning the caress so lightly Jessie almost missed it.

"Thank you," she whispered into the leather.

"No worries," Fran mumbled as she moved a hand comfortingly across Jessie's back.

Jessie shivered, her lips close to Fran's neck, slowly, almost without thought, her face turned to Fran's. She heard Fran swallow, her lean body trembling in Jessie's arms. Jessie stepped back, unsure what was happening, confused by the sudden pull she felt towards her.

Fran didn't make eye contact when they separated. Instead, she glanced towards the door handle, which Jessie pulled open. She walked down the garden path with long strides. Within seconds she was out of sight, leaving Jessie feeling even more alone than she'd felt before.

"Stupid!" Fran scolded herself as she walked briskly down the hill towards the shore. She'd almost kissed Jessie. The sight of her, troubled and emotional, her head tilted towards Fran, the vulnerability in those eyes—it had almost been her undoing.

Why had she gone to Jessie's door? She knew it was difficult to spend time alone with her. Her attraction to Jessie was becoming harder and harder to ignore. She was muddying the waters and sending out mixed signals.

Jessie must've known how close Fran was to kissing her, and Fran was certain Jessie had wanted to be kissed. Oh, yeah. She'd seen it in her eyes. Desire.

Fran rubbed her forehead, a headache forming. She stopped suddenly under a streetlight, rubbed her face with both hands, and pushed her thumbs into the temples. "Get a fucking grip of yourself!" She fumbled in her jacket pocket, removed her cigarettes, and hastily lit one before taking a deep draw.

She leaned back against a high brick wall and took a moment to organise her thoughts. Images of Jessie, vulnerable and alone, swirled around her head. She needed to drive those images from her mind. She craved oblivion, escape, something...anything...that would give her a break from the constant state of denial she had to endure. But she couldn't, or rather, she shouldn't.

She swept a hand across her face and covered her mouth, so deeply frustrated she wanted to scream. She wanted to act out. Or better yet, get absolutely stoned out of her mind. Her heart was racing, and her fingers shook. She wanted to turn on her heel and go back to Jessie's house and find the distraction she needed in Jessie's arms. In her warm mouth and the heat she'd no doubt find between her legs.

She stared up into the starlit sky. "Christ, leave the woman alone, Fran," she whispered. She was twisting in the wind. Every day, every single day, was about denying the things she craved most. And now she could add Jessie Grainger to that list. She flicked the cigarette stub to the quiet road and removed the packet of gum from her pocket.

Chapter 14

Jessie replaced the phone in the cradle and rubbed her forehead, the tension headache that had been threatening to take hold all afternoon was building. Sitting up straighter in her chair, she rolled her shoulders to release the knots, and stretched her arms above her head. It had been a busy week, especially with last weekend spent in Oslo for a friendly international with Sweden, and she was suffering the effects of fatigue. She closed her eyes, leaned her head back against the chair, and tuned out the noise of the outer door opening. Meadow would take care of whoever was there.

"Hi, Fran."

Meadow's enthusiastic greeting carried all the way to the back office. Jessie opened one eye, her attention well and truly piqued. Why would Fran be at the estate agent's on a Friday afternoon? She listened intently, but could only make out snippets of the conversation. She expected Meadow to ring through at any moment to let her know she had a visitor. She waited, but clearly from the flow of the conversation, this visit had nothing to do with her. Since when had Fran and her secretary become friends?

When the pair said goodbye and the door closed behind Fran, Jessie tried to focus on work. She wanted to be finished by five, but it appeared, instead, that she'd be working late again.

She couldn't concentrate. The earlier visit from Fran niggled away at her, disrupting her productivity. She'd hoped Meadow would require assistance, allowing her to casually enquire about Fran without appearing to pry. But she'd remained silent and would be leaving in ten minutes. Curiosity finally got the better of her, and she walked through to the main office with a printout of a new property to advertise in the window. She stopped at Meadow's desk.

"Any messages, Meadow?"

Her secretary smiled. She was always welcoming and cheery. "No, nothing, Jessie."

"Did Fran come in a little while ago?"

Meadow's smile widened. "Yes, she popped in to let me know that Kenny Edwards is playing with his band next Saturday night at the Beachcomber."

Jessie had no idea who Kenny Edwards was, but was even more puzzled by Fran knowing that Meadow liked this musician. When on earth had the pair been chatting? "Sorry, I don't know him."

"Oh, he was in a punk band years ago. He still travels and does gigs, though. I only know about him because my dad was a fan. He played the music all the time when I was a kid. Still does."

"You like punk?" Jessie was astonished at this revelation.

Meadow shrugged and smiled sheepishly, a blush creeping over her fresh face, showing despite the foundation that coated her cheeks.

Jessie wanted to know how Fran and Meadow knew each other. "Do you drink in the Beachcomber?" Jessie asked, as she deposited the printout into the clear plastic sleeve.

Meadow nodded. "Sometimes on a Saturday night if I'm not going uptown, I go there because it's local." Meadow fiddled with the papers on her desk. "Usually the week before I get paid, when I'm running out of money."

"Oh."

Meadow's eyes went wide. "Not because you don't pay me enough. It's because I like to go shopping, and go for nights out up the town. I always run out of money towards the end of the month."

"I can imagine," Jessie joked.

"Honestly, Jessie, by the time I buy a new outfit, because, you know, you can't be seen in the same dress twice, pictures would be all over Facebook and everyone would know." Meadow's gestures conveyed the seriousness of this fashion faux pas. "Drinks are really expensive and taxis, too, but it's a really good laugh."

Jessie didn't know what that was like, and far from being fun, it sounded like a lot of pressure. "Ehm, I'm sure it is." Meadow was only eighteen, but even at that age, Jessie hadn't been one for having much of a night life. She would rather get to bed early and go to the gym in the morning.

"You know what? You should come along." Meadow's voice brightened at the idea.

The suggestion startled her. "Oh, I don't know, Meadow."

"You should. Some of your friends will be there, you know, your teammates. They're really funny."

This was also news to Jessie, but she could guess who these teammates were. Today was full of surprises. "It's not really my thing."

Meadow shrugged. "You'd enjoy it. It's always a good night when a band is on."

Meadow tidied her desk, closing a newspaper, the image on the front catching Jessie's eye. Reaching for the paper, Jessie blinked in surprise. The front page of the *Portobello Reporter* had a grainy black-and-white image of a woman who looked suspiciously like Fran, dressed smartly and smiling.

"Is that Fran?" Her voice rose, relaying her surprise.

Meadow laughed, then said, "No, that's Toni Martin. She owns lots of bars in and around Edinburgh, but her first bar was the Illicit Still right on the corner." Meadow pointed in the direction of the bar in question. "She still owns it."

Jessie was puzzled. This woman, now that she looked closer, was older than Fran, but there was definitely a strong resemblance. "Maybe they are related?"

Meadow frowned. "Toni is my godmother. I'm sure she or my dad would have said something. He works for Toni, they've been best friends for years."

Jessie was at a complete loss, stunned by the numerous revelations her few minutes with Meadow had exposed. It appeared everyone knew everybody else, and she had no idea what was going on. "Does Toni have a brother?"

For the first time since she had hired Meadow, the teenager's face fell, etched in sadness.

"She doesn't talk about him."

"Do you know his name?" Jessie knew she was overstepping a line—she was making a habit of doing that when it came to Fran.

"Ross." Meadow's reply was almost reluctant.

Jessie's eyes widened at the name. It was too much of a coincidence that two strangers in photographs reminded her of Fran.

"Is there something wrong, Jessie?"

"No, no." Jessie shook her head, not wanting to reveal her thoughts. "Listen you get yourself home and have a great weekend. And try not to spend all your pay too quickly," she added.

Meadow laughed. "I'll try, but once I've had a few drinks, I throw caution to the wind." She put her coat on. "I'll see you on Monday. You should come along next weekend. You and Fran are friends; it'd be nice."

Jessie smiled but didn't answer. Meadow left and Jessie locked the door behind her, putting out the lights before returning to the office in the back. It was after five and she still had work to do.

But she couldn't focus on work. Instead, Jessie sat in her chair thinking about Meadow's last words and shook her head. Despite what everyone thought, she and Fran weren't friends. Fran blocked every attempt at friendship Jessie had ever made, and she doubted they'd ever be friends.

No, that wasn't quite accurate. Fran had reached out that one time when Jessie accidentally had driven straight home, forgetting to drop Fran off. That had been different and very unexpected. But still, the second the conversation turned towards Fran, she'd gone running into the night, but not before they'd shared a…moment. For a fleeting second, Jessie thought that Fran had been about to kiss her, and she would have kissed her back.

She wasn't sure what troubled her more. The fact that she would have returned Fran's kiss, or that neither of them had made any acknowledgment of the incident, making Jessie doubt her recollection of the events.

She put the copy of the *Reporter* on her desk and studied the picture of Toni Martin. The likeness was uncanny. Although the picture was black and white, it was clear the woman's hair was dark. But it was her build and the shape of her face that reminded Jessie of Fran. This woman was tall and slim, just like Fran, and the confidence that radiated from her posture was just as striking. But that wasn't what resembled Fran most. She leaned closer to the picture, pored over every detail. Drinking in the similarities to the image of Fran that was so firmly fixed in her mind.

It hit Jessie so suddenly that she could feel her eyes widen. She sat back in her chair. It was that grin. The visage was so serious, until you spotted the upturn at the corner of her mouth. That was what reminded her most of Fran.

Chapter 15

Jessie slowly made her way into the main bar and tried to spot a friendly face amid the sea of bodies. Initially, she'd been reluctant to come to the Beachcomber this evening, but Meadow and a few of her teammates had persuaded her. She hadn't given a definitive yes, but coming along tonight held more appeal than a night alone with Saturday evening television.

"Jessie!"

She turned to where her name had been called and saw some of her teammates gathered around a table waving her over. She should have guessed they'd get here early enough to secure somewhere to sit. They'd all left immediately after the game that afternoon, not hanging around to celebrate their resounding victory against a team near the bottom of the league. Jessie waved and squeezed her way through the crowd towards the back wall.

"Hey, you lot must have got here early." Judging by the cheerful greeting and empty glasses scattered over the table top, they had headed directly to the Beachcomber from the game.

"Would anyone like a drink?" Jessie offered.

"How about port all round?" Morven suggested, causing laughter among the players.

Jessie glared at the policewoman. Morven grinned back at her without remorse, causing Jessie to smile. "I'll be sticking to soft drinks this time."

"You are such a lightweight, Jessie. Four drinks and you're anybody's." More laughter followed that reply as Jessie shook her head.

Shaking a finger in Morven's direction, she replied, "One of these days, that mouth is going to get you into trouble."

"This mouth's been places you could only dream of going."

Jessie knew when to retreat. She was no match for Morven's quick wit, and headed to the bar. "Excuse me" was followed by "thank you," as she made slow progress through the bodies crammed inside the main bar. She waited patiently to be served. There were three staff on tonight, which was just as well given the amount of people here, but there was no sign of Fran. A group of older men, she guessed to be in their mid- to late fifties, stood immediately in front of her. They were dressed in an array of leather jackets and T-shirts emblazoned with what Jessie assumed were names of bands. She couldn't help but overhear some of their conversation.

"Remember the stampede in the Odeon waiting for The Flesh to come on?" a tall man asked, his head completely bald. There was a spiderweb tattoo on the side of his neck.

"Aye, that was mental," replied a man with an impressive red Mohawk.

"Two hours late that night. The crowd got fed up waiting. Every row of seats flattened when we rushed the stage." The bald guy took a gulp from his pint of lager, glee written all over his face.

"They either got on and played, or they were getting a kicking," the man with the Mohican stated.

The bald-headed man grinned. "Man, those were the days."

"Ah cannae believe Kenny's still alive, never mind gigging." Mohawk man shook his head.

The group of men burst into laughter.

Jessie was shocked by the conversation. She tried to attract the attention of one of the bar staff in vain.

"Remember the piles of knuckledusters and knives at the door as they searched everyone going in? Machetes, the lot, some crazy bastard had a samurai sword." The bald man with the tattoos held his hands about four feet apart, apparently demonstrating the length of the sword.

"Good God," Jessie muttered under her breath as she finally managed to squeeze into an empty space at the bar.

"Hi, what can I get you?"

Jessie stared into a pair of mesmerising green eyes that should have looked out of place on the exotic beauty with the full lips and sharp cheekbones. She found herself momentarily speechless. Tall, slim, possibly part Caribbean, Jessie couldn't be sure. It was rare she found a woman so arresting that she literally stopped in her tracks. She cleared her throat and ordered. "I'll have a mineral water, please?"

A full smile beamed back at her. "Sure." The prolonged eye contact combined with the way the barmaid caressed the reply caused a shiver to ripple up Jessie's back and settle between her shoulder blades.

She searched the bar for Fran while surreptitiously stealing glances at the new barmaid, but she was nowhere to be seen. It was unlike Jessie to feel such an instant attraction, and even more out of character for her to want to act on it. But she couldn't stop the image of her leaving with the beautiful woman from popping into her head. She could almost feel the warmth of the woman's hands upon her skin. The twinge between her thighs told her how much she wanted the fantasy to become reality. Though she knew it wouldn't. That just wasn't her. But the woman was stunning, and she was only human. She smiled and hoped it didn't look as shy as it felt upon her lips as she accepted her drink, thanked the beautiful barmaid, and made her way back to her teammates.

"Glad you changed your mind, Jessie. It's good to see you out tonight," Sophie said, making room for Jessie to sit down.

"Well, between you lot going on at me most of the week and Meadow gently encouraging me to come along, I thought I better find out what all the fuss is about."

"Fran told us the band is good and we should come see them," Sophie said.

Great. Looks like I'm the only one Fran didn't invite. "I'll be back in a few minutes. I want to say hi to Meadow."

"Don't you go sneaking back out the door, Jessie," Morven cautioned, and Jessie suspected she was only half joking. She couldn't blame her; she'd already thought about quietly slipping out of the crowded pub.

"I'll be back in a few minutes, I promise."

Jessie thought she'd caught sight of Meadow's long blonde hair in the far corner, near the door. Then again, there were a few girls with blonde hair and skin too tanned for this time of year. As the blonde turned, Jessie recognised Meadow.

"Hi, Meadow." Jessie placed a hand gently on her shoulder.

"Jessie!" Meadow squealed with delight. She jumped up from her chair. "I hoped you'd come." Meadow hugged her in greeting, and Jessie thought it was strange that a social setting totally changed the dynamics of their relationship. Well, it was either the setting or the alcohol. Meadow did appear a little tipsy. "Do you want to join us?" She indicated the table full of pretty young women, all wearing beautiful short dresses and make-up. It was clear a lot of effort had gone into their appearance. Staring at Meadow's feet, Jessie understood why they were suddenly similar in height. How she would manage to walk in those six-inch heels after a few drinks was a mystery.

"I'm over at the opposite side of the bar with a few of my teammates."

"Oh, great. Glad they could make it."

Jessie was certain Meadow was relieved not to be having her stuffy boss join her company, and she couldn't blame her. They got on well as work colleagues, she really liked Meadow, but Meadow clearly enjoyed her social life and Jessie enjoyed her football. It didn't make for a good mix. "I just wanted to say hello and hope you enjoy the band."

"Oh, I will, thanks. My friends don't know the music, but are happy to come along for the cheap drinks before we head into town later."

The table was full of girls in their late teens, chatting and laughing loudly. They were clearly going to have a good night regardless of the music, and a small part of her envied that. She had never been one to go out on weekends to bars, drinking, and meeting people. She didn't enjoy the sensation of being drunk. The lack of control and inhibition felt alien and uncomfortable for her, but she admired their ability to let go and have a good time. Hugging Meadow she said, "Enjoy your night and if I don't get to chat to you again, I'll see you on Monday."

"Bye, Jessie."

Jessie began to make her way back to her teammates, but stopped near the door as Fran entered, followed by two men. The three of them walked to the small stage that was raised no more than a foot from the floor, and started to tune the instruments. Jessie stood with her back to the wall. Clearly, these were the band members. One sat at the drum kit and the other picked up a bass guitar. Fran picked up an electric guitar and began to tune it.

"Is she the roadie?" a man beside Jessie joked as his friend laughed, then made some sexual reference about Fran probably being a groupie who was fucking one of the band members.

Jessie felt the atmosphere in the place shift as the anticipation of the band playing grew with each passing second. The crowd swelled in front of her eyes. People pressed closer to the front of the stage, and the smokers drifted in from outside as the instruments were being tuned. Fran stepped up to the mic.

"Kenny's wrecked."

Those two words caused a cacophony of noise to build. Somewhere a pint glass smashed to the floor, someone shouted out, "Fuck's sake, Kenny! No' again!" Suddenly, the anticipation was gone and the evening had disaster written all over it. The conversation Jessie had overheard at the bar made her fear for the safety of the people in the pub. Some were becoming restless, especially the old punk crowd that had made their way here to support one of their idols. Fran appeared to be deep in discussion with the two remaining band members, pieces of paper in their hands. Jessie hoped she was talking them into playing without Kenny. People were making noises about leaving, and some were finishing their drinks and starting to move towards the exit.

"Fuck this. You fancy a pint in the Central?" asked the bald guy with the spiderweb tattoo on his neck. He appeared menacing and unhappy with the turn of events. The large group of men in his company began to walk past Jessie towards the door.

"Excuse me?" Jessie stopped the bald man by putting a hand on his arm. "Would you give it ten minutes? At least listen to them play a couple of songs?"

"There's no' any point, hen. Without Kenny, they only have a drummer and a bassist."

Jessie sensed that if she could get him to stay, the others would too. "Please, just ten minutes?"

The man smiled, and it softened his features, lighting up his bright blue eyes. "Since you asked so nicely, we'll give it ten, but," he held up his index finger, the knuckle of which had a round dot of Indian ink on it, "if they are rotten, I'm no' hanging about."

Jessie smiled her appreciation. "Thank you."

"What's your name, gorgeous?"

"Jessie."

"Right, Jessie, if we end up staying, you owe me a dance."

Jessie was lost for words as the group of men whooped and whistled.

"Do we have a deal, Jessie?"

She nodded. "We have a deal."

"Wayhey! Gaun yersel', Big Man." His friend gave him a hearty slap on the back.

As the drummer started playing furiously, drawing everyone's attention to the stage, Fran began playing the guitar. The loud wail joined the drums, then bass guitarist added his depth to the mix.

"Is that 'I Fought the Law'?" someone asked.

The older guys started bopping their heads to the beat, all thoughts of leaving forgotten, as they made their way back inside. Jessie stood, gaze fixed on the stage, as Fran played the guitar, competent but uneasy. Jessie could tell she didn't want to be there. The veneer was in place. Fran appeared cool and remote, almost bored, but Jessie had got used to reading her body language. She played the strings with minimum energy expended, but there was tension around her eyes as they flitted from side to side. Fran was uncomfortable.

The bass guitarist was doing most of the singing. It didn't matter that he wasn't the most tuneful. Fran and the drummer were joining in the chorus, and sometimes they were all singing. No one seemed to care as long as they were being entertained.

The night continued amid a chorus of thrashing guitars and furious drumming until Jessie finally recognised a song the band were playing, "Teenage Kicks", and everyone in the room started singing along. Straight after the more upbeat, almost pop-like tune, the band launched into another. This time, Fran was a study in concentration as she picked at the strings to produce the complicated chords. She approached the mic as the slow opening continued, and then began to sing in a heavy, melodic voice. The combination was hauntingly beautiful, almost ethereal. Then, suddenly, the atmospheric tone shifted gears into a thrash of furious strumming and manic drumming. Jessie stood enthralled, and like the lyrics, she was spellbound.

A loud scream of "Gaun yersel', hen!" was bellowed from somewhere near the front. The punk brigade jumped up and down to the furious playing as the song reached its crescendo amid a finale of "Dance! Dance! Dance!". At the end of the song, Fran stood still. The final refrains echoed around the bar, her black hair gathering in thick wet strands, sticking to her cheek. The image took Jessie's breath away. Clearly growing in confidence, Fran sang a couple more numbers. One stood out for Jessie—it was different to all the others, and Fran owned this performance in a way that made the Beachcomber fade away.

Her legs locked, feet apart, head tilted slightly, giving her an imperious, almost arrogant aura worthy of any musician gracing any major venue in the world. Jessie didn't understand what she was seeing, couldn't comprehend the change, but in some way she knew she was seeing Fran. The true Fran. Raw and emotional Fran. Alive and in-the-moment Fran. And this Fran attracted her like no other ever had.

Fran blinked as the song finished, and appeared surprised at her surroundings. Jessie knew she had been in her own world while performing that song. She sensed her begin to shrink away, retreating back behind her walls, even as she remained on stage.

"Nice to see her still playing guitar." The unmistakable London accent croaked out strong, thick and deep.

Jessie turned to an older guy, maybe late fifties, a worn craggy face, hooped earrings, deep blue eyes standing out in stark relief from the many lines and pock marks, and his bleached blonde hair manipulated into short spikes.

"She begged me to teach her when she was two, so I used to play the chords and let her strum the guitar." A look of pride or fondness settled amidst the map of wrinkles. "By her fourth birthday, she could play three-chord guitar songs as well as me. She was better at playing 'Teenage Kicks' than me when she was a toddler."

"Are you Fran's father?" Jessie asked, despite Fran telling her she didn't know who her father was.

He laughed. "No, darlin', I was shacked up with her mother back in the day. Fran was a year old when I met DeeDee."

"Kenny, my man! I fucking came to see you play?" A drunk guy bellowed as he returned from the Gents, still zipping up his jeans.

"I'm sorry mate, I overindulged." His answer carried no remorse, delivered with a shrug and a "just one of those things" attitude.

"How are you still standing? You've been rocking this life for nearly forty years, man."

Kenny held his hands out, "I'm indestructible. My gal's doing great though, ain't she?"

"Just as well or we were all for the off."

Kenny's laugh was cheeky. He put his arm around the man and pointed to Jessie. "I'll see you around, darlin'." He walked off with his friend towards the stage and taking over from Fran to applause and abuse. "Sorry for my lateness, ladies and gents, but didn't Fran do well!" he ground out in his deep, rough voice. "A big hand if you please for Fran. Well done, my darlin'."

Fran deposited the guitar into the hands of Kenny Edwards and departed the stage without acknowledging the applause. She grabbed a glass of dark liquid and gulped some down, before stumbling towards Jessie.

"Fran, you were brilliant!" Jessie proclaimed loudly over the thrashing music. Fran stared at her, wide eyed. Jessie was caught in that gaze. Everything shrank around them as Fran put out a hand towards her.

"C'mon, Jessie, let's dance!"

She was grabbed by the guy she had promised to dance with as Kenny belted out his opening number. Before she knew it, she was being spun around and waltzed to the frenetic music. Through the double doors of the bar, Jessie saw Fran flirting overtly with the barmaid who had caught Jessie's eye earlier. Fran brushed a hand down a long slim, mocha-shaded arm and Jessie felt the tingle all the way across the floor. Then she was spun around again, and they were gone from the hallway when her eyes settled back on the spot. Who could blame the barmaid? Fran had been the star of the show. Jessie doubted there was a man or woman in the room that hadn't paid attention to her teammate on stage.

Fran's gaze again turned to Jessie. She was using her as an anchor. She kept her moored to the spot, otherwise she would be lost while her demons gathered, lurked, and fought for free reign. Her nostrils flared as she saw Kenny stand right behind Jessie, his eyes catching hers, the grin in them unmistakable.

The bastard didn't look like someone who was too strung out only an hour ago to play a set. Anger surged within her as she watched Kenny chatting with Jessie. Fran's jaw clenched, and with a final flourish, she strummed the guitar strings so violently she expected them to snap. But as the final chord rang out around the bar, the strings vibrated and remained intact. Kenny advanced towards the stage as she was already lifting the guitar strap over her head. She thrust the guitar into his waiting hands. His grin lacked remorse, despite knowing what he had put her through.

The thrill of playing thrummed through her veins. Fran was jumpy, on edge. She reached for the tall glass of Coke, her throat was parched. Within two gulps she knew the Coke she had expected was heavily laced with Jack Daniels. She knew she should stop, but she didn't.

She welcomed the burn of the alcohol as it slid into her stomach and filtered into her bloodstream. The effect was almost instantaneous. Fran's gaze twitched around the room. She was in dangerous territory. A sea of grinning, sweaty faces cheered and abused Kenny in equal measure. There were drugs in the room. Fran knew she could find anything she wanted, a pick-me-up, a come-down…heroin. She locked her gaze again with Jessie and stumbled forward on wooden legs. It took great effort to propel herself away from the action, away from the high she craved.

Instead, she lurched towards what she was quickly coming to realise she needed. She reached out an unsteady hand to her, but in the blink of an eye Jessie was gone. Fran dropped her hand back to her side. Her safety net was ripped away without even knowing it, casting her adrift without a life jacket.

Fran clenched her hands at her sides. Someone slapped her on the back telling her how great she had been. A teammate maybe, she wasn't sure, and she didn't care. The words barely registered in her addled brain as she caught sight of Afton. The barmaid whose eyes had been following Jessie all evening. She looked crestfallen as Jessie danced with the guy who had whisked her away when Fran had reached out.

She needed a distraction, and she needed it now. And Jessie was not an option. Fran stood up straighter, and taking a deep breath, she strode confidently towards the barmaid.

"You're wasting your time," Fran stated as she stood close to Afton, a fraction behind her left shoulder.

Afton turned to her, appearing a little embarrassed to be caught staring. "Do you know her?"

"Jessie? We play in the same football team."

Afton sighed. "She's gorgeous."

Fran smiled sympathetically as she nodded towards Jessie dancing with the bald guy. "And straight."

"Ah." Afton's smile was sad, mixed with a hint of surprise. "Looks like I'll be going home alone tonight."

Fran stepped closer, placing her hand on Afton's lower back. "We can't have that." She deliberately used her husky voice, as she ran her free hand slowly down the length of Afton's bare arm, catching the long slim fingers in her own. "Why don't you come upstairs with me?" She whispered into a delicate ear. She sensed the shiver of anticipation as the barmaid turned to stare at her. Fran had seen Afton and Jessie exchange glances all evening from the stage. They'd watched each other when they thought the other wasn't. She'd been jealous, and that had irked her. Jealous that Jessie was interested in the barmaid.

Fran paused. Everything she craved was now inside the bar. It was full of danger and longing. She could remove it all with lust, and in the process prevent Jessie from getting together with Afton. Fran knew that had her hand connected with Jessie, she would've been rebuffed. And who could blame Jessie? Fran spent most of their time alone being deliberately obtuse, but the truth was, Jessie Grainger scared the hell out of her.

She was wildly attracted to her teammate and that could only cause problems for her. She couldn't act upon the attraction. Jessie was too good for her, she knew it, but it didn't stop the longing, the wanting. The need.

No. This was better. Safer. She liked Afton well enough. She was attractive, certainly. But best of all, she was a passing fancy. A fleeting distraction. Not another potential addiction for her to fight.

Fran tugged Afton gently towards the stairs. The barmaid hesitated, glancing toward the bar.

"You won't be missed; the place will empty as soon as Kenny finishes." With those words of assurance Afton followed Fran upstairs.

Contrary to Jessie's earlier fears, the night was successful. Her teammates were bopping along with most of the other clientele, young and old happily dancing away together. Jessie was filled with a sense of warmth. The ageing punk guys had a ball as they danced and frolicked with the football team, students, and Meadow's friends. Nothing overt, just everyone having a great time. It was a shame Fran wasn't around to witness it.

At the end of the night, Jessie collected glasses. The bar staff had struggled to keep up with demand all evening, and only now were people beginning to leave given that the band had finally stopped playing. Kenny sat in the largest corner of the pub, his spiked hair flat, a towel around his shoulders, the veins in his neck and arms standing out ready to pop. He sipped from a glass of water.

"I enjoyed your playing," Jessie said as she collected glasses from the table.

He patted the seat beside him, a tired smile carved into his face. "Come sit with me, darlin'."

Jessie hesitated.

"Come on, it's all right, I don't bite. Humour an old man." Kenny's voice was rougher now than before he started singing.

Smiling, Jessie sat next to him.

"What's your name, darlin'?"

"Jessie."

"You work for Fran, Jessie?" He used the towel to wipe at the rivulets of sweat that continued to drip down his face.

Jessie shook her head. "No, we play in the same football team."

"Oh, nice one. Fran's been telling me a bit about it."

"So you're Fran's stepdad?" Jessie asked, unable to quell her curiosity.

"Well, I suppose I was for three years or so. The word 'dad' would be a stretch, if you know what I mean? It's not like I was a good role model or nothing." The final word sounded like "nuffink".

"Fran said she doesn't know who her father is?"

"Yeah, DeeDee never said and I never asked, so poor Fran don't know." He was staring down at his right hand, rubbing a calloused finger, "Wished I had asked now. Then Frannie might know who her dad was. DeeDee took that one to the grave."

"Were you around when DeeDee died?"

The man's shoulders sagged, his cheerful facade leaving his face along with the sweat still running from his forehead. "I was away on a UK tour, but I got back a few days late. You know what it's like on the road—parties, girls." He scratched at the back of his neck, then continued, "Well, anyway, when I get back to the flat, it's empty. There's dishes and all sorts all over the place, I'm thinking, we've been robbed, but when I went inside..."

He paused, shaking his head. "I knew something wasn't right. I thought she had run off with me best mate. He always was a pretty bastard and he fancied DeeDee. Lots of the guys who hung around the Cave fancied her. She was one of them women the men all flocked to, but DeeDee's first love was heroin. It's like nothing was ever enough for her. If there had been a drug more potent than smack, DeeDee would have been the first one off her tits on it." He held a hand up in apology. "Pardon my French, darlin'." Then his face fell. "Then I found the note left by the police and another from a friend telling me to get in touch right away. Now I was hoping DeeDee had run off with someone while I had been touring, but it didn't feel right. All their stuff was still in the flat."

Kenny slumped further in his seat. "I went down to the cop shop. I mean, I couldn't be minding a toddler. I could hardly look after mesel', you know what I mean?" He pointed to his chest. "Anyways." He shook his head again. "What you have to understand, love, we was all on the drugs back then. Heavy into them, especially when the cheap heroin came in from Pakistan. We all went nuts for the brown powder. DeeDee, she liked smack, she liked it a lot. It was an accidental overdose, stuff was too pure. She was a free spirit, exactly the kind of person that the punk ethos embodied. She didn't give a fuck about establishment rules and class rules. Not quite an anarchist, but a kick-arse, get-it-done type of girl."

Jessie stared open-mouthed at the story.

Kenny rubbed his nose. "Jesus, listen to me running me mouth off. That little pick-me-up's done wonders." He laughed. "Thanks for listening, Jessie. You look after my girl now."

She nodded. "It was nice to meet you, Kenny." She held out her hand and Kenny stared at it before pinning her with those deep-set blue eyes, which cleared, almost sobering him as he focused on her. He took her hand in his rough warm one and shook it gently.

"Lovely to meet you, Jessie."

Jessie continued to clear up glasses as the bar emptied. Fran and the barmaid had not been around since she'd seen them in the hallway. It didn't take much guesswork to figure out where they were. Clearing the table the band had been using, she spotted a crumpled sheet of beer-soaked paper, the ink already beginning to blur. Retrieving it, she recognised the set list and put it in her pocket.

CHAPTER 16

JESSIE HAD NEVER BEEN IN the Illicit Still despite passing it almost every day. It dominated one corner of the main junction and curved elegantly around the corner. The art deco, pink sandstone exterior was offset by large brass-coloured lettering. It fit in well with the buildings around, while maintaining an air of individuality.

Jessie opened the dark oak double doors. She detested entering a strange pub alone, especially one that was frequented by regular clientele. She squared her shoulders, took a deep breath, and stepped inside.

Almost every head in the bar turned to stare at her, justifying her unease. She looked for the dark-haired stranger she'd arranged to meet. She was nervous. More so than she expected to be. Probably because she hadn't been completely honest about the reason for setting up the meeting.

Jessie composed herself and approached the bar. A man of about fifty smiled as he made his way towards her. He had thick brown hair shot through with silver, styled in a side parting, and trimmed neatly around his ears. He wore a pristine white shirt with navy slacks and a perfectly knotted burgundy silk tie. He was handsome, putting her more in mind of a businessman than a barman.

"Hello there, what can I get you?" His smile was infectious.

"I'm meeting Toni Martin. Is she here?"

"Ah, you must be Jessie Grainger, the estate agent. Toni's on her way, held up in traffic. Would you like something to drink? Tea or coffee, perhaps?"

Jessie faltered, slightly flummoxed by the thoroughly charming and knowledgeable bartender. "Coffee would be wonderful, thank you." She opened her purse to remove money.

"On the house." He tipped his head towards the corner. "There's a table over there, behind that partition. Take a seat and I'll bring your coffee over."

"Thank you." Jessie made her way behind the partition where a small wooden table was set with two matching chairs. It would be perfect for either an intimate date or a business meeting. Which was exactly what Toni Martin was expecting to be having very shortly.

Jessie took a seat and closed her eyes, again questioning her judgement at having set up this meeting. Her mouth was dry, making it hard to swallow. It made her even more grateful when the barman arrived with a tray containing a large cup of coffee with a small jug of cream and pot of brown sugar.

"Enjoy."

"Thank you," Jessie said. Her hand shook slightly as she reached for the cream, a ripple of anxiety seeping through her tummy.

"You couldn't resist could you?"

The female voice that carried firmly across the bar stopped the departing barman in his tracks. Laughter accompanied the delivery, as the barman turned to face the newcomer. Jessie couldn't stop herself from listening in.

"Always got to fit in a shift behind the bar."

The barman opened his arms wide. "You know me, I've always felt most at home behind a bar." His smile grew wider as the tall, dark-haired woman approached. She was impressive—lean, dressed in a dark grey trouser suit, with a black, crew-neck top. Black leather ankle boots with a block heel added to her already imposing height. The lightest dusting of make-up covered a handsome face.

"You working here all day?"

"Until six, then the evening staff arrive." He shrugged. "I got the call to provide cover, and I thought, what the hell."

The tall woman gave him a playful shove towards the bar. "Well, I hope you do a decent coffee."

"Of course. I'll bring it over to you. Jessie Grainger's already waiting."

"Thanks, Eddie."

"Toni?" He called to her as she was about to head to the table where Jessie was sitting. "You don't fancy a shift tomorrow?" he said. "Me and you behind the bar, just like old times."

Her laughter again rang out around the pub. "I'm almost tempted, but I have a meeting with the brewery. Now hurry up with my coffee. The service in here is terrible."

Toni Martin walked towards Jessie, a smile still lingering on her lips. She and Eddie were clearly old friends. In a few long strides she was standing in front of her, hand extended in greeting. Jessie stood to accept. Up close, the woman was even more visually arresting—tall, well-dressed, and quite beautiful, with a subtle androgyny, but unmistakably feminine. In all, she was a commanding presence.

"Hi, I'm Toni Martin."

The handshake was firm, confident, and Jessie returned it as her stomach lurched. "Jessie Grainger. Thanks for meeting me."

They both sat and Jessie struggled to start the conversation. She was grateful when Toni Martin beat her to it.

"I've seen your office on the high street. How's business?"

This woman was direct and to the point. Jessie knew she was extraordinary simply by virtue of her success in business, but in the flesh, she found her to be a little intimidating.

"It's going well, thank you. The market is variable, but the rental side is really taking off."

"You're an East Lothian company?"

Jessie nodded. Toni Martin had done her homework. "Yes, my dad, well in fact, my granddad, opened the first office in Haddington over fifty years ago. When my dad took over, he expanded into two more towns in East Lothian. Now I'm branching out further by bringing the business into the city. I want to move more into private rental and especially retail lets." Jessie felt like she was being interviewed.

Toni Martin nodded. "Portobello is a good place to start. It's like a microcosm of what is happening with the economy, always appearing to reflect what is going on. Right now, the place is ripe for small business ventures. That's why I started here." A small smile played on her lips, as her eyes swept the bar.

"How many do you own now?" Jessie asked.

"A few, some clubs and a couple of boutique hotels."

This was the kind of woman Jessie aspired to be. Successful in business, with a knack of knowing what direction her business would be moving in, and obviously not afraid of risk.

"We might do more business in the future."

That statement was like a slap in the face to Jessie, reminding her that this wasn't about business. She had lured Toni Martin here after giving her that impression.

"I'd welcome the opportunity."

Eddie, the barman appeared with coffee for Toni, and Jessie waited while the pair shared barbs. When he was gone, Toni Martin turned her attention back to Jessie.

"So, the Beachcomber. I've admired that place for years. I was always fascinated with it growing up. There's an aura about the place, a nostalgia. I could build a pub that would replicate it, but the Beachcomber's a one-off. A rare commodity. The years of history and tradition appear to ooze from its very walls, building its reputation brick by brick. You can't replicate that." Toni shook her head. "Some bars have character. They take on a life of their own."

Jessie began to sweat as Toni eulogised her love of the bar. This was not going to end well.

"You know what I mean. You sell property, you know what it's like. Every so often, you come across a gem. You must sometimes walk into a house and know there is something special about it. It has a history, a story to tell. You want to know its secrets." She paused for breath and shook her head. "I joked for years with Harry about contacting me if he ever decided to sell up. It's a shame about his stroke. I heard his granddaughter was trying to run the place. I guess it isn't working out."

Jessie swallowed with great difficulty. The gleam in the blue eyes was so intently focused on her, full of gleeful expectation. This woman didn't want the Beachcomber as a business acquisition—she was in love with the place. *Great.* Clearing her throat, she steeled herself for the backlash.

"Ms Martin, the Beachcomber isn't for sale."

Toni Martin appeared puzzled, then frowned as she sat straighter in her chair. The spark disappeared from her eyes as they turned to chips of ice.

"I'm sorry for misleading you," Jessie said. "I actually wanted to talk to you about Fran, Harry's granddaughter."

"I know who she is." Her tone was flat. "I don't have time to help her run the place. An injection of cash we could talk about, but I'm not too keen on part ownership of anything."

"No, it's not that," Jessie added hastily.

The other woman sat back in her chair, arms folded, guarded. It was clear to Jessie she was unhappy at the turn the conversation had taken. She appeared to be weighing Jessie up. She licked her lips and clasped her hands together, before pushing ahead with her questions.

"Did you know Fran's mum?"

"DeeDee? Yes, I did."

Toni was sucking on the inside of her cheek, clearly unimpressed. Jessie produced her phone and located the image she wanted to show. Handing the phone to Toni, she asked, "Do you know them?" The smile that washed over the other woman was distinctly fond.

"Well, that's Ross, my brother, and DeeDee. They went out for about three years, until she buggered off to London with a guy from some punk band. The other two got married. They have a house in Portobello. He's a college lecturer and she's a social worker with three kids." She sighed. "That picture really takes me back. They all hung out at DeeDee's, or wandered around Porty appearing threatening. The four of them were soft as mince." A sadness enveloped her as she pushed the phone back to Jessie. "That was a lifetime ago."

Jessie stared at the picture again, afraid to ask, but knowing she probably wouldn't have a better chance.

"Ms Martin, I don't quite know how to say this, but is there any chance that your brother could be Fran's dad?"

"What?" Toni Martin's raised voice indicated her shock.

"I don't know what your angle is here. Has she put you up to this? I tell you, she was never to be trusted. Trying to get served in my bar, nicking drink from the Beachcomber. Drinking every night and staggering about the prom. She was never any good. Never. She gave her grandparents a really tough time. They provided her with everything she could want, but nothing was enough. Just like her bloody mother. Then she buggered off to London and left them broken-hearted all over again."

Jessie thought Toni Martin was about to leave, and the barman was now staring at them. She needed to talk quickly. "Honestly, she knows nothing about this. I saw the picture and thought your brother resembled Fran. I thought nothing more of it. When I saw you in the *Reporter*, I thought it was Fran at first. I asked Meadow if you and Fran were related, and she said no. So I took it upon myself to contact you."

Toni stared at her for a few moments, then squared her shoulders. Jessie squirmed under her direct gaze. Then Toni shook her head.

"The dates don't work out. DeeDee was off to London a good two years before Fran was born."

"Oh." Jessie deflated like a balloon. She'd hoped, somewhere, her theory would be true.

Toni reached over and held the phone again. "They thought they were going to make records. Turns out, only DeeDee had any talent." Toni shook her head. "But she was always chasing the next big thing. The next thrill. When she met that guy from the band, she was gone. Literally got in the van and went on tour with him. Never looked back." Toni made direct eye contact with Jessie. "It broke Harry and Grace's heart."

"I'm sorry. I'm sorry for bringing you here today." Jessie's knew her face was red. She'd made a mistake and was thoroughly embarrassed.

Toni passed the phone back and sat up straight. Jessie could tell she was back to business. "Meadow speaks highly of you. That's her dad behind the bar." Toni indicated the barman. "I asked about you before this meeting. I always do my homework."

Jessie knew she was being lectured, but saw it for the free advice that it was.

"You play in the same football team as Fran, and obviously you care about her. You're young, talented, and doing well in business. Be careful. Someone like Fran Docherty could end up causing you a lot of problems."

Jessie frowned, but nodded. She'd been foolish to play detective. She knew that. It wasn't her job to try and sort everyone's life out.

"Now, go sell houses," Toni said with a small, tight smile, "and forget this day ever happened."

"Thank you." As Jessie stood, so did Toni, her hand extended. Jessie shook the offered appendage.

"And next time you contact me, make sure it's with a genuine offer." The cheeky wink Toni offered was reassuring despite the chastisement.

⁕

"How are the students settling in?"

Fran rolled her head towards Jessie. "Fine." They were heading home after training, and she'd hoped to make the journey in silence.

"No problems?"

"Place is busier, other than that..." Fran shrugged. In truth, she welcomed the Beachcomber being busier. It was helping to keep her mind off Jessie.

"They aren't too boisterous?"

"I don't mind the noise."

Jessie turned her head towards Fran, amused. "You sure?"

"Makes a change from me and Gary rattling around in the place."

Jessie laughed, and Fran couldn't stop the smile blossoming on her face, until Jessie frowned.

"Who's Gary?"

Fran was surprised Jessie hadn't asked about him before now. "He came with the building."

"Huh?"

"Harry offered him a place to stay. He's been there a few years now. He helps out around the place in exchange for free board."

Fran yawned and rubbed her eyes. She was grateful Gary was working for her this evening. She could get to bed early.

"Fran?"

The soft, yet probing way Jessie said her name put Fran on alert. She swallowed reflexively and turned to Jessie. She said nothing as Jessie's eyes searched hers.

Jessie parked the car in the usual spot at the bottom of the street. "We need to talk."

And there it was. Jessie wanted to have the conversation Fran had hoped to avoid. She closed her eyes and sighed before she clicked open the seatbelt. When she opened her eyes again, Jessie had turned to face her.

"What's going on between us?" Jessie asked softly, confusion lacing her words.

Fran shook her head. What indeed? She knew exactly what Jessie was referring to, but she had hoped she wouldn't want to discuss it.

"I'm not sure." Fran's voice was low. She stared out through the windscreen, avoiding eye contact.

"We've shared a few 'moments' recently."

The way Jessie emphasised the word spoke volumes without needing further explanation. A single word that contained so much depth because of the way she said it. Fran kept her silence, finding more interest in her fingers as she played with them.

"Fran?"

She turned to Jessie. "It's just lust, Jessie."

Jessie shook her head. "I don't agree."

Of course she didn't, and Fran couldn't blame her. She was lying, and they both knew it. There was a definite attraction between them despite her efforts to halt its momentum.

"I'm not looking for a relationship."

Jessie nodded, several emotions crossing her face. Fran thought one of them could even be relief. Jessie sat back in her seat.

"I'm not sure why I brought it up." She let out a short bark of laughter. "Could you imagine us together? I mean, it's crazy."

Crazy? Fran smiled, despite how much it hurt. "We spend a lot of time alone together. It's a fleeting attraction." She shrugged. "It'll pass." It hurt even more to say those words. The more she got to know Jessie, the more time she spent with her, the stronger the attraction became. She was stunned that Jessie had acknowledged it. Shocked that this woman, this beautiful, successful, talented, good woman was drawn to her. Jessie was sorted, together, mature. She was everything Fran wasn't. Everything she knew she'd never be.

"Yeah, I'm sure you're right. It'll pass," Jessie said softly, her voice distant, sadness creeping into it.

"Yup." Fran rubbed her thighs with her palms, anxious to get going, the sensation of being trapped growing with every second she sat in the car.

"I'll see you tomorrow. Same time?" Jessie injected a note of cheer into her words, effectively breaking the tension within the small space.

"Sure." Fran nodded as she got out of the car.

"Night, Fran," Jessie called as Fran closed the door with a small wave, escaping into the night. She was relieved to no longer be pinned down by the honesty of Jessie. Relieved but disappointed that Jessie was once again driving away from her.

Chapter 17

Fran raised her head at the sudden shift in atmosphere in the bar. There, holding the door open for her wife, was Toni Martin. Everyone in the bar who knew them instantly cheered, the gloominess lifted despite the wind and rain that lashed the promenade. They were familiar to her, and the presence of the brunette unnerved her.

She hadn't spoken to either of them since she was sixteen, but they had left a lasting impression. Toni's wife, Shona, was kind and friendly. Fran liked her a lot. But Toni was a different story. She'd marched Fran home to her grandparents more times than Fran cared to recall, and her presence here today was suspicious.

Fran's eyes tracked them as they crossed the bar to her grandfather. Toni and Harry were old friends. The kind who picked up exactly where they'd left off, regardless of time and distance. She'd always found Toni rather aloof, but the way her grandfather's face lit up in her presence was unmistakable.

But Fran refused to be taken in by the sudden "friendly" appearance. The timing was suspicious, and there was no way in hell she would let Toni Martin talk Harry into selling the Beachcomber. She didn't trust Toni as far as she could throw her.

Shona, however, was a different story. Her curly blonde hair was now shot through with silver. Fran guessed she must be in her mid-forties but she appeared younger. Shona had a youthful complexion, the kind of soft skin that didn't wrinkle. She stood at the end of the bar, a smile on her lips, and her intelligent green eyes trained on Fran. The kindness and warmth in those eyes drew her in. Made her feel safe, made her trust. But Fran couldn't afford to trust right now. The vultures were circling.

"Hello, Fran. I'm not sure if you remember me. I used to…"

"I know who you are." Fran was abrupt and regretted being so. She really liked Shona. She'd had a crush on her for years. Long before she was old enough to recognize what it was.

Shona hadn't seemed to notice. Even when Fran was rude, Shona had been patient and understanding. The tilt of her head, the gentle smile, the honest, open expression, all reminded Fran that Shona MacLeod didn't have a malicious bone in her body. She'd always been fair and kind, and Fran knew with certainty that would not have changed over the years.

"How are you doing, Fran?"

Fran felt like a teenager again. Shona had always stopped to talk to her, always been pleasant. She was someone Fran could have reached out to and the response would have been positive.

She would have offered guidance had Fran sought it, but she'd been an unruly teenager, hell-bent on making her own mistakes. Where Toni had seen her as trouble, Shona had seen her as troubled, and had reached out many times.

In the end, it hadn't mattered. Fran had chosen a path of self-destruction. She briefly imagined what her life might have been like had she accepted the help on offer. She certainly would have stayed on at school, maybe even gone to university.

Shona was a woman she could still connect with. Fran could feel it. But there were so many barriers in the way, so many walls erected, so many faulty coping mechanisms...opening up just wasn't an option. Not now.

"I'm okay." Two words, closed, no inroad offered.

"It's good to see you again."

Fran nodded, it was good, but the words had stuck in her throat. She used to follow Shona along the prom just to be near her, and she always spoke to her. She'd never made Fran feel embarrassed or uncomfortable. If she'd been aware of Fran's crush on her, she'd never said.

"My, how you've grown up." Shona smiled. "I remember the very first time I saw you, climbing on the railings outside Mrs Ramsay's guest house. You must've been four years old."

That memory forced a smile on Fran's face. She remembered that day as well. The old bat had come out of her front door screaming at Fran to get down. She'd stuck two fingers up at the matronly woman and told her to fuck off.

"I remember."

"Quite a first impression you made."

Fran nodded. She'd come to hate Mrs Ramsay because of the way she'd spoken to Shona that day. It was only years later she understood that it had been because she was gay. Fran didn't regret a single name she'd called the old bag over the years.

"What would you like to drink?"

"Mineral water, please."

As she poured the water, Fran looked over to where Harry was chatting with Toni Martin. The welcoming smiles were gone, the pair now deep in conversation. Fran's stomach clenched, fearing the worst.

She placed the mineral water on the bar in front of Shona and declined the offer of payment.

"It's on the house."

"Thank you, Fran."

She nodded, but her eyes flitted across the bar to Harry.

"How've you been?"

"Oh, you know, trying to stay out of trouble."

Shona smiled. "I hear you're doing really well at football."

"Pays the bills, I suppose."

Shona's head tilted to the side. "I think you're doing a fantastic job, Fran. Keeping this place afloat and Harry near to what he loves so dearly."

Fran's throat tightened at the heartfelt assessment. The words reminded her of why this woman had been so important to her growing up.

"It's the least I could do."

Shona maintained full eye contact and Fran had to look away. She was ashamed.

She caught sight of Harry. He was white as a ghost. Without hesitating, Fran strode over to where he sat with Toni. She looked between the two of them for answers.

Harry spoke first, his left hand shaking. "Everything is fine, Fran. Me and Toni are just catching up. You remember Toni? Her brother, Ross, used to date your mum." Harry's words unsettled Fran. "Toni, you remember Fran?"

Toni held out her hand. "Nice to see you again, Fran. The last time we met, I was throwing you out of my bar," she joked.

129

Fran tensed, fighting the urge to return the favour.

She shook the offered hand slowly. "I remember." Her tone was flat. Fran hesitated, but Harry's nod reassured her. "I'd better get back behind the bar."

Fran returned to where Shona was sitting on a stool at the bar. Standing next to her, she stared back over at Toni. A warm hand covered her clenched fist.

"Everything'll be fine, Fran."

She stared into those honest green eyes. She wanted to trust Shona. She'd never lied to her; it was Toni she didn't trust. Her breathing was shallow as anger warred with fear. She couldn't settle.

Shona gave her hand a squeeze and then released it. She wanted to ask her what Toni was doing here, but she had too much respect for Shona to put her on the spot. She'd wait and ask Harry.

Fran cleared her throat. "Are you still teaching?"

"Yes, I've been at Edinburgh University for several years now."

Fran nodded. "Nice one." The words sounded pathetic, so God only knew what this intelligent woman thought of them.

"Thank you."

Again, Fran looked over to Harry. Toni Martin stood and whispered something in his ear as her hand squeezed his shoulder. She walked towards the bar, making eye contact with her wife before staring at Fran, a tight smile on her lips.

"Fran," Toni greeted her with a nod.

"All right?" Fran's eyes flitted to her grandfather before returning to Toni's.

Toni nodded. "Yeah, everything's good." She turned to Shona. "Ready to go?"

A smile met her request. "Of course." She turned back to Fran, smile still in place. "It was good to see you again, Fran."

"You too."

"I'll say a quick goodbye to Harry." Shona left the pair of them and walked over to Harry.

Toni remained at the bar. Fran stood, arms spread, as her hands rested on the top of the dark wood. She towered over Toni due to the raised floor, cutting an imposing figure. She was being deliberately antagonistic.

"Everything going okay?" Toni asked.

"Yup."

"If you need any help, or advice, get in touch." Toni placed her card on the bar.

Fran stared at it, then looked back at Toni. "We'll be fine."

Toni nodded as Shona looped an arm around hers. "Ready?" At Shona's nod, she turned back to Fran. "See you around, Fran."

Fran nodded imperceptibly.

"Bye, Fran, take care of yourself."

"Bye, Shona."

Fran's smile was brief, but genuine.

Her gaze followed them as they left. Envy curled in the pit of her stomach. She knew she'd never have what they did. They must have been together close to thirty years. Fran couldn't imagine herself ever in a relationship like theirs. It was the stuff of fairy tales. They just fit together. They had a bond that Fran was certain only death could break.

"Pint please, Fran." Her gaze snapped to one of the regular customers, Dave. "When you're ready."

Slowly, she removed her hands from the bar and stood to her full height. She grabbed a pint glass and began to pump the ale Dave favoured into it. She couldn't keep her eyes off Harry. He looked troubled, and that meant he had something on his mind. She intended to find out.

Placing the full glass in front of him she left the bar, ignoring the £5 Dave was attempting to hand her. "I'll get it later."

She marched over to Harry. She had to know. "Are you selling?"

"What? What makes you think that?"

Fran pointed at the door. "Toni Martin. She must be after something."

Harry shook his head, "No, Frannie, no, I promise you."

Fran slumped into the chair beside him, the use of her childhood name sapping the anger from her. "She offered to help. Said if I needed anything, to ask." Fran gazed into his eyes, hoping he'd understand. "I don't want her help. I want to do this for you. Can you let me have a little more time to show you that?" Fran knew she needed to make it work, for Harry and for herself.

No amount of work could ever repay what he and her grandmother had done for her, but at least this was something she could do in return. It wouldn't erase the hurt she had caused, but she had a chance at redemption.

Toni Martin could run the bar with her hands tied behind her back. They both knew it. But Fran wanted to prove she could do it. She needed to show Harry she was worth something, worth his love and faith.

"Trust me, Fran. Toni Martin doesn't need anything from us, and she wasn't here to take anything from you."

"Then why was she here? I'm doing all right. I know I was struggling at first, but I'm getting the hang of it. I'm finally making enough money to keep the place running and pay for your care."

Fran was confused. She needed to know what was going on, and more than that, she needed to know that Harry trusted her. That he had faith in her to make things work.

"You're doing a great job, Fran. I'm so proud of you. The effort you're putting in, the way you're managing things around here. I knew it was a big ask when I contacted you. A really big ask." Harry gripped her hand. "You've stepped up, Fran. More than stepped up. You're not just getting by here now, you're really making it work. And I truly understand what it takes for you to do that. You've impressed me, lassie. Never doubt that."

"Thank you, Harry." Fran was embarrassed by his words. She wasn't worthy of his praise, doubted that she ever would be.

"Fran?" The gentle, serious tone in Harry's voice was unnerving. She sat up straight. "Toni was here for a reason, but it's nothing to do with the bar." Harry held her hand, squeezing tighter. As tears filled his eyes, Fran was gripped with fear. "It's something else, to do with your mum."

"My mum?" Fran was confused. What could there possibly be to know after all these years? Why would Toni Martin come to speak about her mum now? "I don't understand."

Harry seemed to struggle to find the words, which only added to her confusion and anxiety.

"I'm sorry, Frannie. Listen, it's up to you what you want to do, no pressure."

"You're scaring me, Harry. Just tell me."

"Toni's brother, Ross...well there's a possibility that he's your dad." Harry smiled. "What do you think to that, Frannie?"

She was dazed, totally blindsided. "My dad?" Fran ran a hand through her hair. She was confused, conflicted. She shook her head and stood up abruptly. She frantically searched around the bar. She didn't know what she was looking for and the only thing that called to her was the exit. She ran for it as fast as her legs would carry her.

"Fran! Fran!"

Harry's cries faded into the distance as she hit the cold air and took off running down the wet promenade. She needed to get away from the bar as quickly as possible, to distance herself from Harry's words. But they couldn't be erased despite the distance she put between them.

Chapter 18

Jessie put her feet up on the sofa, laid her head back, and relaxed. She loved to unwind this way. It had become a Sunday ritual of sorts. Comfy sweats and nothing but time on her hands. The patter of rain tapped out a rhythmic cadence on the window. A shiver of appreciation moved through her as she snuggled deeper into the comfortable sofa, grateful to be cocooned inside her warm home.

Business was picking up as the weather changed from winter to spring, and the football season was moving into its final quarter. She loved this time of year and couldn't wait to start another week. She sighed contentedly, reaching for the telly remote control to catch up on the weekend's football highlights.

Knock! Knock! Knock!

She frowned and put the remote back on the coffee table. She padded barefoot to the front door and peered through the spy hole. She was surprised to find Fran on the other side.

She took a step back and allowed herself a moment to compose her thoughts…and her racing heart. When she opened the door, Fran stood, drenched, wearing only a T-shirt and jeans. Her eyes wide and wild as she shivered. She panted, her chest moving up and down rhythmically as she drew oxygen into her lungs.

"Fran?" Jessie instinctively reached out a hand to caress the other woman. Fran flinched back from her touch and Jessie tried to ignore the stab of hurt that struck her. She was concerned. Her imagination conjured all kinds of terrible circumstances that could have brought Fran to her doorstep, soaking wet and obviously troubled. Perhaps something had happened to her grandfather?

"You'd better come inside." She opened the door wider. "Is everything all right?" She closed the door behind her and reached for Fran's hand. She needed to connect with her. She needed the reassurance of physical contact even if Fran didn't. But Fran didn't shrink away from her. Instead, she gripped her hand tightly in return. Her eyes blazed with intensity, her lips parted, and her breath grew more ragged than before.

Jessie stood, frozen to the spot, as Fran closed the distance between them and thrust a cold hand into the hair at the back of her neck. She shivered at the touch of Fran's fingers on her heated flesh, before cold lips closed over hers in a bruising kiss.

Jessie gasped and pushed Fran away. "What are you doing?" Adrenaline and arousal coursed through her veins, thick and fast, a potent cocktail of passion, and it lit a fire in the pit of her stomach. Jessie's breath rasped in her throat as her heart hammered inside her chest.

Fran moved towards her, apparently undeterred by the initial rebuff. Her eyes unfocused. "Please," she whispered, "I need this." Her voice was hoarse, as she held Jessie tightly. "I need you, Jessie."

Jessie placed her arms around Fran as she trembled. Her wet T-shirt clung to her body and Jessie rubbed at her back in a futile attempt to heat the chilled flesh.

Fran drew a shuddering breath. "Please don't make me beg, Jessie. I need you."

The harshly whispered words eroded Jessie's defences. She turned her face and sighed when Fran's lips claimed her. A hot, wet tongue entered her mouth, and Jessie melted into the kiss, giving and taking without question.

The timing was completely unexpected, but she knew what was happening had been inevitable. Jessie had no idea *how* it would happen, but she'd known they would end up at this point somewhere down the line. They'd been headed here from the start.

This was a strange, complicated attraction they'd both been trying to avoid, both trying to fight for their own reasons. Something had caused Fran to succumb. Something had broken her will. She had no idea what had happened and at that moment she didn't care. Jessie was caught up in the emotion and lust that seeped from Fran's very pores. And she was happy to be on the receiving end of the raw passion.

Fran placed her hands either side of Jessie's head and pinned her to the wall. She ground into her and deepened the kiss, her lips now warm as they devoured Jessie's.

Jessie gripped Fran's waist and pulled her closer. She wanted as much of her body pressed against her as possible. She wanted to feel it all. Every delicious inch as her hips pushed toward Fran's in a frantic quest for sweet relief. Jessie wanted…needed her to bring the release her body demanded.

Fran drew back and swiftly pulled the wet T-shirt over her head. Jessie opened her mouth to utter something, but a finger pressed lightly against her lips, silencing her. She swallowed hard at the look of intense arousal in Fran's eyes as the other woman stood before her, topless, and now completely in control of the encounter.

Jessie reached for the button on Fran's jeans, but was left clutching at air when Fran dropped to her knees. She pushed up Jessie's top, and caressed her naked breasts with icy cold hands. Jessie let her head fall back against the wall. She took a deep breath and shuddered as Fran placed light kisses on her stomach. Pain lanced Jessie's bottom lip as she bit into it and released a short grunt before sliding her tongue over the damaged skin. The faint metallic taste indicated she'd broken the tissue enough to draw blood.

Fran slid the jogging bottoms and knickers down Jessie's legs in one efficient motion. The cool air hit her newly exposed flesh as she lifted her bare foot to assist Fran with the removal of her clothes. Fran gripped her hips and placed a kiss on the small triangle of fair hair between Jessie's legs.

Jessie pushed her hand into Fran's wet hair and pulled her closer. She wanted more. Her clitoris pulsed with arousal.

She gasped as soft lips enveloped her, followed by the swipe of a hot tongue. Jessie twitched. She knew she wouldn't last long as her hips surged toward Fran's mouth seeking more, urging Fran on.

Fran sucked her clitoris until she came hard and cried out into the empty hall. Her teeth clenched, and her muscles strained as the intense orgasm ripped through her rigid body. But Fran didn't stop. She continued to tongue her clit until Jessie pushed the dark head away and slid down the wall, her legs no longer strong enough to hold her upright.

As Jessie slumped against the wall, Fran gathered her in her arms and held her close. She kissed her neck and pulled the sweatshirt over Jessie's head. Jessie didn't even have time to catch her breath before Fran sucked her nipple into her hot mouth and urged Jessie onto her knees. Fran's long fingers filled her instantly.

Jessie cried out and her head swam with a wave of dizzy pleasure while Fran thrust deep and strong. Her strokes quickly bringing her to orgasm for the second time in minutes. She panted into Fran's wet hair as Fran held her in strong arms, while she caught her breath. Jessie was barely able to think while Fran trailed her calloused fingers over her exposed flesh and kissed Jessie's bare shoulders.

When her breathing returned to normal and the strength back in her legs, Jessie stirred in Fran's arms. She was far from ready for this encounter to be over. She stood slowly and reached for Fran's hand, pulling her wordlessly to her feet, and then led her to the bedroom.

Fran stood before her, topless and intense. Her damp jeans clung to her legs, but were at least now warmed by her body heat. Jessie reached for the top button and this time Fran allowed her to remove them. The wet denim was hard and rough, and offered resistance.

"Can you sit on the edge of the bed?" Jessie asked and as Fran complied she peeled the fabric from the long legs.

Finally, they were both naked, and Jessie studied Fran as she leaned back on her elbows in the waning light. Her legs slightly parted, and there was a challenge in her blue eyes. Jessie knew Fran was silently asking the question, did she like what she saw?

Fran's pierced and tattooed body had initially disturbed her. She couldn't deny it. It had caused her to judge Fran. But over the weeks and months, Jessie had come to appreciate the body art. The pierced nipples still made her shudder, but she was now pulled towards them as the round steel jiggled with Fran's every movement. In this setting, Jessie found the piercings strangely erotic. She swallowed back the saliva gathering in her mouth and slowly approached the bed. The scent of arousal filled the air. Fran was ripe and ready.

She leaned over her, almost touched her. Almost. She placed her hands on the mattress either side of Fran's shoulders to support her weight and hovered for a moment. She stared straight at Fran, and the challenge in Fran's eyes dimmed, her expression becoming more open, a hint of vulnerability creeping in. Jessie wished she could read her thoughts. She wanted to know what had driven Fran to her door. She could see the answers in her eyes. If only she knew how to decipher them. Later, she promised herself.

Jessie licked her lips, then dipped her head to capture Fran's mouth in a slow languid kiss. She took her time. She needed to taste her thoroughly, savour the moment. She let her tongue explore, memorizing the flavour of her before lowering her breasts to Fran's more modest chest. The contact evoked a murmur of appreciation that caused a jolt between her legs.

Jessie tentatively reached for Fran's breast. She palmed the soft, pliant skin, rubbed a nipple between two fingers, and flicked the steel ring. She looped it through her finger and tugged gently. The bold action elicited a gasp from Fran.

"That gives you pleasure?" Jessie asked.

"Yes," was Fran's breathy reply.

"It doesn't hurt?"

"God, no."

Spurred on by the noises of pleasure Fran made, Jessie lowered her head and traced Fran's areola with her tongue before sucking the jewellery and nipple into her mouth. The warm steel had a metallic tang, there was a clink of metal on enamel as the little silver ball on the ring made contact with Jessie's teeth. Jessie tugged at the steel, pulling the ring between her lips, causing Fran to hiss as she stretched the skin. She was pleasantly surprised to find herself enjoying the added stimulus the jewellery brought to the process, particularly as it was clear how much Fran relished the sensation. She repeated the action.

But the call, the need, to bring Fran to orgasm was too much for her to ignore. She lowered her head, kissed her way down Fran's torso, and drew her tongue along a lightly muscled abdomen. She traced the lines of muscle until she encountered the navel ring. Again she tongued and tugged the metal as she dropped to her knees on the carpeted floor. She placed her hands on Fran's long thighs and pushed her legs further apart. She used the flat of her hands to glide over the smooth skin as Fran's hand went into her hair in an attempt to hasten her journey. Fran lifted her hips toward her and showed Jessie exactly what she wanted and where she wanted her mouth.

Jessie lifted Fran's leg over one shoulder and lowered her head. She traced her tongue along the inside of Fran's thigh, intent on reaching her destination slowly. She slipped her hands under Fran's buttocks, squeezed firmly, and placed her open mouth on Fran's centre. She revelled in the scent and texture of the soft skin beneath her tongue as she licked at her folds. She kept her tongue soft, desperate to enjoy the hot wetness she encountered for as long as possible. When she could no longer resist, Jessie pushed her tongue inside as deeply as she could. Fran moaned and gently thrust her hips, humming with pleasure as she sought relief.

"Suck me," Fran demanded breathlessly, as her free hand gripped the sheet.

Jessie pressed her lips around Fran's clit and sucked while she moved her tongue over the hard nub. Fran's thighs trembled, and Jessie kept up her attentions until Fran's legs stiffened, quivered, and she pulled Jessie's hair in a tight grip. Her voice was hoarse as she groaned through her orgasm until the waves of pleasure subsided.

<hr />

Jessie woke with her arm casually flung across Fran's stomach. It was comforting, despite the unfamiliarity of the situation. She inhaled deeply that carnal, heady scent that clung to their bodies. God, she was tender in areas that had lain dormant for too long.

The brief liaison with a Spanish girl during the Edinburgh festival had been unprofessional of her. The way the tanned, dark-haired beauty had flirted shamelessly when Jessie had organised the month-long let had been too hard to resist. Especially knowing there were no strings attached. A tall, sexy woman looking for a romantic tryst while on holiday had been fun, but nothing like the sex she had just shared with Fran.

Their desire had gone on and on and on. They hadn't been able to get enough of each other; the passion, the deep craving to satisfy and be satisfied was something neither of them had wanted to stop.

It was exhaustion that had finally called a halt to their activities, until she had woken with Fran caressing her breasts, and it had started all over again. Fatigue and hunger claimed them a second time, and it was dark before Jessie opened her eyes again.

Jessie was curious as to what had brought Fran to her door. She still hadn't spoken beyond the occasional "yes", a moan, a groan, a whimper, and the best sound of all...when she came. The sharp groan accompanied by a shudder, before she collapsed onto the mattress or Jessie, depending on their positions at the time. And there had been many of them. They'd both been insatiable.

Jessie trailed her fingers lazily over Fran's stomach, idly drawing random patterns over warm skin. She traced the outline of a tattoo low on Fran's abdomen, the ink patterns barely discernible in the darkness, but Jessie knew each design from memory. A thorny rose, a heart surrounded by barbed wire, with intricate Celtic knots forming a background lattice. Rose stems wound through it, running from Fran's left shoulder, across her ribcage and tapering off towards her navel.

She'd hated them at first. Now the ink drawings fascinated her. She wanted to know more about them. Why had Fran chosen each one? Jessie's hand was captured in a firm grip, causing her to gasp. Her breath caught as she was pulled into Fran's intense gaze. Jessie didn't want the night to end.

The inexplicable attraction between them was real. Despite Fran being everything that normally turned her off in a woman—surly, rude, uncommunicative, detached, moody. The list was huge, yet she still wanted her.

"We need to talk." Jessie couldn't stop the words tumbling out of her mouth. Words that shattered the cocoon they'd wrapped around themselves for the past few hours.

Fran instantly closed off, turning her head away. She pushed the duvet off her long legs and attempted to exit the bed. Jessie's grip on her wrist stopped her. She turned towards her.

What Jessie saw in Fran's eyes made her wish she hadn't spoken, that they could be making love again. Now Fran wanted to flee. Conversation wasn't her strong suit, Jessie already knew that. She suspected talking about emotions would be even harder for her taciturn lover. Fran dipped her head, staring at Jessie's hand. She could almost feel her skin burning beneath that look, but she wouldn't allow Fran to intimidate her, to prevent the conversation they needed to have.

"Look at me." Jessie kept her tone gentle. She didn't want to scare Fran off. When Fran lifted her face, she asked. "Why now?"

Fran was quiet and brooding under normal circumstances, but Jessie knew something was troubling her. *She wouldn't be here otherwise. Not now.* It was a quarter past three in the morning. They'd napped throughout the evening. Recuperating from the energy-sapping sex, before repeating it again and again. Why would Fran want to flee now after everything they'd shared for the last few hours? Granted, she wasn't keen on talking, but surely the simple request to share a few words shouldn't send her running into the night.

Jessie waited patiently as Fran sat on the edge of the bed, unmoving. At least she wasn't running out of the door. She eased her grip on Fran's wrist and waited for her to talk.

Seconds dragged into minutes until finally Fran turned to face her. Even in the dim light, Jessie registered the lines of tension around her eyes.

Fran sighed softly and scooted back up the bed to lean against the headboard.

"I haven't had the best of days." Fran paused, opened her mouth, then closed it with a shake of the head. "Two people came into the bar today. I haven't seen either of them in years." A small smile ghosted over her lips, as she fiddled with the bed sheets. "They were around for most of my childhood, all the years I spent in Portobello. One of them, Shona, was my first crush. I fell in love with her when I was ten." Fran smiled as her tone softened. "I had no idea what it meant. I used to follow her along the promenade whenever she was walking by the Beachcomber." Her expression became pensive. "Anyway, Shona and her wife, Toni, turned up today. At first I thought Toni wanted to buy the Beachcomber from Harry. I still don't trust her motives." Fran shook her head.

Blood rushed to Jessie's head and roared in her ears. She was certain her face must have drained of colour. Fortunately, Fran wasn't paying attention as she continued to speak.

"She was chatting to Harry while Shona and I caught up a little, but I had one eye on her. The woman is all business. Harry spoke to me after they'd gone. It turns out that Toni Martin believes her brother could be my dad." Fran frowned, turmoil swirled in her eyes as she stared at Jessie.

Oh, God. Jessie's stomach churned and she pressed her hand over her mouth. She knew she was the cause. But Toni had been so sure that Ross wasn't Fran's father. She shook her head.

Fran gripped the sheet so tight her knuckles turned white. "Why?" Fran demanded, "Why would she turn up now after all these years and make that claim?" She shook her head. "She wants the bloody pub. It's the only thing that makes any sense. She's a fucking vulture." Fran drew her knees up towards her bare chest. "And what the hell would I do with a dad now? Where the hell has he been for all these years?"

Fran stared at the ceiling. "Some daughter I've turned out to be. The mess I've made of my life. I'm sure I'd be a great disappointment to him." She shook her head. "Anyway, it's not going to happen. No way am I starting a relationship now with some guy who might be my dad. Fuck that."

Jessie thought she was going to be sick. Her stomach roiled and her mouth filled with saliva. Fran had come to her for solace, comfort, and it turned out instead that she was the catalyst for her current anguish. She couldn't let her continue without being honest. She didn't want there to be lies between them. She swallowed back the bile that rose and burned the back of her throat, then gripped Fran's forearm to gain her full attention.

"It's all my fault." Jessie blinked back tears. "I'm sorry," she whispered.

"What?" Fran's voice was low, laced with confusion, the frown deepening.

Sweat broke out on Jessie's body. She wiped her clammy hands on the sheet. "I made the connection."

"What connection?" Fran sat up.

"The day I had a look around the rooms for let, and you found me in the turreted room." At Fran's nod, she continued, "Well, I saw a photograph, the punks on the promenade," Jessie said. "I'm sorry, Fran, I thought one of the boys reminded me of someone. His name was Ross. It was written on the back and he had his arm around DeeDee."

Fran's chest was moving up and down rapidly.

Jessie knew this situation was about to get a lot worse, but she had to tell the truth. "I thought nothing more of it then." She shook her head. Her throat ached with each word she pushed out. "Well, not until I saw a picture in the *Reporter*. I thought it was you at first, the woman looked so much like you. But Meadow told me it was Toni Martin. I, well, it was too much of a coincidence. I asked Meadow if Toni had a brother, and she told me his name was Ross." Jessie covered her face with her hands. The tension and anger radiated off Fran in waves. She rubbed her face and continued. "While I was overseeing the work being done on the rooms, I went back into the turreted room and snapped a picture of the photograph on my phone. Then I contacted Toni Martin and asked her."

Fran was getting of the bed.

"Fran, wait!"

Jessie put a hand on Fran's arm, but Fran shook it off. "Where are my clothes?" Fran demanded, her voice forceful, angry.

"Fran, please let me explain," Jessie pleaded.

Fran strode naked out of the room.

Jessie followed behind her.

Fran grabbed the jeans and T-shirt from the radiator in the hall near the front door. She pulled them on with jerky, fast movements, and continued to ignore Jessie's pleas for her to listen.

"I'll drive you!" Jessie was desperate for Fran to hear her out. The car journey would buy her a few more minutes.

"No thanks, I'd rather walk." Fran's voice was cold and hard.

Jessie stood in front of her, blocking her exit.

"Get out of my way, Jessie."

She tried one last time to get through to her. "Fran, please stay. We need to talk."

"Move, or I will move you."

She knew Fran was serious. The hard, low tone of her voice left no room for doubt. Jessie swallowed the lump in her throat and opened the door. She grabbed a warm jacket and thrust it into the angry woman's hands. "Please take it, it's cold outside."

Fran stared at her, a mixture of anger, hurt, disbelief, and something else on her face, something Jessie couldn't identify. Her jaw worked furiously and Jessie waited for the words that would shred her. They never came. Instead, Fran grabbed the jacket and swept out of the door. She didn't glance back as the gate slammed shut behind her.

Jessie quietly closed the door and sank to the floor. Her body shook as tears of loss and regret rolled down her cheeks. The hallway blurred out of all recognition. It reflected the current state of her life.

━━━━◈◇◈━━━━

Fran stood outside the Beachcomber. The place was in darkness and she had no keys. She guessed it was a little after four in the morning. The promenade was empty as the wind whipped the T-shirt taut against her body. She shivered, but not just from the cold. Temptation lay inside, taunting her like an evil mistress. It would be so easy to get wrecked. She

143

had the perfect excuse. It's what everyone expected of her. It's what she expected of her.

She stared down at her hand. The red bubble jacket Jessie had thrust at her still clutched in her tight grip. The move had surprised her.

She pulled it on and zipped it up, instantly grateful for the warmth it provided. Though it was spring, the temperature had dropped significantly overnight. An early-morning frost glittered under the street light. She was no stranger to wandering the streets late, but sanctuary lay less than thirty metres away and called to her just as potently as Jessie's body had.

Fran stood fighting against the pull of an alcohol-fuelled escape. She wanted oblivion. She craved it. She could taste the smoky banana of Jack Daniels, and it was so close. She could practically feel the glass in her hand. The warmth of it as she forgot her troubles, the tightness in her body disappearing with each gulp of the whiskey. It was so tempting.

"Fuck," she hissed, part anger and part plea. She let out a long shaky breath, as angry tears filled her eyes, and the lights swirled in her cloudy vision. She brought a clenched fist to her mouth and sunk her teeth into the flesh until she tasted blood.

She knew she was in dangerous territory. She was balancing precariously on the precipice. Teetering perilously close to plunging over the edge into her own personal abyss. She wanted it so bad. So bad.

She couldn't let Harry down. His disappointment would crush her. She was terrified that if she slipped again, she wouldn't be able to stop herself. She'd let everyone down. Harry, her godmother, Nikki—they'd given her a chance. *Don't fucking ruin it. Don't. Not this time.* The scream inside her head drowned out her own heartbeat as it was rent from her soul.

She turned and stumbled towards the beach on heavy legs. The waves were invisible in the darkness, but she heard every one as they crashed against the shore. She fell to her knees. The effort it had taken to get this far had been exhausting. She pleaded with anyone who would listen. *Help me…just a few more hours. Please…help me.* She'd only just started to like who she was. Who she could be. The woman she was becoming.

Thoughts of previous nights of excess filled her head. Waking up in strange places with no memory. Clothing soiled. The stench. The strangers. The filth. It was shameful. Fucking disgusting. She was disgusting.

She retched into the sand until her stomach was empty. The cloying scent of Jessie wafted up from the jacket and caused a second wave of nausea. This time bile spilled from her guts and down her nose, burning her nasal passage. Breathless, she fell forward against the wooden groynes, gulping in the cleansing air. She spat out the acidic bile and wiped her mouth with the back of her hand.

She dropped heavily onto the cold, damp sand, and stared into the darkness. She was shocked at how quickly her life had unravelled. Why had Jessie chosen to meddle in her affairs? Why? It was none of her business.

When she'd turned up at Jessie's, she'd needed a friend, some comfort, someone to help her forget for a few hours. Why did she have to go and fuck it all up?

The cold was seeping into her bones as she sat on the sand, but she didn't care. Fran grabbed a handful of the smooth substance and lifted it up. She let the grains fall through her fingers, cascading like scattered thoughts, lost in the vastness of the beach. She couldn't pick out a grain of truth among them. She didn't even know where to start making sense of the revelations of the past twelve hours.

The distant blare of a car horn and the shrill of a siren interrupted the rhythm of the waves. Fran closed her eyes, content to let the cold have her. The crackle of a radio was out of place, but she ignored it, until a torch was shone in her face. She raised her hand to shield her eyes from the obtrusion.

"Hello. You can't sleep on the beach," a male voice stated.

"I'm not sleeping," Fran muttered, wishing whoever it was would go away.

"Stand up please." It wasn't a question. The authoritarian tone was unmistakable.

Fran sighed and eased herself up from the sand, her legs still wobbly.

"What's your name?"

"Fran Docherty." She squinted at the stranger, catching the reflection of the chequered black-and-white band around his hat.

"Do you have somewhere to go, Fran?"

As her eyes adjusted to the dark, she became aware of the presence of a second police officer. She was taller than both of them. Nodding in the direction of the promenade she answered. "Yeah. The Beachcomber."

"Did you get into a fight?" the policeman with the torch asked.

Fran was confused. "What?"

The policeman pointed. "Your head."

Fran reached up to her forehead, it was sticky. "No, I bumped it."

The officers shared a look, one that Fran had witnessed many times before. They were suspicious.

"We'll walk you back home."

Now that it had been mentioned, her head started to throb, and she had no fight left in her. "I'm locked out. I don't have any keys."

"Do you live at the Beachcomber?"

"Yes." *I fucking just said so.*

"Start walking."

Fran did as instructed, and they were outside the front door in little over a minute. "Thanks, I'll be fine."

"Not so fast. Where do you work?"

Fran was losing patience. Now that they were off the beach, she could identify both policemen more clearly. The taller, dark-haired one had yet to speak. He simply stared at her, his face remote. The guy questioning her was only about five-foot-nine and a pest. "Christ, I'm having a bad day. I left my keys and I'm locked out."

"If you don't start talking it's going to get a lot worse," he cautioned.

Frustrated, she closed her eyes and took a deep breath. "I work here and I haven't done anything wrong."

"Trouble has an uncanny knack of finding you, Ms Docherty," the second policeman finally spoke. He must have checked her up on the police database.

"I've done nothing wrong," she ground out through her clenched teeth.

"You're alone, on the beach in the middle of the night, with a gash on your forehead, and a record most seasoned criminals would baulk at," he continued, taking charge.

Fran's breathing became shallow. Despite her best efforts, her past was still haunting her. She spoke slowly, exhaustion lacing her words. "I've had a very bad day. I chose to sit on the beach, freezing my tits off because I'm an alcoholic, and that was the only way I could avoid drinking."

"What happened to your head?"

"I hit it off the groynes while I was throwing up. That's not a crime, is it?"

"And your hand?"

Her right hand hurt, the congealed blood now visible. "I bit it. Call it self harm, if you want. I needed to stop myself giving in to alcohol so I bit my hand." She awaited their response, with her jaw clenched. She was guilty of no crime, and wouldn't allow them to intimidate her.

The silence between the three of them was broken as the front door opened and Gary stood in boxers and a T-shirt. "Fran, where have you been?" He stared at the policemen. "Has something happened?" Then back to Fran. "Have you been assaulted?" Anxiety was clear in his voice.

"Does she work here?" This questioned was asked by the shorter of the two policemen.

"Yes," Gary stated, confusion lacing his answer.

"Can I go now?" Fran asked, nearing the end of her patience with the charade.

"Might I suggest you sleep in your bed instead of on the beach in future," the taller officer added.

"It's a free fucking country."

Gary immediately stepped in. "Officer, everyone is entitled to a bad day." His tone was conciliatory. "Fran's had some difficult news. We all deal with it in our own way." Gary held his hands up in a pacifying gesture, as Fran stood impatiently with her mouth closed.

The shorter policeman turned to Fran, and indicated her head. "You'll need to get that taken care of."

"We have a first-aid kit inside," Gary hastily replied.

He nodded. "Make sure she gets cleaned up and a hot drink inside her."

"I will, thank you, officer."

He turned back to Fran. "Stay out of trouble." A hint of warning in his voice.

"Just trying to get through the fucking night," she whispered hoarsely, as Gary ushered her inside.

CHAPTER 19

FRAN STUMBLED INTO THE ALLEY on rubbery legs. It was dark, the passageway illuminated only by a sliver of streetlight from the main thoroughfare. She leaned against a brick wall, fighting the wave of nausea that threatened to spill onto the cobblestones beneath her feet. Breathing deeply only made it worse as the smell of vomit and urine rose from the uneven cobbles, filling in the gaps like congealed custard.

Sweat beaded on Fran's brow. She was too hot. What the hell had she taken? Her mouth was dry, and she wasn't sure what day it was. Where the fuck was she? London? Yeah, it was London. She recognised the skyline that towered above her, but something wasn't right.

Her vision swam as she staggered back against the wall, hitting her head on the brick. Pain lanced through her skull. Why was she so fucking hot? She panted, gasping for air, but she needed to keep moving. She blinked to clear her vision and steadied herself with a hand on the rough, red brick. She swiped the other hand across her damp forehead and moved forward, her legs heavy and her gait wide in an attempt to stay upright.

The air whooshed from her lungs as sharp pain radiated from her temple. She was face down on the cobbled street with a weight pressing down upon her. Rotten, ragged breath, mingled with her own as a strong hand fisted in her hair. Fran could taste blood in her mouth from a punch to the side of her face. Another glancing blow had slammed her head on the urine-soaked pavement.

She couldn't breathe, couldn't scream. She struggled, her limbs unco-operative and uncoordinated. The heavy weight slowly squeezing the air from her lungs. She spat blood on the road, spluttering, trying to scream or cry out.

She sat bolt upright, gasping as her heart pounded in her chest. It took a few moments to get her bearings.

The room was large and cool, yet she was soaked with sweat. It ran down between her bare breasts. She fell back on the pillows, relieved to be in bed at the Beachcomber. She breathed slowly, trying to calm her racing heart. She swiped a trembling hand across her eyes. A layer of perspiration coated her upper body, running down her legs, as the damp sheets started to cool beneath her. She leaned out of bed to grab the T-shirt she had discarded earlier and used it to wipe her body. She threw the duvet back to allow the sheet to dry, and exited the bed.

She opened a drawer and picked a clean T-shirt, and removed a pair of jogging bottoms from the drawer below. She grabbed her cigarettes from the bedside table, walked to the glass doors on unsteady legs, and pushed them open. She went out onto the balcony and welcomed the cold as it rushed to greet her. Goosebumps pebbled all over her exposed skin. She shivered.

Fran opened the packet of cigarettes. Her fingers trembled as she removed one and lit it. She took a long draw and inhaled deeply, the smoke helping her relax.

A bloody nightmare. Not even a new one. Fran stood barefoot on the balcony. The wind coming off the sea whipped her hair up, and she shuddered as she remembered the details. She had no idea what time it was. There was no sign on life on the beach, and traffic was quiet.

The nightmare always left her unsettled. She didn't know if the events had actually occurred or were a figment of her imagination. It bothered her more that she wasn't sure which of those scenarios troubled her most—real and forgotten, or imagined. If it had happened, what had been the outcome? Had she been mugged, beaten, or worse? Could she really have forgotten something like that? Or had someone come to her rescue and scared off her attacker?

She had no idea. None.

She finished her cigarette, stubbed it out on the wall, and went back inside, closing the balcony doors behind her. She was too wired and unsettled to sleep, so she left her room and hovered at the top of the stairs. It would be so easy to go down. She gripped the bannister tightly and swallowed back the temptation. But it was strong.

"Fran?"

She exhaled at the mention of her name. The quiet word was a lifeline tossed her way. A hand laid gently on her shoulder, the weight of it comforting, the squeeze reassuring. She turned and Gary stood behind her in the dim light, wearing only a pair of boxer shorts. His normally clean shaven face sported a scruffy stubble, but his eyes were warm, compassionate without being piteous. It was almost uncanny the way they appeared to read each other's moods. Perhaps she'd cried out in her sleep as the nightmare had taken hold, alerting Gary to her predicament. She'd never ask and he'd never push, but she knew he'd listen if she wanted to talk.

She knew that her need was laid bare for anyone to read by the honest concern apparent on his face. She felt far too raw to hide any of it. The furious battle raging within her oozed from her pores. She could smell it on herself.

"I'll put the kettle on."

"Sure," Fran managed to croak the word out through a throat tight with want, and a hunger to slake both her thirst and still her trembling limbs. She stumbled towards the kitchen. The craving and nightmare had sapped the strength from her legs. The visions always left her shaken and disturbed.

She sat at the kitchen table, while Gary filled the kettle. She hadn't seen him this naked before. A slight paunch normally hidden by a T-shirt and jumper was visible. He had a lot more hair on his chest than he did on his head. She topped him by a good four inches, but at that moment she felt small and vulnerable in his presence.

He placed a cup of tea in front of her and took a seat opposite before he took a drink from his cup. He sat in silence and waited, ready to listen if she wanted to talk. Fran was thankful for that. Most of the time it was all she needed, most of the time it was enough. So long as they sat here, no matter what hour of the day or night, opposite each other, they would be safe. Another day would pass, adding to the ever increasing tally. Each one difficult in its own way, but somehow she got there. One day at a time.

Across from her, Gary yawned and rubbed at his day's growth. His nipples stood out, skin goose-pimpling from the cold. But Fran knew he wouldn't move. He owed her grandfather as much as she did. This was what they shared—a pact, a bond to both do what was best for the bar and each other. Anything less would disappoint Harry. And so far it had worked, but this time she wasn't sure it was enough.

"What time it is?"

Gary looked at the metal watch on his wrist, his forearms resting on the table as he sat forward in the chair. "Coming up for six."

Fran stared at her hands, wondering if Gary noticed the slight tremor.

"I'll get the bar ready and open up in a wee while," he said quietly.

"Thanks, Gary." She was grateful for the offer. She doubted she could face the world today.

He nodded. "Any time."

When she returned to her room, she craved something else. She grabbed her cigarettes and lighter, and retreated back to the small balcony overlooking the sandy beach below. It was still dark. She lit her cigarette. The first drag burned the back of her throat before leaving a soothing sensation that radiated from her lungs throughout her body as she exhaled. Just like it always did.

The promenade below was lit with Victorian-style street lamps, illuminating the pink-tinged tarmac along with the early-morning joggers and cyclists. Fran saw a familiar figure jogging towards her. She knew every curve on that athletic body. The natural blonde hair, lightly curled, and held back by a thin elastic headband that kept it from her eyes.

Fran had watched Jessie make this journey almost every morning since she'd come to the Beachcomber. Initially she'd been anonymous, but since Jessie found out where she worked, she started to glance up.

Neither of them acknowledged each other this morning, but Fran was certain those keen eyes were aware of her lurking in the shadows. She stubbed the cigarette out on the wall and pushed aside thoughts of her torrid evening and the beautiful Jessie Grainger.

She'd got too close. There was no denying that. Turning up at Jessie's door had been a mistake. She'd known that as soon as she'd walked inside. Before that, if she was being honest with herself. Finding out that Jessie was behind the visit from Toni Martin had been the perfect excuse for her. It made it easy for her to leave without having to explain why it was a mistake.

She'd needed a distraction, and sex always provided that for a few hours. She didn't want to mull over the visit from Toni and Shona, and Jessie hadn't exactly offered her much resistance. Far from it. *She'd wanted it as much as I did.*

But that didn't give her the right to stick her nose in other people's business. She had no right meddling in her life, disrupting her routine, going behind her back. No fucking right at all. Suddenly exhausted, Fran discarded her clothes and crawled back into bed.

＊────◆◇◆────＊

Fran woke from a fitful sleep and rolled onto her back. She stared at the ceiling as memories of the previous day flooded her mind and overloaded her senses. She caught sight of her damaged hand as it gripped the duvet cover, the teeth imprint on the broken skin. She screwed her eyes shut tight and curled into a foetal position.

She'd allowed herself to believe she'd made progress. That she'd taken steps in the right direction. But one incident had dragged her right back to the edge. She was struggling to stop herself from plummeting back into that dark hole. She wavered, trapped inside her bedroom, in a self-imposed prison. She couldn't function outside of these four walls. And inside? Inside, she was barely holding it together.

Fran threw off the covers and walked to the bathroom. She was so tired, emotionally and physically drained.

She glanced in the mirror above the white enamel sink. She looked like shit. Her eyes bloodshot and troubled, dark circles underneath. Gary had cleaned the deep scrapes on her forehead. They'd heal. She wasn't so sure about her heart.

She ran the tap and splashed her face with cold water. She held her head in her hands as her knees gave way, and she crumpled to the bathroom floor. She leant back against the tub and gathered her bare knees to her naked chest.

They'd all let her down. Every one of them. Harry, Toni, and Jessie. But it was Jessie's betrayal that hurt most of all. She'd gone to her because she'd needed someone. No, she'd gone to Jessie because she'd needed *Jessie*. But Jessie wasn't just part of the problem. Jessie had created the whole fucking problem. She didn't cope well with change and she would be embarrassed to meet her dad now. A former addict with a criminal record, she couldn't stomach the thought of more disappointment. His disappointment.

Fran thrust upwards with a burst of energy fuelled by anger. She stormed back into the bedroom, pulled on jeans and a T-shirt, and shoved her bare feet into boots before she grabbed her phone. She wasn't hanging around any longer. She needed to get out of this place. She needed to get away from them. She stopped at the bedroom door, her fists balled.

"Don't do it, don't fucking do it," she whispered harshly. Tears stung her eyes as she bumped her head against the wood. She slid down the wall as the tears fell. Frustration, anger, sorrow...disappointment. They all rolled down her cheeks unchecked.

It seemed like a lifetime had passed before she unclenched her fist and made a call.

"Hello, Fran."

"I need you," she whispered. "I can't do this on my own."

"What's happened?"

Fran swallowed, "I need your help, Nikki. I'm all over the fucking place." Her gaze darted around the room before landing on the red padded jacket. She squeezed her eyes shut tight. "It's all falling apart, they've all fucked it up for me."

"What's happened, Fran?"

Nikki's calm voice helped her focus, but she was distraught. "They are saying Ross Martin is my dad."

"Who is?"

"Harry and Toni and fucking Jessie. My head's all fucked up, Nikki, I'm not in a good place."

"But you have called me...and you're still clean and sober..."

"Barely," she whispered.

"Fran, listen to me. I need you to hold on for the next few hours. I'll be on the first flight to Edinburgh. You hang in there, Fran, I'm on my way. I promise. I love you, darlin'."

"Hurry."

Fran ended the call and laid her head against the door. She hadn't wanted to call Nikki, but she was struggling. Nikki knew her better than anyone. Nikki was her only chance.

Chapter 20

Jessie sat in her car in the football club car park. Alone. She'd waited for Fran in the usual spot, but she hadn't been surprised when she didn't turn up. It had been the same all week. Jessie waited, but Fran had made her own way to training. Still, Jessie persevered. Just in case. She hoped Fran would change her mind.

It was rare for Jessie to be down before a game. Normally she could put anything that was troubling her to the back of her mind. Not today. She could hardly recall a time when she felt as flat as she was right now. Not even when she'd had to endure her three-match suspension. Then she'd been angry and frustrated, not low.

She let her head fall back against the headrest, and closed her eyes. She couldn't blame Fran for being angry with her. She just wished that Fran could understand the interfering for what it was. A genuine attempt to help. Jessie massaged her temples trying to dispel some of the tension gathered there.

A knock on the driver window brought her back to her surroundings. Sophie stood grinning at her. She tried to smile in return, but knew it didn't reach her eyes as she climbed out of her car.

"Everything okay, Jessie?" Sophie's brow furrowed as she scrutinised her intently.

"Yeah, fine. Just a little bit under the weather." She tried to make light of her predicament. She certainly didn't want to discuss her troubles with anyone.

"What's up with you and Fran?"

Jessie shook her head and went to her boot. "Nothing. I made a stupid mistake and she isn't talking to me." She slung her kitbag over her shoulder and closed the boot. Sophie stared at her, concern on her face.

"That's not like you, Jessie. Did Fran do something?"

"Honestly, Soph, it's my fault, and I can't really talk about it. I stuck my nose in where it wasn't wanted and Fran's pissed off. And she has every right to be. She hasn't done anything wrong. I promise. It's all on me."

Sophie stood with her hands in the pockets of her tracksuit bottoms. "You know you can chat to me about anything?"

"I know, but I've messed up. The last thing I want to do is make the situation worse by blurting out her business to anyone else. Do you understand?"

Sophie bit her lip. "Okay, Jessie, but you know where I am if you need to talk, about, *anything*."

Jessie's eyes narrowed as suspicion washed over her. "Who have you been speaking to?" The way Sophie had said "anything", that slight hesitation in her voice, the change of tone, caused Jessie to suspect she may know about her and Fran sleeping together.

"No one, Jessie, honest. I thought maybe you were having a hard time over the divorce. I've been waiting for you to bring it up." Sophie shrugged. "That's what I thought was wrong with you back in January, but you seemed to pick up, until this week."

Sophie appeared earnest and Jessie instantly regretted her accusing tone. "I struggled at the start of the year. It was a shock. I mean, it never crossed my mind that my mum and dad would ever divorce, but they are. Everything's been set in motion. They're just waiting for the formalities and then the signatures. It won't take long as neither of them is contesting anything. They've sorted it all out between them. My mum's staying in the house and my dad already has a new one nearby. His girlfriend's moving in." Jessie stared at the tarmac and kicked a small stone that lay next to her foot.

"Bloody hell!" Sophie exclaimed. "How do you feel about that?"

Jessie leaned against her car and stared up into the blue sky, her mouth open as she tried to make sense of her world that was rapidly spinning out of control. "I suppose he deserves to be happy. I mean, life goes on, right?"

Sophie frowned. "Yeah, but it's weird."

"Oh, God, it's so weird. His girlfriend is only four years older than I am."

"Have you met her?"

"I worked with her up until last year."

Their attention was drawn across the car park as laughter rang out amid car doors slamming, followed by the distinct clop of high heels. Two women who would have stood out in any situation flanked Fran as the trio walked towards them.

With their six-inch heels, dyed hair, one black, the other blonde, and huge sunglasses, these women screamed "don't fuck with me". Dark red lipstick stood out on pale faces along with a flurry of leather and fur, enhancing the dangerous vibe.

Jessie had no idea who these women were, but instinctively she knew they were important. Fran didn't appear out of place walking between them. She looked relaxed, like she fit in with them. Whoever they were, whatever these women represented, this was a world Fran knew and was comfortable in.

The three of them walked into the clubhouse. Fran didn't even look her way. It stung.

"Who the hell was that?" Sophie asked.

As puzzled as her friend, she replied, "I have no idea."

"Those women are kind of familiar," Sophie stated, her eyes narrowed.

"I'm sure we'll find out more inside," Jessie answered as she pushed off the car and they both headed to the club house.

Inside the building a buzz of excitement had been created by Fran's guests. People knew who the two women were, and those who didn't were anxious to find out. Everyone was especially curious about how Fran knew them.

Fran seemed to take it all in her stride. She was unfazed by the attention and completely nonplussed by the effect her two friends were having in and around the clubhouse.

Autographs were being signed for fans who had come to the football game, and photographs taken with the fashionable women. They appeared accustomed to all the attention. Their practised poses were effortlessly struck in between chit-chat with the rest of the team. Every so often, that same uproarious, guttural laugh that had first caught Jessie's attention in the car park would waft across the room. They were having a ball.

In the changing room the players began to get ready for the match. When Fran joined them, they cast questioning glances her way, but she appeared not to notice.

"What the hell, Fran!" Morven exclaimed, her voice a combination of mirth and surprise. "You turn up with a fashion icon and a punk rock goddess, and say nothing?"

Fran shrugged. "They wanted to come to the game." A simple answer that gave no information.

Morven burst out laughing. "But how do you know them?"

Fran removed her T-shirt. As usual, there was no bra underneath. "Nikki's my godmother. She and Madge are friends."

"Oh, that explains it then. Of course, Nikki Demente would be your godmother. It all makes perfect sense now." Morven was mocking, but Fran remained cool.

"Nikki and my mum worked together," Fran replied as she began putting on her football kit, her face turned away from the room. Something in her tone made Morven back off a little. She cast a glance over towards Jessie, who shook her head.

"So, do you know any other celebrities?" Zoe asked.

Fran turned back around to face everyone in the room, she sat on the bench and began to pull her socks on. "One or two." Her reply was a low murmur, but Jessie caught it. Fran studied her hands, not engaging fully in the conversation, obviously not wanting to encourage any more questions.

"Right everyone, let's get our game heads on!" Andrea called out, effectively putting an end to the curious questions being thrown Fran's way. Jessie knew Fran well enough now to know she was grateful for the reprieve.

Jessie sat in Tom's office. The game had been a disaster. One, they should have won at a canter but had somehow contrived to draw with the team currently bottom of the league. Two, crucial points had been dropped, and Tom was mad. She could tell by the way his jaw was set. He'd summoned her here at the end of the game. Jessie sat in silence opposite him, freshly showered, awaiting a dressing-down. Her performance had been awful.

"I want to know what's going on with you. You've been walking around with a face like a wet weekend and it's affecting team morale. Everyone knows something's up and it's become the talk of the dressing room." He stared at her, awaiting her response.

She sat slumped in the chair, chewing on the inside of her cheek. She knew he was right. Her mood had been flat. She owed him the truth. "Fran's not talking to me."

Tom sat forward in his seat. "Look, I know me signing Fran was tough on you, but I thought you'd got past that."

Jessie shook her head. "I have."

Tom frowned. "So, what's the problem?"

She sighed. "I stuck my nose in where it wasn't wanted."

"So this isn't football related?"

Jessie flushed and lowered her head. She stared at her hands. "No."

Tom sat back in his chair. "Okay, I understand this is a private matter and, ordinarily, it's none of my business, but when it's affecting one of my most valuable players, it is. Your performance level has dropped and team morale is being affected because the atmosphere surrounding the pair of you is toxic."

Tom held up a hand as Jessie was about to interrupt. She never could sit quietly for more than a couple of minutes. She closed her mouth.

"I don't want or need details, but I do need you to sort out your problems or, at least, put them aside for the good of the team."

Jessie's trainer-clad foot scraped along the brown carpet. She folded her arms. "I want to sort it out but Fran's not ready or willing to do so."

Tom shook his head. "But Fran isn't letting whatever's going on affect her. She's no different around here. Unless you count sporting a cut head and having two celebrities on your arm different. Other than that, nothing has changed."

Jessie raised her chin. "I can put it aside."

"Good." Tom held eye contact.

She rubbed her face. "I was trying to be helpful. I honestly thought I was doing the right thing." Jessie shook her head as her words came out in a hoarse whisper.

"What's going on, Jessie?" he asked softly.

The tears rolled down her cheeks. She swiped at them. She was embarrassed at her display of raw emotion, but he was her friend. Jessie knew that if she needed him, he'd always be there for her.

Jessie sniffed back fresh tears. "I thought I was doing a good thing, but I've messed up big time." A sad smile accompanied her answer.

"You never liked her from the start but I couldn't help but notice the two of you seemed to be forming a friendship of sorts. What's changed?"

There was a lump in her throat. Jessie covered her mouth with a hand in an attempt to still the words that wanted to tumble from her lips. She was terrified to give voice to them, fearing once they were out there, she could never take them back. Yet she knew if she didn't tell someone, she would be driven mad by her own internal emotional struggle.

She removed her hand and stared at her friend. "I fell in love with her." Jessie's lip trembled as she watched the surprise register on Tom's face. It reflected her own confusion at the truth of her confession.

"Ah, Christ." Tom got up from his chair and walked to the other side of the desk. Crouching beside Jessie, he took her in his arms. He offered physical comfort where words apparently failed him.

Jessie leaned into the warmth of his broad shoulder and let the tears soak into his cotton shirt. She hurt, and knowing she'd hurt Fran only intensified her anguish and sorrow. Fran had come to her in a moment of need and they'd spent an incredible few hours together, but now their relationship was battered and bruised out of all recognition.

She'd made a huge mistake and ruined what had been slowly building between them. As she attempted to sniff back the tears, Tom continued to rub her back, murmuring words of comfort. She hoped he was right and it would all work out.

———— ❖ ————

Jessie spent a few minutes pulling herself together before she left Tom's office. She stood in the corridor, debating going into the hall to sit with her teammates, but her heart wasn't in it. She wanted to get home and put this week behind her. Tom was right. Her actions were affecting team morale. Add to that, Fran appeared to be dealing with the situation far better than she was. The hall door opened and the blonde who had arrived with Fran walked out, a smile stretching across her face when she saw Jessie.

"Hi, it's Jessie isn't it?"

Her English accent was hard to pick. Jessie knew it wasn't from the south. There was definitely a hint of northern England in there. She was stunned and a little concerned despite the welcoming smile and the outstretched hand.

"Yes."

"I'm Nikki, a friend of Fran's."

Jessie shook her hand. Without the sunglasses the woman appeared to be in her late fifties. "Hello."

Nikki studied her for a few moments. Jessie found the silent scrutiny unnerving.

"It's nice to meet you, Jessie. Fran's told me a lot about you."

Jessie swallowed. She expected to be chastised for her part in Fran's recent upheaval, but Nikki's smile appeared to be genuine.

"Don't be nervous. I'm here because she needs me, but that won't always be the case." She rubbed Jessie's forearm. "See you later."

And with those cryptic words she was gone, leaving Jessie perplexed.

A pang of sorrow gripped her as Nikki walked away. Jessie could only dream of sharing the easiness Nikki had around Fran. And the friendship. With a heavy heart, Jessie left the clubhouse as laughter filtered from the main hall, compounding her mood further.

Chapter 21

Just after noon, Jessie entered the office and found the elegantly flamboyant Nikki Demente sitting in reception with an awestruck Meadow. She stopped in the doorway.

"Ms Demente."

The fashionista stood to greet her, hand extended. "Please, call me Nikki."

"Of course, Nikki." Jessie tried the name out for the first time and it was surprisingly easy despite the intimidating appearance of the woman standing before her. "What can I do for you?"

"I was hoping to chat with you before I head back to London."

"Nothing urgent, Jessie, and it is lunchtime," Meadow said, before smiling enigmatically.

"Thank you, Meadow," Jessie offered a bemused smile to her secretary, not missing Meadow's hint regarding lunch. She never took time out to eat, choosing instead to have lunch at her desk or while travelling to appointments. Turning to Nikki, she asked, "Would you like to get some coffee?"

The older woman inclined her head. "That would be wonderful." She turned to Meadow, "It was lovely to meet you, Meadow. Good luck with your studies, and look me up if you find yourself planning any events in London." She placed a card with her details on the desk. "You can never have too many contacts."

"Oh, thank you, that's amazing." Meadow was practically bouncing in her seat as she clutched the card in her hand, waving to them both as they left the office.

"Charming girl," Nikki remarked to Jessie as they walked on the paved street.

"Yes, she is. I'm going to miss her when she leaves at the end of the summer."

"I'm sure. She has a way with people. It will benefit her greatly in her career."

Jessie acknowledged the truth of the statement. Meadow was a people person, friendly and helpful. "It was very kind of you to offer to assist her in the future."

Nikki smiled at Jessie, her designer sunglasses hiding her eyes. "We all have to start somewhere. I know what that's like."

Jessie had Googled the woman walking next to her. The story was fascinating. By all accounts, she simply went to London and, from scratch, with no money, managed to set up a fashion house. Her clients were like a who's who of rock royalty.

"Would you like to sit in somewhere or are you willing to brave the cold?" It was a lovely bright sunny day, but the early spring bite in the air was unmistakable.

"Actually, I would love a walk on the seafront."

"Great. There's a fantastic little kiosk that does coffee-to-go."

Jessie led them down one of the many streets that ended on the prom. She was aware of the stares sent the way of her companion. Even if no one recognised Nikki Demente, her aura was palpable. From her full make-up and beehive-styled, peroxide blonde hair, to the perfectly painted, deep-red manicured nails, this woman grabbed attention. Add to that the black clothing topped off with a leopard print fur coat and designer heels studded with crystals, and you knew she was somebody.

"When do you head back?"

"First thing tomorrow morning. I'm looking forward to getting home, but I'll miss Fran."

And there it was. The reason these two strangers were strolling together along the promenade to have coffee on a cold spring day.

"How is she?" Jessie tried to appear casual, but knew she was fooling no one.

Nikki smiled, removed her sunglasses and replied. "Quiet, which isn't surprising."

There was no censure in Nikki's reply, but it stung regardless. Heat suffused Jessie cheeks. "I know it's my fault. I should have left everything alone." They had come to a stop, standing in a small queue at the kiosk.

"Why didn't you?"

Again, the tone held no hint of censure or rebuke, at least none that Jessie could detect. She shook her head. "I knew I couldn't keep it to myself." She shrugged. "I was aware of the risk involved, but I couldn't not pursue the possibility."

Nikki nodded. "I understand. If I had come upon the same information and made that connection, I would've done something about it too." She paused and raised an index finger. "With one exception. I would've spoken to Fran first."

The chastisement hurt but not because Nikki was saying it. It hurt because she knew she'd messed up. Jessie recognised the truth of the statement.

"With hindsight, I wish I had. But I wanted to spare Fran any anguish if I was wrong. Which it appeared I was. I honestly thought nothing more would come of it, and I'd made the right choice."

"I understand your reasons, Jessie. I truly do."

Nikki's eyes held compassion, which Jessie found to be reassuring. She was aware that this woman could be intimidating if she so chose.

"What can I get you?" a male voice asked.

Jessie turned. A gap had opened while they had been deep in conversation. The young man serving smiled patiently, awaiting their order.

Jessie walked to the counter then turned to Nikki. "Coffee?" At the older woman's nod she ordered two. "Would you like anything to eat?"

"No, black coffee's fine, thanks." Nikki huddled inside her fur coat as a brisk wind whipped along the promenade, leaving sand in its wake across the pink tarmac. Jessie noted that a few strands of blonde hair had fallen loose, softening the edges of the older woman. Jessie picked the coffees up from the counter top, then led them to a nearby bench. "Here, this should heat you up."

"Thanks. I'm not used to all this fresh sea air." She sipped the steaming liquid as she pulled her coat closed. "It's definitely colder up here." Nikki's eyes followed a man walking along the sand wearing shorts and a T-shirt. "You certainly are a hardy bunch."

Jessie laughed at the look of disbelief on her face. "There does seem to be a bit of that in us."

Nikki sipped more coffee, then nodded. "Fran goes around in nothing but a T-shirt, jeans, and that leather jacket, whatever the weather. Stands out on that balcony in just a top, come rain or shine. She must be freezing, but you wouldn't know it." She shook her head. "Crazy girl."

Jessie had witnessed Fran on that balcony many times early in the morning. She wasn't sure Fran was aware she saw her. But on the dark mornings that glow of orange from the tip of a cigarette was unmistakable. Thoughts of Fran caused a fresh wave of sadness to wash over her. "Will she ever forgive me?"

"Give her time, she'll come around."

"Really?" Jessie was sceptical, but also hopeful. After all, this woman knew Fran better than anyone.

"Yeah, she's too bloody stubborn for her own good at times, though."

Jessie loved the regional accent that occasionally popped through. It was slight, but unmistakable, especially when Nikki became animated.

Smiling, Jessie asked, "Where are you from?"

Nikki laughed. "Huddersfield." She dropped the 'H' from the town's name. "God, I haven't lived there since I was seventeen, but whenever I go back, it's like coming home. However, London is the place I'll always reside." The accent lessened and almost disappeared as Nikki fell into her usual cadence.

"Would you tell me a little about Fran's mum?" Jessie asked. She couldn't help herself, especially when it came to Fran. She wanted to find out all she could, and it was highly unlikely Fran would talk about herself.

Nikki's eyes became unfocused as she seemingly retreated into thoughts that Jessie wished she be could be party to. Distant memories, cathartic perhaps, and no doubt treasured. Nikki smiled. "DeeDee was a spitfire— vibrant, energetic. She lived life to the full." She took a sip of her coffee. "You know, she wasn't so much funny as mesmerising. Everyone wanted to be around her. Women wanted to be friends with her, and men, well, they all wanted her."

"But DeeDee chose Kenny?"

"Ah, Kenny." Nikki appeared bemused. "She lived with him, but he was away a lot. The pair of them loved each other, but they didn't have the expectation of monogamy while they were apart." She shook her head. "I don't know how that old fart is still managing to drag his carcass up and down the country making a living. He blames himself, you know, for DeeDee's death." Her voice softened. "He believes if he hadn't spent the extra days away partying, she wouldn't have died." She pursed her lips. "It's no one's fault. DeeDee loved to experiment, but Kenny's soft-hearted. He won't ever forgive himself, but there's no blame." Shaking her head, Nikki continued, "He was a broken man when he lost DeeDee and Fran. He hasn't really ever got over it."

"It's so sad that they both lost DeeDee," Jessie mused, imagining how different all their lives could have been. "Addiction is so awful."

When Nikki didn't reply immediately, Jessie feared she had overstepped the mark. The older woman gazed out over the water.

"Yes, DeeDee was an addict, but she was so much more, very gifted." She turned back to address Jessie directly. "I loved having her work with me." Nikki smiled, softening her normally stern features. "She brought Fran to work with her. We all got on with it back then, no crèche, no health and safety, everybody just mucked in." She crossed her legs. "You wanted to be in a band, you got together with others who wanted the same thing. The ethos was, give it a go, do it yourself, because no one else was going to do it for you." She laughed. "We must've got something bloody right when you consider the amount of successful musicians, designers, artists, and writers to come out of the punk era. There's a lot to be said for the DIY culture. Shame it was so short lived."

Jessie hung on every word. Despite never having had an interest in anything remotely related to punk, she now found herself wanting to know more. "What ended it?"

"Consumerism." Nikki laughed, but it lacked any humour. "The biggest irony of all, punk was killed by its own success. The minute it became commercial and mainstream, the game was up. Punk was dead."

A quiet calm settled between them as they drank their coffee, but Jessie wanted to know more. "Is Fran like her mum?"

Nikki shook her head, as she put her free hand in the pocket of her coat. "Not really. Even in terms of addiction, they differ. DeeDee loved to experiment. Her insatiable craving was for excitement, the thrill. Fran's is about coping with life. With Fran drugs are an escape, a crutch." Nikki took in a deep breath. "DeeDee wasn't a bad mother. Fran was well looked after. She just got a bad batch and overdosed. And that, as they say, was that." Nikki sniffed and blinked back the imminent tears. "I still bloody miss her."

She shifted her shoulders and shook her head before pinning Jessie was an intense gaze. "Don't you give up on my girl. It's not you she's mad at. Not really. She's struggling to deal with the changes in her life. There's a battle raging inside her right now. She's fighting against the urge to reach for a bottle or a pill. That sweet oblivion that will make everything go away for a short time. Only Fran can fight the battles, Jessie. If you want to be in her life at all, you have to face that fact. She has to fight the battles, but we can help her win the war." Nikki smiled sadly at Jessie. "Give her time, love."

<hr>

"Next stop is Paris, and then I fly to New York." Nikki sipped her white wine as the waiter cleared the plates from the table. "Thank you." She smiled at the young Indian man, before turning back to Fran. "I'm doing a bit of travelling in the summer. You're welcome to join me, or pop down to London sometime."

"Maybe. I can't really take any time off, but I'd love to see you again soon." Fran twirled the remnants of Coke in her glass, the dark liquid sloshing against the sides of the tumbler.

"I'll be back up soon, Fran, I promise."

The gentle, caring tone of Nikki's voice caused an unexpected ripple in her stomach. She was going to miss her. "I appreciate you spending the week with me."

Nikki waved off the sentiment. "You know I enjoy spending time with you."

"All the same, I'm grateful to you for coming up at short notice."

Nikki smiled. "What do you plan to do?"

There was no need for Nikki to elaborate Fran knew she was asking about the choices that had cropped up unexpectedly in the last week. She sighed. "Ross Martin's dead, does it matter if he's my father?"

Fran thought back to the conversation she had shared with Harry five days ago. Last Sunday, she'd run off, giving him no opportunity to elaborate beyond stating that Toni's brother could be her dad. On Wednesday, Harry had taken the opportunity to sit her down and give more details. Ross had spent most of his adult life in prison, and had been a long-term drug addict. She winced as she recalled her response—"That's just great, another fucking junkie." Harry went on to explain Ross had died a few years ago of an illness. She knew he was talking about AIDS. It was the way he paused, as if searching for a diplomatic response. She had straight out asked him, and Harry had nodded.

"It matters to Harry whether Ross is your father," Nikki said, playing the guilt card. It did matter to Harry, very much, and it stung. Fran stared at Nikki, her eyes narrowing.

"There's his sister, Toni," Nikki added, apparently not remotely put off by the warning glare.

Yes, there was Toni. Her business card was in the zipped breast pocket of Fran's jacket, untouched since she'd stashed it there. She drummed her fingers on the table as Nikki studied her, waiting her out.

"I need a cigarette." She was stalling, but she needed to be on the move. She felt trapped sitting in a chair.

"Me too. Let me settle the bill."

Fran sat back in the chair. She knew Nikki wouldn't leave Edinburgh without asking the tough questions. Fran tapped her foot impatiently against the dark wooden floor as she waited for her dinner companion to return.

Nikki had gone up to the bar to pay rather than wait for the bill. Fran had long since given up arguing over the bill with Nikki. She always lost. Fran stood and stretched as Nikki made her way back to the table. She picked up Nikki's fur jacket and held it open for her.

"Thank you."

Fran held the restaurant door for Nikki, exiting behind her into the darkening evening. She immediately went to her jacket pocket, removed her cigarettes, and then offered one to Nikki. She lit them both and took a long draw from hers. Nikki linked arms with her, and they began to stroll towards the promenade.

"I like this place, Fran. It has character."

Fran blew a long stream of smoke from her lungs. "Yeah, I suppose."

"Are you going to stick around?" Nikki asked, elegantly tipping ash from the top of her cigarette.

She shrugged. "As long as Harry needs me."

"What about when Harry no longer needs you?" Nikki's tone was gentle.

Nikki had phrased the question delicately, but what she really meant was what would happen when Harry died? Fran didn't want to dwell on that.

"Will you keep running the Beachcomber?" she prodded.

"It's something to do, I suppose."

"Or you could sell up."

Fran shook her head. "No, I couldn't do that to Harry. I'll keep the place open."

Nikki pulled her closer. "I'm so happy to hear that, Fran." She stretched up on her tiptoes and kissed Fran on the cheek.

Fran scowled. "Don't go leaving red lipstick all over me," she objected, and Nikki used her thumb to clean her cheek. They walked in silence for a bit, enjoying the late evening and their cigarettes.

"I spoke to Jessie Grainger at lunchtime."

Fran stopped walking, rocked by the information. "Why?"

"Because I like her and so do you." Nikki's tone was matter of fact.

Fran turned away from Nikki. "She needs to mind her own business."

"She overstepped the mark, true. But her intentions were honest." Nikki turned Fran's face back towards her. "She's hurting, and her only mistake was caring about you."

"I wish she wouldn't." Fran doubted that she had managed to disguise the anguish in her voice.

Nikki rubbed her arm. "We don't get to choose who cares about us."

Fran closed her eyes shut tight. "I'll ruin her life."

"You need to have faith in yourself. You've come a long way, Fran. Take the next step," Nikki urged.

She made it sound so easy. "What if I mess up?" Fran whispered.

"You won't know unless you try."

"No. She deserves better, Nikki, so much better than me."

Nikki took her arm again, and began walking towards the Beachcomber. "At least consider it, and please, think about contacting Toni Martin."

Fran sighed, her face raised towards the dark sky. "You ask a lot, Nikki."

"I know, darling. I know."

Chapter 22

It took Jessie a moment to register the ring of her phone in her sleep-addled brain. She reached towards her bedside cabinet, her hand blindly searching for her mobile. "Hello?" she croaked.

"Hello, is this Jessie Grainger?" A timid female voice sounded in her ear.

Jessie sat up and switched on her bedside lamp, squinting at the brightness. "Yes, who's calling?"

"It's Louise Fisher. I'm so sorry, Miss Grainger, but I've lost my keys and I'm locked out."

The girl sounded distressed, and it took Jessie a moment to realise this was one of the students from the Beachcomber. It was five in the morning and pitch dark outside. The poor girl was obviously scared. "Have you knocked on the door?"

"No, I didn't want to wake anyone up." She was becoming upset now.

"Stay where you are. I'll call someone to come down and let you in. I'll be there soon with a spare key for your room. Okay?"

"Yes." Her breathing hitched as she replied.

"I'll be with you soon, Louise."

Jessie immediately searched her phone for Fran's number and hit dial as she hastily put on some joggers and a sweatshirt. She just hoped Fran would accept her call. Given recent events, she couldn't be certain.

"Hello?" Fran was sleepy, which wasn't surprising given the hour, but a part of Jessie thought she might be awake, standing on her balcony enjoying a cigarette.

"Fran, thank God. I'm sorry to ring you at this hour, but one of the students has lost her keys, she's outside the front door. Could you let her in?"

Fran yawned on the other end of the line. "Yeah, I'll let her in."

"Thank you. I'm going to the office to pick up a spare set of keys, I'll be with you shortly."

Jessie slipped her feet into a pair of boots, grabbed her car keys, and made her way out into the frosty, dark morning.

She arrived at the Beachcomber less than fifteen minutes later, and found the front door open. She entered and made her way upstairs. Louise was sitting at the kitchen table, a cup of tea in front of her, her eyes full of unshed tears. Her dark hair was normally long and glossy, but today it lacked its usual lustre and neatness. Jessie remembered the teenager from her interview. The accommodation she'd been living in had been overcrowded. Jessie had been unsure Louise would find the Beachcomber suitable as it was essentially a bar, but she'd loved the rooms available and let Jessie know just how desperate she was to live there.

"I'm so sorry, I must have left my keys at my parents' house in Aberdeen. I'll call them later and find out for sure."

Jessie sighed as she took a seat at the table. "Let's hope that's where they are." She located the spare key for Louise's room and placed it on the table in front of the student. "Go to the hardware store tomorrow and have a copy of that key made. Then drop the original off at the office."

Louise nodded. "Thank you." She rinsed her cup in the sink, then picked up the key and crossed the landing to her room, and closed the door behind her.

Jessie had hoped Fran would be sitting with Louise when she arrived, but her door was closed. She knew Fran must still be awake. She knocked on the door and waited. It was opened in seconds. Fran stood before her in a T-shirt and shorts, the open expression on her face instantly turning to a scowl. Jessie guessed she must have thought it was Louise.

"I, ah, wanted to say thanks for letting Louise into the house." Fran was sleep tousled, the warmth radiating from her. Jessie was so close she could smell the scent of her warm body. Her fingers itched to touch her.

"It's fine," Fran answered curtly. "Is that all?"

The question stung. It was dismissive and meant to hurt. "Fran..." Jessie spoke as the other woman began to close the room door. "Please, can we talk?"

Fran dipped her head, the door handle grasped in her hand. Jessie waited, hoping. "There's nothing to talk about." She stared at the floor, not making eye contact with Jessie.

"You came to my door, Fran." Frustration and hurt laced her tone. "We slept together."

"It was just sex." Fran attempted to close the door again, but Jessie pushed against it and found herself inside the room. Jessie closed the door behind her to afford them some privacy.

She stared at Fran. "How can you say it was 'just sex'? Believe it or not, I've had sex a few times in my life and I know the difference. What we had, what we shared that afternoon was more than sex, and don't you dare claim otherwise." Jessie's fists were balled so tightly, her nails dug into her palms. Her chest heaved as she attempted to keep the anger at bay.

"Maybe, but it was a mistake." Fran finally looked directly at Jessie. "I turned up at your door because I needed a distraction and you were it."

Jessie moved so quickly she saw shock register on Fran's face as she grabbed her head in both hands. She pulled Fran to her and kissed her roughly, pouring both hurt and passion in equal measure into the kiss. She wanted—no, needed—to provoke a response from her. She needed something to know that what she'd felt was real. That it wasn't just her.

Fran's lips moved against hers, kissing back with abandon as Jessie pawed at Fran's clothing desperately. She pushed her T-shirt up over her bare breasts, exposing them to the cool air, causing the nipples to stiffen instantly. The nipple bars carried the warmth of Fran's body as Jessie fondled her breasts. Their soft warmth caused moisture to pool between Jessie's legs. Shocked by her own actions, Jessie came to her senses and eased away from Fran. She appeared vulnerable, her head back, eyes closed, her breasts exposed.

Jessie's breath rasped harshly from her chest, a mixture of anger and passion fuelling her uncharacteristic actions. She watched as Fran pulled her top back over her chest. Jessie wanted this woman. Despite everything, her body couldn't lie. The attraction was visceral. No matter what her head said or how much she rationalised and reasoned with herself, she wanted her. She knew there were many ways in which Fran was bad for her. Wrong for her. It didn't seem to matter. She couldn't stop thinking about her, and it was driving her crazy.

"I know what sex is," Jessie whispered, a harshness to her voice, "and this is so much more."

"It can't be," Fran croaked as she stumbled. Her movements were unsteady as she made her way across the carpeted floor to retrieve her cigarettes before retreating outside the glass doors.

———◦◇◦———

Fran stood on the balcony, lighting a cigarette. It trembled between her fingers as she brought it to her mouth. The first hint of light was beginning to seep into the sky, silhouetting the gulls against its backdrop, their cries mirroring the pain inside her. Why couldn't Jessie understand that their being together was a bad idea?

Tucking her left hand under her right armpit as she smoked, Fran huddled as best she could against the elements. Spring was here, but it was cold enough for snow. Her right thumb caressed her forehead trying to ward off the tension building rapidly. She stubbed the cigarette out on the wall as she blew out her last puff of smoke, and went inside. She deliberately schooled her features into a cold mask of uncaring offhandedness.

"Are you still here?"

Jessie was sitting on the chaise longue, sipping coffee. Fran saw the hurt rip across her face at the carefully chosen words.

"We need to talk," Jessie stated calmly.

Fran had to applaud her persistence. There was a cup of hot coffee on her bedside table. She picked it up. The warmth that radiated into her hands and her mouth at the first sip was welcome. She would hear Jessie out. It appeared to be the only way to get rid of her. Fran sat on the edge of her bed.

"Firstly, I want to apologise for going to Toni Martin. I should have come to you. I'm sorry. I hope, in time, you can forgive me."

Fran didn't respond.

"I also want to apologise for what just happened. I don't know what got into me." Jessie's face coloured and she took a deep breath. "I don't normally act that way." She shook her head. "I've never acted that way."

It was obvious to Fran that Jessie was uncomfortable being so honest about their encounter. "No need to apologise."

"I wish…" Jessie sighed. "I'm struggling to stay away from you." There were tears in her eyes. "You drive me crazy." Her voice had an edge to it. "I never understood or imagined what that meant until now, but I think of you all the time. The way you smell, the way you taste. I crave more." Her eyes were on Fran, pleading with her to understand. "I don't know if this is anything like addiction, but it's driving me insane. I'm not myself."

"Jessie." Fran's voice was low. Despite her intentions, it was difficult to be cold with Jessie. "Please don't fall for me. You deserve so much more."

"How can you say that? The more you turn me away, the more I want you!" Jessie's voice rose, conveying her anger and frustration. Fran could sense the waves of emotion radiating off her.

"It's lust." Fran was offering her an out. Or maybe it was for herself. Maybe both of them. The situation was too complicated, the stakes too high.

Jessie protested. "You don't know that. I don't only want you physically, I want all of you. I want to know everything about you." Jessie was pleading now, desperate for Fran to react to her heartfelt words, but Fran knew she couldn't. She needed to stop this.

"Trust me, you don't want to have anything to do with me," Fran cautioned again.

"Why?" Jessie's face contorted.

Fran closed her eyes, swallowing against her tight throat, "Because I'm damaged goods, Jessie, a waster. I always fuck things up."

"We can be friends, see where things go?"

Fran cursed. Why couldn't she understand? Why did she have to be so damn stubborn? "Don't you get it? I'm trying to warn you, protect you. I already know how this will end. I've travelled the road many times before."

"I can make my own decisions."

Fran's frustration and pain only increased as Jessie continued not to listen to reason. "I'm no good for you, Jessie. I will mess up your life and you don't deserve that." She let her head fall back, gathered her thoughts, then focused directly on Jessie. "I can't be your friend."

Jessie shook her head. "Why not?"

Whispering, Fran managed to push out her reply past a rapidly closing throat, "Because it would be too difficult."

Jessie approached her, their eyes locked on each other. When Jessie's fingers caressed her arm, Fran flinched at the contact.

"You're attracted to me and I'm very attracted to you. We could make this work."

"I don't trust myself," Fran rasped.

"Don't be a coward. Please. I'm willing to take a chance on us. Why won't you?"

Fran shook off the hand holding her arm. She stood and walked to the centre of the room. She needed space and couldn't bear to have Jessie so close to her. "Don't you get it? I always fuck up." Her voice was stronger now. She needed to make Jessie understand.

"Trust yourself."

Fran rubbed her face. "I can't.

Jessie stood next to her and Fran resisted the urge to physically push her away. She wanted to run. She was trembling and knew Jessie was aware of her predicament.

"I know you want me, and God help me, I want you too," Jessie said. "I'm not giving up on that, I'm not giving up on us. You can't remain hidden away here in your ivory tower forever. You need to engage with the world, not live in a vacuum."

Fran steeled herself. She didn't like opening up, but it appeared that doing so was the only way to make Jessie understand. She turned to face Jessie, her jaw set, eyes blazing.

"I've been addicted to drugs and alcohol. I've spent time in prison." She stared into Jessie's eyes, making sure every word she said hit home. Keeping her own eyes hard, she continued, "I have been in prison for drug possession, selling drugs, and theft. When you're an addict, you will do anything, *anything,* for a fix. I have fucked men for drugs and money." Fran swallowed. "There are periods of my life that I cannot recollect. I probably don't want to. I've soiled myself and not cared. Slept many times in my own piss and vomit, more times than I can count. Imagine being so wasted that it doesn't bother you?" She swallowed and pushed on. "I've injected heroin." She paused allowing that fact to sink in. The look of horror on Jessie's face telling her it had. "I'm now facing up to who I am, what I've done, and who I've been. My behaviour was excused for years because of my mum." A burst of ironic laughter leapt unexpectedly from her throat. "Sure, she died of an overdose, but she had a job and a life. I'm sure she would have been greatly disappointed in me."

Fran struggled to keep the emotion from creeping into her voice.

"People stopped caring and I don't blame them for that. I was self-destructing. When I left prison almost two years ago and Nikki was outside,

I knew she was all I had left in the world. She was giving me one more chance. One more chance that I didn't deserve, but she was doing it for my mum. Don't get me wrong, I'm grateful that she was there, but I got clean for me. To get some self-respect back. To prove to myself that I could get clean, but let me tell you, every day is a struggle. Every single fucking day the urge to get wasted is strong. It's been my coping mechanism for so long that I'm naked without it. I'm laid bare for everyone to pick over and even I don't like what I see. So why the fuck would anyone else?" She ended harshly, her voice raw. She stared at Jessie whose eyes were wide. Fran knew she had shocked her, but she needed to. Life was shocking. The truth was shocking. And Jessie needed to hear it in all its gutter glory.

She turned away, unable to bare the revulsion any longer. "Go home, Jessie. Go home to your nice, ordered, perfect life."

Fran refused to look at her. Instead, she kept her back turned until the door closed. She wanted Jessie like she'd never wanted anyone else in her life. And that terrifying fact was exactly why she could never have her. It was too big a risk to her stability and sobriety. But most importantly, she didn't deserve Jessie. She wasn't worthy of her love. Jessie deserved so much better.

Jessie stumbled from the Beachcomber onto the promenade, swiping an arm across her face to wipe away the tears that were streaming down her cheeks. Her legs felt like rubber, and she wasn't fully in control of her body as she struggled to avoid an early-morning jogger. He chose a wide arcing manoeuvre, keeping well out of her way. She shook her head and pushed on. She wanted to run, but her legs wouldn't cooperate.

She got to her car and fumbled in her pocket to locate her keys. She opened the door, and sat in the drivers seat. Jessie stared out the window, she was numb. How had her life spiralled this far out of control? Since her parents had informed her of their divorce on Christmas day, it had been one disaster after another. All she'd ever wanted was to work hard and play football. Now she was trying to come to terms with her parents' split and somewhere along the way she had fallen in love with a woman she would never have imagined being a part of her life. And never would be, judging by the conversation that had just taken place.

Normally, when something went wrong in her life, she went to her mum, but she hadn't visited her since New Year's day. She missed her terribly. She'd been avoiding her mother, blaming her for the marriage breakdown and making her father miserable. But if Jessie had learned anything in these past few weeks, it was that life was never black and white.

Fran was right about one thing—up until now, she'd enjoyed a near-perfect life. But since Fran Docherty had arrived in it, it had tumbled out of her control. It was coming apart at the seams, and there was not a damn thing she could do about it.

Well, she could start making up with her mum, and that was what she intended to do. She needed someone to talk to, someone who would listen and not judge. Someone who wasn't too close to the situation. Someone who loved her unconditionally. Right now, her mum was the only person who ticked all those boxes.

Chapter 23

Jessie opened the door and was immediately assaulted with the smell of a Sunday roast cooking. Her stomach rumbled appreciatively and her mouth watered as she inhaled the pleasant aroma.

"Hello?" she called out, making her way down the hall towards the kitchen.

"Jessie!" her mum exclaimed, as she wiped her hands on a dishtowel. She took Jessie in her arms. "It's so good to see you," she said. She held her tightly. "Oh, Jessie, I've missed you." Her voice cracked.

Jessie hugged her mum and inhaled the familiar scent of the light perfume she favoured. It was both comforting and grounding. It was like coming home, and she was home, but it would never be the same now that her dad had moved out. A wave of sadness swept over her, and she swallowed back the lump in her throat.

"How have you been, Mum?" Her tight throat affected her voice, making the words raw.

"Oh, you know, doing okay." Her mum used the tea towel to dab at the corner of her eye. Her smile was sad and her chin quivered.

The silence stretched out until an awkwardness hung in the air, she was acutely aware of the distance that had grown between them in the past weeks. But Jessie needed to have her mum in her life, especially now. She couldn't stay angry with her forever.

"I'm sorry I haven't been around in a while." Jessie swallowed back her torment, determined to push through the barriers.

"I've missed you, Jessie." There were fresh tears in her mum's eyes, and Jessie felt a pang of guilt at having put them there.

Her mum's bottom lip trembled. "I never wanted to hurt you, I'd never intentionally hurt you, I swear." She took a shuddering breath.

Jessie shook her head. "I know, Mum. I just couldn't understand. I guess I still don't, but you're my mum and I love you, and I don't want it to be like this anymore."

Her mum grasped her hand and led her to the kitchen table, where they sat down. She took both of Jessie's hands before she spoke. "I was suffocating inside." She shook her head. "I was going through the motions, and I felt like I was standing outside of my body watching as life passed me by." She squeezed Jessie's hands tighter. "I know you're disappointed in me, Jessie. And I know I've hurt your dad, but I was dying a little more with each passing day." Her mum sniffed back tears, her lips pressed tightly together as her thumbs rubbed the back of Jessie's hands.

Listening to her mum talk candidly about herself was unusual. Jessie had never been privy to these thoughts. The woman sitting before her was, in some ways, a stranger. Yes, this was her mum, but Jessie was witnessing a whole new side to the woman who had raised her.

"What will you do now?" The question held no hint of anger or petulance. Jessie genuinely cared.

Her mother shook her head. "I don't have a plan. All I know is that I'm happier than I have been in a long while. I'm looking forward for the first time in ages." Her eyes softened as they captured Jessie's. "I know you don't understand, but if I had stuck it out with your dad, I would have been doing it only for you. I now it's selfish, but I couldn't pretend any longer."

Jessie stared down at their joined hands, taking a moment to gather her thoughts. She raised her head and answered. "I'm trying to understand your decision, Mum. To make some kind of sense of it. But I won't lie to you, it's a struggle." She licked her lips. She needed to be honest. "It's like part of my childhood was a lie." Now that Jessie had said it out loud, she understood that was one of the main problems she had with the divorce.

"That's not true," her mum interrupted. "Until these past eighteen months, I was happy. Then something changed. I'm not sure exactly what. It wasn't an incident, or anything that your dad did. It was something inside of me." She laid a hand on her chest, emphasising the point.

"A midlife crisis?" Jessie knew she shouldn't have said it, but it was difficult not to be harsh in the circumstances.

"Oh, Jessie, you've always had such a rose-tinted view of the world. I'm sorry that this has shaken you so much. I suspect some of that comes from having had such a stable upbringing."

Jessie stopped in her tracks at her mum's words. Her upbringing had been idyllic, balanced. She was a well-loved, spoilt on occasion, an only child. It struck her that Fran from the age of four had also been offered stability, but it hadn't been enough. How did losing her mum affect her? Was it the reason she had demons leading her to addiction and self-destructive tendencies?

"Jessie?"

She blinked back to the present. "Sorry, Mum, I was miles away."

Her mum tilted her head to the side. "Tell me what's going on with you?"

Tears sprang to her eyes so quickly, they stung. Jessie tried to blink them back. Her mum could always pick up on her mood, especially when something was troubling her. Even now, when the principle problem was the divorce, she had scratched beneath the surface and unearthed another difficulty hidden in the dirt. Jessie linked her fingers together and ran a thumbnail over the inside of her palm, something she did when she was troubled.

"I've got myself into a little bit of a mess." She peered into her mum's green eyes. The furrow of her brow conveyed concern, the slow nod encouraging Jessie to continue. "I don't even know where to start really. So much has happened." Jessie bit her bottom lip. "I've fallen in love." She shook her head. "I never saw it coming, Mum. She, this woman, she drives me mad, and not in a good way. The first time I met her was on a football pitch and her antics got me sent off." Jessie smiled at the memory. "Then Tom signed her up for the club. I couldn't believe it, I had never wanted to lay eyes on her again, and there she was, one of my new teammates."

She fiddled with the ring on her finger. "I disliked everything about her. The way she dressed, her attitude, her tattoos, the fact that she smoked. I could go on but you get the picture." At her mum's, nod she continued, "She lives and works in Portobello, so I ended up giving her a lift to games and training. It made sense. It also meant she would get there on time. Which had been a problem too. She's running her granddad's bar, the Beachcomber. I had to go in and get her when she was late for her lift one morning." She recalled that morning, the images burnt into her brain. The bar with patrons in it from the night before, sleeping, and Fran sprawled naked across her bed with a foul-mouthed woman. "She doesn't talk unless she absolutely has to. It's infuriating." Jessie sat back in her chair, exasperated at recounting that part of the story. Her mum raised an eyebrow. "Yes, I know, she also asked me not to talk on a two-hour drive."

"That must have been very difficult for you." Her mum's attempt to conceal her mirth failed.

Jessie smiled. "Anyway, she's different. And she doesn't want to be in a relationship with me." Sadness crept into her voice.

"Oh, Jessie, I'm so sorry. But why is that?" Her mum appeared puzzled.

"Fran is a very complicated woman, to say the least. She has a past that's *colourful*." Jessie's diplomatic choice of words was in part due to her mother being unlikely to approve of Fran's past behaviour. She knew if a friend were describing Fran to her, she would tell them to run and keep running. "She's had problems with drugs and alcohol." Jessie waited for her mum to digest that information. It certainly made her sit up straighter in her chair, her face radiating concern.

"I know that doesn't sound good, but she's worked hard at getting her life back on track. I believe that's part of why I'm drawn to her."

"Will you pursue her?" Her mum was frowning.

"She won't enter into a relationship with me." Her mother appeared relieved at that, and Jessie couldn't blame her. "She says I'm too good for her, that she'll ruin my life." She sighed. "Oh, Mum, Fran's full of self-loathing and terrified of messing up. She's been concentrating on proving to her grandfather that she's a changed person. I know it's awful to hear that she's had problems with addiction, but if you knew her and some of the things she has been through…" Jessie shook her head. "I'm not trying to make excuses for her behaviour. She's hurt people, but now she genuinely wants to change her life." She leaned forward, placing her forearms on the table.

"She's obviously been a very troubled young woman."

Nodding her agreement, Jessie continued, "I know she has feelings for me, Mum, but she continually pushes me away."

The soft, warm hand that caressed her cheek was comforting, as was the thumb that wiped away the tear that trickled down.

"If I know my daughter, and I think I do, you won't give up on her." Her mum's smile was encouraging, her voice comforting, but that's what mums were meant to do. That's why she'd come here.

"It's so difficult, Mum. How can I change her mind? I don't know what to do. I love her, I want her. I want her to give us a chance." Frustration laced Jessie's words.

"Perhaps she needs to sort out her life before she can begin to move forward. I suggest you give her time."

Jessie sagged in her chair. "That's what Nikki said." She traced a pattern on the wooden table.

"Who's Nikki?"

"Nikki Demente."

"You know Nikki Demente?" Her mum sounded confused, like she didn't quite believe what Jessie said.

Jessie threw her hands up. "Am I the only person who didn't know her? Even Meadow knew who she was."

"Sorry, Jessie, you've lost me. When were you speaking to Nikki Demente?"

"We had coffee at the kiosk on the promenade."

Her mum's brow furrowed. "Did you bump into her there?"

"What?" Jessie shook her head. "No, she came into the office wanting to chat about Fran. Nikki is her godmother."

"Nikki Demente is Fran's godmother?" Her mum repeated slowly.

"Yes, and some punk guy called Kenny Edwards is kind of like her stepdad, or at least he was for a little while. I've met him too, he's...interesting. Anyway..."

"Hang on." She held up her hands. "Let's back up a little. You've met Nikki Demente and Kenny Edwards?"

"Yes! I just said so." Jessie was becoming irritable.

"Wait," her mum said. "Can you please explain this more thoroughly so I can begin to understand how this has come about?"

"Mum—" Jessie was running out of patience.

"Jessie, you can't name-drop icons from my youth and expect me to take it in my stride. Imagine if I told you in passing that I met Mia Hamm and Ronaldo, then acted like it was nothing." Her mother's eyes were wide, a hint of sarcasm in her voice.

"Okay, I get your point." When she put it like that, Jessie supposed it was a bit difficult to take in.

181

"Fran's mum headed down to London at sixteen. She took off with some singer in a punk band which was touring the country. Anyway, things with this singer didn't work out, but she'd met Nikki and started working for her. At some point, she got pregnant and had Fran. Then she met Kenny Edwards and they were together until DeeDee died from an overdose when Fran was four."

"Oh, how awful for her, losing her mum so young."

"I know. I can't even imagine what that must be like." She paused, her mum's expression mirroring her own heavy-heartedness. "A few weeks ago, Kenny was playing at the Beachcomber. Well, he was actually off his face and Fran had to step in and play or everyone was going to leave. She is a brilliant guitarist. Kenny started teaching her when she was a toddler. I was at the Beachcomber and while Fran was playing, he appeared behind me and started chatting about Fran."

"Okay, so Nikki was there too?" Her mum was obviously eager to learn more about Nikki Demente.

"Ah, no." Jessie took a deep breath, she wasn't going to omit any facts while telling this story. "I helped Fran rent out rooms in the Beachcomber to students. She needed to make more money as her grandfather's nursing home fees are so expensive." Her mum nodded, so far following the story. "While I was surveying the rooms, I found one that was completely different. It was fascinating. At first I thought it must've been Fran's room as a teenager, but when I looked at the contents, it was clear this room was from another time. Turns out it was Fran's mum's room, and it was exactly as she'd left it the day she headed to London. There were records, clothes, posters, school books, it was amazing. I couldn't stop myself from having a nosey around." Holding up a hand she continued, "I know, I know, I should've left, but I didn't. I snooped."

The look of chastisement cast her way was unmistakable. She remembered it well, but hadn't witnessed it in a very long time. "I saw a photograph of four punk teenagers on Portobello promenade. They were menacing, well, they were trying to be." Jessie recalled Toni Martin's take on the photograph, which presented an altogether different image. "One of the guys looked familiar. I didn't know him, but he reminded me of someone. There were names on the back of the photograph. One of them was Fran's mum, but no one else I knew of. I thought nothing more of it until I saw a woman in the *Portobello Reporter*. I thought it was Fran all dressed up, but Meadow laughed and told me it was Toni Martin—"

"What!"

Jessie smiled and nodded, "I've met her too. Meadow's dad and Toni are best friends. He works for her." Jessie was getting frustrated with the constant interruptions, "Now if you'd let me finish…"

"Please continue," her mum said. "But Toni Martin is a very successful woman."

"So I gather," Jessie added, exasperated. "Anyway," she went on, glaring at her mother, "I asked Meadow if Toni had a brother, and it turns out, she does, Ross. That was the name of the guy in the photograph who reminded me of someone. Now I knew Fran had no idea who her father was and I thought, what if?" Jessie paused, making sure her mum was following.

"I'm with you so far."

"I contacted Toni Martin and met her at the Illicit Still." Jessie didn't add that she had lured the woman under false pretences. The story was not painting her in the best light as it was. "She said Ross couldn't be Fran's dad as the dates didn't match up, so I thought nothing more of it. I thought I was wrong." Jessie shrugged. "But later, Toni remembered something and went to the Beachcomber and spoke to Fran's grandfather. She said Ross could be Fran's dad. He told Fran of the possibility and she sort of freaked out." Jessie briefly debated how honest to be with her mum about what happened next.

"Your face just turned an interesting colour, Jessie. I'm your mum, you can tell me anything. I won't judge."

Jessie scratched her forehead. "I know, but it's not easy for me to be so open about my life." At her mum's nod, Jessie knew she understood. "That afternoon, Fran turned up at my door. I had no idea why and we didn't exactly talk…" Jessie faltered. She cleared her throat. "We ended up in bed." Her mum showed no outward sign of any surprise, but Jessie still squirmed to have had to reveal that information. "When we did talk later, she told me what had happened. Oh, Mum, I felt awful when she said 'Why now? Why are they only telling me this now after all these years?' She was so hurt and confused, but I couldn't keep the truth from her. So, I confessed to my part in it."

"You did the right thing, Jessie."

Jessie rubbed her face. "I wish I'd never gone into that room. If I hadn't seen that photograph, none of this would've happened." Her voice was raw, full of anguish and sorrow.

"Don't be so hard on yourself. You had good intentions."

Jessie sighed. "But it created a lot of instability in a life that needs a solid foundation. Since then, Fran's struggled with her demons again. Hence, Nikki coming up from London to support her through the difficult time." Jessie paused. "That's how I met Nikki Demente. She came to one of our games. Madge Adams was with her. They're old friends." Jessie knew her mum would get a kick out of that detail later. "Nikki introduced herself to me that day and then turned up in the office to chat with me about Fran before she returned to London. That's when we had coffee."

Her mum sat back in the chair, surprise evident on her face. "Well, I may be the one who wants to take her life in a new direction, but you've certainly beaten me to the punch, darling."

Jessie nodded and smiled, but it faded quickly as she thought about the tension that currently existed between herself and Fran. "I want her, Mum, like I've never wanted anyone before. It's new and exciting, and it hurts like hell. Being rejected, especially when I know she feels it too—I can't accept that. It's driving me crazy."

Chapter 24

"What a day!" Jessie declared, as she wrestled with the office door, her hands full of brochures. Looking up when no answer came back her way, she was surprised to find the usually cheerful Meadow crying.

"Meadow? What's wrong?" Jessie deposited the brochures on the nearest available surface and went immediately to her distraught secretary. The teenager sniffed as she held a newspaper towards Jessie, before bursting into tears again. Jessie laid the newspaper on the desk while standing next to Meadow. She frowned as she searched for the article that had caused such upset. She saw the headline, with a picture of Fran inserted within the article. She was on the football pitch—it had been taken during the weekend.

WHERE ARE THEY NOW?

Fran Docherty grew up in the Portobello area of Edinburgh and left home at the age of sixteen to pursue a career in London. She experienced success early, and by her seventeenth birthday she was modelling and appearing in music videos, before briefly fronting the band Cannibal Roses. Cannibal Roses had been hotly tipped for success, and after a well-received tour of the UK, a major record label signed them. A young Fran Docherty was on the precipice of a life-changing career.

That's where the success story ended. Their first album was never completed after Docherty was sacked by the label on account of her increasing unreliability due to drug use. A gifted guitarist and singer, she worked as a session musician and toured sporadically with various bands before her habit spiralled out of control, and she disappeared into obscurity and a life filled with drugs, homelessness, and crime.

She busked around London, frequently ending up in police cells for drunk and disorderly behaviour until finally being imprisoned for selling drugs to fund her own habit. The judge at the trial stated that Docherty had "run out of chances", as he passed a sentence of five years.

The Docherty family are no strangers to disappointment and tragedy. Docherty was brought up by her grandparents after her mother died from a drug overdose when Fran was only four years old. Debbie "DeeDee" Docherty had also left home at the age of sixteen to head for the bright lights of London in the post-punk era. She worked with top fashion designer Nikki Demente until her untimely death at age twenty-two.

Fran Docherty is now back in town, running the Beachcomber bar after her grandfather, Harry, suffered a stroke last year. She is also to be found turning out each week for Lothian Thistle, the ladies' football team currently second from top of the Scottish league.

Has Docherty finally got her train wreck of a life back on track, or is it simply a matter of time until she pushes the self-destruct button again?

Jessie experienced a wave of dizziness. She knew this article would be devastating for Fran. Her sordid past was now laid bare, her secrets splashed all over the newspaper for everyone to read and titter over. Fran was immensely private, with good reason. Jessie's hands trembled as she swallowed back her anger at the injustice of Fran's life being invaded without any regard for the consequences.

"Why would they say that, Jessie? Poor Fran. It's terrible, and losing her mum like that."

Meadow held her face in her hands, shaking from the renewed sobs wracking her slender frame as Jessie rubbed her back. The article was dreadful.

"She should be left alone to get on with her life. This is horrible. They make her sound awful and she's not." Meadow's voice broke into a higher pitch on the final word.

Jessie nodded as she continued to comfort Meadow, pulling more tissues from the box on the younger woman's desk and handing them to her. "I agree, she doesn't deserve this."

"Why? Why are they doing this to her?"

Jessie shrugged. "There's been a lot of media attention around the club. We're doing well. Combine that with Nikki Demente showing up, I guess they've been looking for juicy stories."

"It's not right. They shouldn't be able to do something like this to someone."

"No, they shouldn't." Jessie knew what she wanted to do. "Meadow, will you be okay on your own for the rest of the afternoon?"

Meadow glanced up at her through red-rimmed, watery blue eyes. "Yes. Are you going to visit Fran?" She blew her nose.

"I am." She handed Meadow her mobile. "Take my work phone, cancel the two appointments I have booked for this afternoon. Family emergency. Tell them I'll call back tomorrow."

Meadow appeared to pull herself together a little. "You go, Jessie. I'll make sure it's all handled here. And tell Fran I send my love."

"Of course." Jessie hugged her. "It'll be all right. I'll see you tomorrow."

Jessie got into the car. She wasn't so sure that it would be all right, despite her reassuring words to Meadow. Fran, as she had found out, didn't deal well with bad news. She wasn't sure how welcome she would be but she knew she wanted to offer her support. She took a deep breath and drove to her destination.

She entered the Beachcomber, but Fran was nowhere to be found. Jessie stood outside the door to the main bar, debating her next move. Gary caught her eye as he handed a gentleman his change and momentarily stopped and stared at Jessie. She bit her lip, unsure of her next step until Gary inclined his head towards the stairs.

Jessie didn't hesitate. She took the wide stairs two at a time and headed for Fran's room, only to find it empty. She frowned as she paused in the doorway. Then it came to her. She knew where Fran likely was. She headed up to the top floor and stood outside DeeDee's room to catch her breath before she slowly opened the door. Grateful to find it unlocked, she quietly slipped inside.

Fran lay on the bed with her back to Jessie, wearing her usual faded jeans and T-shirt. Her worn, suede ankle boots were carelessly discarded on the wooden floor. Jessie removed her jacket and shoes, then cautiously walked across the room on the balls of her feet and gently tucked in behind Fran on the bed. She put her arm around Fran's waist and lay there, motionless. She was unsure if Fran was even awake, until a hand covered hers. They lay close together in silence on the single bed, Jessie offering comfort and Fran quietly accepting the gesture in the dull, grey spring afternoon.

Jessie stirred and opened her eyes. She'd been dozing but knew exactly where she was and who she was with. She had no idea what time it was or how long she'd been asleep as Fran lay snoring softly beside her. She closed one eye and managed to focus on her watch only six inches from her face. Nearly four thirty in the afternoon. Her stomach rumbled, but she had no desire to eat. She was happy to simply lie next to Fran, keeping her cocooned and protected from the pain that lurked outside. She idly caressed Fran's hip and considered her predicament. But she couldn't protect her. She was unable to imagine what it must be like to have all your darkest secrets revealed for everyone to read.

"What time is it?" Fran's voice was raspy from sleep.

"Four thirty," Jessie replied, her voice low.

Fran turned to her, their lips so close that Fran's breath ghosted over her face as she exhaled.

"I take it you've read the paper?" Fran asked.

"Yes." Jessie stared at her face. She had become adept at searching for clues there because she said so little. Right now, her eyes were dull, the whites murky, and the lines around the eyes radiating pain and tension.

Fran sighed. "I'm never going to be allowed to move on. Now everyone knows about my fucking past." She closed her eyes, appearing defeated. There was no anger in her voice, more a resigned weariness.

Jessie laid a palm on Fran's cheek. "It's not fair. Most people get to choose who they tell their secrets to, not have them splashed all over a newspaper."

Fran eyes were focused somewhere across the room as she answered. "I'm not most people."

"No. You're not." *In so many ways*, Jessie thought. "I'll stay with you if you'd like someone around."

Fran pushed up on her elbows. "We have training."

Jessie sat up, surprised that Fran wanted to train. "Sorry, I thought that you might want to give it a miss tonight."

Fran sat on the edge of the bed and rubbed her forehead. "I have to face everyone some time. Might as well be today." Her shoulders were slumped.

Jessie was impressed that Fran wasn't going to hide away. "I'll give you a lift."

Fran turned to Jessie. "Thanks. I appreciate that."

"What'll the reaction be?" Fran asked as they neared the turn for the training ground. She hadn't missed a session all season, and Jessie knew no one would blame her for not turning up tonight. Instead, here she was, ready to face everyone.

Jessie knew most of the team well, and she hoped that they would come through for Fran. In past situations, when a player was having a difficult time, the team tended to offer support. She hoped it'd be no different with Fran, and tonight she'd find out what being part of this team was really all about.

"You might be surprised." It wasn't exactly reassuring, but it was the best Jessie could come up with in the circumstances.

Jessie drove into the car park and shut off the engine. About to unbuckle her seatbelt, she hesitated, making sure they were alone. She turned to Fran. "Ready?"

Fran took a deep breath, released her seatbelt, and opened the passenger-side door, exiting the car.

Fran and Jessie rounded the corridor and found Ruth standing outside the lounge with the door open.

"I'm willing to bet neither of you have eaten since breakfast, so you'd better get in here and at least have some fruit before you train." Her no-nonsense tone indicated she wouldn't take no for an answer.

Neither Fran nor Jessie protested and followed Ruth into the hall where she guided them to a table.

"Now, sit down and I'll bring you both something over."

"Thanks, Ruth," Jessie replied as Fran managed a weak smile. The older woman cast a concerned glance Fran's way before leaving to fetch some food.

Zoe and Sophie approached them from the corner of the room. As they walked past, each gave Fran's shoulder a firm squeeze before making their way out of the hall. Fran was puzzled or maybe surprised, Jessie couldn't quite tell, but she was encouraged by the gesture from their teammates.

Ruth returned to the table with a plateful of sliced fruit and a jug of water. "You two make sure you eat all of that. Can't have you fainting while training." She lingered a moment and Fran looked up at the diminutive woman. "You stay strong, Fran, you hear me? We look out for each other here. We all have a past. Every one of us. It's what we do now that matters, and you're doing fine." Ruth's voice cracked as her emotions shone through.

Jessie knew the older woman cared very much for the players and had been hurt by the personal attack on Fran. "It's a bloody disgrace putting that stuff in the paper," she added. Then she walked off, clearly upset, her hand going to her eyes, wiping at the gathering moisture.

"We'd better at least try and eat something," Jessie suggested.

Fran nodded.

When they both entered the changing room twenty minutes later, Fran's kit was laid out neatly and her cupboard had been tidied. Maggie was standing, waiting to sort out Fran's piercings. Despite the quiet of the changing room, the atmosphere was filled with a resilient positivity that was collectively emanating from every player and directed towards Fran.

Fran walked over to her spot, spoke briefly with Maggie, and began to prepare for training.

The changing room door slammed into the wall due to the force it was opened with, shattering the silence.

"Have you lot seen this fucking article in the newspaper!"

Morven's outburst died on her lips as she stood with the paper in her hand. The door closing behind her. Every eye in the room staring at her. She cleared her throat. "Oh, I didn't expect you to be here, Fran." Morven's sudden switch from ranting to a strategic retreat would have been comical in normal circumstances but not now.

Jessie looked from Morven to Fran, who had stood up, her gaze darting around the room. Everyone remained quiet.

Fran swallowed. "Just so you all know, everything in the paper is true." She met the eyes of all her teammates.

"It's your business, Fran," Andrea said. "Whatever you did, you served your time, no need for it to be plastered all over the paper." There were murmurs and nods all around.

Fran's eyes stayed on Morven. Jessie knew the pair had built up a friendship and, with Morven being a police officer, perhaps Fran was especially wary of her reaction. As the two women met each other's gaze, everyone else waited.

Morven was silent for a few moments, before she raised the newspaper that was bunched in her fist, squeezing it tightly. "And that bit at the end was unnecessary. That makes it personal. That fucking reporter better be staying well within the boundaries of the law," she warned.

Some of the others became more vocal in their agreement with Morven's summation. "Bloody right!"

Fran shook her head. "I don't want any retribution, please. I just want to get on with my life."

There were nods, before the changing room quietened. But Morven, while slowly nodding along with the rest, didn't give the impression to Jessie that she was ready to let the matter drop.

"In that case, let's get out there," Andrea added. She clapped her hands together. "Move it, ladies, we've a big game at the weekend!"

With that, the team started to file out of the changing room. Tom was standing in the corridor. "Jessie, can I have a word please?"

Jessie hung back at Tom's request. He waited until all the players had left the room and stepped inside.

He leaned with one hand pressed against the wooden door and asked, "How is Fran?"

"Quiet, but resilient." Jessie thought that was a fair summation. "I was surprised she came tonight".

Tom nodded. "I wouldn't have blamed her, but it's good she faced the music head on."

"And the girls have pulled through for her. I think that'll help." She studied Tom, unsure how much of Fran's past he had known before today. "Did you know?"

Tom nodded. "She alluded to certain incidents when I spoke to her about signing for us. I told her it wasn't anyone's business." He rubbed at the short beard he'd been growing for the past few weeks.

"And now?" Jessie asked, needing to know if the revelations would make any difference.

"We go on as usual. She's been exemplary since she signed. Passed every drugs test, never missed training. I've no issue with this. But she might come in for some heat from the press sniffing around for more dirt." Tom chewed his bottom lip

"No doubt."

His expression remained pensive. "Keep an eye on her, will you?"

"Of course." Jessie intended to do just that if Fran would allow her.

Fran rubbed her face as Jessie pulled into the side street next to the Beachcomber. It had been a long day. She was physically and mentally drained, and grateful for the silent journey home. When the engine stopped, she fumbled with the button to release the seatbelt. Jessie's hand covered her own, stalling her. She turned to Jessie, whose expression was open, sincere, welcoming.

"I'm here for you."

The simple words, spoken so softly, were almost her undoing. A lump sprung to her throat. The car was too small, suffocating her. Fran needed to get out. She nodded and pulled her hand away. She opened the car door and stepped out into the night air. She gulped it in.

Fran's legs were shaky, but she managed to move in the direction of the promenade. She eventually sat down clumsily on one of the pale green, wooden benches, her long legs splayed out in front of her. She stretched her arms along the back of the bench and tipped her head towards the dark sky. It was the first time she'd relaxed in hours. A day of tension and temptation had passed, and she was still sober.

The display of unity at training had been touching but overwhelming. Jessie's offer of support was just too much. Spending the day right by Fran's side and then telling Fran she would be there for her…she didn't deserve it. She didn't deserve her. But here she was, regardless of what Fran thought.

Since her frank confession a few weeks before, Jessie had said nothing. Quietly going about her business, courteous, but keeping her distance. Just like Fran had wanted.

But in truth, she hurt a little more every day as realisation dawned that she'd managed to drive Jessie away. She hadn't wanted to. In an act of rare unselfishness, she'd done it because she'd believed it was right for Jessie. She cared for her too much to want to hurt her. Pushing her away would save Jessie a world of pain in the long term. Now, knowing Jessie was still there for her was both heartening and terrifying.

Her boots scraped along the terracotta-coloured tarmac as she pulled her legs back in towards the seat. Leaning her elbows on her thighs, she sat forward on the bench. She stared at her hands, fiddled with her fingers, and tried to make sense of her life.

She knew she'd reached an impasse, but she wasn't sure she could move forward. She wasn't sure she was ready—or strong enough—to take the next step. Yet the thought of remaining as she was held no solace. She was stagnating, allowing life to pass her by. Jessie was right. She'd shut herself away. Even though she worked each day and was part of the football team, she made no effort to integrate or take part beyond what was absolutely necessary. Instead, she remained distant and closed off.

So why did the thought of taking another step forward terrify her? Her stomach clenched as she turned it over in her head. It had been so long since she'd allowed herself to feel. So long that she could no longer be certain of the signals her body was sending. Was it a pang of anxiety or anticipation?

Fran stood, attempting to shake off the thoughts, but found herself stopping. She was running again, she realised. Perhaps she needed to allow the thoughts to roam freely in her head. Perhaps that way, she could make progress. Take a step, however small, and find out where it led.

She had to do something. She just had to. Because keeping busy and hiding in plain sight no longer held the appeal it had a year ago. Now there was Jessie.

Chapter 25

"Fran!" Meadow exclaimed.

Jessie smiled. She'd hoped that Fran would pick up their routine again after the past weeks of her making alternative arrangements for training and games. After shutting down her computer, she made her way to the front office and couldn't help overhear the conversation.

"I'm so glad to see you. That newspaper story was terrible."

Meadow was hugging Fran when Jessie entered the front office. She was a little envious of her secretary's ability to easily show her affection in public. Fran was returning the hug, rubbing Meadow's back.

"I'm fine, Meadow." She smiled at Jessie over Meadow's head. Then stared at Meadow. "Really, I'm fine," she reassured the young woman.

Meadow nodded. "Good," she said, and offered a watery smile.

The pair parted, Meadow retreating back behind her desk to begin closing the office for the evening. It was approaching five o'clock.

"Come on, Meadow, time for you to leave. I'm closing up," she cajoled her secretary into leaving a few minutes early, smiling to emphasise her appreciation of the young woman's dedication and commitment. She was really going to miss Meadow when she finished up at the end of August.

Meadow slipped on her jacket and closed her bag. "Bye, Fran. Bye, Jess." She waved as she opened the door.

"Later, Meadow," Fran replied, as Jessie added her goodbye.

They were alone as the door closed behind Meadow, and Jessie took a moment to study her friend, for that was what they had surely become over the last few days. She just hoped it stayed that way.

"How are you *really* doing?" Jessie asked.

"Fine." Fran stood with her hands in the front pockets of her faded, black skinny jeans.

Jessie doubted that was true. She knew Fran was struggling with demons after the week she had endured and was still enduring.

"Don't you have a thing, you know, an oath about honesty as part of your recovery?" Jessie asked.

Fran shook her head. "Honesty is overrated."

"I disagree. Honesty allows people to know exactly where they stand." Jessie was fed up with the mixed signals. She knew Fran was fighting an internal battle, but remaining patient while she struggled was difficult. Fran was still staring at her. The dark smudges beneath her puffy eyes could almost pass for an injury, but Jessie knew the cause was a lack of sleep.

Fran had endured a week of hell. Her privacy had been invaded in a manner that was usually reserved for celebrities or politicians. Few people would ever experience the type of exposure Fran had had in the past few days. Added to that, there had been a steady influx of curious customers to the Beachcomber. Fran was the latest exhibit in town, and people were lining up to view it. Jessie had expected Nikki to appear at some point, but she hadn't been around.

"Well, if you need to talk, you know where I am." Jessie supposed Fran would always be a frustrating mix of silence with occasional bouts of reluctant verbal disclosure. And today she clearly wasn't in the mood for talking. Jessie knew she had to respect Fran's wishes and pushing wouldn't get her anywhere.

Training was going well. The press were easing up on searching for a story and beginning to concentrate once again on the team's fight for the title. Thistle were two points behind the league leaders, with two games left in the season. But the title was in their own hands. They played the current leaders, last year's champions, on the final day of the season, at home.

Two wins and the title was theirs. Jessie was excited and could hardly wait for the games to come around.

Fran sat next to her as she drove back towards Portobello. Fran had remained quiet throughout training. Her knack of being withdrawn while surrounded by others was infuriating, but Jessie had learned that Fran needed her space. She pulled up to the kerb. The evening was still light, the nights getting longer. She resisted the urge to sigh.

"Do you have time for a coffee?" Fran asked.

Jessie attempted to hide her surprise at the unexpected invitation. "Yes, of course."

"Great."

Fran got out of the car. Jessie blinked before she followed.

The Beachcomber was quiet as they made their way through the foyer to the stairs. When they reached the top, Fran led them to the kitchen where four of the students were having a late dinner. They greeted Fran warmly, then collectively stiffened when Jessie appeared behind her.

"Don't worry, I'm here with Fran. Enjoy your supper." Jessie smiled, but the students remained quiet.

Fran inclined her head towards her room. "I'll bring the coffee in."

Jessie was thankful for the escape. Remaining in the kitchen while the tenants ate dinner would have been uncomfortable for all of them. It appeared that they either weren't aware that Fran was their landlady, not Jessie, or simply didn't treat her as one. Jessie smiled to herself, knowing that was no doubt the way Fran wanted it.

Fran entered the room a few minutes later, two mugs of hot coffee in her hand. Jessie was in her usual place on the chaise longue. Fran handed her one, then took a seat on the edge of her bed and kicked off her suede ankle boots. She leaned back against the headboard, one leg stretched out in front of her, the other bent at the knee. She took a sip from her cup.

Jessie remained quiet, hoping that Fran would talk.

"These past few days have dragged up a lot of memories for me. It's...unsettling."

Jessie peered over the top of her cup of coffee, pleased that Fran was opening up. "I'm sure. It must be awful having your life splashed all over the media."

Fran studied her hands as she pressed the tip of each finger on her left hand individually between the thumb and forefinger of her right, a habit Jessie had observed many times over the past months. Raising her head, she stared at Jessie, her eyes narrowed. "Do you remember the night Kenny played here?"

How could she forget? "I do."

"That's the last time I had a drink."

The impact of that statement hung in the air. Jessie had naively assumed Fran had been clean and sober all season.

"It was an accident. I was drinking Coke while I was performing. Someone must have assumed there was Jack Daniels with it. When I finished playing, I was really thirsty and picked up what I thought was a full glass of Coke and gulped it down. I'd drunk half the glass before I realised. It was strong, must have been a double, but I didn't stop. I drank the whole glass." Fran paused, picking at some lint on her jeans. "I knew I was in trouble, and I needed an outlet. I use sex as a distraction. A coping mechanism to get me through some difficult hours." Fran's eyes moved to Jessie.

Jessie let that fact sink in, remembering the Sunday Fran had turned up at her house and pounced on her.

"I was wired, and there was a bar full of alcohol and drugs. The barmaid..." Fran shook her head, a small grin on her face. "Her eyes had been tracking you all evening. I was jealous." Fran paused, and Jessie thought that must be difficult for her to admit. "You were dancing with a guy and she was crestfallen. I seized the opportunity. I'm sorry."

Jessie's eyes narrowed. "I was pissed off when I saw you both head upstairs. I was attracted to her and you knew it, didn't you?"

Fran nodded her acknowledgement. "She spoke about you, asked me if I knew you. I told her you were straight." Fran's admission was accompanied with a slight upturn of the corner of her mouth.

Jessie opened her eyes wide. "That's outrageous!"

She shrugged, apparently unrepentant. "I didn't like the idea of the two of you together."

Jessie halted the sip of coffee she had been about to take. The mug suspended an inch from her mouth as she stared, unmoving, at Fran. Fran didn't like the idea of her being with another woman.

Jessie placed the mug of coffee on the wooden floor, the drink forgotten. The silence between them stretched out, until Fran turned to pick up her own mug, breaking the intensity of the moment. But the words had been spoken, the impact of them startling. Jessie couldn't quite believe Fran had uttered them, but she had, and she'd created an opening between them.

Without directly referencing it, Fran had now twice alluded to the time she'd arrived that Sunday afternoon, wet from the rain and restless. Jessie pondered what might have happened afterwards had she not been the one to cause Fran's predicament that day. Would they have seen each other again? Or, as Fran had already implied, would it have simply been sex as a distraction for a few hours? Jessie could've been any warm body, until Fran said she'd been jealous of the attraction she'd seen between Jessie and the beautiful barmaid.

Jessie swallowed, and spoke for the first time about the incident that led to that Sunday a few weeks ago. "I regret not coming to you first with the information about Ross Martin."

Fran raised her eyes from the coffee cup she cradled on her stomach. "I know."

Jessie took a deep breath and forged ahead. "I was wrong. I thought by going directly to Toni Martin, I would be sparing you any unnecessary stress if my hunch was incorrect." She paused. "I'm sorry."

Fran tipped the mug, apparently examining the coffee remaining inside, before turning her eyes to Jessie, the mug again resting on her flat stomach. Jessie observed Fran's tongue slide across her front teeth, as her top lip rippled with the movement underneath.

"I didn't appreciate the subterfuge. I prefer people are upfront with me."

They held eye contact. Jessie nodded. "I understand." And she did. She had broken the fledgling bond she had created with Fran and she understood that it had interrupted the gradual trust that had been developing between them. She instinctively knew that Fran did not trust easily and rebuilding that confidence would take time. Was she being offered the chance?

"I watched your old music videos on YouTube." Everyone in the team had been watching them, along with thousands of others, given the escalating view counts since the newspaper article. When Fran had stood in for Kenny, Jessie had really had no idea what to expect, maybe some punk rock or indie rock. But that wasn't Fran's style. There had been a soulfulness underpinning her performance that evening.

Placing her empty mug on the bedside table, Fran answered, "I haven't seen them in years." She yawned as she pushed her fingers into her hair, messing it deliberately, the style she preferred. She stretched and rested her clasped hands on top of her head.

Jessie wasn't convinced by her laid-back demeanour. "There's a promo video for a single, 'The Ghost of You'." Jessie recalled viewing it when she'd got home the night when the exposé had been in the paper. She had tapped her foot to the beat as a teenage Fran performed with a mixture of raw attitude and passion. When the song finished, she had sat open-mouthed, before muttering a silent "wow".

"It's beautiful." She frowned, biting her bottom lip. "Is it about your mother?"

Fran nodded, exhaling loudly. "Yes." She crossed her legs, stretching them out. "I'd gone down to London to be close to her. To get a sense of where she went and why." Fran stalled, lines creasing her forehead. "Turns out, I was chasing a fucking ghost." The harsh words were laced with a bitter undertone. "I spent my time meeting people who knew her in places she had been, and all I heard was how wonderful she was. How they missed her and what she could've become. There I was, in the same world. The music and the fashion had changed. But the only real difference with the drugs was that there were more of them. And I liked ecstasy. A lot. I started on that. It was brilliant. I felt totally alive and full of love. Life was amazing. Clubbing every night, parties, the music, the girls—I couldn't get enough of it."

"You're glorifying drugs." Jessie was surprised, a hint of censure in her voice.

Fran sighed. It was long and heavy. "Until you try drugs, you'll never really understand what using is like."

"I know drugs are addictive," Jessie protested.

Fran nodded. "Some drugs are addictive because the body adapts to them. When you stop using them, the body's in a state of flux, because you've created a chemical imbalance. That's withdrawal. Nicotine, heroin, alcohol, they all do that, but that's only part of the story."

Jessie sat in rapt attention as Fran became the orator, stringing sentences together, opening up for a rare conversation.

"A habit is hard to kick and withdrawal is hell; that much is true. But drugs are enjoyable. Heroin is addictive, but the craving of that ultimate high, that feeling of invincibility," Fran shook her head, a soft smile on her features. "It's immaculate, as Jim Morrison once said." Fran appeared to relax purely at the memory, while Jessie was horrified.

"People take drugs for many reasons, and you hear a lot about addictive personalities and needing a fix to escape, but what you aren't told is how wonderful drugs can be. I'm not addicted to heroin at this moment, but knowing how amazing it can make me *feel*. And, well, that's a whole different temptation. It's never black and white, Jessie, that's what people don't get. It's never just about one thing. There are as many shades of grey as there are addicts and ex-addicts in the world."

The way Fran said the word "feel" conveyed so much. The emphasis she placed on those four letters. The way she dragged on the F, as her face slackened and her eyes became hooded was both enlightening and terrifying to Jessie, that the mere thought of this drug could create such a response in Fran. She shook her head, and replied, "I can't even imagine taking drugs."

Fran smiled. "I know. You don't crave that danger or added excitement. As I said, I got hooked on heroin, and after the band failed, heroin was all that interested me for large chunks of my life. I got some work as a session musician, but the drugs were getting in the way and the offers quickly dried up. I was unreliable and that was no use to the studios that were offering me work. I left Nikki's because she was trying to help and I didn't want it. I started busking for drugs money. I got robbed and beaten up a lot." She smiled a bittersweet smile. "I was a mess. I went back to Kenny's thinking he'd leave me alone, but he tried to help too. On at me every day, telling me my habit was out of control." Fran shook her head. "There's a reason Kenny is still on this planet and touring most of the year. He's a smart user. He never lets it spiral out of control. When you have other drug users telling you how bad your habit is, you know you're in a terrible place."

Fran shuddered, as though shaking off some horrible memory. Jessie sat quietly, not wanting to interrupt the flow of words.

Fran continued, "I ended up on the streets, in squats, hostels, shelters. Sometimes wherever I fell. Periods of my life are blank. Just totally blank. I have no idea what happened during those times. I have flashbacks and nightmares. I struggle to separate what's real in them, which in itself is fucking disturbing."

It appeared Fran couldn't stop. Jessie was surprised, but eagerly lapped up every word as Fran finally opened up about her past.

"I got into a cycle of getting clean and getting work, which led to me touring with bands where the drugs and alcohol flowed freely, and I'd end up back on heroin. Then the cycle would start all over again. Countless times I've been through this. So many attempts to get clean, I don't know exactly how many, maybe ten, fifteen? I've failed every time." She raised her eyes to the ceiling. "I've tried it all, Jessie. Smack, speed, coke, and everything else you can imagine in between. That's why my only choice is to stay clean and sober. It's the only way for me. I want to succeed this time."

Fran rubbed her face with both hands. "I've been arrested a few times. Mostly for possession, but there have been breaches of the peace, drunk and disorderly conduct." She took a deep breath and let it out. "I'm not proud of any of it. When the charges racked up, I ended up in jail for the first time. A short stretch, that time. I was twenty-two and hooked on heroin again. I'd been avoiding jail with stints in rehab, but this judge'd had enough of me." She laughed, but there was no humour in it. "It's ironic really. It's as easy to get drugs inside as it was on the street. I've been on methadone, but it never helped me kick the habit. When I was released last time, Nikki was outside waiting for me. She asked if I wanted to have one last go at getting clean. No clinics or methadone this time. She said, 'If you're serious, get in the car. If not I'll be at your funeral'. Then she just sat in her car waiting for me to decide."

Fran pinned Jessie with eyes full of intensity. "I've been clean since, and by some miracle, got no infectious diseases." She settled back against the pillows. "I wasn't always careful. I was lucky. I wouldn't have slept with you if I had anything." Fran appeared tired, weary.

Jessie was relieved. Knowing now what she did, the possibility that Fran may have a drugs-related illness had niggled somewhere in the back of her head. She was left with one burning question. "Fran, how on earth did you become a footballer?"

Fran raised both eyebrows and pursed her lips. "Just have a talent for it."

Jessie was still puzzled. "Are you telling me you only took it up when you left prison?"

Fran laughed, genuinely this time. "No, I've been playing it for years. I've not always been off my tits. I went through periods of sobriety and I've always enjoyed football." She licked her lips. "When I got clean this time, I believed it would be a good way of instilling discipline and order into my life. A constructive distraction." She shrugged. "It helps."

When she left the Beachcomber a short while later, Jessie's head was spinning with the amount of information Fran had imparted. She was also stunned at the way Fran had opened up to her. As was often the case, some of her words made Jessie uncomfortable, especially the manner in which she'd spoken of drugs. Fran had appeared turned on as she'd waxed lyrical about the immaculate state heroin could achieve. Jessie shivered, trying to shake off the disconcerting memory, but it was too disturbing for her.

CHAPtER 26

As play stopped to allow treatment to an opposition player, Jessie anticipated that Tom would call her over to issue instructions. He stood on the sidelines, arms folded, looking more relaxed than usual. She supposed he could enjoy the match—they were winning 3-0, and the points were all but ensured for today. That just left the final match next week against the team top of the league. It'd be an all-or-nothing game against the current champions. She couldn't wait.

This was what they'd worked towards all season. Losing in the quarterfinals of the cup earlier in the season had been disappointing, but it had allowed them to focus all their energies on the league run instead. As much as Jessie would've loved to do the double, she knew losing in the cup was a blessing in disguise. The league was within touching distance, team morale was at an all-time high. But there were no certainties in football.

So she intended to enjoy the rest of the game, the three points secure. With less than fifteen minutes to go, she couldn't imagine any way back into the game for today's opponents. Picking up a water bottle, she took a long drink, then headed back to the centre of the pitch.

"Ow!" Jessie grimaced as she was taken down late in a challenge. She didn't want to get injured before next Saturday. She got back on her feet a little gingerly, and hobbled towards the sideline for treatment.

Tom's eyes narrowed as he scrutinised her movement. Turning to the bench he said, "Elaine, get stripped." Elaine Travers had been an able replacement in the absence of Jessie when she had served her three-match suspension at the start of the campaign. Jessie stepped back onto the pitch, knowing she was going to be subbed shortly.

Fran moved out of defence to confront an onrushing midfielder. Jessie frowned. Fran was out of position, which was unlike her. As Fran took the ball, her follow-through wiped out the opposition player. There was a long shrill blast on the referee's whistle, which brought a stop to the play. The ref brandished a yellow card at Fran, who didn't complain—she had been expecting it and Jessie knew why. She had cleaned out the player who'd fouled Jessie not two minutes before, exacting her own brand of revenge.

The resulting free kick from the foul was swung into the penalty box. It sailed into the middle and Fran rose above everyone else to clear it, taking an elbow to the face for her troubles. As Fran lay on the grass holding her head, Jessie ran twenty yards to push the player who'd elbowed Fran. Jessie reacted before she thought about it. Amid the pushing and shoving, Sophie had put her arms around Jessie and removed her from the melee.

"Take it easy, Jessie," she cautioned.

Jessie closed her eyes, knowing she had made a mistake. "I'm okay, Soph.".

"Ref! Ref!" She could hear Tom shout, trying to get the official's attention, but he simply held up a hand as calm was restored, not ready to deal with Tom. Jessie and the opposition number three, who had elbowed Fran, stood to one side awaiting his decision. The referee brandished each player a yellow card. Jessie's third of the season. She was rarely carded.

"Ref! Subs!"

The referee turned to Tom and gave a nod before signalling to the sideline to allow the substitutions to take place. Maggie was on the pitch helping Fran, who'd sustained a cut to her head. Fran was standing and appeared to be okay, but it was hard to tell. Maggie walked with Fran to the side of the pitch and continued to treat the wound. The two substitutes stood waiting for Jessie to make her way to the sideline, before being waved onto the pitch by the ref. As Jessie walked past Tom, he narrowed his eyes. She didn't linger, but went directly to the dugout where she received the congratulations of her teammates. She watched as Mo joined Tom, her eyebrow raised in question. Jessie couldn't hear the conversation, but got the distinct impression it involved her and Fran.

At the end of the game, Tom entered the treatment room. Jessie was sitting, waiting while Maggie examined the cut on Fran's head.

Maggie tutted. "I'm not happy about this, Fran. I'd prefer you go to hospital to be fully checked out."

Jessie scrutinised the gash on Fran's head, above her left eye. The swelling wasn't too bad, not surprising given how much it had bled.

"I'd prefer you stitch it here. I'm not going to hospital."

Jessie doubted Maggie was going to change Fran's mind. The physio frowned deeply as she once again used a penlight to check Fran's pupils, then asked her to touch her own nose. Maggie then held up one of her own fingers and asked Fran to touch it.

"You appear fine. I'll stitch it if you agree not to work this evening and have someone with you overnight."

"I'll stay with her," Jessie answered immediately, hoping Fran would agree.

Maggie nodded before starting the preparation to stitch Fran's cut. Tom leaned against the wall, arms folded, remaining silent as Maggie worked. Fran barely winced as the needle pierced her skin.

"I'd like to chat to you both before you leave," Tom stated.

Jessie knew they were in for a dressing-down from Tom. She and Fran shared eye contact as Maggie continued to work, unconcerned with matters outside her remit. The room dipped into silence while five stitches closed the gash in Fran's skin.

"That's you done, Fran, I'll give you some pain medication to take away with you."

"Cheers," was the quiet reply.

As Maggie cleared up, Tom took the opportunity to talk. "Whatever is going on between you two, is not my business." Tom held up a hand to stop Jessie interrupting. Her mouth closed and she nodded. "Personally, I'm happy you're finally getting along, but," he said and held up a finger, "when your private life starts affecting what you do on the pitch, that becomes my problem." Fran remained quiet, but Jessie was bursting to answer. "Fran, you took retaliation on a player because she fouled Jessie. That resulted in a yellow card for you." Fran shrugged, her legs dangling over the side of the treatment table. There was no denial. "Not only that, one of their players then elbowed you," he pointed towards her stitched head, "resulting in the injury and a possible concussion."

He turned to Jessie. "You ran *twenty* yards to push the player that elbowed Fran and got yourself a booking." Jessie's face heated, her head bowed. "None of this would have happened if you were both thinking clearly. Obviously emotions are…" Tom shook his head, apparently searching for the correct words. "Well, they're affecting your judgement. We have one monumental game left. I need both of you fit and focused. If one of you is fouled, let the ref deal with it. No retribution or remonstrating. Be professional." He paused, but Jessie knew he wasn't finished. "Your actions today, both of you, could have resulted in red cards, a ban, or serious injury. You'd have let yourselves and the team down, and I know neither of you want that." He took a breath. "Please, we have one last game. Don't mess it up." He glanced from her to Fran and back.

"I'm sorry, it won't happen again," Jessie spoke, contrite, not objecting to what Tom had said. He was right.

He turned back to Fran, who simply nodded slowly.

"Okay, well, enjoy the rest of the weekend and I'll see you both at training."

Maggie reappeared with the medication for Fran. She had made herself scarce while Tom had been speaking to them. Fran took the tablets, and she and Jessie left the treatment room.

CHapteR 27

JESSIE DROVE TOWARDS PORTOBELLO. SHE wished she was privy to the thoughts going through Fran's head. The tension in the car was strange, though not unwelcome. But she couldn't hold her tongue any longer.

"He thinks we're sleeping together."

"Yeah."

Taking her eyes off the road, she studied Fran, gauging her reaction to the statement. She appeared contemplative, possibly reflective. Her head tilted towards the passenger-side window, her injury currently hidden from view, and Jessie thought Fran had never looked more beautiful.

"How's the head?"

"Fine." Fran turned to face Jessie as she answered.

Jessie waited for the traffic lights to turn green. In just a few more minutes they'd be at the Beachcomber. She'd have loved to chat more to Fran, but Fran wanted silence and Jessie had learned to take her cues from her. The lights changed and Jessie drove towards the turning for the Beachcomber, only a hundred metres away.

"Can we go to yours?"

Jessie blinked in surprise and continued past the turn. "Of course." She hadn't expected that. She'd thought they would go to the Beachcomber where Fran would tell her again that she was fine. That there were plenty of people around to keep an eye on her. It meant Fran could rest properly and Jessie could move around without bumping into the students staying at the pub. She was getting fed up with the way they stood to attention whenever she arrived, hastily washing dishes and cleaning the kitchen.

Parking in front of the house, they both exited the car and made their way inside.

"Make yourself at home," Jessie said. "I'll get us something to eat."

Fran sat on the sofa and removed her boots and jacket. She appeared tired, her face drawn, and she winced as she sat down, the first indication of how much pain she was in.

"I'll get a glass of water so you can take those painkillers."

"Cheers."

When Jessie returned from the kitchen, Fran was stretched out on the sofa, eyes closed, lines etched around them. Jessie moved a side table over and put the glass on it. She contemplated nudging Fran awake but chose to leave her. She could take her tablets later. Jessie checked her watch. She'd wake her in an hour with some food.

Fran appeared rakish with the cut and the swelling above her eye. In a weird way, it suited her. It fit the image she portrayed to the world. Tiptoeing, so as not to disturb her, Jessie gently draped a blanket over Fran before heading to the kitchen to prepare dinner.

"Fran." Jessie spoke softly, but received no response. So she gently shook her shoulder. "Fran."

Deep blue eyes blinked open, confused and disoriented. Fran sat up, and rubbed at her eyes to rid them of sleep. "Ow," she muttered.

"Careful, you have stitches, remember?"

Fran shook her head and focused on Jessie. "I forgot."

"Your tablets are on the table." Jessie indicated the water and strip of painkillers. "I made us dinner. You want me to bring it through here?"

"No," Fran replied. She gestured towards the kitchen. "I'll join you."

Jessie was pleased by Fran's decision. Part of her still feared that she was going to flee at any moment, realising this was not where she wanted to be.

"Great. It's just soup and sandwiches. I hope that's okay?"

"Perfect," Fran murmured as she followed Jessie into the kitchen and took a seat at the table. The same one she'd occupied on a cold January evening only a few weeks ago. She'd surprised Jessie that night by reaching out, albeit in her own awkward way. Jessie had enjoyed the company. Fran was akin to a jigsaw puzzle and Jessie felt she was slowly fitting the pieces together. Just as she was making progress, the board would tip, scattering all the pieces back onto the large pile waiting to be picked up again and fit into place.

"How are you?" Jessie asked, as she stirred her spoon through the thick vegetable soup.

Fran swallowed the spoonful she had consumed. "Fine."

Jessie hadn't expected Fran to elaborate, but it was polite to ask. It also broke the silence, for a short while anyway. Jessie resisted the urge to sigh, and bit into her sandwich as she watched Fran eat. She had her head down, focused on the food in front of her, not making eye contact.

"What's prison like?" She'd been desperate to ask ever since Fran had told her she'd been locked up. It had been an attempt to sicken her, to prove that she was no good for her, and Jessie had struggled for a short while with the news. But in a strange, warped way, it only made her want to know more about Fran now.

Fran stopped eating, her spoon clinking against the bowl, discarded in what remained of the soup. She frowned and raised her eyes to meet Jessie's as she asked, "Why would you want to know that?"

Jessie swallowed. She knew she was back on treacherous ground. Sitting up straighter in her chair, she replied, "I want to know more about you."

Fran's expression didn't change as she continued to stare at Jessie. Jessie's heart rate increased, and she sensed that this was an important moment. Fran had shared some of herself with her. Now she was asking for more.

Fran sat back in her chair, her posture softening. Jessie resisted the urge to smile. She took it as a sign that the other woman was going to open up in some way. Fran was going to answer her question.

Fran rubbed the top of her left bicep, her right hand disappearing under the sleeve of her T-shirt. "I served three years of a five-year sentence for having a quantity of drugs in my possession that was too big for personal use. It was heroin and, yes, I was selling it." Fran paused and Jessie took the time to absorb that information. "I was in Holloway prison. You've probably heard of it." Fran leaned so far back in the chair her head touched the wall. "Some days, you could almost forget you were locked up. You get used to the routine. Nothing much happens beyond the usual. You start to filter out the everyday prison sounds. The constant jangling and click of keys turning in locks, the clanging of metal doors. Daytime in prison is usually uneventful, and often boring." Fran took a deep breath. "At night it becomes a place of human misery. Shouting, screaming, crying. There's just so much pain. Sometimes anger or threats, but mostly it's all about the pain."

Fran stared off somewhere. Jessie knew her eyes weren't focused on anything in particular.

"That's the part of prison that gets to you. Hearing the suffering and anguish that comes in the dark."

Fran sat forward in the chair, her forearms resting on the table. "Most of the women in prison shouldn't be there. I mean, an unpaid debt, probably because there were children to feed. A lot of women are in prison because they got involved with the wrong guy." Fran shook her head and continued as Jessie sat, rapt in the moment. "I could give you statistics, but they don't even begin to tell the story of domestic violence, drug abuse, mental health disorders, vulnerability, and guilt. A lot of the women suffer guilt, usually because they have children on the outside. Children who've been put into care. It eats you up to bear witness to it. The self-harm, the suicide attempts."

Fran stared intensely at Jessie and slowly turned her forearms to show the inside of them. Now Jessie knew why there were so many marks there. She willed herself not to cry, but the thought of Fran deliberately damaging herself hurt. Each mark on that lovely skin caused a mark on her own heart. Still, she said nothing. She knew Fran didn't require or want sympathy. Only understanding.

"Anyway, there are two things you can be certain of in prison—drugs and a warm body to keep you company. What more could a drug-addicted lesbian want?" Fran's laugh was mirthless. "There are educational classes and leisure activities. Christ, there's even gardening and hens to take care of, and some prisoners do well. They really do. But most will reoffend."

Jessie thought about that. Would Fran end up back in prison? Could she be one of the few who do their time and never go back? She'd already faltered once.

"I have a chequered past, Jessie. I don't know what the future holds, but I don't want to end up back there. The key to that is to stay away from drugs and alcohol." Fran paused. "Even prescription drugs."

That explained Fran's reluctance to take the pills Maggie had given her, but it gave Jessie hope. She could only imagine the emotional scars Fran carried deep within her. Some had manifested physically, the result of a life long lived outside the realms of what society perceived normality to be.

Fran stood and started clearing the dishes from the dinner table, a sign the conversation was over. Jessie gathered the leftover food and put it in the recycling bin as Fran started to fill the sink with hot, soapy water. Jessie didn't stop her, enjoying watching her perform the domestic task. It humanised her in a way no words could.

With the kitchen cleaned, they moved into the sitting room, Fran on the sofa and Jessie in an armchair.

"Do you want the television on? The football highlights will be starting."

Fran stretched. "I don't watch TV."

"Ever?"

"Not in a long time." She lay back on the sofa, tucking a cushion under her head, her face turned towards Jessie. "You go ahead."

Jessie shook her head, "No, I'm all footballed out for the day."

Fran smiled, then closed her eyes. Jessie sat in the dim light and again observed her for a few minutes. Fran's breathing evened out as she fell asleep.

Jessie got up quietly and retrieved her laptop. She pulled a footstool over, opened the machine, and checked her emails. It was difficult to concentrate on work. She moved some mail into a folder to answer later, others she deleted, but her eyes kept returning to Fran.

She closed her laptop and picked up her iPhone. Some texts had come in while they'd been in the kitchen. Mostly from teammates asking how Fran was. Jessie returned the texts with the same message: "Fran's okay, I'll text you tomorrow." She glanced at the clock. She was shocked by late hour—it was almost midnight. She hadn't expected Fran to stay and she still might leave at any moment. She rubbed her eyes. When she opened them and found Fran staring at her.

"You should go to bed."

"I promised Maggie I would keep an eye on you."

Jessie wanted to suggest that they could both go to bed, but she didn't want to push or risk rejection. They'd been getting along well since the newspaper article, but beyond Jessie holding Fran that afternoon in the turreted room at the Beachcomber, there'd been no physical contact between them.

Fran stood from the sofa and held out her hand. "Come on."

Jessie stared at the hand in silence, the tension building with each passing second. Was Fran going to simply put her to bed or was she going to join her? Jessie knew what she wanted. She took hold of the hand and was guided to her feet before being led to her bedroom.

Jessie hesitated as they stood next to her bed. Fran still held her hand. She turned and searched Fran's face for a clue as to what she wanted, but her face was partly hidden in shadow from the only light spilled in from the hallway. It left Jessie more confused.

When Fran placed a warm palm on her cheek, Jessie swallowed and welcomed the abrasiveness of her skin. She had become used to the roughness of Fran's hands, the scars mixed with callouses, which she now knew were from playing guitar. Her breath hitched as Fran dipped her head, closed the gap between them, and captured Jessie's lips in a soft kiss.

She welcomed the connection. She'd wanted this to happen again after the many weeks since they'd made love. Because that was what it was, despite Fran's claims to the contrary. Jessie knew it had been more than sex. Everything they did, every conversation, every silence they'd shared had been underpinned with the fragile attraction between them. It was undeniable, and now it appeared that Fran was embracing the fledgling relationship, inch by precious inch.

Jessie moaned as Fran deepened the kiss. The slow, languorous give-and-take between them was blissful. The quiet, darkened room disturbed only by a soft sigh as they held each other. The kiss gradually came to an end, a healing of sorts, a sign she had finally been forgiven. Jessie accepted the change, this shift in their relationship.

Fran may have tried to drive her away with stark realities of the seedier excesses of life, but ultimately, that knowledge had only left Jessie wanting more of Fran. Wanting more of the woman she was now. Far from being repulsed by Fran's past, it impressed upon her just how much progress she had made in her battle with addiction, in moving forward with her life. Confronted with the flaws, Jessie was scared, but she didn't want to run. No, what she wanted was to be part of Fran's journey. To embrace the future with her. If there was a hiccup along the way, she believed they could face it together. As Fran reached for the hem of her T-shirt, Jessie hesitated, unsure if they should take this further.

"Your head," Jessie protested, but was silenced with a finger placed on her lips.

"I'm fine," Fran whispered.

"But…"

"Shh." Fran prevented any further protest by placing her lips over Jessie's, kissing her, as she slowly raised the T-shirt over her breasts. They pulled apart long enough for her to remove the top completely, before she kissed Jessie again, deeply. Her calloused hands roamed the soft skin of the newly exposed flesh. Rough fingertips brushed the underside of Jessie's breasts, then trailed down across her stomach, to unbutton her trousers.

Jessie's heart beat furiously in her chest. The deep-seated desire in the pit of her stomach ignited at the thought of making love to Fran again. Her breath caught as Fran's hands slowly peeled away the layers of clothing until they stood together naked, the hurt falling away with each discarded item.

Jessie shivered with pleasure as their bodies touched the length of each other, their breasts pressed together. They began to explore each other anew, reacquainting themselves, as hands searched and caressed.

Fran devoured Jessie's lips, sucking and pulling at them with her lips and teeth, before pushing her tongue deep into Jessie's mouth. Jessie caressed and licked Fran's tongue, while pressing a muscled thigh between her legs, eliciting a gasp of pleasure from her. Slick juices coated her thigh as Fran pressed against her, thrusting her hips, while she grabbed Jessie's buttocks, grunting as her rhythm increased.

"Oh, fuck!"

Jessie knew Fran was close, but she didn't want her to come just yet. Manoeuvring Fran onto the bed, she lay back on the cool sheets as Jessie settled on top of her. She searched Fran's eyes, needing to be sure that this was more than a fuck to take the edge off. What she saw was an open, wanton expression that spurred her on.

She caught Fran's lips in a searing kiss as she pushed her hand between Fran's parted thighs. She was so wet. Jessie pressed the tips of two fingers against Fran's opening, pausing a moment before entering her in one smooth motion. Fran's head pressed back against the sheets, her mouth open.

"Oh, yeah," Fran hissed as her walls contracted around Jessie's fingers, pulling them inside her hot centre.

Jessie began a steady rhythm, pumping her fingers in and out, as Fran grunted on each deep stroke. She picked up speed to match Fran's dancing hips. Sweat beaded on her forehead as her own hips pushed against her, their bodies grinding, Perspiration coating their heated skin as Jessie took Fran harder.

"Fuck me, yes, fuck me," Fran demanded through gritted teeth.

Jessie stilled her fingers and Fran's eyes opened wide, an objection on her lips halting as Jess encouraged her to turn onto her front. Fran needed no more instruction as she raised herself on her knees, her face buried in the pillow as Jessie pumped her fingers harder and deeper until Fran's muffled cries of passion filled the room.

Jessie slowly removed her slick fingers, as Fran lay spent, face down, breathing rapidly. She smoothed her palm over the sweat-soaked back, running her hand all the way up into the damp hair at the back of Fran's head. She swallowed back the lump in her throat as she caressed the back of Fran's neck, relishing this rare moment of vulnerability.

Fran turned over and took in a deep breath, a small contented smile on her face, eyes hooded as she reached for Jessie. "I'm done."

Jessie smiled, leaning over her lover. "Lift your leg for me," she requested, releasing a shuddering breath as Fran's thigh connected with her pulsing clit.

Jessie was so turned on, she couldn't wait any longer. She took Fran's hands and pinned them above her head, rocking faster, her heartbeat matching her thrusts, strong and rhythmical. She stared, open-mouthed, at Fran, before climaxing and collapsing on her. Jessie finally released Fran's hands as the last of her climax ebbed, leaving her limp, a smile on her bruised lips, and her heartbeat slowly returning to normal.

Fran held her, smoothing her palms over Jessie's back and shoulders, as she lay, silently absorbing her weight. Jessie snuggled into Fran's neck, the pulse beating strongly beneath the skin. She took most of her weight off Fran's body and left an arm strewn across Fran's waist as she drifted off.

"Tell me more about your life?" Jessie asked, her head on Fran's shoulder, as they lay in the dark. She had woken a few moments ago, delighted with Fran's hand slowly moving over her back, lazily drawing patterns on her skin.

Fran shrugged. "Nothing much to tell."

Jessie knew that was an outright lie. "Tell me more about London. You said you went to be close to your mum?" She rubbed her palm over Fran's chest, enjoying the bare, smooth skin.

Fran took a long breath and exhaled through her nose, her hand in Jessie's hair, massaging her scalp. "I was young, sixteen, almost seventeen, but I looked older, and I thought I was mature." Fran snorted, indicating, she was anything but. "I finished school. My grandparents wanted me to stay on until I was eighteen, and hopefully go to university, but I knew better than anyone else." She gave a small shake of her head. "I hated school. I hated the strict regime imposed upon me, especially in a place like George Heriots. I was always flouting the rules of the uniform, adapting it, being rebellious. It came naturally to me. I rebelled against my grandparents, school, anything that was constraining. I'd planned to head to London the year before, made up my mind, and nothing was going to change it. I knew Kenny would offer me a place to stay. He was a soft touch, always has been." Fran yawned.

"I told my grandparents I was going for the summer. I already knew I wasn't coming back, but the lie made leaving easier. I know they must've feared the worst, especially after going through the same thing with my mum." Rubbing her face, Fran continued, "I regret hurting them, I really do. I was young and selfish. All I thought about was my own satisfaction and freedom. I grabbed my guitar, packed a holdall full of clothes, and took the train to London."

She became silent and Jessie waited, hoping there would be more.

"I went with a plan," Fran continued. "I would stay with Kenny. I knew he and Nikki would introduce me to people down there. They have lots of contacts. I got some modelling work through Nikki. She said I could make a career out of it if I chose to, but I only did it for the money. What I really wanted was a career in music. Kenny asked me to join him for part of his tour, but I wanted to stay in London, not be travelling all over the UK, spending less than twenty-four hours in any one place. I loved London. There was so much going on. The club scene was amazing and I had no problems getting into venues. Before long, I was partying almost every night, and recreational drugs went hand in hand with the club scene. Pretty much everyone was doing coke or ecstasy, and I enjoyed them too.

Sometimes both. That's called a bluelight. Highly dangerous, but it's so smooth if you get it right."

Fran dipped her head to stare at Jessie. "I was wild. Totally out of control, living life to the full, or at least, my seventeen-year-old version of living life to the full. Soon I was being ejected from clubs for my wild behaviour, getting a bad reputation." Fran pursed her lips. "Then Nikki first stepped in. She moved me out of Kenny's place and into hers. Put me in contact with some of her friends. That's when I got the band together. Nikki advertised for musicians to send us recordings of them playing, and then we asked the ones we liked to come and audition. Nikki did everything. I doubt I would have got a band together without her. We chose three guys, all in their early twenties. I had always envisioned fronting a male group. The guys were good, and by then, I was pretty decent on lead guitar. The one thing that had interested me all through school was the guitar, and I'd had lessons right up until I left school. I started to write songs and we rehearsed for weeks before we did our first gig at a small venue in London. We developed a following, and before long we were being noticed. When we signed an album deal, we had several offers to choose from. Everything was going in the right direction. I was on the precipice of achieving all I dreamed of. We were about to make it big if all the music magazines and critics were to be believed."

Jessie was amazed. Fran had been on the brink of stardom and had lost it all. She waited as Fran appeared to be gathering her thoughts, staring up at the ceiling.

A soft sigh left the taller woman's lips. "Unfortunately, in my seventeen-year-old brain, that meant acting like a complete brat. I thought I was already a star. We hit the recording studio, but the album was never finished. My drug habit saw to that." Fran scratched her head. "Had it been any other band member, they could've been replaced, but I was the frontwoman and despite all my dreams of stardom, the bottom line was that fame didn't sit well with me. I was using heavily to try to cope with being thrust into the limelight, and we hadn't even hit the big time. My dreams were about to come true, but I couldn't handle it. By my eighteenth birthday, I had a heroin habit and the record company cut their losses. They knew there was little chance of me holding it together to tour and make them money.

We were dumped and I was such a mess I didn't even care." Fran laughed mirthlessly. "Truth be told, I was relieved."

Fran became quiet, and Jessie knew she was finished talking. She knew not to ask anything more at this time, despite wanting to. What a pity that Fran had not fulfilled her dreams, her potential. Her talent would remained largely untapped, her songs never to be heard by mainstream music audiences. From Fran's telling, attempting to fulfil her goals simply wasn't something she was wired to cope with. The pressure that a high-profile music career would bring had just been too much for her.

"It's such a shame you didn't make it." Jessie spoke quietly, but there was no reply.

Chapter 28

THE CHANGING ROOM WAS CHARGED with anticipation and nervous energy. Jessie could feel it coming from her teammates in waves.

They needed to win today. The highest position they'd achieved thus far was third last season. This time they could win the league. Anything less would result in another season without a trophy. They'd never been in this position before. Experience was on the side of those in the away changing room today, but Thistle had the home advantage.

Jessie removed the training kit she'd used in the warm up and began the methodical process of putting on her strip. The flutter in her stomach wasn't unwelcome; yes, she was nervous, but she was keen to get out on the pitch and give her all. She'd hold nothing back. She just hoped it would be enough.

First, the neatly ironed shirt, turquoise blue, with a navy trim, her name printed boldly on the back in navy letters, the sponsor's logo emblazoned across the chest. Jessie pulled it over her head, shrugged her shoulders, and let it settle in place before tugging her shorts up her legs.

She walked to a bank of mirrors to check and redo her hair, making sure it was secure behind her headband. The face looking back at her in the mirror was focused, serious, determined. Jessie walked back to the bench, sat down, and slipped her socked feet into a pair of lime-green football boots before securing the laces. Finally, she pulled two navy sweat-bands onto her wrists. She was ready.

Jessie looked at Tom. He was dressed smartly in one of his many skinny suits, light grey this time, with a bright white shirt and a slim striped tie that reflected the club's colours. He took up a prominent position inside the changing room. He glanced around, catching the eye of every player and nodding slowly, his hands tucked in his pockets.

"This is it," he said. "Our whole season will be defined by the next ninety minutes." He paused. "We've worked all week on the game plan. Every one of you knows how to execute it." The players nodded silently. Tom removed his hands from his trouser pockets, clenching his fist. "You, all of you, are good enough," He pointed to himself. "I know it." He thumped his fist to his chest. "I know it and so do you." Tom let his words sink in. "You've all worked tremendously hard this season." He nodded as he looked around. "You're a fit, dedicated, talented team." He placed a finger in his left palm as he counted off the points he made, the last one making a slapping sound. He grasped the three fingers in his left hand, holding them tightly. "You deserve this title." He looked each of them in the eye. His gaze rested on Jessie. "All of you. Now go and make it yours!" He clenched his fists as he delivered the final words. The dressing room exploded with a cacophony of noise as players shouted and released some of the nervous energy.

Tom held the door open and patted each player on the back as they passed. There was no more need for words. What they had left to say would be said on the pitch.

Jessie stretched her arms behind her back as the players lined up in the tunnel. There were claps and shouts from some of the players as they psyched themselves up. Jessie jumped up and down a few times trying to settle her nerves. This was the biggest domestic game of her life and she couldn't wait to get started. She'd never won a league title. This was her best chance.

She clapped her hands together as she shouted, "C'mon!", before taking a deep breath and blowing it out. She puffed out her cheeks, rubbed her hands together, and bounced a few more times. As they were about to leave the tunnel she glanced back and found Fran staring at her.

Fran inclined her head and Jessie nodded.

The team ran out to the pitch. The crowd was the biggest of the season, including a large contingent of travelling supporters on the opposite side to the home fans in the main stand. Jessie guessed there must have been around two thousand people. She'd played in front of far bigger crowds, ninety thousand at Wembley stadium when she represented Great Britain at the London Olympics, but here the fans were so close. She could see their faces, recognise individuals, in some ways, the intimacy added to the atmosphere. Thistle fans also stood behind each goal. Jessie knew her parents were in the crowd. It was the first game they had attended together all season. Usually her dad popped along to catch some of the home games, but they'd both informed her they'd be here today, offering their support.

After the coin toss and the respective captains had decided who would kick off and which end to defend, the Thistle captain Andrea Miller called the players towards her. They formed their customary huddle as she delivered her final words prior to kick off.

"We've worked for this, we deserve it. Let's do this for ourselves, girls. One hundred per cent commitment. No fear! Let's get the job done!"

The players dispersed with a spring in their step, and Jessie made her way to the centre circle. Thistle was kicking off the first half. She stood, hands on hips, with her boot resting on the ball, awaiting the referee's whistle. Her mouth was dry and her heart rate up. She wanted this so badly. They were ninety minutes from glory, but she couldn't afford to think that far ahead.

Jessie closed her eyes and inhaled through her nose, regulating her breathing. She took a few seconds to herself, allowing the sights and sounds around her to recede. She needed to be in the moment, to focus. Her shoulders relaxed as the tension ebbed. Jessie opened her eyes. She was ready.

When the whistle came, she calmly rolled the ball to Danika and set off for her position as today's lone striker. Tom had opted for a 4-4-1-1 formation, gambling on the opposition pushing for an early goal, then hitting them on the counter-attack. The strategy was to soak up pressure at the back and frustrate the opposition into a mistake as they over-committed.

As the match progressed, Tom's tactics seemed to be working, but a goal had eluded them. Fran dominated the central defence and headed clearances into the heart of the Thistle midfielders, Sophie and Andrea. They worked the ball out with short, crisp passes, and set up the counter-attacks Tom had asked for. Jessie had come close with a snap shot from outside the box that was tipped over the crossbar by the goalkeeper.

She was being marked closely, but she waited. Her patience paid off when the opposition defender was booked midway through the first half as she crashed into Jessie one too many times and the referee brandished the yellow card. With her marker playing more cautiously, Jessie began to find space to work in.

Another counter-attack followed a strong headed clearance from Fran. Sophie played a quick one-two with Andrea before floating the ball into her path. Jessie beat the defender, and closed in on the goal. The second central defender crossed over to cover her.

Instinct took over. Jessie knew Danika was making a late run into the box. She could feel it, she didn't need to look. She knew her teammate wouldn't let her down.

Jessie feigned to go outside again and played the ball inside instead. Right into Danika's path. Her finish was sublime. The onrushing goalkeeper went to ground, and Danika clipped the ball over her into the net.

Thistle were ahead 1-0.

Danika ran towards Jessie and jumped into her arms, wrapping her legs around Jessie's waist. Jessie held her, suspended for a few moments as they grinned at each other, before they were brought to the ground by the rest of their teammates.

The match was in their favour and their first title was in their hands. Andrea urged them to keep focus and remember the game plan.

At half-time the team sat in the dressing room, catching their breath and taking in fluids, while Maggie tended various aches and pains. Tom offered words of encouragement. They were doing well, executing the strategy, but they needed to remain focused. The pressure would mount, and Thistle had to be prepared for the onslaught.

"Great play, Fran," Tom said.

Fran raised her head from her seated position.

"Your clearances have been great, but they know what's coming. Their manager will be working on a way to deal with you. They weren't expecting it and it worked for the first half."

Fran said nothing as she waited for Tom's instructions. "I want you to find Zoe or Morven with your clearances for the second half." He looked away from Fran. "That goes for anyone else in defence who is clearing the ball. Find Zoe or Morven. We'll attack the wings and give them something different to think about. They're going to throw everything at you. They need a goal. Be prepared, and don't do anything rash. If you don't have a pass on, play the ball into the channels. Jessie'll be running them. Don't get nervous, don't panic."

Jessie knew it was a good tactic. Tom was always planning ahead, solving a problem while creating a new one for the opposition. Her stomach fluttered again as she had time to imagine winning the league. No. She couldn't think that far ahead, she needed to be back out on the pitch.

She rubbed her knee where she had taken a kick earlier in the game. It hurt, but nothing that was going to trouble her. She picked up a drink bottle, opened the top, and drank the sweet liquid, before washing it down with water. She extended her legs, pulling her toes up to stretch her calves. Tom went around individual players, offering final pieces of advice and instruction. When he got to Jessie, he crouched down beside her.

"Good first half, Jessie, great energy. We need more of the same. It could be a frustrating second half for you. We'll be on the back foot. If a chance comes your way, bury it."

Jessie nodded. She knew what was coming, but if she could find a way to nick a goal, it would certainly ease the nerves that would build throughout the second half. She held eye contact with Tom, her features set, full of determination.

"Great assist, and you've handled the centre half brilliantly." He squeezed her shoulder as he stood up. "Right, ladies, one big effort. This is it. Believe! You can do this!"

The players left the changing room in a more muted fashion than at the start of the match. They were nervous. It wasn't surprising, but they needed clear heads. The one player who never appeared to be fazed by anything was Fran. Her commanding presence at the centre of the defence was the reason Jessie knew they had a shot at this. She was unflappable.

She caught Fran's eye and smiled at the short nod of encouragement. Fran wasn't demonstrative, and the small show of emotion was more settling than any words could've been. The fluttering in her stomach receded as she focused on the job ahead—the final forty-five minutes of sweat and hard endeavour. There'd be tears. Jessie hoped they'd be joyful ones.

The second half started as Tom had predicted. Inchcolm United had changed tactics, but Fran continued to perform heroics in defence. Jessie didn't get much of the ball, but she selflessly chased down everything in her area of the pitch. She hurried defenders into passes and rushed the goalkeeper, hoping for errors.

The minutes passed by, and the team's only focus was defending their lead, not creating chances. Tom shouted from the sidelines for the defence to push up. To ease the wave after wave of attack. Jessie was tempted to get behind the ball, but she knew Tom would scream at her to stay farther up the pitch.

With fifteen minutes to go, the opposition were camped in the Thistle half, laying siege to the goal. Panicked clearances and misplaced passes showed the rampant nerves running through the team, escalating and spreading like a summer wildfire. The air was thick with the tension that echoed on the faces of the home supporters. Lips were bitten, hands went to heads, and each close shave etched an agony in the lines of every face. Pauline blocked the ball with every part of her body, making save after save, while Fran cleared everything she could get a foot or head to.

Inchcolm mounted another attack, pulling Fran out wide to intercept a player burrowing down the left wing. Fran won the ball and played a short pass to Andrea, who turned to play the ball forward, but lost her footing in the soft turf. Her unfortunate slip surrendered possession to Inchcolm.

Jessie held her breath. Inchcolm were two on one with the goalie. Fran was out of position, leaving a gaping hole in the defence. Lana didn't have the pace to get across in time to cover the second striker. Fran stretched out a long leg and clipped the heel of the player with the ball. She tumbled to the ground and the ball trundled harmlessly into the arms of the goalkeeper.

Jessie's hands went to her head as people screamed for a penalty. All eyes focused on the referee who was running to where the incident took place. The ref stood on the edge of the box and indicated a free kick, before going to her top pocket and brandishing the red card at Fran who sat on the grass fixing her socks, clearly in no hurry to leave the pitch. Jessie couldn't disagree with the sending off, Fran had illegally prevented a clear goal scoring opportunity. As the Inchcolm players argued for a penalty, Jessie ran across to Tom, who was gesticulating furiously with his arms towards her.

"Danika drops into central defence in place of Fran. You slot into her position. No crosses into the box, especially from the wings. Tell them to block everything! Force them to play through the middle." He grabbed a hold of Jessie's top as she was about to run off. "If you manage to get the ball, take it for a run, and eat up as much time as bloody possible."

He shoved her in the direction the Thistle players had gathered on the pitch. Fran was just getting to her feet, deliberately giving the team time to reorganise. Jessie relayed Tom's instructions as Fran finally, slowly, walked from the pitch.

The last ten minutes were frantic. Thistle players threw their bodies in front of everything that came their way, kicking the ball clear only for it to return time and again. They were encamped on the edge of their own box. Jessie put in as many tackles as the rest of her teammates.

One clearance went to the opposition central defender who dribbled the ball back into the danger area. Jessie got a foot to it, stayed on her feet, and chased it. When she looked up, there was only one defender to beat. The players behind her couldn't catch her. She only had one thought, and ran for goal.

As the defender came towards her, Jessie tapped the ball through her legs, collected it, feigned a shot to the right, then calmly stroked the ball into the bottom left corner of goal. She turned back up the pitch, arms aloft in jubilation.

Inchcolm were on their knees, the fight sucked out of them, while Thistle found a new gear. They were running, en masse, to greet her. Within seconds, she found herself at the bottom of a ten-player pile-up.

When the final whistle blew three minutes later, Jessie dropped to her knees, hands over her eyes, and sobbed. Her body shook with the force of the emotion. Relief and joy. The tension evaporated from her body. Each hiccupped breath a testament to a long, hard season, full of effort and hard work.

The tears ran down her cheeks as she finally realised her dream. But Jessie also wept for the off-field crisis she'd endured for the second half of the season. She was emotionally and physically spent. She'd left everything on the pitch today in more ways than one.

Scenes of joy unfolded before her eyes, pure euphoria erupting among the Thistle players and staff who ran onto the pitch to celebrate. Thistle fans were sportingly applauding the opposition as they trundled from the field, before turning their attention to the home team.

Many of the players sought out friends and family in the crowd. Jessie spotted both her parents, standing together in front of the main stand, their smiles beaming with pride. She ran towards them, as they both opened their arms wide to envelope her in a fierce congratulatory hug.

"Well done, Jessie, you were fantastic! The team was brilliant!" Her dad said enthusiastically, as he shook her.

Her mum added, "I'm so pleased for you, Jessie. I know how much this means to you."

"Thanks. Thank you both for coming along." She was smiling widely. "I hardly know what to do with myself," she laughed.

Her dad pointed towards the centre of the pitch. "Well, you'd better get ready for the presentation. It looks like they are about to make it."

Jessie's hands flew to her head. "We've done it!" Her parents again shared her joy and laughter. She waved and turned from them to make her way towards the players who were being ushered into a line to receive their winners' medals. Fran was a little ahead of her, quietly making her way towards the rest of the team. Jessie caught up with her and squeezed her shoulder. "Well played, Fran. I've never been so happy to see one of the team sent off. You were incredible." Fran bringing down the player just outside the penalty box had been crucial.

Fran shrugged off the praise. "Just doing what I'm paid to do."

Normally, Jessie would have bristled at that answer, but she saw it for what it was. Fran couldn't deal with praise and the attention it brought. She smiled at her sulky teammate.

"Yeah, well, well played anyway." In return she received the slightest flick of a smile. It was enough to warm her heart.

Chapter 29

Jessie sat at the long table surrounded by her teammates at the end-of-season dinner. Everyone associated with the club was in attendance, well, almost everyone. At the top table sat the staff who held the club together, including their main sponsor, Mr Laidlaw. He was making a rare appearance to hand out the awards. Jessie had earlier picked up the award for top goal scorer, and all that was left to be presented was the main accolade, the player of year, voted for by the team in a secret ballot. The excitement increased as they discussed who it would be this year. The room descended into silence as Mr Laidlaw approached the mic.

"Ladies and gentlemen, if I can have your attention please." He paused to allow the last remnants of chatter to recede. "I'd like to thank everyone for the huge effort that has gone into making this the most successful season Lothian Thistle has had to date. The capture of our first league title means we will play European football next season for the first time in our history. As you know, the Champions League games will be televised."

He waited to let that fact sink in. Jessie and everyone on the team was aware of this. Their star would rise, and some of them would become targets for the bigger clubs in Europe and America. It also meant that the club would have increased revenue to attract players in return. Jessie glanced up and down the table, knowing that some of them would be missing next season and new people would arrive—the bittersweet story of sporting success.

"I want to thank each and every one of you for the effort you've put in this year. It's been monumental." Applause rang out around the hall, not for the first time that evening.

"Of course, the players didn't do this all by themselves." Laughter rippled among those in attendance. "And I would like to take this opportunity to thank the people who, on a daily basis, help make this all possible."

Jessie joined in the applause as all members of staff—from Ruth, who did a great job in the kitchen, to Maggie, the physio—were individually thanked and invited up to the stage to receive a small gift.

"Finally, I'd like to thank one last person. When this man applied for the job of managing the team, I thought it was a wind-up." Mr Laidlaw moved his arm towards Tom. "This guy played at the highest level in the English premiership but, as we all know, his career was cut short. Instead of licking his wounds and feeling sorry for himself, Tom set about gaining his coaching badges. I think everyone would agree with me when I say that his drive, ambition, and considerable knowledge, have made the difference in the two years he has been here and made us the winning outfit we have become."

The room erupted again for Tom, who appeared a little bashful despite his years of attending award ceremonies on a much larger scale than this one. Jessie smiled at his discomfort in the limelight.

"He could've gone into football punditry. I mean look at him, is that not a face made for television?" More laughter rang out as Tom began to squirm in his chair. "Tom, I want to thank you for the job you are doing for this team. I don't know how long we'll be able to hang on to you, especially after winning the league, but you're doing one hell of a job, son. Everyone, put your hands together for Tom Matthews!"

Jessie clapped as loudly as she could. There was no doubt in her mind that no other available manager could have taken them to a league title this quickly. Tom's passion for the game, combined with his tactical knowledge and ability to pick players, would ensure he succeeded with teams far bigger than Lothian Thistle.

"Tom, if you'd like to come up here to present the final award of the evening?" Tom stepped up to the stage and joined Mr Laidlaw. "Right, ladies and gentlemen, we've reached that time when we present the final award to the best player, as voted for by the players themselves." Mr Laidlaw removed an envelope from his jacket pocket, opened it, and took a moment to read the name, before he nodded his agreement. "This year's player of the year is Fran Docherty!"

Everyone clapped and cheered, and Jessie momentarily brightened. She glanced towards the door in expectation of Fran breezing in to collect her trophy. Wishful thinking, as Tom stood with the trophy in his hand, smiled, and addressed the mic.

"As you may have noticed, Fran couldn't be here to collect this award in person. So, knowing that she isn't big on socialising—"

"She's done more socialising than all of us put together!" The heckle got a few laughs.

"As I was saying, knowing Fran couldn't be here, I gave her a call to ask her what she would like to say if she won this award." Tom smiled as he studied the trophy in his right hand. "As you can imagine, it wasn't a long conversation." He waited till the laughter had subsided. "She did have some words to share. Firstly, she wanted to thank me, yeah, I know, but it's true. She also wanted to thank all the staff. Ruth and George, who've looked after her so well, making sure her kit was ready, and making sure she got a few hot meals." Tom smiled over at the couple who were enjoying a rare night off to join in the celebrations. "She wanted to thank Maggie for all your hard work keeping her fit and taking care of her piercings." There was more laughter. "I promise you, I didn't make any of that up. She also wanted to thank Mo, for handling everything outside of football, and a big thank you to the fans for all the support."

Again, Tom paused to allow a few whoops and cheers. "Finally, she wanted to say a special thank you to all the players. You've all made her welcome and you stuck by her in her time of need." His expression became serious. "I'd like to add a few words about Fran. I already shared them with her in private, but I would be saying them if she were standing here now." He raised his chin slightly and swallowed. "I contacted Fran almost a year ago to ask her to play for us. She wasn't enthusiastic, some would say she has never shown any enthusiasm, but we struck a deal. It's no secret that Fran agreed to play for two years, for personal reasons, not for the love of the game. I know that fact wasn't to everyone's liking. Some were initially opposed to her joining us, and after the first weekend of pre-season training, it looked like the doubters were right. God knows, she cut it close a few times. I could go into all the incidents, but we don't want to be here all night." The room collectively laughed again.

"She proved us all wrong. She quietly and effectively went about her business. Turned up to every training session and every game. On the pitch she was professional and dependable. Fran added skill and a calmness to our defence that we have been lacking, and she's been a key factor in us winning the league. We've had the least goals scored against us of any team. We didn't score the most, but we were rock solid in defence. She could easily play in the national squad, but she's turned down the opportunity. We know her reasons—she can't give the commitment. I've had offers for her from all over the world, and she's turned them all down. She's going nowhere. She deserves this trophy and every one of you voted for her. Apparently, that's a first. I've been told we have never had a unanimous vote for player of the year. She's not here, but we all appreciate her, so let's hear it for Fran!"

Everyone in the hall stood and clapped for a player who wasn't even there. Fran had cast her spell over them all, and Jessie couldn't help but be amazed at how that had been achieved. Fran wouldn't want it, she wouldn't believe herself deserving of it, but everyone who had come into her life in the past ten months was on their feet applauding her.

As the evening wore on and the time nudged past eleven, Jessie hoped she could make a dignified exit, leaving the partygoers to move on to a nightclub. There was no way she was going to be dragged along this time. She still hadn't quite forgiven some of them for the kidnapping after the Christmas night-out.

"Jessie?" Tom called her as she was slipping out of the main room in the plush hotel in the centre of town.

She stopped outside the door, holding it open for Tom to exit into the hallway. He smiled at her. "I knew you'd be sneaking off about now."

Jessie shrugged. "You know me, I don't like to stay out too late at these things."

Tom raised his hand, which held the trophy that had been awarded to Fran. "I suspect you'll be seeing Fran before me. Would you give this to her?"

Jessie's face flushed despite her attempts to remain composed. Tom raised an eyebrow.

"Perhaps in the next hour or so?"

Jessie rolled her eyes as she snatched the award from Tom's hand. "Fine."

Tom laughed. "I never saw it coming. All that complaining you did about her…just look at you now."

Unbidden, a smile broke out on her face, and she shook her head. "Had anyone even suggested it prior to Christmas, I would've been indignant."

"Christmas?" Tom questioned, apparently surprised by this admission.

Jessie pursed her lips, nodding. "That's when I first started to see Fran as something more. Don't get me wrong, I wasn't imagining a relationship, but I thought perhaps we could be friends, of sorts." Jessie studied the award in her hand, a fond smile on her face. "I never imagined this happening when Fran first arrived at the club." Though she raised the award in her hand, she was referring to both that and the fledgling relationship they were pursuing together. "Anyway, I'll make sure she gets this."

Tom hugged her. "I'll be in touch soon. As you know, I'm going on holiday for a few weeks." He kissed her cheek.

Jessie wagged a finger at him. "Remember, you promised one more year."

"Don't worry, Jessie, I'll be back at pre-season training."

"See you soon. Have a great holiday."

———— ✧ ————

It was a little after midnight, and Fran was clearing out the last of the stragglers. The bar was stuffy after a long, hot day and airless night. Outside, there was barely a breeze to disturb the air. She was sticky and sweaty. As she swiped the back of her hand across her forehead, she saw Jessie entering the bar. They hadn't made any arrangements, but she'd hoped Jessie would pop in. She took a seat at an empty table and waited as Fran walked the last group of patrons to the main door of the Beachcomber and locked it behind them.

"You look nice," Fran complimented. Jessie had on a little black dress that fitted her in all the right places. She was beautiful—muscular and strong, with just the right mix of femininity.

"Thank you, I come bearing gifts." Jessie placed a trophy on the table. "I believe this belongs to you. Nice speech by the way." She raised an eyebrow in silent question.

Fran took a seat at the table. It was the first time she'd been off her feet all evening. Dipping her head, she studied the trophy. It stood about a foot high, a gold-plated cup on a solid oak base, engraved with her name and the year. "Thanks."

Fran was sure Tom had given a good speech on her behalf. Did it really matter if she didn't have much input into it? She'd agreed with the content that Tom had run by her. Had she been there, her acceptance speech would have consisted of the one word she had just spoken to Jessie, "Thanks", or maybe, "Cheers".

"Busy night?"

Fran leaned back in the chair. "Not too bad. A lot of people stood outside, though I doubt it was any cooler out there." She yawned, stretching her arms above her head.

"Well, I'd better be heading back. You need your rest." Jessie stood, lifting her clutch bag from the table.

Fran had expected Jessie to stay. She sat forward in the chair, surprised by the sudden turn of events.

"Or I could keep you company?" Jessie added.

Fran stood and held out her hand. Jessie took it and they walked upstairs to her bedroom.

"Would you like anything to drink?" Fran asked. She needed a cold drink herself.

Jessie smiled. "Water would be great, thanks."

When Fran returned from the kitchen, she stood in the doorway of her room, caught by the sight of Jessie standing barefoot at the open balcony door. She was staring out over the Forth estuary, a hand lifting the hair from the back of her neck. Quietly, Fran entered the bedroom and gently closed the door. Walking up behind Jessie, she placed a glass of cold water in her hand and wrapped her free arm around Jessie's waist. Slowly, she let the stress and strain of a busy evening behind the bar ease from her body.

They stood there, quietly absorbing the warmth of each other. Fran rested her cheek against the side of Jessie's head, inhaling the sweet scent of her shampoo. She placed a delicate kiss on the tip of the Jessie's ear, eliciting a shiver from her lover.

"You smell so good," Fran whispered, as she moulded herself into the curve of Jessie's arse, slowly grinding against the firm muscles.

"Mm," Jessie murmured, her head tilted to the side, offering Fran more access to her neck.

The moan of pleasure from Jessie spurred Fran on. She snaked her free hand lower on Jessie abdomen, drifting towards the juncture of her thighs.

Jessie laughed lightly, as she caught Fran's wandering hand. "If you keep that up, I'm going to drop my glass."

Fran didn't intend to stop. She'd wanted Jessie from the moment she entered the bar. From the day she had first encountered Jessie on a football field, if truth be told. But she'd never imagined wanting her again and again. Every day, or at the end of a busy evening behind the bar, instead of seeking her comfortable bed and a night of rest, she wanted Jessie. She needed her. She reached for the almost empty glass in Jessie's hand. "I'd better take that then," she whispered into her ear, making Jessie gasp.

Fran walked to the bedside table and put the two glasses down. She turned to stare at Jessie, only to find her staring back over her shoulder. The room was suddenly too hot. Fran couldn't stand the clothes sticking to her skin.

She reached for the hem of her T-shirt and pulled it over her head, leaving her bare chested. Fran swallowed as Jessie's eyes remained on her, dipping to her breasts, before returning to meet Fran's intense stare. Without taking her eyes from Jessie, Fran reached for the top button on her jeans, popped it, and slowly slid down the zip. The audible gulp from Jessie caused Fran's nostrils to flare, moisture gathering between her legs. Jessie reached for the zipper at the back of her dress, but Fran wanted to be the one to do that.

"Leave it," she commanded. Jessie's hand stopped, then dropped to her side.

Fran pushed the denim down her legs, pulling her boots and jeans off in one movement. She walked, naked, back to the open doors, where Jessie stood silently, waiting.

A hint of a breeze filtered in, disturbing the still air and ghosting over Fran's skin. It failed to cool her heated flesh.

Fran reached for the zip of Jessie's dress. Her hand trembled. She fumbled with the tab, before she got a hold of it and slowly pulled the zip open, the individual teeth separating audibly, increasing the tension in the dark room.

Fran carefully pushed the open dress off Jessie's shoulders, assisting the silk on its way down Jessie's bare arms, gathering at her waist. She ran the backs of her hands down the newly exposed flesh, before easing the dress over Jessie's firm backside to pool at her feet. Jessie stood with her back to Fran wearing only skimpy black underwear, her head turned to the side.

"You're so beautiful," Fran whispered, as she placed a soft kiss on Jessie's shoulder. She ran her hands over the smooth skin of Jessie's upper back before she unclasped the black lacy bra and pushed it slowly from Jessie's shoulders. The flimsy garment dropped silently to the wooden floor. Fran stepped into Jessie, her arms snaking around Jessie's waist, pulling her back into her lean frame. A soft sigh escaped Jessie's lips at the contact.

Fran absorbed the warmth from her lover's body, and ran her palms up Jessie's smooth torso, over her ribs, to rest on the underside of the Jessie's breasts. The weight of the pliant flesh filled her hands. Fran closed her eyes and pressed her lips to Jessie's neck. She sucked and licked at the pulse point as Jessie offered more of her neck. She grazed the flesh with her teeth before licking the abused skin.

Jessie arched her back, pressing her breasts into Fran's hands, as she reached behind and pulled Fran's hips closer. Fran gasped. She knew she wasn't worthy of this woman, but she couldn't help herself. Jessie turned her on like no one ever before. She squeezed Jessie's breasts, the softest part of the otherwise toned body. The nipples hardened under her fingertips, demanding more attention.

"You feel so good," Fran rasped.

Jessie turned her body quickly and met Fran's lips in a hungry kiss. Hands finally free, they roamed over Fran's naked form, down her back to mould her buttocks, again pulling her closer.

Fran thrust a thigh between Jessie's parted legs, pulled her onto the length of taut muscle, as Jessie ground her pelvis into the long limb. There was no time to make their way across the floor to the bed. Their need was too acute, too demanding. Instead, Fran manoeuvred Jessie onto the chaise longue that dominated the top of the room. She reached for the final barrier between them and pushed the lace knickers down Jessie's legs, desperate to taste her, wanting the essence of Jessie's passion on her tongue. She still couldn't believe that Jessie—amazing, beautiful, wonderful Jessie—allowed Fran's soiled hands to touch her precious body. She lowered her head to the juncture of Jessie's thighs.

"Oh God, I need to taste you too," Jessie whispered, her voice strained with passion and desire.

Fran didn't hesitate to grant the request. She turned her body and lowered her pelvis towards Jessie's mouth as she claimed Jessie with her own. She groaned as she encountered the unique taste of Jessie while her engorged clit twitched between Jessie's lips.

Fran tried desperately to concentrate on Jessie as her own pleasure built. *Christ, she has such a fucking talented mouth.* Fran tumbled towards orgasm, determined to bring Jessie with her, she held on until Jessie began to convulse beneath her. They both came, tongues swiping erratically between groans and sighs of pleasure.

———⬦———

Fran sat bolt upright, gasping for breath. The room was warm, though the balcony door was open. Not a breath of air disturbed the stillness of the night. It took Fran a moment to realise she wasn't alone. She glanced to her right, barely making out Jessie's features in the early dawn light. She used the back of her hand to wipe the sweat gathered under her chin as she rubbed the damp hair at the back of her neck. She took a deep breath, and her heart rate began to settle into a normal rhythm. She swung her legs over the side of the bed, her bare feet hitting the dark wooden floor, and sat naked as she passed a trembling hand over her face.

"Fran?"

Fran jerked as her whispered name was accompanied by a warm hand caressing the centre of her back. Eyes shut tight, she rubbed her temples, then kneaded her scalp, attempting to regain some composure. Another fucking nightmare. The remnants of which were still whispering around her brain, unsettling her as echoes from the past ghosted into her present, stealing her breath and invading her dreams.

"Are you okay?"

The hand had returned to her bare flesh, rubbing gently at the overheated skin, offering comfort. Fran sat up a little straighter, not yet ready to face Jessie. "A bad dream." She stood, opened a drawer, and hastily pulled on the first T-shirt she laid a hand on. She followed up with a pair of shorts, before grabbing her cigarettes and lighter, and making her way to the balcony.

Fran lit up and took a deep draw. The smoke filled her lungs and settled her frazzled nerves. The nightmares never stopped coming. They were all disturbing in different ways, but this one…she hated. Dreaded. As the gulls squawked their early-morning call, Fran shivered. But not from the cold. She remembered the expression her granny had used, "like someone had walked across her grave". She pulled the final drag from her cigarette. The smoke streamed out of her nostrils on a noisy exhale. She was ready to face Jessie. She no longer had a choice.

Inside, she found Jessie sitting up in bed wearing one of her T-shirts and sipping a cup of coffee. Her eyes tracked Fran as she made her way across the room, replaced her cigarettes on the bedside table, next to the steaming hot cup of coffee waiting for her.

"Thanks," she said, as she sat on top of the covers, picking up the cup for a much-needed mouthful of liquid.

"You're welcome." Jessie took another sip from her mug.

Fran knew Jessie was probably desperate to ask, but she remained silent. She gave Fran time, for which she was grateful. They sat up in bed, drinking coffee, each keeping their own counsel, and trying to ignore the elephant in the room. Fran weighed up her options. Should she have a conversation now or wait until next time? And there certainly would be a next time and a time after that. Placing her mug back on the bedside table, she turned to Jessie.

"I have nightmares."

Jessie nodded. "Do you want to talk about them?"

Fran shook her head and laughed bitterly. "No, but, I suppose I should." She wasn't sure which one of them was more surprised, but it didn't matter. She closed her eyes and took a moment to gather her scattered thoughts. She opened them and turned to Jessie. "I have a few recurring nightmares." She shook her head and pushed on. "Tonight…" She wrung her hands, uncomfortable with sharing, "Tonight's was the worst one." Fran's hands were cold, despite the warmth in the room. She licked her lips, her mouth dry. She reached for her mug and took a sip before continuing. "I was alone with my mum when she died." She searched Jessie's face, concern written all over it as a quiet "Oh" slipped from her lips.

Fran settled herself before continuing with the story. "I got up in the morning and tried to wake her because I was hungry, but she didn't respond. That wasn't unusual, but it wasn't an everyday thing either, you know?" Jessie nodded and Fran continued. "I know now it was because she was smacked out of her head. Sometimes she'd be unresponsive for a while. I shook her arm and she was cold. In my four-year-old head I thought I should make her warm. I went to the bedroom to fetch my blanket. It was pink, with silver stars on it and white fluffy clouds." It always amazed her how vivid her recollection was of that day was. "I put it over my mum. She always told me when she tucked me in at night that it would keep me warm and safe. That's what I wanted to do for her, keep her warm and safe, so I used my blanket."

Fran had never discussed this with another living soul. The counsellors in rehab had time and again tried to get her to open up, but this part of herself she had always kept locked away. Stuffed deep down, never to see daylight, it was too big, too horrible. Not even Nikki spoke of those days, four in total.

"It was a long weekend. Everyone was on holiday from the Thursday until the following Tuesday."

Jessie sat absolutely still across from her. Fran had never understood the benefit in opening up to a stranger. Why should she? It was none of their business, and they had no right to be party to her deepest darkest secrets. But Jessie…was worthy. Fran knew anything she told Jessie would be kept safe and treated with care and respect. Her secrets wouldn't be discussed, pulled apart, or analysed to make sense of her behaviour.

Jessie was still sitting quietly, not pushing, waiting patiently.

Fran swallowed back a lump in her throat and continued, "We were together over four days. I cried, shouted, pleaded, begged her to wake up. I tried to give her drinks, played her favourite records. I hoped she'd get up and dance to them like we usually did. When I was exhausted, I lay down beside her. She was cold. So cold. I think deep down I knew she wasn't going to wake up, but I wasn't going to give up on her." Her chest tightened as her voice cracked. Jessie swiped at her own tears as they tumbled down her cheeks.

"Eventually, Nikki showed up on the Tuesday. I have no idea what time. She shouted through the letterbox when there was no answer. She told me it was okay, to come, and let her in." Fran swallowed with difficulty, her throat tight. "I stood on the other side of the door talking to her, telling her Mummy was asleep, and that she was cold. Nikki had already worked out that she was dead. She told me that if I opened the door she would get some help." Fran sniffed and swiped at the errant tears with the back of her hand, anger edging out the anguish. "Why would she do that? What mother takes heroin while responsible for a fucking child?" Fran paused and tried to regain some composure. "Everyone's always telling me how great she was, how talented, vibrant, beautiful. But I can't get my head around the overdose. Accidental, that's what I was told. It was an accident. But they don't know that, do they? She could have been checking out, leaving me. No one knows because none of them were there. I was, and I sure as hell don't fucking know."

She rubbed at her face. "Sometimes it's like living with a fucking ghost," Fran whimpered, torment in her voice. "I hear about her all the time, from so many people, how she was a great mum..." She turned to face Jessie, her eyes wet. "Was she? Was she really? She fucking left me with a lifetime chasing shadows and highs."

Fran's face contorted with pain and frustration, the bitter tone in her voice giving way to raw emotion. She shook uncontrollably in Jessie's arms. She allowed herself the simple pleasure of being comforted. Jessie guided her back to bed, pulled the duvet up over her body, and then spooned her. She tucked an arm tucked around her waist, and held her safe. Along with the confusion, the pain, the what-ifs, and the what-might-have-beens, there was Jessie. She was listening and offering comfort. And that was more than Fran knew she deserved.

Chapter 30

FRAN LEANED AGAINST THE DOORWAY of Harry's room in the care home. She watched him as he read a morning paper. He wasn't yet aware of her presence. She took a moment to study the knick-knacks he'd brought here—the small photos in ornate frames that she recognised from the Beachcomber, pictures of her grandmother and her mother in happier times.

She hated that he was here but knew it was the best place for him. It smelled old. There was that faint whiff of incontinence and something else she couldn't define. Like school dinners with the distinct sting of disinfectant fighting through, yet still failing to fully mask the more unpleasant odours.

"Hey old man, you up for a roll and a stroll?" Fran asked, injecting cheer into her voice.

"Fran, come in," Harry said. He placed the newspaper on the small table next to him.

She stepped into the room. It was spacious and light, the high ceilings giving an airy sensation to the surroundings. "What're you doing hiding away in here?" Fran accused, her hands in the front pockets of her jeans.

Harry removed his reading glasses with his good hand. A look of distaste crossing his features. "The class they run after breakfast, that music and movement thing? I hate it." He waved his glasses around emphasising his point.

After so many months chatting with Harry, Fran had no problem understanding him, despite the damage from the stroke. She had no issue with Harry skipping the class either. She wouldn't enjoy it herself and couldn't imagine being wheeled in to participate and having no means of escape.

"Let's get you out of here for the day then." Fran inclined her head towards the door, indicating their route of escape.

Harry's face lit up at the prospect and Fran thought, not for the first time, that maybe she was doing the wrong thing paying for his care. It was suitable, it catered to his needs, and provided therapy. But she knew Harry wanted to be in the Beachcomber. That was his home. She sat in the vacant chair, usually reserved for visitors, resting her elbows on her knees as she leaned close to Harry. "Do you want me to take you out of here? I mean for good?"

Harry's eyes became watery, his mouth twisting to form a lopsided smile. "Fran, I'm an old man who can't take care of himself." He used his good hand to take hers. "You're doing all you can. I don't belong in the Beachcomber anymore, and I don't want to become a part of the fixtures and fittings. The tables are more useful than I am."

"Oh, Harry," she protested.

He squeezed her hand, stopping her objection. "Come on, Frannie, we both know this is the best way. I'm well taken care of here, and I spend my afternoons with you in the bar, catching up with the boys."

Fran smiled at his use of the term. The "boys" were a bunch of retired men who were all less than a decade younger than Harry. "You let me know if you want to come home."

"I'm fine here. Now you promised to get me out for the day." Harry released her hand, indicating he wanted to get going.

Fran stood. "How do you fancy a trip along the prom?"

"Aye, it's been a wee while since I was along the far end."

Fran nodded. "It's a nice morning, we'll go as far along as you like." She opened Harry's wardrobe, searching for a light jacket. "Let's get you ready then." She put his coat on, the way the staff had shown her, dressing his affected arm first, then popped a woollen flat cap on his head.

She stood in front of Harry, put her arms under his shoulders and lifted him to his feet, literally hugging him, then eased his slightly shorter frame into the wheelchair. She'd performed this manoeuvre so many times over the past year that it had become second nature to them. Fran had quickly got over her discomfort lifting Harry, and Harry in return had got over his own awkwardness at requiring her assistance. They were like a well-oiled machine.

They slowly made their way along the promenade, enjoying the sunshine as they took in the familiar sights and sounds of Portobello. The mums and toddlers passing them on their way to and from the swimming baths, the dogs and their walkers on the sand and the tarmac, the runners and the cyclists carefully picking their way among the casual walkers, the kids in buggies, and the people in wheelchairs. The good weather had brought everyone out for a glimpse of the yellow orb and its first rays of summer. It cast up memories for Fran of her early years spent on this very stretch of promenade. She supposed it wasn't a bad place to have grown up. It had character and there was a vibrancy about it.

"You warm enough?" Fran asked, as they neared the end of the main stretch of promenade.

"I'm fine, Frannie," Harry replied in a tone that warned her not to fuss.

Fran continued on to her destination, waiting for Harry to notice the latest change on the seafront.

"What the hell is this?" Harry complained.

Fran smiled. It hadn't taken long. She knew Harry would be vocal about the new buildings. "Luxury flats."

"Aw, Fran, I hardly recognise it along here anymore." Harry turned as best he could to stare at her. She stopped pushing and stood beside him. "This part used to be a hive of industry and activity," he said, frowning. "There were factories here, the brickworks, and the potteries. When they finally closed, it became the fun fair. Remember? I brought you here in the summer. You loved it."

She did remember. She had very fond memories of her trips to the shows. Harry would bring her along on Saturdays during the good summer weather. He would take her on the dodgems and the big wheel, then he would buy her ice cream or candy floss.

She patted him on the shoulder. "Progress, Harry."

He huffed. "Right." He appeared deflated, his earlier good mood evaporating rapidly.

"Come on, I want to show you something." Fran pushed Harry towards the gap between the new flats and paused, waiting for his response.

"Well, would you look at that." Harry's voice held a hint of wonder. "They kept them."

Fran knew he would be happy that the two pottery kilns had been retained as a feature amidst all the modern bricks and mortar. She liked them herself.

"I'm pleased. They're a reminder of what's been here before." Harry sat in silence as he took in the beauty of the kilns. "You know, Fran, I would say that I was going to miss this place, but the truth is, most of it's already gone. The people, the businesses, they're already memories."

Fran hated when Harry spoke this way, but she didn't interrupt him. She simply laid a hand on his shoulder.

Harry sighed. "I'm ready to head back now." He sounded weary.

Fran bit her bottom lip. She wasn't ready to return to the Beachcomber just yet. She pushed Harry over to a vacant bench overlooking the sea. Putting the brakes on the wheelchair, she sat next to him on the bench. Removing her pack of cigarettes, she gave one to Harry.

"Now, Frannie, you know I'm supposed to give these up," he jokingly chastised.

"That makes two of us." She had been trying, and was down to five a day, give or take the odd one here or there. She lit the cigarettes and they sat enjoying the smoke, glancing out over the water as it lapped at the shore. The quiet was interrupted by the occasional dog barking and the cries of the circling seagulls hovering in the breeze.

After a few minutes, Fran broke the silence. "I've been in contact with Toni Martin." She turned to Harry.

Harry's hand stalled, the cigarette inches from his mouth, fingers trembling.

She swallowed and nodded. The hope in Harry's eyes so clear, she wouldn't draw this out. "I might be her niece."

Harry frowned.

"Let me explain." She flicked ash from the tip of her cigarette. "I've actually met up with her a couple of times. I didn't say anything because I didn't want you to get your hopes up."

"Well, go on," he said. His tone was impatient.

"We met at the Still, had a chat, and Toni asked if I wanted to do a DNA test. She explained to me that without Ross's DNA we could never have a conclusive result. She'd already looked into the possibility of any samples of blood or tissue belonging to Ross being retained or stored anywhere, but there was nothing." Fran shook her head and swallowed. "She made arrangements, and we both went to a doctor who took samples from each of us. That was a couple of weeks ago. Toni called me yesterday with the results. Basically we're probably related—that's the best that can be done without any sample from Ross."

Harry took a moment to digest the information. "So, Toni is your auntie? Ross was your dad?" Harry's hand shook, a long gathering of ash teetering on the end of his cigarette.

Fran nodded. "Probably."

"All those years Toni spent looking out for you, Frannie, and it turns out she's your auntie." There was a hint of surprise in his voice.

Fran pondered that as Harry took a draw of his cigarette while staring out across the grey water, a faraway look in his eyes. Toni Martin had tried numerous times to point her in the right direction. Perhaps she'd recognised something in Fran that had caused her to care, while Fran had always assumed Toni had been vigilant around her for the sake of her grandparents. She'd always viewed her as a meddling pain in the arse, frequently ruining her fun. She had a knack of knowing exactly what Fran was up to and where to find her.

Fran took her and Harry's cigarettes, and stubbed them out on the lid of a nearby bin.

"Don't set fire to the bloody bin," Harry cautioned.

Fran sighed. "I was twelve, Harry. My pyromania days are over."

Harry grinned, the familiar twinkle back in his eye. "You were always a wild one, just like your mother." He wiped at an errant tear. "Bloody wind."

She shook her head. "Right, old man, you ready for lunch?"

Harry nodded. "Aye."

Fran released the brakes on the wheelchair and started to push Harry back towards the Beachcomber. With a bit of luck, they wouldn't bump into too many folk who knew Harry, and they could be sitting down to lunch in twenty minutes.

Chapter 31

"Why are we all wearing Hawaiian shirts?" Jessie asked as she pulled out the front of her top and glared at Morven. The policewoman had been adamant that they all wear the garments.

"Because I'm going to Hawaii for my honeymoon," Morven replied, popping a lei around Jessie's neck.

Jessie sat back in her chair as Fran entered to deliver another round of cocktails to the Beachcomber's lounge. Morven's hen night was busy. Not wanting to be caught staring at Fran, Jessie averted her eyes when her lover put a cocktail in front of her. She did offer a murmur of thanks, which Fran barely acknowledged, before leaving the lounge.

"I can't believe not one of you has slept with her," Morven stated loudly, her words aimed at every member of the football team, not her friends and colleagues in attendance. "Or have you?" Morven glanced around, her keen eyes checking faces for any sign of guilt. Jessie sipped her tequila sunrise, careful not to make eye contact with the razor-sharp policewoman. She had an uncanny habit of sniffing out information. Jessie knew that was the reason Morven attempted to provoke her so often. She hated to be teased, and it was Morven's nature to exploit any weakness for all it was worth. "If I were single, I'd have been right in there," the policewoman declared.

Jessie rolled her eyes at Morven's bravado as a few others heckled the bride-to-be.

"Oh, I saw that Jessie," Morven waggled a finger at her. "We all know Fran isn't your type, but I wonder who is?"

Jessie refused to be baited, hoping Morven would soon focus on someone else.

"Come on, Jessie, what kind of woman do you go for? Or are you still undecided on the gender thing?" she mocked, before pursing her lips, apparently giving her own question some thought. She pointed a finger at Jessie. "I bet you go for someone like yourself. Foreplay is probably hanging up your clothes and folding your underwear." Laughter erupted around the room.

Jessie bit back. "Says the woman who prefers the gentle touch."

"Ooh, Morven!" Sophie laughed, as did most of the room, Morven's eyes narrowed in warning.

Jessie continued unperturbed. "Oh, stop, that hurts. Stop! Ahh!" Everyone was laughing as Jessie mimicked Morven. But only Jessie, Morven, and one other person knew why.

"She had her elbow in my arse!" The policewoman protested loudly.

"Ew, TMI, Morven!" Zoe shouted, already drunk on her first cocktail.

"I'm talking about Maggie, you dirty bitches. I was at physio!"

"You're a wimp, Morven," Maggie stated.

"Thanks, Maggie. Now my reputation is in tatters."

Maggie smiled as she sipped her piña colada. Jessie thought it was a pleasant change to see Morven on the receiving end. She was merciless with everyone else.

"I'll get you back, Jessie Grainger," Morven warned.

"I don't doubt it," Jessie replied, smiling, knowing she would pay dearly, but the exchange had been worth it.

"Drink up everyone, we're leaving for the restaurant in twenty minutes," Sophie called out.

"Just one thing before we go, Morven." Sophie stood behind the policewoman, placing her hands on her shoulders to keep Morven in the middle of the room.

It was fun to observe the woman who normally instigated everything about to have the tables turned on her. Several of their teammates converged upon Morven, Jessie included. The policewoman searched for a means of escape, but there was no exit available. Within seconds they'd overpowered her. They removed her Hawaiian shirt amid screams of protest. The aqua blue, hibiscus patterned garment was thrown into the air as Morven valiantly wrapped her arms around her chest, pleading for her bra to be left alone.

"Not my bra, get your bloody hands off me!" Morven thrust out her elbows as she protected the flimsy garment.

It appeared as though the team members were about to show some mercy, until Sophie made the call. "We have a better bra for you, Morven. Either remove that little black number, or we'll rip it off you."

Amid chants of, "Take it off! Take it off!" Morven squared her shoulders as the rest of the team stood in a tight circle, protecting her modesty.

"Come on, it's not like we haven't seen you naked before," Zoe taunted. While that was true, everyone knew it was a question of perspective. Stripping off in a changing room was one thing, getting naked when everyone else was clothed with all eyes on you was quite another.

"Where is this top you have for me?" Morven asked. She continued to shield her chest with her hands. "Jessie, you can undo my bra."

"I'm honoured," Jessie mocked, as she stepped closer to Morven and unclasped the silky garment. As the bra slackened, Morven held it tightly to her breasts, not yet ready to remove the final barrier.

Sophie stepped forward with a coconut bra, holding it in front of Morven.

"Fuck off! I'm not wearing that!" Morven spluttered.

"You wanted a Hawaiian theme. The bride shouldn't wear the same as everyone else, so you're going to be a hula girl." The team members could barely control their laughter, and Jessie was enjoying every moment of Morven's plight.

"Would you like me to tie the string, Morven?" Jessie asked politely, knowing her offer of help would further piss Morven off.

"Thank you, Jessie. How kind." Sarcasm dripped from every word.

"Now your skirt. Take off your trousers, but you can keep your knickers on." Sophie produced a green grass skirt. "Take your shoes and socks off too. We have some flip-flops for you to wear."

Morven removed the items as requested, before putting on the skirt and flip flops. She stood in the middle of the lounge as the finishing touches were added to the costume—a lei, with matching floral wristlets and anklets.

"Looking good, Morven. Come on give us a wee dance," Sophie coaxed

Morven began to overcome her embarrassment and started to get into the fun of the costume. She attempted a hula dance as everyone in attendance clapped and shouted encouragement.

"We need to get more alcohol in you, that was rubbish," Sophie teased as she put a strawberry daiquiri into Morven's hand. "Drink that. The bus'll be here in a few minutes to take us to the restaurant."

"I'm going to be bloody mortified walking around like this," Morven protested as she sipped the slushy, pulped concoction. "Oh, that's nice," she added, distracted by the drink.

Sophie placed a flower in the policewoman's hair. "Right, that's you all set. The bus is outside. Everyone drink up, the restaurant's booked for eight."

Sophie was Morven's pick for best woman/maid of honour, and Jessie thought she was a great choice, especially given the outfit change. Morven had wanted a Hawaiian theme…she was going to get one.

"Fran, come and see Morven's outfit," Zoe called from the open door of the lounge, beckoning the bar woman through.

Fran stepped into the room and made a show of studying the bride to be. Folding her arms, she remarked dryly, "It's sexier than your other uniform," before smirking and walking back to the main bar.

"Thanks, Fran!" Morven called to the retreating figure, pulling a face, as the rest of the hen party laughed.

—◆—◇✕◇—◆—

The basement restaurant specialising in Polynesian cuisine was garish and busy. Morven's appearance was greeted with applause and catcalls. The alcohol flowed, served in an array of brightly coloured tiki-style mugs, and plate upon plate of food arrived to be shared. The hen party became louder and more boisterous, competing with the traditional Hawaiian music drifting from the speakers.

The staff were encouraging and tolerant in equal measure, assisting an increasingly drunk Morven with her hula dancing, while turning a blind eye to her to use of a table as a surf board. Jessie sat back in her chair, sipping her fourth cocktail of the night.

She didn't particularly enjoy alcohol, especially drinks that were laced with more than one type of it. She wasn't drunk, though the alcohol was definitely affecting her mood. While most in the company were loud and boisterous, Jessie was becoming increasingly quiet and withdrawn, the drinks causing her mood to flatten.

She glanced at her watch. It was after eleven, and she knew she could sneak away shortly. The bill had been settled and they were all at the bar, enjoying the music and the company. Jessie watched her teammates, the closeness they shared, and envied some of them their ability to let their hair down once in a while. She'd never felt comfortable relinquishing that control. Even on nights like this, where the expectation was to have a good time, it was more of a burden to her, a pressure to enjoy yourself, and to her it just didn't come naturally.

Sophie and Zoe were chatting, sitting close together, something about the way their thighs brushed caught her attention. Zoe was leaving the club. She had been offered a full-time contract in the English top league, and she deserved it. She had been excellent the past season and she was young. There was so much more to come from her. The prospect of playing in a more competitive league and training full-time had been too good an offer to resist.

"What's up, Jess? You look depressed," Sophie said as she shifted and sat next to Jessie.

"I'm just tired, Soph. It's time for my bed." Jessie used the excuse easily.

"You sure that's all? You seem a bit off tonight."

Jessie shook her head. "Are you and Zoe together?" she asked, deftly changing the subject.

Sophie smiled. "Since she signed the contract with Sunderland, we both realised we are going to miss each other. A lot." She shrugged. "We've been seeing each other for the past three weeks."

Jessie smiled. "Congratulations. Sunderland isn't too far away. You'll be up and down the A1 after weekend matches." Jessie paused. "Unless you're leaving too?"

Sophie shook her head. "No, I'm happy where I am. This is new to us. I'm not running off anywhere. We can get together around playing and training. We plan to take this slowly, see where it goes."

Jessie was relieved. The prospect of Sophie leaving the club hadn't crossed her mind until now. Players left for all sorts of reasons—study, work, and sometimes relationships were also a factor in the club they chose to play for. Zoe joined them, sitting on Sophie's knee, affirming their relationship to anyone who took notice.

Jessie thought back to earlier in the evening at the Beachcomber. She and Fran had barely acknowledged each other despite the fact they were sleeping together. She wished she shared the same openness as these two did, or Morven, who was soon to be married. The pang of disappointment wasn't new. She wanted to tell Sophie she was with Fran, had been for weeks, but she remained quiet, keeping it to herself and planning her exit.

———————— ✦✧✦ ————————

Jessie stood outside the Beachcomber, exhaled slowly, and tried not to sag as the air seeped from her lungs. Fran hadn't invited her back here tonight, but she was certain she would be welcome. Or at least hoped she would be.

So why were they sneaking around behind everyone's back? Here she was standing outside waiting for the bar to empty. She'd left Morven's hen night when it was time to hit a nightclub, feigning tiredness. Knowing she was coming back to where they started their evening. Her thoughts were beginning to irritate her. Jessie walked inside and loitered at the entrance to the main bar, waiting to catch Fran's eye.

She plastered a smile to her face. This wasn't her, waiting around, sneaking behind everyone's back. But if she didn't turn up, she wasn't sure Fran would make the effort, and that bugged her. She was tired and wished she'd headed home, but she wanted to be with Fran. She wanted to spend time with her, get to know her more.

"Hey," she greeted Fran who made her way towards her.

"Hi."

Well it wasn't exactly welcoming, but then, Fran never was.

"Is it okay that I'm here?" Jess enquired, wishing she could stop walking on eggshells around Fran.

Fran shrugged. "Sure." Then walked past Jessie into the lounge to retrieve empty glasses.

She stared at Fran's retreating figure, then walked into the main bar and picked up glasses to make herself useful.

They worked in silence, only the clinking of the glasses punctuating the air in the now-empty bar. The atmosphere was underpinned with a tension that made Jessie uneasy. Her mood was well and truly sour by the time they'd finished, and her earlier anticipation disappeared with the slops down drain.

Jessie stood waiting as Fran removed the till tray and locked it in the safe. Perhaps they were both tired, she mused, as Fran returned from the small room that housed the safe. Jessie smiled at her, but there was a tension in Fran, a stiffness to her demeanour, a tightness around her eyes.

"Is everything okay?" she asked. Perhaps Fran's evening hadn't gone well after the hen party left.

"Fine."

"I doubt that's true."

Fran remained silent.

Jessie could no longer hold her tongue, frustration and anger getting the better of her. "What the hell's going on?" Fran refused to make eye contact, which fuelled Jessie's ire. "What the hell is this we have?" she gestured between herself and Fran. "I sat tonight among our friends while you worked, and whenever you came into the lounge we both acted like we don't mean anything to each other." Jessie needed to vent her anger. "I mean, what am I to you? Are we in a relationship? Am I your girlfriend?" She wanted to scream her frustration. "Why am I a secret?"

Fran shrugged. "I'm not a fan of having everything labelled and defined."

Gritting her teeth, Jessie clenched her fists. "So, what? We sleep together and that's it?"

"What else is there?" Fran appeared puzzled.

Jessie took a moment to calm herself, trying to expel some of the tension from her body. "I know you're a bit of a free spirit, but I would prefer to build something with you. Be a part of your life. Have a long-term plan. Not hang around on the fringes, never knowing where I stand."

"What is it that you want from me?" Fran words were cold, a harshness to them.

Jessie shook her head, unable to believe Fran's failure to comprehend her predicament. She took a deep breath before answering. "Dates, friendship, spending time together, supporting each other, building a future together." She searched Fran's face for a spark of hope as she reeled off the list.

"Traditional. Conservative. Everything I never wanted for myself. Is that your idea of a relationship?"

Jessie spluttered. "Well, yes. Yes, it is. That's how I always imagined it would be."

Fran's face was set in stone, there was no chink of emotion, no reaction to the words. It was chilling for Jessie to observe the detachment. "Well I didn't."

Jessie blinked, her head swam with questions, unable to make sense of the sudden change from Fran. This was a woman who had kept Jessie on her toes from the first moment they met. Nothing had ever been smooth. Every inch gained was swiftly and clinically taken back, leaving Jessie floundering, unsure where to plant her foot. Never remaining on solid ground.

"I see."

And she did. Fran was running. She was scared and sabotaging what was new. She was uncomfortable with change and there was not a thing Jessie could do about it.

She knew not to push. That would only drive Fran further away. She lifted her head, and pinned Fran with a gaze of utter determination. "Well, when you figure out what you do want, you know where to find me." She turned and walked out of the Beachcomber, not looking back.

She refused to cry. She couldn't make Fran be with her. Fran's defensive mindset was a coping mechanism, but Jessie had shown Fran enough of who she was to warrant more than she was being offered in return. She'd wait, get on with her life, give Fran time to work out the direction she wanted to take. Jessie knew she needed more from Fran, but she was damned if she was going to do any more pushing to achieve it.

Chapter 32

Fran's stomach fluttered with a pang of anxiety that had built steadily the closer the train got to the outskirts of London. When she arrived at Kings Cross, she hopped on the Tube for the twenty-minute, sardine-packed journey to Knightsbridge. The June weather in London was stuffy, that cloying, rancid heat at the end of a busy work day. The short walk from the station to this affluent square in Knightsbridge helped clear her head a little. The claustrophobic streets packed with commuters receded as she walked along the wide Kensington road to the leafy Ennismore Gardens.

Fran took the six steps that led up to the glass door entrance quickly, but hesitated a fraction of a second before pushing the bell. She recognised the doorman through the heavy glass door, and he smiled as he approached, pressing the button to unlock the door.

"Miss Docherty, how lovely to see you again," he greeted her cordially.

Fran smiled in return. "Hello, William."

He tipped his hat as she entered. "Might I say, you're looking well."

"Thank you." Fran was never comfortable with compliments, but William had always struck her as a genuine man. She supposed she probably did look well considering some of the states he'd seen her in.

He walked behind the reception desk. "I'll let Miss Demente know you're here."

"Would it be okay if I were to surprise her?" Fran knew it wasn't protocol, but she'd lived here on and off for years, and there was good and bad in that. William had witnessed her fluctuating behaviour, turning up at all hours of the day and night. Sometimes drunk, often high, but he had been one of the more understanding doormen, assisting her whenever she allowed.

He hesitated a second. "I'm certain that she would be extremely happy to see you." He smiled and nodded towards the wide staircase. "Enjoy your visit, Miss Docherty."

"Thanks, William," Fran replied before taking the stairs two at a time, eating them up with her long strides.

Standing before the heavy wooden door painted a deep red gloss, Fran lifted the rarely used brass knocker and tapped twice. She knew Nikki would be inside, frowning, trying to work out how the hell someone had got past reception and as far as her front door. This wasn't the kind of place where your neighbours dropped in on you for a cup of tea or to borrow some sugar. You barely saw anyone else and, even then, no one spoke to each other.

Over the years, Nikki had witnessed many neighbours come and go. She'd lived here longer than anyone, and now the place had changed beyond all recognition. No longer inhabited by academics and bohemians, it was the domain of city workers who stayed during the week and headed off to the country at weekends. Nikki was an eccentric surrounded by a mass of conservative consumerism. Everything she loathed.

The door swung open. "Fran!" Nikki exclaimed. "What on earth are you doing here?" She stepped forward to hug her and squeezed her tightly. Fran held Nikki in return, sinking into the welcoming embrace. When they parted, they stood grinning at one another.

Nikki was obviously staying in for the evening. Her usual unique clothes were replaced with a simple, long-sleeved cotton top, linen drawstring trousers, both black, and a pair of white slippers that had probably been complimentary in a luxury hotel. Fran shrugged. "You said to come visit any time."

Nikki frowned. "I didn't expect you to turn up at my door unannounced." She stood aside and beckoned Fran inside. "Come in. Don't you have keys?"

"I wanted to surprise you."

Nikki closed the door and led Fran towards the sitting room. "Well you've certainly done that. How did you get past the doorman?"

"William."

"Ahh," Nikki said with a smile. "He's always been fond of you. Always asks after you."

"I like him too." Fran put her dark canvas rucksack on the wooden floor and took a seat on one of the large brown leather sofas.

"Why didn't you call me? I could've been out," Nikki admonished, taking a seat opposite.

Fran removed her leather jacket, placing it on the sofa beside her. "I only decided this morning to come down."

Nikki scrutinised her carefully, likely searching for any problematic signs. She relaxed back into the sofa, tucking one leg beneath her in a casual pose.

"What's in the bag?" Before Fran could answer, Nikki interrupted, "No, don't tell me, let me guess. Two pairs of jeans, a handful of T-shirts, and a few pairs of black socks."

Fran shrugged. She was nothing if not predictable when it came to clothing.

"How did you get here?"

"Train."

Nikki's eyes widened, obviously surprised by the answer. "You spent five hours sitting on a train?"

Fran indicated her rucksack. "There's a couple of books in there too."

"And everything's okay with you?" Nikki's eyes narrowed again.

"Really, Nikki, I wanted to spend time with you." Fran opened her arms wide, indicating she had nothing to hide.

"How's Jessie?"

The question caught Fran off guard, her hesitation clearly alerting Nikki. She was like a bloodhound, sniffing out trouble. Fran took a deep breath. "Jessie's fine."

"Does she know you're here?"

Fran couldn't lie. "No."

Nikki sighed. "Does anyone know you're here?"

"Harry and Gary."

Nikki rolled her eyes. "At least that's something."

Fran drummed her fingers on her thigh. "I needed to get away for a few days and I do miss you."

She leaned back against the leather sofa and stared up at the ceiling. Nikki never would let her get away with any bullshit. She was loyal and stood by Fran, but she was direct. She'd never let Fran hide away under the guise of a surprise visit. She'd push to the heart of the matter. Fran lowered her eyes back to Nikki. "I need a little time to work things out in my head. I always do that best when I'm with you."

Nikki rose from the sofa. "Well, you know where the guest bedroom is. I'll put the kettle on."

Fran smiled at the accepting words and the fondness they held. While Nikki was always welcoming, she liked to know upfront what she was dealing with, and Fran enjoyed the comfort of familiarity. Picking up her rucksack, she headed to the room that had been hers many times over the years. She placed her rucksack on the bed, not bothering to empty it, and threw her jacket onto a chair.

When she returned to the kitchen, Nikki was making tea the old-fashioned way, in a teapot. The strainer sat on the tray, waiting to catch the loose leaves, and Fran picked up the fragrant scent of bergamot. She smiled to herself. Earl Grey. She didn't mind all the little peculiarities and eccentricities that made up Nikki. To her, they enhanced the experience of spending time with her.

"How long are you staying?" Nikki asked, as she placed the strainer over a fine china cup, heavily patterned with turquoise and gold.

"Dunno, two or three days maybe."

Nikki placed a cup and saucer in front of Fran. "In that case I want to spend as much time with you as possible, unless you have plans of course." She waited for a clarification.

Fran shook her head. "Nope, I'm all yours."

"Good, tomorrow I have a thing and I'd very much like it if you came along."

"What kind of 'thing'?" Fran was suspicious.

Nikki waved her hand as if it were nothing. "A music-video shoot."

"Nikki." Fran drew out her name. "You know what these shoots are like."

"You can't control every environment." Nikki blew on the hot tea.

Fran sighed. "I don't trust myself."

"Fran, you stand in a bar full of alcohol every day."

"But this is London," Fran protested.

"Exactly, the place of all your past demons. So why have you run here?" Nikki raised her chin in challenge. "What's so terrifying back in Edinburgh?"

Fran shook her head. "Where is this bloody video shoot?" She wasn't ready to discuss the main reason she had travelled here.

Nikki raised an eyebrow. "This conversation isn't over."

"Sure," Fran answered before taking a sip of her tea.

"The car will pick up us up at eleven. I'll be busy off and on. I hope you don't mind."

Fran shook her head. "Nope, I like hanging out with you. Even when you're busy."

Nikki pointed a remote at the flat-screen television mounted on the kitchen wall. "I know you don't watch it, but I still like to catch the news," she said by way of apology.

Fran hid her smile behind the cup she was about to sip from. Pausing, she asked, "You still enjoying capitalism?"

Nikki frowned. "Don't be vulgar."

"What's this place worth now?" Fran teased. She knew the price of Nikki's flat was a constant source of embarrassment to her. Purchased in the late eighties for a six-figure sum, it was now worth millions. "You must be voting Tory now."

Nikki swung her gaze from the news presenter who was reporting the government's latest budget cuts. "Like bloody hell I am! We need to reawaken the electorate. The country's sleepwalking into this austerity scam!"

Fran failed to smother her grin.

"Don't rile me up. God, sometimes I really miss the old days. People took an interest in politics. A peaceful revolution, Fran, that's what this country needs. A democratic revolt." She pointed her finger in the air for emphasis. "It saddens me the way many people believe everything in the mainstream media. Everyone is so self-serving. I mean, where is the love?"

Fran shrugged. Politics were never her thing, but she did admire Nikki's passion and vigour for the subject. She genuinely cared what happened in society.

Nikki sighed. "It's soul destroying. We need hope." She shook her head. "I'm getting old; perhaps I'm out of touch."

"Never. We need more like you if we are going to get this peaceful revolution started. You need a manifesto."

Nikki laughed. "You might have the right idea not watching the news. It makes me so angry." She drank her tea, then laughed again. "This evening isn't any different because you're here. I usually shout at the news when I'm on my own."

Fran grinned. "I know. I've heard you many a time."

"Seriously, Fran, it really gets to me. And have you seen the latest thing, the Sex Pistols credit card? I mean what the hell? Punk! On a credit card! Nothing says 'Anarchy in the UK' like the Sex Pistols. Now they're on a credit card. I despair!" Nikki placed her cup on the saucer, then sighed. "Anyway, the entire point of this is, I'm a socialist. Regardless of how much money I have, my values will always remain firmly in the working-class trenches when it comes to class warfare."

"I've never doubted that," Fran remarked without malice or poking fun.

Nikki finished the last of her tea and put the dishes in the sink. "Remember, we leave at eleven. Everything you need is in the bathroom." She walked to Fran and kissed her on the cheek. "It's great to see you, darling."

"You too, Nikki."

CHaPtER 33

FRAN OPENED THE GLASS DOORS that led out on to the railed balcony. It had been a long, eventful day at the video shoot. The night was still warm as the sun set on the pristine square surrounded on all sides by the Georgian granite houses. The central gated park was immaculately manicured. She'd gazed over this view many times, but it no longer held the appeal of her youth and her mixed-up, drug-addled twenties.

Fran was stunned. She longed to be back at the Beachcomber. But, more than that, she wanted to be back with Jessie. Heading down to London, she'd been fearful. Full of trepidation as she approached the city that had been the scene of so many low points in her life. She'd worried she'd slip back into the ease of the lifestyle that ran through the heart of the city. In the circles she'd moved in—the circles Nikki moved in—temptation was everywhere and offered as freely as a cigarette.

It had been difficult to resist when it was right under her nose. And even though it remained difficult, Fran had resisted. She took comfort from that. Another skirmish won in the constant battle with addiction.

She turned at the clip-clop of heels behind her. Nikki, sans make-up, her black kimono wrapped tightly around her waist, joined her on the balcony.

"Want one?" Nikki held out an open packet of cigarettes. "I've hardly noticed you smoking?"

Fran shrugged as she removed a fag from the packet. "I'm down to three or four a day." She placed the cigarette between her lips as Nikki offered her a light, puffing on it a few times before inhaling deeply.

"Sorry about today."

Fran observed Nikki out of the corner of her eye as she exhaled the lungful of smoke. "It wasn't so bad."

Nikki raised an eyebrow. "If you say so."

A silence descended upon them, each lost in her own thoughts. Fran stared up at the slowly darkening sky, took a drag on her cigarette, and blew the smoke into the still air. "I had an interesting chat today." She turned to Nikki, who was staring at her, her face unreadable as she took a short puff on her cigarette, barely inhaling, before blowing the smoke back out.

"Well, are you going to keep me in the dark?" Nikki gestured with her cigarette as she complained.

Fran smiled at her impatience. "The guy with the band, Freddie, recognised me from my time with Polydor. You know? Before it all fell apart." She casually flicked ash from the tip of her cigarette.

"Freddie Trent? What did he want?"

Fran knew Nikki's suspicious tone was for her benefit. She was always protective of her when the record company artists and repertoire people came sniffing around, looking for her to record again. "Relax, he just asked me what I thought of the band."

"Not much I assume?" Nikki interrupted.

"I told him they look the part," Fran remarked dryly.

Nikki laughed. "That was diplomatic of you."

"We chatted a bit more and he let me listen to their other stuff."

"And?"

Fran shrugged. "Nothing that would be a decent second single."

"Pity."

"I told him the band needed to work with a songwriter and get some decent riffs."

Nikki chuckled. "What did he say to that?"

"He asked me to manage the band."

The cigarette paused on its way to Nikki's lips. "He what?" she asked, clearly stunned.

Fran shook her head. "I turned it down. The last thing I want is to be back in that world."

Nikki nodded her agreement. "No doubt, you have the talent, Fran, but—"

"I know."

They both fell silent again. Fran could guess what Nikki's thoughts were. How different her life could have been had she coped with the fame and controlled her habit. The faraway look in Nikki's eyes mirrored one she had sported herself many times. "I've agreed to work on their material though. On my own. Back home." And for the first time she realised that home wasn't just the Beachcomber. It wasn't the place that held so many memories for her. It was the person she wanted to build memories with. It was the woman she wanted by her side. It was Jessie.

Nikki's eyes shot to her, wide, surprised, searching Fran's face.

"I also agreed to let them record 'Slow Soul'."

At that, Nikki's mouth dropped open and moisture gathered in her eyes. "Oh, Fran."

"There are some contract negotiations to smooth out." Fran shrugged. "I like the idea of my music finally being out there. I may not perform it myself, but," she hesitated, "it'd be a shame for it all to go to waste."

Nikki stubbed out her cigarette, then threw herself into Fran's arms, crying. Fran held her close and kissed the top of her head as she rubbed the silk-clad back comfortingly. The warmth of her body seeped through the cool material.

When Nikki gathered herself together, she sniffed and stood back, making a show of smoothing out Fran's clothes. It felt motherly and, to Fran, Nikki was the closest thing she had to a mother.

"I love you, Fran. I'm so very proud of you." Nikki's voice cracked, but she held the tears at bay as she nodded, emphasising the importance of her words.

———⊙⬦⊙———

"So, when are you heading back to Edinburgh?" They were sitting having lunch in a quaint French bistro in Knightsbridge, a short walk from Nikki's flat.

Fran stopped chewing, regarding Nikki with suspicion. Nikki held eye contact as Fran finished her mouthful of food. "Friday."

Nikki nodded. "So we have one more day together. What would you like to do?"

Fran shrugged. "I don't mind. I just want to spend it with you."

Nikki speared a piece of broccoli with her fork. "Charmer."

Fran played with the food on her plate, not particularly hungry. She was over chewing and each bite was sticking in her throat.

"What's on your mind, Fran?"

She raised her eyes from her plate at Nikki's words. She'd been staring at the food, not really focusing on it, her mind miles away. "It's nothing."

Nikki placed her knife and fork on the plate, and sat up straighter in her chair. She pinned Fran with her narrowing, hazel eyes. "Don't tell me nothing. We both know you have something on your mind. Is it the business from yesterday with Freddie?"

Fran blinked. She hadn't even thought about that today. "No, I'm okay with all that." Her words held a hint of surprise at the truth of her statement.

Nikki was doing that thing that unnerved Fran. Her hands were clasped under her chin, her head tilted slightly, and Fran knew her mind was working overtime, evaluating and inspecting her every twitch and flicker.

"Jessie then?"

Fran slouched in her chair, her fork discarded. "We had words before I headed down here."

"You're in a relationship with her?"

"Yeah, well, sort of." Fran paused to consider that. "At least, we were. Now I don't know."

"Why don't you know?"

She sighed, recalling the night of Morven's hen party, the pretence between them, ignoring each other while everyone was around. Jessie coming to her later that night after the bar was closed, as she had been doing frequently. "We've been seeing each other for a few weeks." Fran scratched her stomach. "It's been a secret. I don't know why, though, we just haven't told anyone." It wasn't in her nature to tell anyone her business, but she hadn't been welcoming any time Jessie was in her presence unless they had been alone. At Morven's hen night, they'd acted like strangers, not lovers. "Jessie wanted to know exactly what we were doing. You know, were we in a relationship, where was it going, that kind of thing."

"And?" Nikki prodded.

Fran rubbed her face with her hands. "I don't know. I suppose we are, or were." She was so frustrated. "I told her I thought things were fine the way they were." Shaking her head, she continued, "But that wasn't enough for Jessie."

"So what happened?"

"She accused me of being scared, lacking commitment." She pushed her fingers through her hair. "I told her I couldn't do it anymore."

Nikki frowned, her head cocked to the side. "But you've been in relationships before?"

Fran closed her eyes. "Not like this." She opened them, certain that her friend could peer straight into her heart. She felt naked. Nikki's face softened, a soft smile appearing on her lips.

"You've fallen for her." It wasn't a question, more a statement, to help Fran get to the heart of what was troubling her.

"I've never felt this way about anyone before." She stared at Nikki, her eyes pleading, confusion and fear swirling in her stomach. "I don't know what to do with it, Nikki. I'm frightened."

"Oh, Fran." Nikki's smile was sad, the corners of her mouth turned down.

"What if I fuck it up?" Fran put her hands on her head. "Jessie deserves better, Nikki, so much better than me. She has a nice life; I shouldn't bring all my crap into it."

"You've come so far, Fran. You need to forgive yourself. Jessie knows who you are. Let her make her own decisions."

Fran thought back to the words Nikki had said the last time she was in Edinburgh, *We don't get to choose who cares about us*. But Fran was deciding for Jessie by her actions, pushing her away.

"I'm terrified, Nikki," she whispered. "Afraid to be that wrapped up in someone. So I pushed her away. She finally had enough and told me to figure out what I want."

"Then help Jessie understand," Nikki suggested.

"I've tried opening up, but I hate being so exposed. I feel naked." Frustration underpinned every word.

"Do you trust her?" Nikki asked.

Fran blinked. "Yeah, but I've never been any good at it. I've told her things, but I don't feel lighter, unburdened." She struggled to find the words to properly explain the sensation she was left with. "It makes me dirty and unworthy."

"You need to tell her, Fran, or you'll lose her." Nikki spoke gently, but firmly.

Fran shook her head. "I can't find the words, it's all locked up." She rubbed her chest. "It hurts to get them out. It's so exhausting." She took a deep breath. "I'm so fucking tired. I'm terrified to let go, but she keeps chipping away." Fran leaned back in her seat, closing her eyes, a weariness sweeping over her.

"You need to have this conversation with her."

She rolled her head to the side. "I know." She glanced down at the discarded food on her plate. Her appetite gone, her stomach churned as her mind milled over the options available to her. She needed to have a conversation with Jessie if they were to move forward, but Fran wasn't sure she was strong enough. Life would be less complicated if she took the coward's way out.

Chapter 34

MORVEN AND HER NEW WIFE Amanda cut the wedding cake. They were both stunning in their white dresses. Morven's was a sheer silk fitted number that finished above the knee. The spaghetti straps accentuated toned shoulders. Her blonde hair was cut neatly into a bob. Amanda had chosen a full-length, white-embroidered lace dress. Her dark hair was piled high on her head, with a ringlet hanging elegantly on either side of her face. They were beautiful. Amanda was the taller of the two by a couple of inches and a dress size smaller, a firewoman, with a no-nonsense attitude. Morven tended to be better behaved around her new wife. Thank God someone could tame the mischievous policewoman.

Jessie sat at the table full of her teammates and their dates. She'd been surrounded by people she knew well all day, but she was lonely. It never usually bothered her. Despite knowing that Fran didn't attend functions and events, she had hoped, deep down, that they would have come together today. Let everyone know they were a couple. Since the night of Morven's hen party a week ago, the complicated woman hadn't been in contact.

"Cheer up, Jessie, it's a wedding."

"Hmm?" Jessie turned to Sophie, who was seated next to her. "Sorry, miles away," she said. She tried to hide her subdued mood.

Sophie nudged her with a shoulder. "Everything okay?"

Jessie attempted to appear cheerful. She plastered a smile onto her face. "Yeah, really, I'm fine."

Sophie's expression became serious. "I suppose being at a wedding when your parents are going through a divorce must be a wee bit sad."

Jessie hesitated for a second, she hadn't even thought about the divorce today. She shrugged. "What can you do?" She didn't know what else to say and felt a little guilty for allowing Sophie to assume the divorce was the cause of her blues.

"New season soon though, Jessie. That'll cheer you up."

It did. "Defending our title this season. I'm excited."

The lift in her mood was short-lived. Slices of cake arrived at each table, and Jessie picked distractedly at the thick marzipan icing. The plates and cups were cleared away, and the lights dimmed for the music to continue. Jessie's thoughts started to drift towards when it might be acceptable to leave. It was a little after nine. She would probably have to stay at least until the two brides left. She wasn't sure what time they were going, in which case, maybe eleven would be okay.

"Jesus! Look at Fran," Zoe said.

Jessie's gaze immediately tracked Zoe's. She saw Fran talking to the newlyweds, a small, neatly wrapped gift in her hand. She was smiling, and kissed both Morven and Amanda on the cheek. Jessie's breathing hitched, her mouth slightly open. Not because Fran was casually chatting while offering her congratulations. No, Fran resembled someone who had arrived straight off a catwalk. She was stunning.

Jessie's eyes roamed the fitted, tapered, feminine tuxedo. It must have been made for her—a snow-white shirt beneath, with a small batwing collar, the top three buttons open. A pair of pointed leather ankle boots with three-inch heels finished off the outfit. Fran's hair had been cut and dyed jet black to add a glossy sheen to the normally unruly style.

Jessie wasn't surprised to find many eyes, both friends and strangers, on Fran. Those who knew her were stunned at the transformation from scruffy to elegant. Those who didn't know Fran were probably curious, because, like Nikki Demente, Fran carried the air of someone famous. Someone important. This wasn't a woman who wanted to appear invisible, this was someone who wanted to stand out.

"That woman is so fucking sexy," Sophie said. She sounded slightly breathless.

Jessie couldn't argue with Sophie's assessment; Fran was bloody sexy. Her stomach fluttered. Her traitorous body betrayed her needs and wants despite her attempts not to react to the presence of Fran. Jessie sipped on the glass of white wine in front of her, dipping her gaze, determined not to stare any longer.

Fran approached the table. A sensation washed through Jessie. The back of her neck tingled in anticipation as Fran walked towards her. Jessie held her breath. Fran was right next to her. So close that Jessie sensed the heat radiating from Fran's body.

"Fran!" Zoe said, "Come sit with us."

The sensation disappeared as Fran walked past Jessie to the top end of the table and sat down next to Zoe. Jessie could hear her teammates all remarking on how fabulous Fran looked, how well she scrubbed up.

Amid all the fussing, Fran raised her head and made eye contact with Jessie. Her face was unreadable. Jessie stared at her, waiting, hoping. Then, suddenly, Fran's attention was drawn elsewhere. Jessie swallowed and looked out over the dance floor, her earlier flurry of anticipation receding with each beat of the band.

Jessie surreptitiously followed Fran's every movement, who she chatted with, who came over to talk with her. She wanted to be sitting right next to her, but Jessie's pride wouldn't allow it. She had told Fran to come to her when she figured out what she wanted. Having heard nothing all week, Jessie assumed that was an answer in itself. It irked her, though, that Fran hadn't said hello on her way past. Or casually brushed her shoulder as a show of acknowledgement. Jessie had thought for one moment that Fran was about to sit next to her. Perhaps she had been, but Zoe's interruption meant Jessie would never know. As the minutes ticked by, she was convinced it had been wishful thinking.

Fran stood and headed towards the bathroom, then on her way back, stopped and chatted to Andrea, smiling at something their team captain said. Fran was different this evening, not only her appearance. Yes, the clothes transformed her, brought out her beauty, but there was a casualness to her. She appeared to be more comfortable with her surroundings, with being around people. She wasn't exactly the life and soul of the party, but she was relaxed, talking, and even smiling on occasion. Jessie should be happy for her. But seeing Fran this way and not being a part of it only soured her mood further.

Jessie sipped her wine. She was a little bit tipsy after a long day starting with bucks fizz, then champagne for the toasts, and wine with the meal. But now that Fran was here, Jessie didn't want to leave. Why she was putting herself through the torture of Fran sitting a few feet away, she wasn't sure.

No, she was. She wanted Fran to say something to her, anything, even a nod or a smile. But nothing meaningful had passed between them.

The night was drawing to a close, her wine glass was empty, and the floor was filling up with couples for a slow dance. Morven and Amanda stood in the centre, smiling lovingly at one another. A dark-clad figure stood before Jessie, blocking her view. She raised her head to complain and was confronted with Fran, a hand extended in invitation.

"Dance with me?"

Jessie remained seated, staring into Fran's eyes. They softened.

"Please."

Jessie couldn't resist. She accepted the hand and was gracefully helped to her feet. Fran led the way to the dance floor and placed her free hand around Jessie's waist, pulling her close. Jessie welcomed the familiar sent of mint, with a hint of smoke, combining together to create the unique aroma that hung around Fran. She tucked into Fran's body, and rested her head below her chin. The warmth radiating from Fran caused her to tremble.

"You're beautiful," Fran whispered into her ear, her breath causing a new shiver to ripple through Jessie.

Jessie raised her head. "Thank you. And you're stunning."

Fran didn't reply to that. Instead, she pulled Jessie closer. Their bodies pressed together from thigh to breast as they moved to the music, slowly swaying as one. When the song finished, Jessie raised her head. Their gazes met and Jessie knew Fran wanted the same as she did. She wasn't sure who moved first as their lips touched softly. The kiss was not much more than a caressing of lips, but enough to make anyone aware that it was far from chaste. When they parted, Jessie was breathless and Fran held on to her hand.

"I'd very much like to take you home." Fran's voice was hoarse.

Jessie nodded. "I'd like that too." She led Fran from the dance floor to the table they had been sitting at. Several of their teammates were watching them, some smiling, others staring open-mouthed. Jessie smiled briefly as she retrieved her clutch bag and gave a small wave goodbye. She and Fran walked out of the hotel and into the dark, still night, where a queue of taxis stood waiting.

In the back seat of the black cab, Jessie thought she must be losing her mind. They sat side by side, with the taxi hurtling towards her house. She imagined Fran sliding her hand under the hem of her dress, between her legs and into the heat that was driving her crazy. She squirmed in the seat, attempting to alleviate some of the need building within her. Jessie was so turned on that if Fran made a move, she would let her take her right there on the back seat.

Fran squeezed her hand. It was almost as if she could sense Jessie's predicament. The contact offered comfort and calm. Jessie turned to Fran, who was sitting ramrod straight, seatbelt in place, staring ahead at the empty road. Her clamped jaw was the only indication of emotion. Jessie's breath quickened, her arousal climbing, knowing they were going to be together.

Fran had come to her. Whatever had happened during the last week, something had changed. Jessie wasn't in a hurry to find out what. She wasn't in the mood for talking.

As soon as they got into the house, Jessie set about Fran like a woman possessed. Her appetite was ravenous, drunk on a heady mix of lust and want. Being this close to Fran triggered all her senses. This woman did something to her. Jessie couldn't explain it, couldn't define it. It was carnal and basic, instinctual, frightening, and exhilarating. She claimed Fran's mouth with confidence, knowing exactly what she wanted. She slipped her hands inside the black jacket, palming Fran's breasts. She knew instantly there was no jewellery in the stiff nipples.

Fran groaned and Jessie pulled her mouth away. She licked Fran's neck as she began to push the jacket from her shoulders. Her head was swimming, drunk on desire.

"Jessie," Fran whispered, which urged Jessie on more, until her industrious hands were captured in Fran's. "Jessie," she hissed again.

Fran stalled her onslaught, gently but firmly restraining her wrists. She blinked and stared at Fran, confusion warring with the heightening passion surging within her.

"We need to talk."

"Talk?" She couldn't believe Fran was extinguishing the fire burning between them, the heat rolling in waves from both of them. "Now?" She was still struggling with the change in direction.

Fran rubbed her thumbs across the inside of Jessie's wrists, a comforting gesture, soothing. "I want to be with you, but it'd be better if we talked first."

Jessie nodded, her mouth open, panting as her breathing began to return to normal. "Okay," Jessie said, her good manners kicking in. She shook her head in a futile attempt at trying to clear the lust that fogged her thoughts. "Would you like some coffee?"

Fran's smile was genuine. "Yes." She kept hold of one of Jessie's hands and they walked to the kitchen.

Fran took a seat at the table as Jessie fussed with the kettle and removed two cups from a cupboard. Jessie needed to keep busy. She didn't want to consider what Fran might have to say. All the signals had been positive, but Fran wanted to talk now. That was unusual.

She poured the boiling water into the cups already containing instant coffee and milk, and stirred the hot liquid before depositing the spoon into the sink. She lifted the two mugs, placed them on the table, and sat opposite Fran.

"Thank you." Fran took a sip of coffee. Jessie left hers, doubting she could push the liquid past the growing lump in her throat.

Fran sat comfortably in the chair, fingers linked together. "I'm a selfish prick, but I don't want to be any longer."

Jessie stared at her, unsure if she was expected to reply. She was surprised by the profound statement.

"I've often been told that unresolved grief can be a factor in addiction." Fran pursed her lips. "I have a lot to tell you. So much that it's hard to know where to start." Fran laughed, but it was a nervous laughter. "Toni Martin's probably my aunt."

"Really?" Jessie's heart rate picked up.

Fran nodded. "Only a paternity test is one hundred per cent conclusive, but Toni and I share enough DNA markers to say we are probably related."

Jessie absorbed this new information, cautious as to Fran's thoughts and how she might be taking the news. She was mindful of her part in all of this. Fran had been completely unimpressed by her meddling. "So, Ross is your father?" Jessie spoke hesitantly.

Fran shrugged. "Probably, but you can't do a paternity test on a corpse."

Jessie's vision swam. Another death, another disappointment. Her fault. "I'm so sorry," she whispered. She shook her head, biting back the tears that sprang forward. Meadow had told her Toni didn't talk about her brother. She should have asked her why at the time. The silence spread out between them. Jessie opened her mouth to say something, but hesitated, finding herself lost for words. There was no emotion readable on Fran's face.

"AIDS, a few years ago. Another drug addict." She shrugged. "The addiction gene certainly runs strongly in my family. Both my parents were junkies."

Jessie covered her mouth with her hand. "I'm sorry, Fran. I am so sorry." She didn't know what else to say. She'd opened this can of worms, served up another disappointment on a silver platter to sit right along with all the others in Fran's life. But this wasn't a side order. It was a main course with all the trimmings.

Fran sat back in her chair, appearing thoughtful. "I never imagined I would meet my father. It rarely even crossed my mind, but now that all hope is gone, somewhere, deep down, I'd been carrying a little piece of it." She paused. "The day after I found out Ross could be my father, Harry told me he was dead. But now, knowing he was my dad, it's strange." Fran took a healthy sip from her cooling coffee. Jessie's remained untouched. She wanted to weep. Inside, her stomach was churning. Acid burned at the back of her throat. Jessie couldn't move, she was rooted to the seat.

When Fran had opened up about the days she spent with her mother alone in the flat, Jessie had thought being with DeeDee's body could in part be responsible for Fran's demons. She had considered the experience might even be the root cause of Fran's addiction. Now, knowing both parents were addicts, it was hardly surprising. How could Fran escape its claws? Genetics must surely play a part, and Fran was saying that her grief was a trigger. Did that mean knowing Ross was dead would lead to the pattern repeating itself all over again?

"When you get clean and sober, sometimes the things you're struggling to cope with are no longer a problem." Fran pushed a hand into her hair. "I struggled to cope with burgeoning fame. I'm not famous. I don't have the tools to cope with that kind of pressure, that's why I turned to drugs and alcohol. It's never been about losing DeeDee, but that was always a convenient excuse for my behaviour."

Jessie was stunned by the honesty.

"I've been in London," Fran stated.

269

Jessie didn't know whether she was coming or going. All this information being imparted left her head was spinning, trying to keep up with everything.

"I went to visit Nikki." Fran appeared relaxed, adopting her slouched posture as she sunk lower in the chair.

"How is she?"

Fran nodded. "Good. Asking about you."

"Did you enjoy your visit?" Jessie was almost scared to ask.

Fran pursed her lips. "It was interesting." She rubbed her stomach, the crisp white shirt taking on a ruffled look. "Nikki dragged me along to a video shoot."

Only Fran could make something that most people would find exciting sound so mundane. "How was it?"

"Ah, the usual—a band, models, groupies." Fran shrugged. "That sort of thing."

Jessie knew there was more by the way Fran's eyes slid to the side. She had something on her mind. "Did anything happen?" She had to ask. She could only imagine the temptation that had surrounded Fran in London, especially at a music video shoot.

Fran smiled slightly. "I agreed to help the band a little." She laughed, appearing bewildered. "Some A&R man recognised me. He asked me what I thought of the band." Fran raised her eyebrows. "I'd spoken with them earlier. I liked them, but their music is shit. I agreed to write for them and offered one of my songs."

Jessie sat, stunned. So much had happened since she had last spoken to Fran. It had only been a week ago that they'd had words, but with all this news it felt more like months.

"I'm done with London. I told them they have to come up here. Freddie gave me a laptop, said it can all be done on that." The scowl on Fran's face indicated she wasn't convinced.

"I could help you with the laptop," Jessie offered.

"Cheers." Fran stood from the table. "Do you mind if I have a smoke?"

Jessie stood quickly to open the patio doors. The night was cool, the fresh air rushed into the kitchen, giving them both a chance to clear their head. "May I join you?"

"Sure." Fran walked out onto the decking.

Jessie slipped off her heels and walked out barefoot, enjoying being out of the shoes for the first time that day. The light from the kitchen spilled through the open patio doors, allowing Jessie to study Fran. She looked thoughtful but relaxed as she blew smoke up into the air. Jessie stood beside her, leaning on the wooden railing as Fran enjoyed her cigarette. A grin appeared on Fran's face.

"What's so amusing?"

Fran's smile remained as she shook her head. "I was remembering a story my granddad told me."

"Would you share it with me?" Jessie was keen to hear the tale, especially since it put a rare smile on Fran's face.

She gazed at Jessie for a few moments. "Okay." She stared up into the dark sky, a crooked grin making her appear devilish. "You know the show *Top of the Pops*?" When Jessie nodded, Fran continued. "The intro music, it's Led Zeppelin, 'Whole Lotta Love'." Fran hummed the tune as she mimicked playing guitar, and Jessie recognised it instantly and nodded. "Well, my mum loved the show. When the intro music came on, she would dance around the room, jumping and doing the pogo, and my gran would always comment about the music. Something along the lines of 'Jesus Christ, Harry, it's that show, it sets them mad'." Jessie assumed the voice Fran affected was the way her gran spoke. "She would then shout at my granddad to turn off the TV and he would shout back at her to turn it off. Meanwhile, my mum was screaming, laughing, hugging the TV. She picked it up, telling them she was taking it to her room." Fran paused and smiled as she pushed a hand through her hair, massaging her scalp. "My granny then started to beat my mum with a rolled up newspaper, demanding that she put the telly back on the stand." Fran laughed. "This was the late seventies, it must've weighed a tonne." Taking a deep drag of her cigarette, she continued, "Anyway, my gran and granddad are now both on their feet telling her to put the TV down, and she says, 'Back off old people, I'm taking the TV'." Jessie joined in Fran's laughter as she imagined the scene.

"They'd then agree to let her watch it if she left the television in the front room," Fran continued. "My mum would then put it back on its stand and assume a position sprawled out in front of it to prevent the channel being changed. She'd sit there for the next half hour absorbed in the music and fashion on the show. Singing along to the songs with my granny making comments in the background like, 'Pity you don't know your homework as well as the song lyrics'." Fran again mimicked her gran. "Harry told me that they always did that to tease her. As my mum sat, enthralled by the show, they would be winking at each other as they tried to come up with the best one-liners to tease her more. Then when the show was finished, my mum would leap around the room, sometimes even stomping a booted foot in the coal fire, and run out of the door to meet her friends."

Jessie loved the story. Fran's retelling was full of warmth and affection, but now her face was tinged with sadness as the heavy weight of loss hung in the air. "Your mum sounds like she was quite a character."

Fran took a deep breath, her shoulders sagging as she exhaled. "I suppose." She stubbed out her cigarette in a metal container Jessie had left outside for Fran's use when they first started seeing each other. "Anyway, I wanted to let you know about Ross and Toni."

"I'm sorry it turned out the way it has." Jessie wasn't sure what else to say. No words seemed adequate.

Fran slipped her hands into the pockets of her trousers. "I'm not."

Jessie blinked, surprised.

"At least I won't spend the rest of my life wondering who my dad was, and Harry's delighted. He has so much respect for Toni. Knowing she's my aunt has really cheered him up."

"And what about you? How do you feel about Toni being your aunt?"

Fran scratched her cheek. "I think I'm okay with that."

Jessie smiled. "She's quite formidable."

"She's not so bad. I was a nightmare growing up. I suppose she was only looking out for me and trying to help my grandparents."

"Maybe she saw something in you back then, something that made her care, a resemblance or similarity," Jessie suggested.

"That's what Harry believes."

Jessie shivered as she rubbed the goose-pimpled flesh on her bare arms. Fran removed her jacket and placed it over Jessie's shoulders, the warmth instantly seeping into her. "Thank you." She placed her hand in the pocket and felt something in there, a card. She took it out and held it in her hand. "May I?"

Fran shrugged. "Sure."

DEFENSIVE MINDSET

To Fran,

"For all tomorrow's parties."

Love, Nikki xx

The handwriting was bold. Jessie stared at Fran, hoping that she would elaborate on the message.

"Lyrics from a song we both like. Nikki made me this tux, sent it up a few weeks back when I said I had a wedding to attend. She put that in the pocket."

"I don't know the song."

Fran smiled. "I'll play it for you sometime."

Jessie was happy on so many levels with that answer. It offered both acceptance and hope.

Fran placed an arm around Jessie's shoulders. "Come on, it's getting colder out here." She led them back into the warm house.

Jessie removed the jacket and hung it over the back of a kitchen chair. Unsure how to proceed, she opted for safety. "Would you like more coffee?"

"Sure," Fran replied, as she stood awkwardly in the kitchen.

"I'll bring it through to the sitting room. Make yourself comfortable." The suggestion would allow them both a little space, some time to regroup. As Fran left the kitchen, she busied herself making two more cups of coffee.

Her thoughts turned to the events of the evening. Fran arriving late, keeping her distance, then asking Jessie to dance, effectively announcing their relationship to everyone with a kiss. Jessie had assumed they'd be making love by now. Instead, Fran wanted to talk. The one thing Jessie had pushed for from the moment they shared their first car journey and Fran had resisted. Now that she was opening up, she suspected Fran wasn't finished. She appeared to have a lot on her mind when they came back into the kitchen a few minutes ago.

Jessie entered the sitting room to find Fran perched on the edge of a sofa. She placed a mug of coffee on a coaster on the table in front of Fran.

"There you go."

"Thanks."

Fran sipped the coffee, then placed the cup back on the coaster. She ran a hand through her glossy hair before placing her elbows on her knees, leaning forward towards Jessie. "I'm sorry about last week." She rubbed her forearm. "It happened because I'm scared." Fran licked her lips. "I've never felt like this before. The way I feel about you. I deliberately pushed you away." She stopped, and Jessie took a moment to let those words sink in.

"Okay."

Fran sighed. "This is new to me, Jessie." She indicated the space between them with her hand. "It terrifies me, but I want to be with you." She cleared her throat. "I'm in love with you."

Jessie's heart began to pound in her chest as her mouth became dry. The words hung in the air. Fran was in love with her. How she'd longed to hear those words. "I love you too." She could barely get the words out without rushing them.

Fran smiled and blew out a long breath. "I can't guarantee you an easy life. I fight hard to stay clean and sober." She clasped her hands together. "Sometimes I want to get high; some days I come so close to giving in." She bit her bottom lip. "I don't want to fail. I don't want to disappoint you." Her voice had become anguished as she rubbed her face with her hands. "I don't want to lose you if I fuck up."

Fran's expression was pained, and Jessie knew this was a major concern for Fran. She understood that she was afraid to commit for fear of failing and losing her. She was laying herself bare, and Jessie knew it was taking a lot for her to do that.

Jessie knew her answer. "If you falter, I'll be there to pick you up. I've seen enough of who you are to understand the battle you're constantly fighting." She reached over and took Fran's hand in her own. "I've come to know you well enough to trust that any slip-up will be temporary. I don't expect you to falter, but if there were to come a time, for whatever reason, and you turned to drugs and alcohol, I'll be there for you in any way you need."

"You can't be sure—" Fran choked on the words.

Jessie interrupted, "I won't lie to you and say that the prospect of that ever occurring doesn't fill me with dread. It does. But should it happen, I believe we can get past it. The progress you've made in the past year has been impressive. I believe in you, Fran."

Fran's eyes closed and she swallowed. "Thank you," was the hoarse reply.

Jessie stood and urged Fran to join her. They held each other, absorbing the warmth, melting into one other, connecting through touch. As Fran trembled, Jessie held on tighter.

———◆◇◆———

Fran was humbled. She had no idea why Jessie wanted to give her a chance, but she welcomed the opportunity to be a part of her life, to make a life with her. Fran dipped her head and caught Jessie's lips, kissing her softly, slowly, savouring the moment. She poured emotion into the kiss. All the words she failed to find that would explain perfectly how much she loved this woman, she hoped to convey through her actions. When the kiss ended, Fran leaned her forehead against Jessie's, catching her breath as she pulled Jessie closer. Jessie's hands that had earlier been so lively and eager, searching out Fran's flesh, were now moving slowly over Fran's back.

"Can we go to bed?" Fran asked.

Jessie nodded, and Fran took her hand, leading her to the bedroom, neither of them in a rush. Jessie understood they had all the time in the world. Fran was offering more than just a night of passion. She was ready to commit to their relationship.

This time Jessie unbuttoned Fran's shirt slowly. She untucked it from the fitted trousers before turning to offer the zip of her dress to her. Fran kissed Jessie's bare shoulders as she peeled the dress open. She savoured the moment, taking time to appreciate each layer of this wonderful woman. The scent of her, the softness of her skin, the firmness of her body. Fran trembled as each piece was revealed to her. This time, it was for real.

Jessie turned and smiled, kissing her again as she unzipped Fran's trousers. They both stepped out of the discarded garments. Jessie slipped off her underwear, and they were both naked in the darkened room.

Fran stepped forward and pressed her body the length of Jessie's. She sighed at the contact, savouring the warmth of Jessie's naked form against her own. Her heart beat quickly and her breathing became a little ragged.

"I love you," she repeated, and Jessie made a noise in her chest. No words, but Fran understood the affect her proclamation had on Jessie. The importance of saying it again. "And I very much want to make love to you." Fran captured Jessie's lips. She'd kissed many women before, but never had she experienced this depth of emotion, the swelling in her chest, the indescribable pleasure this woman brought to her. The need she evoked within her.

They lay on the bed and she gazed at Jessie as she stroked her towards orgasm. Fran blinked back the moisture that gathered in her eyes and swallowed back the lump in her throat.

"I love you," she whispered again, as Jessie surrendered to the pleasure being given.

Jessie reached for Fran and pulled her close. Fran lay her head on her chest. She could hear the strong beat of Jessie's heart beneath her ear, the cadence regular and visceral. Fran was awestruck that Jessie was brave enough to place it in her unworthy hands. She knew now that it belonged to her. That knowledge chased the last fragments of her demons away. It left her own heart full of joy and something that words could not describe. The sensation overcame any lingering fear and terror. Fran knew it must surely be love. That all-encompassing, inexplicable craving for another.

Jessie ran fingers through Fran's hair and a smile ghosted across Fran's lips. She was relaxed and content; exactly where she wanted to be. There was no urge to run, to hide, or deny anymore.

She was safe. She was home.

About Wendy Temple

A passionate Scot, Wendy grew up in East Edinburgh. As a child it was her dream to live on the historic Royal Mile, which she did for a number of years before returning to the seaside a few years ago.

With an academic background in Community Education; Healthcare & Physical Education, she has held numerous jobs in these fields and is a passionate advocate of keeping access to further education & healthcare free for all and lessons in physical education available to all schoolchildren.

A sports fanatic, Wendy played hockey & volleyball competitively & five-a-side football for leisure. Her hobbies include watching lots of sport, reading & writing; genealogy & history.

Wendy started writing fanfiction in 2005 to impress a woman…

CONNECT WITH WENDY
Facebook: www.facebook.com/wendytempleauthor
E-Mail: weebod@mac.com

Other Books from Ylva Publishing

www.ylva-publishing.com

THE SET PIECE

Catherine Lane

ISBN: 978-3-95533-376-8
Length: 284 pages (70,000 words)

Amy gets an irresistible offer: Become engaged to soccer star Diego Torres to hide that he's gay and in return get a life of luxury. The simple decision soon becomes complicated. Diego is being blackmailed, and Amy needs to find the culprit. It doesn't help that Casey, his pretty assistant, is a major distraction. Will Amy watch her from the sidelines or find the courage to get back into the game?

FOUR STEPS

Wendy Hudson

ISBN: 978-3-95533-690-5
Length: 343 pages (92,000 words)

Seclusion suits Alex Ryan. Haunted by a crime from her past, she struggles to find peace and calm.

Lori Hunter dreams of escaping the monotony of her life. When the suffocation sets in, she runs for the hills.

A chance encounter in the Scottish Highlands leads Alex and Lori into a whirlwind of heartache and a fight for survival, as they build a formidable bond that will be tested to its limits.

WELCOME TO THE WALLOPS

(The Wallopps – Book 1)
Gill McKnight

ISBN: 978-3-95533-559-5
Length: 242 pages (67,000 words)

Jane Swallow has always struggled to keep peace, friendship, and equanimity within the community she loves, but this year everything is wrong. Her father has just been released from prison and is on his way to Lesser Wallop with the rest of her travelling family. Her job is on the line, and her ex-girlfriend has just moved in next door. Only a miracle can save her.

JUST MY LUCK

Andrea Bramhall

ISBN: 978-3-95533-702-5
Length: 306 pages (80,500 words)

Genna Collins works a dead end job, loves her family, her girlfriend, and her friends. When she wins the biggest Euromillions jackpot on record, everything changes...and not always for the best. What if money really can't buy you happiness?

COMING FROM YLVA PUBLISHING

www.ylva-publishing.com

UNDER PARR

(Norfolk Coast Investigation Story – Book 2)
Andrea Bramhall

December 5th, 2013 left its mark on the North Norfolk Coast in more ways than one. A tidal surge and storm swept millennia-old cliff faces into the sea and flooded homes and businesses up and down the coast. It also buried a secret in the WWII bunker hiding under the golf course at Brancaster. A secret kept for years, until it falls squarely into the lap of Detective Sergeant Kate Brannon and her fellow officers.

A skeleton, deep inside the bunker.

How did it get there? Who was he…or she? How did the stranger die—in a tragic accident or something more sinister? Well, that's Kate's job to find out.

WENDY OF THE WALLOPS

(The Wallopps – Book 2)
Gill McKnight

In the second cosy romance from *The Wallops*, there are worrying times ahead for community police officer Wendy Goodall. She is seconded by sexy Detective Inspector Diya Patel to work on a witness protection plan in the Wallops. Flushed with her new gayness, Wendy also has a mad crush on the adorable, yet reclusive Dr. Lea James. And could wily Girl Guide leader, Kiera Minsk be connected with the human traffickers working along the south coast?

As if life wasn't crazy enough, her twin brother Will announces that their birth mother wants to make contact!

Defensive Mindset
© 2017 by Wendy Temple

ISBN: 978-3-95533-837-4

Also available as e-book.

Published by Ylva Publishing, legal entity of Ylva Verlag, e.Kfr.
Ylva Verlag, e.Kfr.
Owner: Astrid Ohletz
Am Kirschgarten 2
65830 Kriftel
Germany

www.ylva-publishing.com

First edition: 2017

Credits
Edited by Andrea Bramhall and Lee Winter
Cover Design and Print Layout by Streetlight Graphics